Also by Beth Ciotta

Her Sky Cowboy
His Broken Angel
(A Penguin Special)

His Clockwork Canary

THE GLORIOUS VICTORIOUS DARCYS

BETH CIOTTA

A SIGNET ECLIPSE BOOK

SIGNET ECLIPSE
Published by the Penguin Group
Penguin Group (USA) Inc., 375 Hudson Street,
New York, New York 10014, USA

USA | Canada | UK | Ireland | Australia | New Zealand | India | South Africa | China

Penguin Books Ltd., Registered Offices: 80 Strand, London WC2R 0RL, England
For more information about the Penguin Group visit penguin.com.

First published by Signet Eclipse, an imprint of New American Library,
a division of Penguin Group (USA) Inc.

First printing, June 2013
10   9   8   7   6   5   4   3   2   1

SIGNET ECLIPSE and logo are trademarks of Penguin Group (USA) Inc.

ISBN 978-0-451-23999-0

Printed in the United States of America

PUBLISHER'S NOTE
This is a work of fiction. Names, characters, places, and incidents either are the product of the author's imagination or are used fictitiously, and any resemblance to actual persons, living or dead, business establishments, events, or locales is entirely coincidental.

The publisher does not have any control over and does not assume any responsibility for author or third-party Web sites or their content.

ALWAYS LEARNING   PEARSON

To my editor, Jhanteigh Kupihea,
who gives my imagination free rein and champions my
adventures with genuine and inspiring enthusiasm

ACKNOWLEDGMENTS

I'd like to share my heartfelt appreciation with everyone at Penguin for supporting this series and helping to bring the Glorious Victorious Darcys to life! Your creativity and expertise help to fuel my own imagination and enthusiasm.

I especially want to acknowledge my amazing editor, Jhanteigh Kupihea, as well as my dazzling copy editor, Michele Alpern. Thank you for helping me to make this story shine!

A special shout-out to my agent, Amy Moore-Benson—my champion, my friend. Thank you for keeping me sane.

A huge, sloppy thank-you to my critique partners, my sister and fellow author Elle J. Rossi and my cherished friend and fellow author Cynthia Valero. You ROCK!

My love and appreciation to my biggest supporter—my husband, my hero, Steve. Thank you for everything, always.

To my many wonderful and supportive friends and family members, loyal readers, and enthusiastic Facebook friends—thank you for brightening my days and enriching my life. To the hardworking bloggers and reviewers who help to spread the word—thank you for your thoughtful time and energy. And to all of the wondrous librarians and booksellers who live and breathe and promote literature—thank you for being.

Greetings, fellow romantics and daring adventurers,

I don't know about you, but one of my most cherished possessions is my imagination. It's taken me to some wondrous places, but none so personally thrilling as the alternate world I created for *Her Sky Cowboy* and the subsequent stories in the Glorious Victorious Darcys series.

Imagine the 1960s. Race riots. Vietnam. The Cuban Missile Crisis.

Imagine a group of fanatical peace activists happening upon a means of time travel and jumping back to the source of departure, the mid-1800s, in hopes of altering the future and avoiding specific global atrocities.

Imagine their good intentions going horribly wrong and, instead, the two centuries melding, setting the world on an unknown course.

I imagined and ended up with a spectacular and endearing alternate era—the Victorian Age meets the Age of Aquarius.

Every decade, every era, and every world has its own lingo. In kind, there is terminology specific to the GVD universe. I've included a glossary for easy reference should you desire clarification. Also for those who have not read *Her Sky Cowboy*, the first installment in the series, I'd like to offer some history on how this world came to be. If you prefer to discover while reading, then skip this part. But for those who prefer background, this is for you!

Spectacularly Astonishing Exclusive Peeks into Marvelous Historical Facts (sort of)

1851—Great Britain. The Great Exhibition is held at the Crystal Palace. Prince Albert encourages the celebration of inventions and technology. Engineer/visionary Briscoe Darcy introduces his one-of-kind time machine, vowing to journey forward in time and to return with a futuristic marvel. He vanishes in front of thousands of people, never to be seen again. Historically, Darcy is known as the Time Voyager.

1856 (a leap year)—A caravan of twentieth-century time travelers arrives in the nineteenth century via a time vehicle dubbed the Briscoe Bus. Their mission: to alter history for the preservation of mankind. Known as the Peace Rebels, these Mods spread the message "Make love, not war."

Hungry for knowledge regarding technological marvels of the future, Prince Albert embraces the PRs, causing a rift between him and his old-fashioned wife, Queen Victoria. The PRs' loose morals and advanced knowledge threaten their original goal. Some PRs are corrupted, selling knowledge to power-hungry Vics. Soon society is divided into two main factions: Old Worlders and New Worlders.

1860—The Peace War breaks out, and when the dust settles . . . a hybrid of the 1860s and the 1960s is born.

—Beth Ciotta

ALTERNATE WORLD GLOSSARY

Terminology and definitions exclusive to the Glorious Victorious Darcys (and related spin-offs)

aero-hangar—a cavernous shelter used for housing and repairing airships.

aeropark—a public or private airfield.

ALE—acronym for Air Law Enforcement. A legion of law enforcers who police the skies in airships.

Aquarian Cosmology Compendium—an elusive journal compiled by the scientific faction of the time-traveling Peace Rebels. According to legend, the ACC features designs and scientific data pertaining to twentieth-century technological wonders, as well as engineering details of a functioning time machine.

automocab—a hired road conveyance powered by steam or petrol (e.g., taxicab).

automocoaches—road vehicles of various size and construction, powered by steam or petrol. Often a cross between late-1800s mechanics and mid-to-late-1960s designs (e.g., steam-powered Beetle Bug).

Book of Mods—an extensive compilation of sketches, essays, and cautionary tales pertaining to culture, politics, technology, and significant events of the twentieth century. Written by a faction of the original Peace Rebels, this published journal was once widely read, but is now banned.

clockwork propulsion engine—a unique engine, originally designed by Briscoe Darcy, enabling a vehicle to travel through time.

corneatacts—cosmetic optical lenses utilized by Freaks to disguise their kaleidoscope (rainbow) irises. Constructed to fit over the cornea, *corneatacts* create the illusion of normal, unicolor irises.

Disrupter 29—a modified derringer (pocket pistol) enhanced by twentieth-century technology. An advanced weapon available for purchase only on the black market.

Flatliner—someone who cares only about his/her future and not the future or welfare of mankind.

Freak—the offspring of a Vic and a Mod. Cross-century humans with varied supernatural gifts. *Freaks* are born with kaleidoscope eyes (irises that swirl with a rainbow of colors) and a unique blood type. A powerful and unpredictable minority, *Freaks* are regarded as a curiosity and/or a threat. As such, their civil rights are restricted by law.

Freak Fighters—any person belonging to the underground organization fighting for the emancipation of Freaks.

Freak Rebellion—a brewing revolution intent on winning equal rights for Freaks.

Her Majesty's Mechanics—highly trained, highly covert agents who "fix" sensitive and controversial matters for the British government and its sovereign.

Houdinians—a secret "security" team.

Mod—any person born of parents from the twentieth century.

Mod Tracker—similar to a bounty hunter. Someone who tracks and locates Mods for monetary gain.

ModVic—a cross-century clothing trend; 1960s Bohemian meets 1880s Victorian.

New Worlder—liberals who embrace advanced knowledge and technology in hope of creating a better tomorrow.

o'blaster—a black market weapon similar to a shotgun. Instead of pellets, the cartridge is packed with razor-sharp metal shards and heated by a core-propulsion blast.

Old Worlder—conservatives who shun radical change and fear divergence, preferring to move forward with the natural march of time.

Peabody 382—an enhanced gentlemen's pistol. Pretty but deadly.

Peace Rebels—twentieth-century peace fanatics from the fields of the arts and sciences who traveled back to the nineteenth century, intent on altering history and circumventing future chaos and destruction . . . and ultimately Armageddon. As time went on, also a moniker for any Vic who joined their cause.

Peace War (1860–1864)—a four-year transcontinental war stemming from advanced twentieth-century knowledge that led to corruption on both sides of the Atlantic, infecting Americans and Europeans, Vics and Mods, blurring politics, culture, and beliefs. As a result, society divided into two factions—Old Worlders and New Worlders.

Remington Blaster—a nineteenth-century revolver enhanced with twentieth-century technology.

skytown—floating pleasure meccas composed of three to five airships. "Above the law," these traveling hippie circuses offer illegal and outlawed entertainment and welcome equal fraternizing amongst Mods, Vics, and Freaks . . . and assorted criminals.

stun cuff—a common weapon of defense. A highly charged metal bracelet that "zaps" the attacker with a jolt of electricity. Works through the same concept as a twentieth-century stun gun.

telecommunicator—a handheld communication device that transmits coded messages.

tele-talkie—similar to a twentieth-century walkie-talkie; a personal two-way radio device.

Thera-Steam-Atic Brace—a steam-powered prosthesis.

Time Voyager—Briscoe Darcy, nineteenth-century engineer/visionary who invented a time machine and traveled into the future, ultimately enabling the twentieth-century Peace Rebels to travel back to the 1800s.

time-trace—a supernatural skill. The ability to experience another person's memories.

torchlight—a battery-powered tube of light similar to a twentieth-century flashlight.

Vic—any person born of parents from the nineteenth century.

CHAPTER 1

Since the day he'd been born (three and a half minutes later than his twin brother), Simon Darcy had been waging war with time. He had either too much of it or not enough. Somehow his *timing* was always off. Bad timing had cost him much in his thirty-one years. Most recently, his father, Reginald Darcy, Lord of Ashford.

The proof was in his pocket.

Simon didn't need to read the abominable article—he had it memorized—yet he couldn't help unfolding the wretched newsprint and torturing himself once again. As if he deserved the misery. Which he did.

The London Informer
January 5, 1887

MAD INVENTOR DIES IN
QUEST FOR GLORY

The Right Honorable Lord Ashford, lifelong resident of Kent, blew himself up yesterday whilst building a rocket ship destined for the moon. Ashford, a distant cousin of the infamous Time Voyager, Briscoe Darcy, was rumored to be obsessed with making his own mark on the world. Fortunately for the realm and unfortunately for his family, Ashford's inventions paled to that of Darcy, earning him ridicule instead of respect, wealth, or fame.

Simon's gut cramped as he obsessed on the article that had haunted him for days. For the billionth time, he cursed the Clockwork Canary, lead pressman for the *Informer*, as heartless. The insensitive print blurred before Simon's eyes as his blood burned. Instead of tossing the infernal sensationalized reporting of his father's death, he had ripped the article from the London scandal sheet, then folded and tucked the announcement into an inner pocket of his waistcoat, next to his tattered heart.

For all his guilt and grief upon learning of his beloved, albeit eccentric, father's demise, Simon had stuffed his emotions. His mother and younger sister would be devastated. Especially his sister, Amelia, who shared their papa's fascination with flying and who'd lived and worked alongside the old man on Ashford—the family's country estate. For them, Simon would be a rock. As would his ever unflappable twin brother, Jules.

Simon had made the trip from his own home in London down to Kent posthaste. He'd remained stoic throughout the constable's investigation of the catastrophic accident, as well as through the poorly attended funeral. He'd even managed a calm demeanor whilst listening to the solicitor's reading of the will—unlike his dramatic and panic-stricken mother. Although upon this occasion, he could not blame her for the intensity of her outburst.

The Darcys were penniless.

Simon and Jules had their personal savings and fairly lucrative careers, but the family fortune was gone, and as such, Ashford itself was at stake.

Even after sleeping on the shocking revelation, Simon couldn't shake the magnitude of his father's folly. His mind and heart warred with the knowledge, with the implication, and with the outcome. Because of Simon's ill timing and arrogance, his mother and sister were now destitute.

"Do not assume blame."

Simon breathed deeply as his brother limped into the cramped confines of the family dining room. "Do not assume to know my mind."

"Has grief struck you addle, brother?" Dark brow raised, Jules sat and reached for the coffeepot. Like their father, the Darcy twins had always preferred brewed coffee over blended teas.

Simon flashed back on one of his father's quirky inventions—an electric bean-grinding percolator—which might have proved useful, except, as a staunch Old Worlder, their mother had refused to allow Ashford to utilize electricity.

Destitute and living in the Dark Ages.

Riddled with emotions, he pocketed the blasted scandal sheet and met his twin's steady gaze. But of course Jules would know his mind. The older brother by mere minutes, he always seemed to have the jump on Simon. Even so far as guessing or knowing his thoughts. Simon was often privy to Jules's notions as well, and sometimes they even had what their little sister referred to as "twin conversations." Whether spurred by intuition or some bizarre version of telepathy, they often finished each other's sentences. It drove Amelia mad.

"I could've been working alongside my mentor on Tower Bridge," Simon said. "Instead I chose to pursue my own *brilliant* idea."

"You doubt the merit of a public transportation system high above the congested streets of London?"

"No." Simon's monorail system inspired by the Book of Mods would have eased ground traffic and air pollution caused by the rising population and number of steam-belching and petrol-guzzling automocoaches. It would have provided an affordable mass transit alternative to London's underground rail service.

It would have afforded Simon the recognition and respect he craved.

"I regret that I boasted prematurely about my project. Had I not bragged, Papa would not have invested the family fortune." Sickened, Simon dragged his hands though his longish hair. "Bloody hell, Jules. What was the old fool thinking?"

"That he believed in you."

"When the project failed, I Teletyped Papa immediately. Railed against the injustice of political corruption. Wallowed in self-pity. What was I thinking?"

"That he would damn the eyes of the narrow-minded and manipulative Old Worlders. That he'd side with you. Ease your misery." Jules looked away. "He excelled at that. Building us up. Making us believe we were capable of whatever our hearts and minds desired."

For a moment, Simon set aside his own heavy remorse and focused on his brother, who had always been darker in coloring and nature than the more fair and frivolous Simon. Though presently residing in London, where he worked as an author of science fiction novels, Jules Darcy was retired military, a decorated war hero. Details revolving around the skirmish that had mangled his legs and left him with a permanent limp were classified. The period of rehabilitation had been extensive and also shrouded in secrecy. Even Simon was clueless as to those peculiar days of Jules's mysterious life. Although he was often privy to his brother's moods and inclinations, he'd never been able to read Jules's mind regarding the covert nature of his service to the Crown.

"Coffee's bitter," Jules said, setting aside his cup and reaching for the sugar bowl.

Everything had tasted bitter to Simon for days, but he knew what his brother meant. "Eliza made the coffee. Be warned—she cooked as well."

Frowning, Jules glanced toward the sideboard and the steaming porcelain tureens. Though an excellent housekeeper, Eliza was famously ill equipped in the kitchen. "What happened to Concetta?"

The skilled though crotchety cook had been in their mother's employ for months. "Mother dismissed her this morning. Said we could no longer afford her services."

"Did she not offer the woman a month's notice?"

"She did. Along with excellent references. But Concetta's prideful. She ranted in her native tongue, and though I'm not fluent in Italian, I understood the intention. She's leaving today."

"Damnation," Jules said.

In this instance, Simon knew the man's thoughts. Things were indeed dire if Anne Darcy, a conservative woman obsessed with old ways and upholding appearances, had resorted to dismissing servants. Another kick to Simon's smarting conscience.

Just then Eliza's husband, Harry, appeared with two folded newspapers in hand. "As requested," he said, handing the *Victorian Times* to Simon, then turning to Jules. "And the *London Daily* for you, sir." The older man glanced at the sideboard, winced, then lowered his voice. "I could fetch you fresh bread and jam."

If anyone knew about the poor quality of his wife's cooking, it was Harry.

Simon quirked a smile he didn't feel. "We'll be fine, Harry." The man nodded and left, and Simon looked to his brother. "We'll have to sample something, you know. Otherwise we'll hurt Eliza's feelings."

"I know." Distracted, Jules seemed absorbed by the front page of the *Daily*.

Simon immediately turned to the headlines of the *Times*—a respectable broadsheet, unlike the *Informer*.

The Victorian Times
January 10, 1887

ROYAL REJUVENATION—A GLOBAL
RACE FOR FAME AND FORTUNE

In celebration of Queen Victoria's upcoming Golden Jubilee, an anonymous benefactor has pledged to award a colossal monetary prize to the first man or woman who discovers and donates a lost or legendary technological invention of historical significance to Her Majesty's British Science Museum in honor of her beloved Prince Albert. An additional £500,000 will be awarded for the rarest and most spectacular of all submissions. Address all inquiries to P. B. Waddington of the Jubilee Science Committee.

Simon absorbed the significance, the possibilities. "Blimey."

"I assume you're reading what I'm reading," Jules said. "News like this must have hit the front page of every newspaper in the British Empire."

"And beyond." Simon fixated on the headline, specifically the words FAME AND FORTUNE. He wanted both. For his family. For himself.

"Pardon the interruption, sirs." Contrite, Harry had reappeared with three small envelopes. "It would seem sorrow regarding the loss of Lord Ashford has muddled my mind. These were in my pocket. I picked them up at the post whilst in the village this morning." He handed an envelope to each of the brothers, then placed the third near their sister's place setting. "This one is for Miss Amelia," he said. "That is, if she joins you this morning."

Since their father's death, Amelia had been grieving in private.

"We'll see that she gets it," Jules said. "Thank you, Harry."

The man left and Simon struggled not to think of their young sister locked away in her bedroom—mourning, worrying. Yes, she was a grown woman, twenty years of age, but she'd led a sheltered life, and though obstinate as hell, Amelia was tenderhearted. At least half of Simon's worries would end if she'd relent and marry a good and financially stable man. Alas, Amelia's fiery independence was both a blessing and a curse. Frustrated, Simon focused back on what appeared to be an invitation. "No return address."

He withdrew the missive in tandem with Jules and read aloud. "Given your family's reputation as innovators, adventurers, and visionaries—"

"—you have been specifically targeted and are hereby enthusiastically invited to participate in a global race for fame and fortune," Jules finished.

"Royal rejuvenation."

"Colossal monetary prize."

"Legendary technological invention," they said together.

"Is your missive signed?" Simon asked.

"No. Yours?"

"No." He glanced from the mysterious note to the *Times*. "Apparently the anonymous benefactor thought us worthy of a personal invitation. Do you think it is because of our association with Briscoe Darcy?"

"Yet again it's assumed that because Papa knew the Time Voyager, he must have had knowledge regarding Briscoe's time machine."

"Also natural to assume Papa would have passed along that information to us," Simon said. "Which he did not."

"No, he did not. If he had any."

"Unless . . ." Simon looked to the envelope next to Amelia's empty plate.

"If Papa had pertinent information regarding Briscoe's time machine, he would not have burdened Little Bit with such knowledge," Jules said. "Too dangerous."

Indeed. No invention was more historically *significant* than the one constructed by their distant cousin Briscoe Darcy. A time machine used to catapult Briscoe into the future (1969), which ultimately enabled a group of twentieth-century scientists, engineers, and artists to dimension-hop back to the past (1856).

Intending to inspire peace and to circumvent future atrocities and global destruction, those dimension-hoppers, also known as the Peace Rebels, preached cautionary tales throughout the world, most notably in America and Europe. Unfortunately, a few were corrupted and soon leaked advanced knowledge that led to the construction and black market sales of modern weapons, transportation, and communications. The globe divided into two political factions—Old Worlders and New Worlders. Those who resisted futuristic knowledge and those who embraced it. The Peace War broke out and the nineteenth century as it should have been was forever changed.

The Victorian Age met the Age of Aquarius.

For years and for political reasons Simon and Jules resisted the urge to explore anything having to do with Briscoe Darcy or time travel. Not to mention time travel had been outlawed. However, this Race for Royal Rejuvenation, coupled with their family's unfortunate circumstances, motivated Simon to break their childhood pact. "It is true Papa never shared any secrets with me regarding Briscoe and his time machine, yet I do have an idea of how to get my hands on an original clockwork propulsion engine."

Jules raised a lone brow. "As do I."

"Are we in accord?"

"We are. But first, let me Teletype this P. B. Waddington, as well as a personal contact within the Science Museum. I want verification that this treasure hunt is indeed official."

Simon's pulse raced as his brother left the room. With every fiber of his being he knew the response would be affirmative. His brain churned and plotted. Only one of them needed to find and deliver the clockwork propulsion engine in order to avenge their father's name and secure the family's fortune. But, by God, Simon wanted it to be him.

CHAPTER 2

"Willie!"

Wilhelmina Goodenough, known socially as Willie G. and professionally as the Clockwork Canary, refrained from thunking her forehead to her desk due to the booming voice of her managing editor. She did, however, roll her eyes. She could always tell by the timbre of Artemis Dawson's bellow whether she was being summoned for a good reason or bad. This was bad. Given her foul mood of late, this could mean a bloody ugly row.

As lead journalist for the *London Informer*, Britain's most popular tabloid, Willie had earned a desk in close proximity to Dawson's office. Lucky her—or rather *him*—as was public perception.

For the last ten years, Willie had been masquerading as a young man. Sometimes she was amazed that she'd gotten away with the ruse for so long. Then again, she was slight of frame as opposed to voluptuous. What womanly curves she did possess were easily concealed beneath binding and baggy clothing. Her typical attire consisted of loose linen shirts with flouncy sleeves, a waistcoat one size too big, and an American-cowboy-style duster as opposed to a tailored frock coat. Striped baggy trousers and sturdy boots completed the boyish ensemble. A vast selection of colorful long scarves had become her trademark, as she always wore one wrapped around her neck in a quirky style no matter the season. When outdoors, instead of a bowler or top hat, Willie pulled on a newsboy cap and tugged the brim low to shade her face. She'd chopped her hair long ago, a shaggy style that hung to her chin and often fell over her eyes. She was by no means fashionable, but she did have a style all her own.

And not a bustle, corset, or bonnet to her amended name.

Once in a great while she yearned for some kind of feminine frippery, but she was far more keen on surviving this intolerant world than on feeling pretty.

"Willie!"

Blast. "Best get this over with," she said to herself, because no coworkers were within earshot of her somewhat sequestered and privileged work space, and even if they were, she wasn't chummy with any of the blokes. Willie had two confidants in this world: her father and her journal. One hidden away and one locked away—respectively.

Out of habit, Willie checked the time on her pocket watch, then consulted the timepiece on her multifunctional brass cuff. Her preoccupation with time had prompted the "Clockwork" portion of her professional name, and was often a source of unkind jest for fellow journalists. Their assessment of her peculiar habit meant nothing to her, whilst knowing the precise time and how much time had passed between certain events was of vital importance.

Abandoning her research on significant technological inventions, Willie pushed away from her scarred wooden desk. Her home away from home, the desktop was crowded with stacks of books, piles of documents and files, scores of pens and pencils, her typewriter, her personal cup and teapot, and a working miniature replica of Big Ben, otherwise known as Clock Tower. Dawson often wondered how she found anything, but she did in fact know the precise whereabouts of any given item. Organized chaos: just one of her many gifts.

On the short walk to her boss's office, Willie breathed deeply, seeking solace in the familiar scents of the newsroom—ink, paper, oil, cigarette smoke, sweat, and assorted hair tonics. Scents she associated with freedom and security. This job enabled her to pursue her passion as well as provide for herself and her addle-minded father. Forsaking her gender and race had seemed a small price to pay in the beginning. But lately she teemed with resentment. Bothersome, that. She had no patience for self-pity.

To her own disgust, she strode into her boss's office with a spectacular chip on her shoulder. "You bellowed?"

Dawson looked up from his insanely neat and orderly desk. "Where's the story on Simon Darcy?"

Bugger.

Certain her palms would grow clammy any second, Willie stuffed her hands into the pockets of her trousers and slouched against the doorjamb. "What story?"

Dawson's eyes bulged. "The story I asked for days ago. The story that's *late*. The interview with Simon Darcy regarding the collapse of Project Monorail!"

"Ah, that."

"Yes, *that*."

"The timing seemed off."

"Off?"

"He's been away, attending his father's funeral, comforting his family."

"Yes, I know, Willie. The father who blew himself up whilst building a blasted rocket ship! Two Darcys suffer ruin due to two fantastical projects one day apart. One week before a global race is announced that promises to stir up interest in *outlawed* inventions, if you know what I mean—and I know that you do!

"The timing, dear boy, is *perfect*! Pick Simon Darcy's brain whilst he's vulnerable. Get the scoop on his failed project and his father's bungled invention. Probe deeper and dig up buried family secrets. Go where no man has gone before and ferret out never-disclosed-before details regarding Briscoe Darcy and his time machine. If anyone can do it, you can!" He pounded his meaty fist to his desk to emphasize his point.

Willie felt the force of that blow to her toes. Her temples throbbed and her pulse stuttered. Aye, she could do it. But she did not want to. The subject of their discussion was too close to her well-guarded heart. Though she said nothing, Dawson clearly read her reluctance due to her obviously not-so-guarded expression.

Narrowing his bloodshot eyes, the portly man braced his thick forearms on his desk and leaned forward. "Close the door."

Gads. This was worse than bad.

Willie did as the man asked, then slumped into a chair and settled in for a lecture. She resisted a glance at her cuff watch. As long as she didn't make physical contact with Dawson, time was irrelevant. Meanwhile her keen mind scrambled for a way to get out of this pickle.

"The *Informer* is no longer the most popular tabloid in the country. We've been edged out by the *Crier*."

"The *City Crier*? But that's a Sunday-only paper. We are a daily. Not only that . . ." Willie tamped down her pride, snorted. "You're jesting."

"Our investors are not happy," Dawson went on, grave as a hangman. "The publisher and executive editor are not happy. Which means . . ."

"You are not happy."

"Get the dirt on Darcy or dig up something even more titillating." He jabbed a finger at the door. "Now get out."

Although Dawson could be a curmudgeon, he'd always had at least a sliver of good humor hiding beneath the guff. Willie sensed no humor now. The pressure from above must be severe indeed. Pausing on the doorstep, Willie voiced a troubling notion. "When did I stop being your favorite?"

"When you went soft on me. That original piece you typed up on Ashford's death was fluff. And the revision wasn't much better. Our readers want sensational, Willie, not respectful. They can get that from the quality press." After a tense moment, Dawson sighed. "You've had a good run at the *Informer*, Willie. Some people think you've gotten too comfortable. Too arrogant. Most people don't know you as well as I do, and even *I* don't know you that well. But I do know that you have a special gift. I'd hate to lose it."

Sensing freedom and security slipping away, Willie spoke past her constricted throat. "You'll get your story."

SOUTHEAST OF LONDON
PICKFORD FIELD

"Rough landing."

An honest observation, not a criticism. Still, Simon bristled at his brother's greeting. Jules had taken the train from Ashford to Pickford Field—a private aeropark outside of London where they'd agreed to rendezvous. Simon had commandeered the ramshackle airship designed by their father, a small boat modified with a hot-air balloon and steam engine components enabling the vehicle to fly—albeit without great altitude or grace.

"The engine stalled twice and the steering mechanism seized," Simon said whilst descending the splintered gangway. "It is fortunate that I landed at all. I anticipated crashing every five minutes of that two-hour flight, which, by the way, should have taken but an hour." Adrenaline pumping, he wrenched off his goggles and stalked toward the aero-hangar owned by their mutual friend Phineas Bourdain. "Considering Papa's shaky design and my mediocre piloting skills, you should be *applauding* my wretched arrival."

He realized suddenly that Jules was not on his heels but lumbering behind. Damn the injury that had left his brother with a stilted gait. Pretending not to notice, Simon paused and jammed a hand through his wind-ravaged hair. "The *Flying Cloud* is a flying death trap."

"Yet Amelia would have utilized that death trap in order to join in the race without a second thought."

"The only reason I took the damned thing."

Jules clapped him on the shoulder. "You're a good man."

Simon's conscience twinged. Their father was dead due

to his arrogance. How good could he be? "I'm a lunatic, clearly. But at least Amelia is grounded and safe at Ashford with Mother."

"Let us hope she stays there." Jules squeezed past him and into the cavernous hangar.

Simon glanced over his shoulder, noted the murky silhouette of the city's edge, the buildings cloaked in a wintry gray and the persistent haze from the countless smokestacks and culminating fumes of ground transportation and industrial factories. Had Project Monorail flourished, pollution would have diminished by at least a third. Resentment churned as he turned away from his failed vision.

Moving into the aero-hangar, he noted two sizable dirigibles, one in complete disarray. He expected their friend to emerge from behind the exposed steam engine, tools in hand, grease smearing his face, but there was, in fact, no sight or sound of the crack machinist. "Where's Phin?"

"Somewhere over Yorkshire," Jules said as they side-stepped scattered engine components and cluttered work areas. "Last-minute booking."

Retired military, Phin was not only a skilled machinist but a bloody impressive pilot. He'd been operating a private aero-repair and charter business for two years, and making a damned fine living. Simon followed his brother into the man's cramped but tidy office. Shoulders tense, Simon shrugged out of his greatcoat whilst Jules helped himself to Phin's brandy and poured them both a glass.

Simon drank to warm his chilled bones. He assumed Jules indulged to subdue his chronic pain—not that the proud man ever admitted the need for medicinal spirits. Instead Jules allowed his friends and acquaintances, as well as their mother, to believe his fondness for liquor and various drugs was rooted soundly in hedonism. As he was a novelist—a science fiction writer no less—no one questioned his eccentric ways or decadent lifestyle. Indeed, they expected such folly from an artist. Out of respect for his brother's dignity, Simon supported the illusion.

"I could not speak freely at Ashford," Jules said.

"Because of Amelia?"

"Because of anyone." Jules poured more brandy, then leaned back against the weathered chair, glass in hand. "You said you had information pertaining to the clockwork propulsion engine."

"Not precisely. But I know where to find specific instructions on how to *build* the clockwork propulsion engine."

"The Aquarian Cosmology Compendium?"

Simon nodded. The sole and elusive journal that included designs and notes compiled by the scientific faction of the time travelers, known as Mods. "Amongst other scientific data, that compendium supposedly contains details regarding the dimension-hopping heart of Briscoe's time machine, as well as the Peace Rebels' Briscoe Bus." The vehicle that had enabled the Mods to time travel.

"So you intend to find the legendary compendium and replicate the engine? Your engineering skills are exceptional, Simon. I've no doubt that, presented with the design, you could construct a working model, yet—"

"It would be a replication, not a historical find. Hence my plan." Simon leaned forward and lowered his voice even though they appeared to be alone. "If I build the clockwork propulsion engine to Briscoe's specifications, I can test it. Utilizing a time machine of my own construction, I'll travel back to 1856 and pinch the Briscoe Bus's *original* clockwork propulsion engine and then return to our time to collect our due fame and fortune. Other than Briscoe's time machine, surely the Peace Rebels' time machine is the invention of unparalleled significance and will therefore win the Triple R Tourney."

"That is your plan."

Sensing skepticism in his brother's voice, Simon frowned. "I confess it is not without challenge. Locating the Aquarian Cosmology Compendium—"

"—would be a damned miracle."

"I realize no Vic has ever laid eyes on those notes," Simon said, using the Mod term for the rightful citizens of Queen Victoria's England. "But the compendium is referred to in the Book of Mods. Therefore it must exist."

"Searching for the ACC is a waste of your valuable time."

"You have a better idea?"

"I do." Jules swilled the remnants of his glass, then leaned forward as well. "According to my sources—"

"What sources?"

"Government sources."

"You're retired."

"But still connected to people in high places. What I'm about to tell you—"

"Is highly confidential." Simon had long suspected his brother still dabbled in stealth campaigns, but he'd never known for sure or in what capacity. Just now his senses buzzed with curiosity and a hint of danger. Pretending nonchalance, he raised one cocky brow. "Fascinating. Do tell."

"It is possible that the Mods' clockwork propulsion engine was not destroyed along with the Briscoe Bus, as reported, but that it was whisked away and hidden. There's reason to believe the knowledge of the secret location is guarded by three reclusive Mods known as the Houdinians."

"An odd and unfamiliar title." Simon frowned. "Who are these Houdinians? And why have I never heard of them?"

"Because they are a closely guarded secret."

"Yet you're privy to this secret."

"I'm privy to a lot of secrets." Jules checked his pocket watch. "Time is of the essence." He passed Simon an envelope. "Three Houdinians. Three names. There is a curiosity shop in Notting Hill. It's run by a retired Mod Tracker, although few are aware of his past vocation."

"You're one of the few."

"I am." Jules corked the liquor bottle. "If anyone can give you a location on a Houdinian, it's Thimblethumper."

"Queer name."

"Bogus name."

"Why am *I* talking to this Thimblethumper? Why not you?"

"Because I'm increasing our chances of success by going after another clockwork propulsion engine."

"Not—"

"Yes."

"But the original device—"

"Is trapped in the future. I know." Jules reached inside his coat and passed Simon a palm-sized gadget with a hinged cover. "It's an experimental tele-talkie. Agency restricted. Show it to no one and only use it to communicate with me in times of dire need."

Simon thumbed open the cover and marveled at the intricate mechanism.

"Point-to-point verbal communication. Earphone, microphone, antenna," Jules said, noting various and curious components. "Power button and toggle. Left to transmit, right to receive."

"No cords?"

Jules shook his head. "It's a hybrid of the Mods' walkie-talkie. A personal two-way radio device." He produced a matching silver and bronze tele-talkie and thumbed the power button, causing Simon's device to squawk, then squeal.

Simon winced at the high-pitched sound as Jules limped out of the office and a goodly distance away. Suddenly, he heard his brother's voice as clear and loud as though he were still in the same room. "Good God," Simon said, toggling left to transmit. "Can you hear me as well?"

"Ingenious, is it not?" Jules asked. "Powering off to conserve energy."

Simon powered off as well and joined his brother in the cavernous work area. "How—"

"No time to explain, and as I said, it's experimental and—"

"Agency restricted." Simon angled his head. "What agency would that be precisely?"

Jules paused as if deliberating the wisdom in sharing that information, then slipped the tele-talkie into a leather pouch attached to an intricate harness worn beneath his greatcoat. "The Mechanics."

Simon absorbed the name and significance. He knew his brother traveled in scientific and fantastical circles, but the

Mechanics were *so* fantastical and mysterious, many thought them an urban legend. "You're telling me that you have personal connections with Her Majesty's Mechanics?"

"I *am* a Mechanic."

Highly trained, highly covert agents who "fixed" sensitive and controversial matters for the British government and its sovereign. It's not that Jules didn't have the keen intellect and military training. "But—"

"My leg." Jules quirked an enigmatic smile. "I manage."

Blimey. Simon could scarcely believe his ears. "How long—"

"Since my recovery."

"Then you are not retired."

"Oh, but I am. Officially."

Simon shoved a hand through his hair. "If you were recruited upon techno-surgical recovery, then you have been operating undercover for six years. Why did you not tell me?"

"Because it was not sanctioned."

"And now?"

Jules thumbed a switch on the knob of his cane and Simon watched, fascinated, as the walking stick retracted to the length of a screwdriver. "Although I consider myself fairly invincible, I am not a magician. Should I fail upon this mission, I shall be stuck in the 1960s along with our not-so-dear and troublesome cousin Briscoe." Jules's expression darkened. "Papa died believing me to be a struggling writer, racked with demons and wrestling with addictions. If I do not return . . . I'd prefer you, Mother, and Amelia to remember me in kinder regards."

Simon struggled to make sense of his brother's words.

"Professor Maximus Merriweather holds the key to my futuristic voyage," Jules said, whilst buttoning his coat. "And he, I have learned, is in Australia. Should there be a dire reason, you can reach me using the tele-talkie."

Simon glanced at the advanced device burning a hole in his hand and his ever-curious mind. "A wireless signal that transmits over fifteen thousand kilometers?"

"Lest you forget, the Mods put a man on the moon."

"Are you saying the Mechanics have recruited an original Peace Rebel? A twentieth-century scientist? An engineer? Someone from NASA? The GPO? Wait. You are traveling to speak with Professor Merriweather? *The* Professor Merriweather?"

"A difficult man to track and even more difficult to engage."

Simon bristled with envy. Merriweather was a legendary physicist and cosmologist. A Mod who'd preached about the wonders and downfalls of the future before disappearing with his young daughter in a bid for safety and anonymity. Someone who would understand, support, and—given his education and origin—possess the knowledge to perhaps advance and enhance Simon's Project Monorail. "What I wouldn't give for an hour alone with that genius."

"Yes, well, I require more than an hour," Jules said, "and should Merriweather slip my grip, you will have a Houdinian at your disposal."

Before Simon could remark, Jules pushed on. "The tele-talkie should function for as long as I'm in this dimension. After that . . ." He grasped Simon's shoulder in an affectionate squeeze. "I suppose we shall have to rely upon our twin sensibilities." He smiled, then stepped back. "Good luck in your quest, brother."

A thousand questions crowded the tip of Simon's tongue, but he stood speechless as Jules disappeared before his very eyes.

LONDON

He appeared out of nowhere, pushing in behind Willie just as she unlocked her door, forcing his way inside her lodgings before she could engage the customized clockwork safety lock.

On instinct, she grabbed the first weapon within her reach and whirled.

The intruder blocked her swing, and the bronze Buddha with the clock in his fat belly flew out of her hand, crashing into her new electric table lamp. The glass shade and incandescent bulb shattered, time stopped, and Willie's bravado wavered. Physical contact had been brief. Not long or focused enough to effectively time-trace into his past, but enough to catch a glimpse of a memory. A group of men convening in a darkened room and the whisper of two disjointed words—*assassination* and *Aquarius*.

Heart pounding, Willie scrambled back, assessing the situation.

She'd been walking off her frustration. Ruminating Dawson's order to get a story on Simon Darcy or to hit the proverbial street. She'd been lost in thought, lost in the cold fog rolling in with the depressing dusk. She knew not if this odious thug had been following her or perhaps lurking in the shadows of the meager lodgings she rented near Blackfriars Bridge. What she knew was that she was now trapped inside her dimly lit parlor with a dangerous masked stranger.

"I mean you no harm," he said as if reading her mind. "If I did, the deed would be done."

"Comforting," she snapped.

"Cheeky," he replied. "Indeed, I find your fighting spirit . . . stimulating." His lip twitched as his gaze landed on her newsboy cap, then dragged south to her worn boots. "The name is Strangelove."

Willie forced her knees steady and willed her tone not to spike in pitch. "I'm not partial to blokes," she said, assuming Strangelove had a predilection for young men.

"Neither am I." Still smiling, he gestured to her worn and faded chaise. "Do sit, Miss Goodenough."

It was, in fact, good advice, as her legs fairly buckled at the mention of her real name. Practiced at pretending and desperate to maintain her guise, Willie slouched against the chaise in her lackadaisical boyish style, whilst contemplating potential weapons within her reach. "I'm afraid your eyesight's impaired by that mask, sir. The name's Willie G. and I'm a chap same as you."

"Spare me the pretense. I've neither the time nor patience." Strangelove sat in a chair with the grace of a titled gentleman. His dark clothes, cape, gloves, and top hat were of fine quality, his speech and manner refined. "Wilhelmina Goodenough," he said, leveling her with a narrowed gaze meant to intimidate. "Daughter of Michelle and Michael Goodenough, a twentieth-century security expert and a nineteenth-century merchant. A Mod and a Vic. Which makes you, Miss Goodenough, aka Willie G., aka the Clockwork Canary, a first-generation Freak."

She sat frozen, her lungs convulsing in trepidation. He knew who she was and, worse, *what* she was. Born of parents from two dimensions, all Freaks possessed various supernatural abilities that magnified and sharpened with age. Feared and/or shunned by polite society, her altered race was denied numerous rights, ofttimes including the opportunity to pursue the profession of their choosing. Hence her ten-year ruse. Strangelove knew she was a woman, knew she was a Freak. Did he know about her time-tracing skills? Did he mean to exploit her gift of tapping into people's memories? His intent was clearly nefarious. At the very least the wretched toff had the ability to shatter her sculpted world. "If you mean to blackmail me—"

"I do."

"Pressmen make very little money."

"Obviously." Strangelove glanced around the clean but cramped and cluttered living space Willie called home. "I've no need of your exiguous finances, Miss Goodenough, but I do require your time and skills. I have it on good authority that Simon Darcy is joining the Triple R Tourney. I want you to join him on his quest and to report to me the moment he's acquired whatever historical technological invention he seeks."

Willie stared. Yet another person intent on pushing her into Simon's world. The timing was surreal, if not suspicious. "What makes you think—"

"You had an illicit affair with Darcy when you were but sixteen," he persisted. "Surely you can charm your way back into his life. Although I suggest a gown instead of trousers. And your hair—"

"I have no intention of revealing my true identity," she blurted. Never mind serving up her heart on a silver platter. Her gaze skipped to a sentimental keepsake propped upon a fringed pillow on the corner chair, the only *girly* item in the room. A doe-eyed china doll given to her by Simon. The only evidence that he'd ever been part of her life. How did Strangelove know about the brief but torrid love affair that crushed her soul? No one, aside from her parents and brother, knew.

Or so she'd thought.

"Then concoct a ruse as the Clockwork Canary. I care not how you follow and report on Simon Darcy. Only that you do."

Willie met and held the man's steady and unsettling gaze. A man of purpose. A man of power. She tested her limits. "And if I don't?"

"I will obliterate your ruse, Miss Goodenough. Rob you of your reputation and livelihood, your journalistic means of perpetuating the Freaks' emancipation, as well as your ability to support your father and to shield your rebellious brother from harm's way." He smiled when she tensed. "Ah, yes. Your Freak brother, Wesley. Did I fail to mention my knowledge of his gift and crimes?"

Who *was* this man? How was it that he knew so much about her and her family? If she could touch him and focus, she could time-trace into his past, experience his memories as though she were an invisible bystander. Learning pieces of his life, his secrets, his deeds, might help to reveal his true identity and purpose. Why was the word *assassination* tied to one of Strangelove's memories? Was this a past transgression or a plotted crime? She stole a peek at her cuff watch.

One focused touch . . .

But the man kept his distance, even as he tossed her a shiny rectangular device. "This is a telecommunicator. I will brief you on the practical use and codes. It is a direct line to me. Show it to no one, especially Darcy."

Her pulse flared. The Darcy family was famous for their association with the Time Voyager. Simon himself had garnered a fair amount of attention regarding Project Monorail. He was, in fact, quite unpopular with Old Worlders. Gaze fixed on the futuristic device, Willie feigned nonchalance. "Do you mean Simon harm?"

"Only if he stands in between me and a certain invention. You can assure Darcy's safety by using your wiles, your gift, and my telecommunicator, Miss Goodenough."

Oh, how she wished he'd stop calling her that. How could so much misfortune rain down upon her in one blasted day? First Dawson had threatened her job if she did not get a story on Simon, and now this man, this Strangelove, threatened her reputation, the safety of her father, her brother, and the man she had once loved.

Willie balled her fists, damned fate, and searched her soul. She would do anything to protect her father and brother. As for Simon, as much as she resented him, she did not wish him harm. Putting her heart at risk seemed a trivial sacrifice. But she was not a pawn. Never a pawn. Perhaps she could protect all those at risk and advance her own interests as well. "I'll do as you ask, Strangelove, but considering it means a sabbatical from my regular job at the *Informer*, I have a price."

The vexing toff studied her at length. "You're in no position to bargain, but I will do what I must to advance my goal. If you cross me, however—"

"You will crush me."

"Cheeky *and* smart."

Oh, but she despised the Vics who thought to manipulate her kind. In spite of her foul mood, Willie smiled. "Aye. I am."

CHAPTER 3

By the time Simon had made the journey from Pickford Field into London, it had been too late to visit Thimblethumper's Shoppe of Curiosities. It had also been too late to visit pertinent libraries in order to research the Peace Rebels and any mention of the Houdinians, the Briscoe Bus, or the clockwork propulsion engine.

Instead of visiting his gentlemen's club for dinner or popping into a neighborhood pub for a pint and a chat with friends, Simon had retired directly to his town house in Covent Garden. The vexing failure of Project Monorail was too fresh, as was the sensationalized report of his father's death. Presently Simon would be the talk of his circle and not in a way he fancied or craved. He loathed being the center of pity or scorn or a source of curiosity—most assuredly and especially in cases based solely on his connection with the Time Voyager. For the umpteenth time in several days, Simon damned the Clockwork Canary for shining a light upon that showboating and infamous inventor whilst diminishing the life and death of Reginald Darcy and by extension dragging Simon, as well as Jules and Amelia and their mother, Anne, through the mud. The more Simon heaped his anger upon the *Informer* and that bloody, unfeeling journalist, the less he focused on his own guilt regarding his father's ghastly death. The less he obsessed on the corrupt Old Worlders who'd damned his epic engineering marvel.

By narrowing his scope of fury and frustration, Simon had hoped to recoup the sleep that had eluded him since enduring the double blows of crushing loss. Instead he'd wrestled with new and additional quandaries. Foremost, the knowledge that his brother was a Mechanic. A legendary and esteemed post. Yet again, and even with a bum leg, his older twin had exceeded any accomplishment Simon had yet to make. Yes, he was proud of Jules, but he was also damned envious. Knowing his brother plotted the improbable—traveling into the future, absconding with Briscoe's original time machine, and traveling back home—filled him with wonder and hope but also, dammit, *envy*.

On top of that, one of the Houdinians' names dogged Simon like a tenacious foxhound.

Mickey Goodenough.

Goodenough alone, although unique, would not have rattled Simon, but for the fact that Thimblethumper's Shoppe was in Notting Hill. A neighborhood he used to frequent and now avoided, as it conjured memories of Wilhelmina Goodenough—*Mina*—his first and only love. Her father's first name had been Michael. Mickey for short? Except he'd been a Vic merchant, not a Mod rebel. At least not to Simon's knowledge. If one parent had been a Mod and the other a Vic, that would make Mina a Freak. Yes, she'd been a bit of an enigma, but a *Freak*? Surely he would've sensed if he'd made love to an altered being. And her eyes ... They'd been a solid and seducing flash of meadow green, not the rainbow of swirling colors indicative of a Freak. Perhaps this Mickey Goodenough was a distant cousin or, more likely, no relation at all.

Regardless, the possibility haunted Simon throughout the night and throughout his morning routine. By the time he left his town house in Covent Garden and, via the underground, traveled to Paddington Station, he was in a foul mood indeed.

He'd waited for her. *Here.* At this railway station. Their agreed-upon meeting place. They were to elope to Gretna Green. Only Mina never showed.

Simon navigated the crush of morning travelers whilst shoving aside the smarting memories of the redheaded sprite's betrayal. His heart had long since healed, but there was a lingering sting to his pride. He'd been so sure of their love, so sure of *her*. True, she'd been young—sixteen to his nineteen—but her keen mind, adventurous nature, and worldly views had rendered the two of them kindred souls.

Or so he'd thought.

Leaving Paddington, Simon signaled an automocab, and a scant few minutes later abandoned the foul-smelling, gear-grinding vehicle, choosing to walk the remaining distance rather than waste time in congested traffic. Glancing up, he briefly envisioned the tracks of a monorail system and mentally calculated the advantages the alternate mode of transportation would have upon this thriving area.

There were times, by God, when Simon felt as though fate had deemed him undeserving and schemed to rob him of notable success. Resentful, he shut down his dream and focused on his immediate goal. Unfortunately, navigating the cobbled streets of Notting Hill threw him back in time, intensifying his prickly mood. He envisioned Mina's playful smile, her long vibrant red tresses, and brilliant green eyes. Taking her innocence before marriage had been reckless and irresponsible, but blimey, she'd stirred his blood, seducing him with her striking beauty and kinetic spirit. This moment his senses sparked as though she were hot on his heels. Absurd, as she had moved to Scotland years ago with her parents. Still, he couldn't shake the feeling of being followed.

Simon pulled his derby low over his brow, then glanced at the shop's display window to his right. Indeed, he spied a familiar reflection. Familiar because he'd noticed the ill-tailored bohemian when he'd stopped to purchase the morning newspaper and then again on the train, slouched in a seat close to his own. Dipper? Newshound? Or perhaps the disgruntled brother of a woman Simon had dallied with. Indeed, he had no shortage of lovers.

Even though Thimblethumper's was just ahead on the corner, Simon crossed to the other side of the street. Sure enough, the peculiar chap followed.

Simon stopped and whirled, attacking the puzzle head-on. "What's your game, boy?"

"I . . ." The bloke met Simon's gaze and dithered, stumbling back two paces and into the path of a steam-powered automocoach.

Cursing, Simon yanked the flustered chap from harm's way and into a sheltered alcove. "Get a grip, man," he said, although it was his turn to falter. His body responded to their close proximity in a curious and bothersome manner. In a heartbeat, Simon assessed the smooth skin and slight bone structure of the face all but hidden beneath a floppy newsboy cap and obscured by shaggy ink black hair. "I say, *are* you a man?"

The kid shoved at Simon's shoulders, pushing him back whilst tugging his cap even lower. "I'm no Miss Nancy, if that's what you're suggesting."

Indeed it was not, but that would explain the effeminate aura. It did not, however, explain Simon's keen sexual awareness. Although adventurous in the bedroom, he had never been attracted to another man. "Why are you following me?"

The kid fussed with his colorful scarves, stealing a glance at his bronze time cuff. "I have a proposition."

Simon raised a brow.

"Not *that* kind of proposition."

"Do I know you?" Simon couldn't shake the sense of familiarity even though he was most certain he'd never met this dark-eyed bohemian. A pretty boy with an intense, caged energy. A source of increasing fascination.

"Undoubtedly, you know *of* me." He offered a worn gloved hand in greeting. "The name is Willie G.," he said in a clipped, gruff tone. "Known professionally as the Clockwork Canary."

Simon ignored the proffered hand and grabbed the Canary by his ridiculous lapels.

"Cheese and crackers!" the kid exclaimed.

Simon froze. He hadn't heard that particular curse in a long time. Another reminder of Mina. *Damnation*. Shaking off a bout of déjà vu, Simon whisked the Canary into the alley. Blood boiling, he pinned the focal point of his fury against a brick wall and glared. "You made a laughingstock of my father."

"I apologize."

"Not accepted." Simon stared into the Canary's wide eyes. The damnable pressman trembled beneath his touch. Was he a coward as well as a nance? Meanwhile, Simon's own heart pounded with something more troublesome than rage. He couldn't get that curse, *Mina's* curse, out of his mind. Unsettled, he released the lad and distanced himself posthaste. "What do you want?"

"I have it on good authority that you are joining the Race for Royal Rejuvenation."

"So?"

"I want to tag along."

"To report my misadventures?"

"To chronicle your journey. Your success."

Simon narrowed his eyes. "What makes you think I'll succeed?"

The Canary gave a cocky shrug. "You'll have me as your secret weapon."

Simon snorted. Of all the cheek.

"If you need answers, I can get them. Information? Scoop? I can be of service. It is what I do. What I am good at. Ferreting out data. Have you never read one of my candid interviews?"

"I prefer respectable broadsheets to the *Informer*." He had in fact skimmed random accounts. And if he hadn't, they were often the subject of tavern gossip. The Clockwork Canary, though sensationalistic, was a perceptive interrogator and a gifted writer.

"I'll pay you," the Canary blurted. "That is, the *Informer* will pay you a generous sum if you allow me to experience and chronicle your expedition. A serialized version highlighting the more adventurous and romantic elements."

Simon crossed his arms over his chest. "Romantic?"

The Canary copied his stance and cocked his head.

"Your endless affairs and scandalous liaisons are almost as famous as your engineering flop."

The insult would have stung more if Simon had been less intrigued by the cutting delivery. By God, the kid sounded jealous. "How much?"

The Canary blinked and then mumbled a hefty sum.

"That much?"

"You are a Darcy. Therefore, you command great interest and high payment."

Difficult to ignore a lucrative offer that would greatly benefit his mother and sister. Still, of all the pressmen. The damnable Clockwork Canary? Did Simon's recent ill luck know no bounds? "Your condescending tone suggests this feature is not of your choosing."

"My job was threatened, if you must know." The kid stared daggers into Simon's skeptical gaze. "Secure a posh story on Simon Darcy or else, I was told."

That snagged Simon's attention, if not sympathy. Knowing he was a person of interest buffered many a recent sting. He shifted his gaze from the arrogant pressman to Thimblethumper's Shoppe. "Advance my cause with a certain merchant, Willie G., and you have a deal."

Astounding.

Willie was still shaking in her boots minutes after Simon had pinned her to a wall. She'd been so stunned by his aggression that she'd blurted a curse from her youth. It was as if the physical interaction with Simon had thrown her back in time. *Gads!* She hadn't expected their first encounter in years to be easy, but she'd been knocked arse over teakettle and blown to the moon and back. How could one manage combustible feelings of anger, resentment, and knee-buckling ardor whilst maintaining a calm and cheeky facade? A most difficult challenge, although not as difficult as maintaining her boyish guise. Simon Darcy seduced every fiber of Willie's feminine being. Much like a moth to the proverbial flame—only this time she refused to get burned.

She'd suspected trouble the moment she'd spied him loping down the steps of his modest yet keenly located Georgian town house. When she'd last seen him, twelve years prior, he'd been a free-spirited, handsome young college student. Now he was a devastatingly gorgeous, finely built man who emitted an arrogant streak and a dash of danger. She'd fairly swooned when he'd smiled and chatted up a ragamuffin newsboy hawking papers on the corner. That smile. Those *lips*. The lips that had whispered endearments into her ears. The mouth that had brushed over hers, melting her limbs and searing her difficult world with tender passion.

After boarding the train, she'd slumped in her seat, feigning interest in the business pages of the stuffy *London Daily* whilst sneaking peeks at Simon, who'd been reading the equally stuffy *Victorian Times*. How dashing he looked in an unconventional though precisely tailored suit. A daring style that bordered on ModVic—Victorian attire influenced by the futuristic threads of the "love" generation. Pointy-toed Beatle boots, black and burgundy striped trousers, an embroidered velvet Nehru frock coat featuring gold buttons and a stand-up collar. His black wool greatcoat and matching derby were more conventional, though the paisley winter scarf hinted of a rebellious nature. His longish unkempt golden brown hair clashed slightly with his darker, impeccably and closely trimmed beard and yet somehow matched his overall roguish style.

But mostly Willie was mesmerized by Simon's sinfully handsome face.

When he'd whirled and she'd locked gazes with him, up close and dead on, the breath had whooshed from her lungs. Her traitorous heart had swelled and raced, and her world had tilted in a most fierce and troubling manner.

Astonishing.

Appalling!

How could she be so disgustingly attracted to a man who'd rejected her based upon her race? As someone who'd grown more aware of prejudice and injustice as she'd come of age . . . as someone who worked surreptitiously yet vehemently to obliterate intolerance, she felt that ancient snub sting with blinding ferocity. How disconcerting that her stomach fluttered and her pulse skipped with amorous yearnings. How massively revolting.

Balled fists stuffed deep in the pockets of her oversized duster, Willie warred with her conflicting emotions as she followed Simon inside his point of destination. Thimblethumper's Shoppe of Curiosities was a curious place indeed. She glanced around the tiny store, noting various antiquities and peculiar collectibles. On any other day she might have been fascinated by what looked to be a seventeenth-century lantern clock or the doll-sized clockwork automaton that, when activated, scrawled a message with her quill pen upon the page of her vintage lap desk. However, this moment a replication of a Mod toy captured Willie's rapt attention. The palm-sized double-disk and string device, known by many as a *bandalore*, had been around for centuries, although it would not gain vast popularity until the 1960s, and by then would be called a yo-yo. Willie's mother had traveled back in time with one—something she'd fiddled with to alleviate stress or when she was puzzling through a problem. Willie had been charmed by the toy and had been severely disappointed when her mother had passed the yo-yo down to her son. Then again, Wesley had always been Michelle Goodenough's favorite.

Someone tugged on Willie's scarf, yanking her out of the past. "Are you with me or not, Canary?"

She blinked up at Simon's irritated expression and realized she'd lagged behind. Without comment Willie brushed past him and ahead, spying the balding head of a man hunched over a desk and tinkering with some geared gadget.

"Thimblethumper?" Simon asked whilst nudging her aside.

"What can I do for ya?" the elderly man asked without looking up from his work.

Simon slid him a piece of folded paper.

Thimblethumper set aside his tool and swapped one set

of loupes on his cumbersome spectacles for another. Even with the help of thick lenses, he squinted at whatever was written on the page. His right eye twitched; then, after a tense moment, he looked up and frowned. "Who are ya?"

"Simon Darcy."

Thimblethumper clenched his jaw and narrowed his milky gaze. "And your friend?"

"Associate," Simon amended without sparing her a glance. "Mr. G."

"A Darcy, huh?" he noted, ignoring Willie. "One of *the* Darcys?"

"Fortunately or unfortunately," Simon said whilst sweeping off his derby, "but undoubtedly."

"Bane of my damned existence. The lot of you," he said cryptically, then, "Close kin to the Darcy who blew himself up recently?"

"That would be my father," Simon said as he shoved an impatient hand through his hair. "And to be more precise, he blew up a rocket ship and suffered the consequences of said accident."

Willie bristled. Even though Simon wasn't looking at her, she knew that correction had been lobbed in her infernal direction. As if she hadn't done her research properly. She had, by gads. It was Dawson who'd spun her words for the worse.

"Sorry for your loss," Thimblethumper grumbled, then blew out a breath. "Guess that means you're related to Jules, which explains this list. Damned agency's a pain in my tookus," the older man complained. "I'm retired."

"But knowledgeable. I need to speak with one of these people. Can you help?"

Thimblethumper drummed his fingers on the dusty desktop, clearly perturbed, clearly unwilling.

What people? Which agency? Willie ached to touch the reluctant merchant, to trace a memory and to snag a piece of pertinent data, but with the deep desk and a mound of gadgets and tools between them there was no clear and natural way. Unless . . .

Willie noted the time, then took off her gloves. She pulled her worn leather wallet from the inner pocket of her coat and procured a tantalizing bribe. Strangelove had provided her with a significant bankroll, finances to see her through the sabbatical from the *Informer*, finances to advance his cause. "We'd be obliged if you could aid us in our search." As was her usual quandary as a reporter, she was fishing for facts in a dark and mysterious sea. She had no idea who or what they were searching for—but Thimblethumper did.

She offered the money, hoping the exchange would allow her enough time to mentally connect and time-trace. She was focused, prepared, but then Simon shifted, his arm brushing hers. Her concentration shattered just as Thimblethumper snatched the money. Had the merchant touched her at all? She couldn't be sure. She'd been compromised by the merest connection with Simon. Not that she'd seen into *his* memories. Just like when Simon had snatched her from the path of the automocoach, when he'd rushed her into the alley and trapped her against the wall. She'd been too aware of the present to connect with the past. Too emotionally unsettled. Too sexually primed.

Pocketing the bribe, Thimblethumper trailed a finger down Simon's list, a list shielded from Willie's view. "Dead. Missing." He paused, then grunted. "Underground."

"In hiding?" Simon asked.

"On the job."

"Where?" Willie asked just as the bell above the door tinkled, announcing a new customer.

"Edinburgh."

"I lived in Edinburgh," she said, pulse tripping. "Where precisely?"

"Don't know precisely."

"Vaguely," Simon pressed.

"Old Town," Thimblethumper said in a gruff whisper, flipping up the visual loupes and casting an anxious gaze toward the three shoppers perusing a nearby collection. "Know this, Darcy. The Houdinians swore to protect and they kill to do so. Proceed at your own risk."

Before Simon could comment, before Willie could blurt her next question, the man veered off and on to his potential customers.

"We're done here." Simon grabbed and stuffed the paper with the list of names into his pocket, nabbed Willie's arm, and guided her through the clutter, toward the exit.

Her curiosity and journalistic instincts demanded more information. *Who are the Houdinians? What do they protect?* She spied the yo-yo. "One moment." She snatched up the nostalgic toy. "Wait here," she said to Simon. *No distractions.*

"Excuse me, ladies," Willie said with a gallant and apologetic smile. "I am anxious to purchase this toy for my brother. Fascinating, yes?" she asked whilst demonstrating the "sleeper"—one of the only tricks she'd mastered, unlike her mother, who'd been a whiz. Tempering a wisp of melancholy, Willie blinked back to the present and Thimblethumper. "Could you tally my purchase, sir?"

Frowning, the man rushed back to his desk, utilizing the mechanical till as he named a ridiculous price.

Dipping into her wallet once more, Willie passed over the cash. "An invigorating purchase," she said, noting the time on her cuff as she offered her hand in a proper gesture of gratitude. "I thank you. For this and for your assistance regarding the other matter," she added, prompting Thimblethumper to reflect on the Houdinians.

Properly focused, the moment he clasped her palm, Willie traced Thimblethumper's past, a semimeditative trance where she experienced a portion of the "transmitter's" life. A vibrant memory. It felt as though she were there, but she was not. Seemed to last for hours, but it did not. She blinked back to the present, blinked at her cuff watch. She'd been away but five seconds. Registering that reality, Willie breathed easier and backed away with her yo-yo, a location, and an exhilarating discovery.

Heart pounding, Willie caught up with Simon and prodded him toward the door. "*Now* we have what we need."

CHAPTER 4

Oddly invigorated after yet another insomnious night, Simon approached the platform assigned to the Flying Scotsman. The newly enhanced (and somewhat famous) steam locomotive would speed him and his confounding *associate* from London to Edinburgh on this cold and dreary day. Given the faithfully dismal weather in Scotland, no doubt they'd be greeted with icy rain or a snowstorm by the time they reached Waverley Station later this evening. Simon's valet, Fletcher—bless his vexatious, meticulous soul—had insisted upon packing as though Simon were visiting Antarctica.

Tickets purchased and pocketed, Simon set his overstuffed traveling valise alongside his booted feet and checked his pocket watch. Ten minutes to boarding. Surely the Canary was already here somewhere. Given the sensational story waiting to be told, and the fact that the journalist's job was at stake, Simon had every faith the kid would show. Perhaps he was purchasing fruit for the ride or a penny dreadful to help pass the hours.

Simon searched the mob, looking for the dark-haired bohemian with his colorful scarves and voluminous duster. The cavernous station served as the London hub for the Great Northern Railway, and as such teemed with a goodly quantity of travelers. Voices of passengers and vendors mingled and bounced off the vaulted ceilings and glass panes. Iron wheels screeched. Steam engines coughed and hissed.

Simon vibrated with the thrill of the chase and a possible colossal triumph. One of the three Houdinians—Jefferson Filmore—was living and working "underground," protecting *something*, hopefully, possibly, according to his brother, the Briscoe Bus's clockwork propulsion engine. Simon hadn't mentioned the precious and banned time-traveling device to the Canary, but he suspected the pressman knew precisely what he was searching for, either from research and deduction *or* from that curmudgeon Mod Tracker.

Shortly after leaving Thimblethumper's the previous morning, Simon and Willie had parted ways—but not before exchanging heated words. The infuriating pressman had refused to share whatever specifics he'd learned from the retired Mod Tracker, saying, *I'd rather not risk you embarking on this expedition whilst leaving me in the dust, Darcy. No offense, but I don't trust you.*

Of all the cheek. Especially since Simon now suspected the kid of a colossal lie.

They'd agreed to take the rest of the day to prepare for the journey and to meet this morning at King's Cross Station for the ten o'clock express. Simon had visited his bank as well as his solicitor. Once again, he'd avoided his gentlemen's club, although he had slipped into Lambert's Literary Antiquities, owned by his trusted friend Montague Lambert, who'd reluctantly allowed Simon to borrow his banned and now rare copy of the Book of Mods. Simon's own treasured edition had been pinched by someone at the Institute of Civil Engineers, a personal violation that rankled to this day.

Sequestered in his home library, Simon had burned the midnight oil, reviewing the fascinating compilations of futuristic sketches, essays, and cautionary tales, written by a faction of the original Peace Rebels. He had searched every page, every sentence, hoping to find mention of the Houdinians. There had been none, although admittedly Simon's mind had wandered time and again. He could not shake his intense and undeniable physical attraction to the quirky pressman who irritated and fascinated him simultaneously and beyond measure.

At least he'd managed to deduce that he was not, in fact, attracted to a boy. During their parting row, Simon had taken intense notice of certain physical details. The Canary possessed no stubble, no signs of shaving, and the kid was certainly old enough to have facial hair. At one point the fabric of the kid's scarf had slipped enough to reveal a slender neck—no Adam's apple. Not to mention the kid's feet were overly small for a man. The more he thought about it, the greater his certainty.

Willie G. was a fraud. A woman passing as a young man. But why? Androgynous? Gender confused? Or perhaps simply motivated by a desire to excel in a man's world, earning a man's wages and rights. Simon could think of a few reasons and he mulled over each one. He also contemplated the niggling feeling that he'd met the Canary before. Something about him . . . *her.* The way she'd exclaimed, *"Cheese and crackers!"* The vision of her finessing that yo-yo with shaky skill. Just prior to dawn and in a state of delirious exhaustion, Simon had entertained a bizarre speculation.

The physical attraction he felt toward Willie G. was much like the instinctual and intense pull he'd felt toward Wilhelmina Goodenough. Could they be one and the same? The hair and eye color were wrong. The skin tone was off as well. Mina's complexion had been most pale, whilst Willie's was ruddy. Mina had also been shorter in stature, although, at sixteen summers, perhaps she had not reached her full height, or perhaps Willie had inserted lifts inside her boots.

Willie had a slight Scottish lilt and a crude vocabulary, whereas Mina had spoken eloquently—her most vulgar expression being the infamous "Cheese and crackers!" Then again, Mina had moved to Scotland with her family. Depending on how long she'd lived there, that could account for the odd and wholly undefinable accent of the Canary. If they were, indeed, the same person. It boggled the mind, and yet Simon could not rid himself of the possibility.

Another glance at his watch. Five minutes to boarding.

A newsboy appeared hawking the morning edition of the *London Informer*. Unable to resist, Simon purchased a copy. Just as he unfolded the wretched tabloid, someone snatched it out of his hands.

The Clockwork Canary.

"You don't want to read this," the kid said.

"Oh, but now I must." Simon retrieved the newspaper and focused on the front page.

EXCLUSIVE SCOOP—THE CLOCKWORK CANARY TO SING DARCY'S EXPLOITS!

The *Informer*'s star reporter has taken a sabbatical in order to chronicle the exploits of the Honorable Simon Darcy, London's most controversial civil engineer (and relation of the infamous TIME VOYAGER), as he joins the Race for Royal Rejuvenation—now known as the Triple R Tourney! The Clockwork Canary will record a firsthand account of Mr. Darcy's adventures, to be published in serial form upon completion of the expedition. Prepare to be dazzled by tales of risqué romance, high drama, and nail-biting intrigue! Will Mr. Darcy dazzle and deliver like his notorious cousin? Or, like his unfortunate father, will his dreams go up in smoke?

Simon's temper sparked and snapped like the malfunctioning turbine on the *Flying Cloud*. Strangling the Canary would only land him in prison—or worse. In addition, the blasted pressman possessed knowledge that Simon very much needed. Tempering the urge to kill, he glanced over the top of the paper at the red-faced sensationalist. "If I were a violent man—"

"But you are not."

"How do *you* know?"

The kid's cheeks burned even brighter. "I've done my research. You have no prior record or history of physical violence."

"There's always a first time." Simon folded the paper and shoved it in under his arm. He leaned in, glowering down at the dark-haired, dark-eyed, ruddy-skinned bohemian. An intimidating move meant to allow him closer, intimate proximity. His body responded in a familiar, intimate way. Bleeding hell. *Mina?*

"I did not write it," the kid gritted out. "That particular article, that is. My editor assigned someone to take my place. Whilst I'm away. With you."

Simon merely watched as the Canary fidgeted beneath her coat. *Her* coat. Oh, yes. He would bet his comfortable town house this pressman was indeed a bird. And quite possibly his former betrothed. Question was, what was she playing at?

"Did you purchase our tickets?" Willie asked as a whistle blew and a conductor invited passengers on board.

"I said I would."

Looking anxious to distance herself from Simon, she tightened her grip on her valise and tugged down the brim of her floppy cap. "What car—"

"The same as mine."

"Row—"

"Compartment."

"But—"

"My expedition. My rules," Simon said. "I don't want you out of my sight, Canary. Deal or no deal, I don't trust you."

Flabbergasted. That's what she was. Flabbergasted, that fate could be so cruel. Jaw clenched so as not to spew curses, Willie moved into the private compartment, a confined area consisting of opposing upholstered bench seats, hinged doors on either side, and windows affording a view of the passing scenery. The inner door snicked shut, effectively trapping her within close quarters with Simon Darcy for the next nine hours.

Gads.

Simon's valise was already stored in an overhead rack alongside his neatly folded greatcoat and dashing black derby. *He* was seated facing north.

Sitting next to the infuriatingly charismatic engineer was unthinkable. Sitting across from him was nearly as daunting. She'd be forced to look at him for the entire journey. Worse, he'd have a clear and close view of *her*.

Irritated, Willie eyed the rack over the empty bench and considered the difficulty of hoisting her weighty carpetbag over her head.

"Need help?" Simon asked, sounding amused.

Had he known she was a woman, he would have taken her baggage even before they'd boarded the train. Apparently, he merely thought her a puny-muscled bloke. At least her masculine ruse was secure. *For now.* Feeling Simon's eyes burning into her back, she plopped the bag on the end of the bench and hunkered down next to it. "I prefer to keep my belongings within easy reach."

His mouth quirked. "Might want to take off some of those layers," he said, indicating her outerwear. "It's a long ride."

"Mind your own comfort, Darcy," she said, even as she broke into a sweat. "As to the duration of this rail trip, if you had booked passage on a private or commercial airship, we could have cut our travel time by half, if not more."

"Look at it this way, Canary. More time to get to know me. I assume you intend to pick my brain as part of your exposé."

Interrogation was indeed part of her plan. Not only for the serialized account that would ensure her position at the *Informer*, but as a way of learning more about Simon's targeted invention of historical significance in order to appease Strangelove and to protect her family. The task was daunting, albeit exhilarating. "Indeed I do have questions," she said as the train jerked out of the station.

"As do I." He leveled her with a hard stare that made her weak in the knees. "What did you learn from Thimble-thumper?"

Willie forced herself not to fidget or to look away. She'd spent most of the night wide-eyed and weary with thoughts regarding Simon Darcy, many of them sexual. This man had stroked her bare flesh. He'd made her body sing and soar. He'd made her weep with the beauty of their tender albeit scandalous lovemaking. The memories were vivid and mesmerizing and she'd spent several restless hours talking herself out of a rekindled infatuation . . . and failing. In the hazy delirium of near sleep she'd concocted a plan on how to deal with the man as well as her unwelcome yearnings. So far that plan was floundering.

"I reserve the right to relay that information until such a time when I trust you will not wing open the outer door of this compartment and boost me out upon the countryside. Now," Willie said, pulling off her gloves and procuring an ever-ready pad and pencil from her coat pocket, "as to my questions."

"After a nap."

Willie blinked as Simon stood and shrugged out of his stylish frock coat. "But it is midmorning."

"I kept late hours."

"Dallying with drink and women, no doubt," she blurted.

Another infernal twitch of his gorgeous mouth. "No doubt." He settled back onto the cushioned bench, crossed his arms, and stretched out his legs. He closed his eyes, abandoning all talk, leaving Willie hot tempered and out of sorts.

For a moment she simply stared. No waistcoat. No cravat. No scarf. Just a white muslin shirt with generous sleeves. How very Mod. The shirt lay open, exposing his neck and a hint of his glorious chest. At once she remembered cuddling with Simon upon stolen occasions. She recalled laying her cheek to that chest, hearing his heartbeat, smelling the scent of soap mingled with a tinge of manly essence. Her face burned as she remembered her youthful, brazen behavior. Adventurous, impassioned, she'd kissed his collarbone, his chin, his stubbled jaw, his . . . "Blimey," she murmured, jerking her gaze from Simon's mouth.

"Problem?" he asked without opening his eyes.

"It's blooming suffocating in here." Willie sidled over to lower the outside window.

"It's freezing out there," Simon said, guessing her intent. "Take off your blooming coat."

Indeed, Willie was perspiring most uncomfortably. Between the binding, her layers of clothing, and her sizzling thoughts regarding the night she'd seduced Simon into taking her innocence, she would like nothing more than to stick her head outside in an effort to shock her system. Clearly, she was sleep deprived and delirious.

Definitely cranky.

She wrenched off her long wool duster. She shed her mismatched sack coat as well. What could it hurt? Every piece of clothing on her body bagged to conceal her feminine assets. Her trousers, her shirt, her blue velvet waistcoat—all garments one size too large. Plus, she'd bound her breasts tightly so she appeared as flat as a crepe.

Or a boy.

As long as she maintained her slouching posture, blunt vocabulary, and lowered pitch, she could maintain the ruse. She'd fooled thousands of people over ten long years. She could fool one ancient lover.

Breathing somewhat easier, Willie tugged off her cap and sleeved sweat from her brow. Looking over her shoulder, it appeared as though Simon had indeed drifted. She heaped her coats upon the rack, although she laid her cap nearby and kept her long purple scarf looped around her slender neck. She did not, under any circumstances, want to fall prey again to staring at Simon's person and fantasizing.

Distraction was vital.

Carefully, quietly, Willie dipped into her carpetbag and procured her cherished Book of Mods. She'd painstakingly re-covered the journal and its treasured contents so that it appeared to be a novel written by Mary Shelley.

"*Frankenstein*?"

Willie started as Simon shifted to her side and snatched the book from her hands. Her heart thudded due to his close proximity and the delectable smell of soap. "I thought you were sleeping."

"Resting." He flipped through the pages. "Biological and nuclear weapons? Civil rights riots? Antiwar protests?" He cut her a glance. "Monstrous indeed, but not Shelley. Where did you get this?"

"I own it." She snatched back the one thing her mother had bequeathed her and hugged it to her chest.

"The reprinting and selling of that book was outlawed long ago."

"It's a first edition and I did not buy it. Nor did I pinch it," she added, striving not to squirm under his intense regard.

"The content is considered dangerous."

"Old Worlder propaganda," Willie said with a snort. "Considering the progressive nature of Project Monorail and your family's fascination with futuristic marvels, I'm surprised you don't own a copy of the Book of Mods."

"I did. Until someone pinched it." He nodded to the book. "Pleasure? Research?"

"I was looking for a mention of the Houdinians."

"You won't find it." He thumped a finger to the spine. "This was the source of my restless night."

He'd spent the night with a book, not a woman? She shouldn't care, but she did. She almost smiled. "You said your copy was stolen."

"I borrowed one from a friend."

Still clutching the book and the hidden keepsake inside, Willie unleashed her curiosity. "What do you know about the Houdinians?"

"That there were three. That one is dead, another missing, and"—his lip twitched—"the last one underground."

"Where did you get the list?"

"Classified."

"I know the third name, the man we're looking for in Edinburgh. Jefferson Filmore. I learned that much from Thimblethumper." She learned much more, but, for now, chose to withhold the information. Instead, she sought to pick Simon's brain in hopes of filling some mysterious gaps. "What are the other two names?"

"Classified."

Willie snorted. "Top secret? Do you moonlight as a spy, Darcy?"

"No. But I know someone who does." He angled and leaned back, his arms folded over his chest. Apparently he would not be returning to his own bench seat any time soon. "What else did you learn from Thimblethumper?"

"That the Houdinians protect an engine. The engine that catapulted the Briscoe Bus through time. Although of course that can't be true."

"Because according to legend—"

"And the Book of Mods."

"—the Peace Rebels destroyed the bus soon after arriving in this century."

"In order to prevent anyone from using it to hop into yet another dimension and creating further havoc." Willie had heard the story a million times.

"What if they destroyed the bus, but not the engine?" Simon asked.

"But they did. They blew up the entire time-traveling vehicle, including the clockwork propulsion engine."

"How can you know that for sure unless you were there?"

Because her mother had witnessed the detonation and explosion firsthand.

When the fire died out, the Briscoe Bus was nothing more than a burned-out, melted mass of charred metal.

Willie shook off the memory of her mother's voice, her face. "Why would they salvage the engine?"

Simon shrugged. "Insurance? In case they wanted to return home? The bus was but a shell, easily re-created by many a skilled Vic or Mod. But the engine . . ."

"Was as unique as the one built and utilized by your distant cousin Briscoe Darcy. A significant invention indeed," Willie said. "But the original time-traveling engine is trapped in the twentieth century and therefore unattainable."

"It would take a miracle," Simon said.

Willie narrowed her eyes. "I have never heard of the Houdinians." And her mother had told her and Wesley many a tale about the 1960s, as well as the Peace Rebels' mission. "Thimblethumper mentioned an agency. What agency? And he mentioned your brother, Jules. As if he was somehow connected." She frowned, considered. "The spy you spoke of. Is it your brother? A decorated war hero would no doubt qualify. Although one would think his injured leg a hindrance."

"Fascinating."

"What?"

"The way your mind works. You're quite clever, Canary. Undoubtedly gifted in finessing people to talk about themselves or to perhaps unintentionally share information."

She averted her gaze, returned her BOM to her carpetbag. "It's a gift."

"What else did you learn from Thimblethumper? Something specific to Filmore's whereabouts?"

Indeed she did. She eyed the outer door and the scenery whizzing by as the train chugged north.

"I'm not going to toss your bloody hide once you tell me," Simon said, losing patience. "Who would write my dazzling tales of risqué romance, high drama, and nail-biting intrigue?"

She smirked. Just then the train lurched, and off-balance, Willie toppled into Simon's lap.

He steadied her by her forearms, his strong hands searing her skin through the thin fabric of her shirt. He searched her face, her eyes. "Who are you?"

Willie blinked into his mesmerizing gaze. "Don't be daft. You know who I am."

"Do I?"

"The Clockwork Canary."

His gaze slid to her mouth. "I venture you are more than you seem."

Willie's heart fairly burst through her ribs. He suspected her true gender. He would not hold another man this close for so long. At least he did not know her true identity. Instead of shielding her kaleidoscope eyes with green corneatacts, she'd switched to brown. Her hair was chopped short and now black, not cherry red. And she'd darkened her pale skin, at least all visible skin, using a Mod-enhanced lotion that she'd bought on the black market, a tanning agent called QT.

"Ever kiss a man before, Canary?" Simon asked in a low, dangerous tone.

"No," she lied, deciding to brazen it out. "You?"

"No." He righted her then and pushed to his feet, looking down at her as though he couldn't decide whether to ravage or throttle her. "But there's always a first time."

With that, he nabbed his frock coat and exited the compartment, leaving Willie alone with her traitorous yearnings and sizzling blood. "Cheese and crackers," she whispered in her own higher-pitched voice, lowering the window and pressing her face into the icy fierce wind.

Tales of risqué romance, indeed.

CHAPTER 5

Strangelove.

The name echoed in his ears along with the tinny grunts emitting from Renee, his voluptuous robotic domestic who doubled as his housekeeper and sex servant. Taking the life-like automaton from behind, he envisioned two very human women—both vexing in nature, both whetting his sordid appetite. Miss Amelia Darcy and Miss Wilhelmina Goodenough. The latter more easily manipulated and most fresh in his devious mind.

Ridding Miss Goodenough of those mannish clothes would have pleased him. Feasting his eyes upon her naked flesh. Forcing her onto her knees. Bingham had never fornicated with a Freak. Surely it would be more stimulating than pumping the greased and geared Renee. The automaton, though fetching in face and figure, was far too submissive. Surely a Freak, especially one as feisty as Miss Goodenough, would put up a fight.

The mere thought of a struggle in which he would dominate triggered an explosive release. With a guttural growl, he smacked the synthetic flesh of Renee's lush arse and shoved her face forward upon his massive bed.

Without a word, she rolled onto her back and stared up at the ceiling. Still and naked. Quiet and waiting for her next order. In many ways, Renee was the perfect woman.

Especially for a man with sadistic fetishes. Most especially for a man who despised opinionated women with utopian ideals. New Worlders like Amelia Darcy.

"To think I'd contemplated marrying that outspoken liberal," he said aloud, then sneered. "Although I would not mind taming her." Not wanting to obsess over the female Darcy and her role in the Triple R Tourney, he fondled Renee's pleasing assets whilst contemplating the latest developments in London.

"Maintaining anonymity and multiple aliases is essential to my well-being and master plan," he said to the cold-skinned robot. "But I confess I sometimes wish that I had a confidant. Someone with whom to share my assessments and brilliance. My impatience and frustration."

"Confidant," she repeated in a monotone. "The Dowager Viscountess Bingham."

"Ah, yes. Mother. Indeed I trust her with my secrets, but her intrusive manner and incessant nagging grows tiresome." He rolled to his side and propped on one elbow, looking down at Renee's attractive albeit engineered face. "I, Lord Bingham, viscount and visionary and, it might be said, nefarious entrepreneur, appoint you, a programmed minion and acceptable lover, as my number two confidant." He quirked an arrogant grin. "I do not know why this did not occur to me before, as *you*, my dear, are the perfect sounding board."

"Sounding board," she said. "Experiment to test new idea."

"Indeed. Let us see how you do. I shall now sound off, as I have much on my mind, much to assess. I would ask that you at least nod occasionally to indulge my venting."

She nodded.

"Well done." Bingham smoothed a hand over his impeccable hair and considered the last two days filled with surreptitious deeds. He was most pleased and impressed with his efforts. "Given the nature of my ambition, I am not often at liberty to conduct business as myself. I've been *Mars* as well as *Strangelove* for two different yet connected reasons: to dominate the global market of Modified products. Weaponry, communications, and transportation. Thus far, my plan is on target. Although this latest trip to London taxed my patience on many levels. Shall I tell you why?"

His number two confidant nodded.

"Let us start with Aquarius."

"Eleventh astrological sign in the zodiac, originating from the constellation Aquarius," Renee recited from her data resource implants. "Age of Aquarius. Mod terminology pertaining to period of transition—inventions, machines, worldwide organizations, international collaboration, and the fellowship of humankind."

"Or in this case," Bingham said, "a secret society, comprised of nine titled men of science and industry, united in an effort to embrace and cultivate Mod technology. Men of peace, all but me, yet they plot to assassinate the queen. A nasty but necessary endeavor."

"Queen. Queen Victoria—"

"A simple nod would suffice." When she complied, Bingham pushed on, his annoyance rising. "Queen Victoria remains rigid and polices progress with an iron fist. She continues to blame the Peace Rebels for the death of her beloved Prince Albert, banning time-traveling devices and other Mod products. As if by slowing time, she could go back in time," he snapped in disgust. "Romantic rubbish.

"The divide between Old Worlders and New Worlders widens by the day," he went on. "Meanwhile, a Freak rebellion brews in the background. Astonishing that an altered race believes themselves worthy of equal rights," he said with a derisive snort.

Renee jerked her head right, narrowed her eyes.

By Christ, had he hit a nerve? Automatons had no nerves. No feelings. Surely he was mistaken.

"Old Worlders," she said. "Conservatives who shun futuristic knowledge and the technology that, according to the Book of Mods, steered mankind toward the brink of destruction. New Worlders. Liberals. Utopians. Knowledge is power."

"Indeed. And knowing what 'could be,' they choose an alternate path, using technology only for good. Or so they profess." A staunch Flatliner, Bingham cared only about what futuristic knowledge could do for him. As far as he was concerned, this assassination was long overdue. The sooner Her Majesty Queen Victoria bit the dust, the sooner his rise to global industry kingpin. Stacking the odds in his favor, Bingham had set his sights on personally traveling into the future in order to garner progressive ideas beyond the scope of the Book of Mods or the elusive and legendary Aquarian Cosmology Compendium. If *any*one had a whit of information regarding time travel, logically and historically it would be a Darcy.

Bingham fell back on the bed, bored with Renee, who struck him this moment as little more than a voluptuous encyclopedia. Of course she couldn't understand the magnitude of his handiwork. Exhausting civil measures, he'd employed drastic tactics, establishing himself as the anonymous benefactor of the Race for Royal Rejuvenation. Unbeknownst to the Jubilee Science Committee, they'd aided Bingham in pushing Lord Ashford's offspring, as well as multitudes of other adventurous and greedy souls, into action. True, any number of people could possess vital knowledge pertaining to the outlawed time machine, particularly an original Peace Rebel. Although most of the PRs were dead or in hiding, he'd employed Mod Trackers to sniff out the whereabouts of Professor Maximus Merriweather—a twentieth-century physicist and cosmologist and the most qualified contender. As for the Darcys, Bingham had eyes and ears everywhere. Including Wilhelmina Goodenough.

He smiled as confidence and arrogance pumped through his blood, fueling a fantasy and the swelling of his shaft.

Rolling on top of Renee, he pinned the automaton's hands above her head. "You serve me well, number two." He entered her swiftly, and looking into her vacant eyes wondered what it would be like peering into the kaleidoscope eyes of Miss Goodenough. He imagined and indulged most vigorously.

CHAPTER 6

THE FLYING SCOTSMAN
EN ROUTE TO EDINBURGH, SCOTLAND

It was the longest journey of his life.

Simon had left the compartment several times. To shake off his anger. To shake off his lust. Although he would bet his prized drafting tools that his traveling companion was a woman, and though he suspected she was someone with whom he had already been intimate . . . he could not force his attentions. She had to make the first move, or at least a slip. Even an unintentional invitation would be better than no invitation at all.

All this angst over a kiss. And yes, this moment, a kiss was what he craved above all else. A craving more intense than any sexual desire he'd experienced in the last several years.

It boggled the mind. Boggled the mind and vexed his patience. Yet whilst pacing the connected corridors of the train, it occurred to Simon that he was not alone in his suffering. His companion had also excused herself, frequently escaping to the primitive yet functional public loo. Either she had a minuscule bladder or she too needed space to clear her head and cool her desires. There was no mistaking her sexual interest, even though she tried to hide it. If the Canary was experiencing even a modicum of Simon's discomfort, he would be a happy man. A spectacularly delirious man. The solution to his dilemma was suddenly clear. The more miserable her mood, the happier his.

He reentered the compartment, surprised to find her wearing dark-tinted spectacles and fumbling with the yo-yo she'd purchased from Thimblethumper. "A little late in the evening for sunshades," he remarked whilst closing the door.

"I have a blinding headache," she said, winding the string around the middle of the disks. "Light, whether natural or artificial, intensifies the throbbing."

Frowning at her pained expression, Simon reached up to douse the already dim sconce. "Then let there be darkness."

"No! I mean, that isn't necessary. The sunshades suffice and I don't wish to inconvenience you should you wish to continue your drafting."

Since the Canary had returned her rapt attention to the Book of Mods, and then to jotting notes in a journal, Simon had passed much of the time executing freehand drawings in his sketchbook—a design he'd been contemplating as an alternative to a mechanical lift. He'd yet to work out the kinks in his "mobile staircase," and his mind was not fully invested, but anything was better than pondering Project Monorail. Would he always connect his pride-and-joy design to his father's death? Would he always feel responsible for the disastrous explosion? Turning his thoughts from morbid images, he focused on the Canary's miserable efforts. "What *are* you trying to do?"

"A trick."

"Perhaps you should perfect the basics first."

"I know the basics."

"Perhaps you should reacquaint yourself."

Her head jerked up, and though he could not see her eyes, he was pretty sure she was glaring. "Just because you are an expert . . ."

Simon raised a brow as she trailed off. He had indeed mastered the art of the yo-yo as a young boy. "How did you know—"

"I assumed. Given your arrogant attitude and the fact that, by trade, naturally you would be intrigued by the workings."

"Mmm."

"No matter," Willie said, shrugging off the moment. She glanced at her time cuff, something she did a lot. "We'll soon be arriving at Waverley."

As she pushed off the wall and started to pocket the yo-yo, Simon moved in behind her and wrapped his hand over hers and the toy. "It's all in the technique," he said close to her ear.

There was a moment of silence in which he noted her ink-stained hands, the scent of hair freshly soaped, and a slight, almost imperceptible, shudder of her body. A moment of delicious sexual tension . . . followed by a swift jab to Simon's gut. Damned if her elbow didn't strike hard and true.

"You may be worldly in matters of free and diverse love, but I, sir, as mentioned before, am not interested." Agitated, the Canary reached up and snagged her coats. "That is not to say I judge. I do not. To each his own," she said whilst pulling on extraneous layers. "But I do not appreciate your attempts to shock, intimidate, or seduce, or whatever the hell your intention. I am here, with you, for one reason only, Darcy. To get a story. A story for which you will be handsomely compensated."

Simon bristled. First of all, he would not be the only one benefiting from this tabloid serial. The *Informer* would profit banking on the Darcy name, and the Canary would gain even more recognition and glory.

Second: How long would the infuriating pressman persist with this boyish ruse? And *why*? The pretense and lies did not bode well and he rankled at the thought of being made a fool. Again. Simon backed away, but continued to turn the screws. "I once knew a girl whose little brother performed yo-yo tricks with ease. A yo-yo passed on to him from the mother, a gesture that injured the girl's heart, as she coveted her mother's yo-yo . . . and approval. I promised to teach that girl the proper technique that would enable her to master many tricks, but I never got the chance."

The Canary tugged her cap over her shaggy hair just as

the Flying Scotsman hissed and screeched to a full stop. "Disappointed you, did she?"

Simon nabbed his own belongings, intrigued and incensed. "Indeed," he said, disembarking on the kid's heels.

Hoofing it through the bustling station, heavy bag in tow, the Canary gave Simon her back. "Something tells me the feeling was mutual."

It had been many a year since anyone had discombobulated Willie so thoroughly. She was confident and competent and, out of necessity, wily. Because of an unfortunate series of events, she'd locked down her emotions years ago. Through practiced control and camouflaging trickeries, she had fooled the masses for a decade. A consummate actress, she'd successfully maintained a male persona, in part by engaging in a reclusive lifestyle. Her most frequent interactions were with her coworkers at the *Informer*, and prompted by professional envy, most of them kept their distance. Friendship was a foreign concept, so she was in no danger of having her cover blown due to slipping up with a chum. As a journalist, she typically narrowed her interviews to one personal visit. As a supporter of the underground efforts to garner equal rights for all Freaks, she corresponded with like-minded souls through coded Teletypes or via occasional meetings in the nearest skytown. Even then, she adopted yet another costume and persona. She thrived on anonymity. It kept her liberated and employed. Kept her motivated and useful. It kept her brother safe and her father from landing in a mental ward or poorhouse. She would not endanger any one of those things by admitting her true identity to Simon Darcy.

Somehow the man had deduced who she was, and it galled that he was toying with her. Still, even if he out-and-out called her on the ruse, she would fight for all she was worth to deny the truth. As much as she would like to blast him face-to-face for jilting her because of her race and thereby tainting the love they once shared, the confrontation was not worth the cost.

Shoulders squared and back to the infuriating man, Willie hustled through Waverley Station, breaching the doors and moving onward toward Waverley Bridge—an iron-latticed thoroughfare that would lead them to Cockburn Street and beyond to High Street, also known as the Royal Mile.

A frigid wind and colossal snowflakes assaulted Willie as she hailed a conventional coach.

"Cockburn Hotel is within walking distance," Simon said as he moved in beside her. "I reserved rooms—"

"We're not staying at the Cockburn."

"We're not?"

Led by a blanketed horse, a hansom cab rolled in and Willie informed the coachman of their destination. Meanwhile Simon wordlessly took her valise and hoisted it up into the cab along with his. Further proof that he was aware of her *gentler* gender. She scrambled aboard before he could offer his hand—and raise the coachman's brow. Once they were both seated and the coachman urged the horse forward, Willie divulged the data she'd traced from the Mod Tracker.

"I booked lodgings near St. Giles' Cathedral on High Street," she said whilst massaging her throbbing temples. "There's a pub close by. Spirits & Tales. Filmore works there during the day, dispensing pints of ale and local ghost stories. I assume he patrols an underground passage at night, supposedly protecting the clockwork propulsion engine, but I do not know which passage. The section of Edinburgh known as Old Town is comprised of many wynds, closes, and vaults."

"Considering you were alone with Thimblethumper for a scant few seconds, you learned much," Simon said, sounding suspicious. "Anything else?"

"Only that even though Thimblethumper dislikes Filmore, he considers Filmore's job as a Houdinian relevant."

"Yet the man willingly divulged Filmore's location."

Not so willingly, Willie thought with a frown. The retired Mod Tracker had voiced vague information and had indeed misled them by not offering Jefferson Filmore's alias. The name he went by in Edinburgh. Had she and Simon asked after Filmore, they would have left Edinburgh empty-handed. No, she had time-traced to ferret out this more precise data, not that she would admit as such. "I suspect Thimblethumper felt pressured by that agency he mentioned to divulge pertinent tracking data to you, the brother of an influential agent." She glanced over. "Who did you say Jules works for?"

"I didn't say."

Willie grunted and shrugged. "Can't blame a pressman for trying. Readers would be even more riveted by your adventure were there a secret agency tie-in." Never mind *her* burning curiosity.

"I don't intend to put my brother at risk by indulging you or your readers' morbid need for sensation. Focus on me and my story, Canary, or take flight."

"Touchy."

"Intrusive."

"You're one to talk," she mumbled. He'd encroached on her personal space on the train, not once, but twice. She hugged herself, shivering in response to the memory of Simon's provocative touch, as well as the freezing temperature.

"An automocab would have offered a semblance of generated heat," Simon pointed out.

"In order to preserve the historical integrity of Old Town, petrol- and steam-fueled transportation is prohibited on the Royal Mile. Foot and horse traffic only."

Simon looked out at the moonlit cobbled streets and centuries-old buildings as the carriage horse clopped uphill toward High Street. "How long did you live here?"

"Two years," Willie answered honestly. Then her family had transplanted to America for two years and then back to England. Not long after her mother had died, Wesley had run off and her father's mental health had declined. She'd been scrambling to keep her own marbles ever since. Between the stress of dealing with Simon, the pressure of being blackmailed by Strangelove and threatened by Dawson, and the melancholy inspired by thoughts of her family, Willie felt her mood darken by the second.

The throbbing in her temples and behind her eye socket didn't help. She'd worn her corneatacts too long this day. Influenced by modern technology, the small tinted lenses fit over her cornea and disguised her kaleidoscope eyes, giving the appearance of a single-colored iris. Ingenious. Expensive. *Temporary.* Although she'd worked hard to build up a tolerance to the discomfort, Willie could bear to wear corneatacts for only four hours before her eyeballs began to hurt and her head to ache. That's when she typically took an afternoon walk, swapping the lenses for her sunshades and giving her eyes a rest. A half hour did the trick, but she hadn't been able to break away from Simon for more than ten minutes without him knocking on the loo door, ribbing her about being up to no good.

Now she was paying the price.

The piercing pain and relentless pounding promised a migraine. Desperate to head off a bout of nausea, she'd removed the corneatacts when Simon last left the compartment. But the effort had come too late, and relief would not be coming anytime soon. She needed a dark room and sleep. Lots of sleep.

"You don't look well," Simon said.

"You're one to talk with those puffy shadows beneath your eyes."

"You can make out shadows beneath my eyes? How can you see anything at all wearing those dark glasses in a pitch-black cab?"

She could not explain it, but she could, in fact, see fine. Something about her heightened sense of night vision. A peculiarity born to some Freaks, but not all. For instance her brother did not possess enhanced night vision. The traits of Freaks, a new breed, were inconsistent and unpredictable. In addition, whatever supernatural gift they possessed intensified with age. With every year, Willie honed her time-tracing skills. Who knew what she'd be capable of in ten years? *No one.* The same applied to those gifted in telepathy, accelerated healing, shape-shifting, and weather manipulation, to name a few *skills.* No one knew the extent

of their future powers. Hence the fears of many an Old
Worlder.

MUTANT RACE THREATENS TO
DOMINATE EARTH

That had been one of the more extreme headlines, ignorant propaganda distributed via leaflets in Piccadilly Circus,
a bustling, touristy portion of London's West End.

Mutant. Is that how Simon had thought of her when he'd
learned of her true heritage?

Suppressing an ancient hurt, Willie ignored the man,
peered out the window, and absorbed the historical sights
and pungent scents of Old Town. Oh, how she loved this
city. Her family had rented lodgings on Haymarket, not far
from High Street. The first year she'd existed in somewhat
of a haze, heartsick over Simon's rejection, pining over what
had been and what she'd dreamed would be. But then she'd
settled into numb acceptance and then a period of blessed
healing. She'd explored the wonders, the mysteries, and the
history of Edinburgh with passion. This city had soothed
her soul.

St. Giles' Cathedral came into view and Willie's chest
tightened with a twinge of melancholy and a hint of nostal-
gia. She had attended services here with her father. Influenced by her mother, Willie had never committed to one
faith and instead embraced all. However, her father asked
so little and his wife and son had given even less. It had
seemed a small and easy sacrifice to Willie to accompany
her father to services on Sunday mornings. Thereafter
they'd wander over to Dunbars for a late breakfast. She
smiled a little, remembering how she'd reveled in the full
Scottish fare, including haggis and black pudding, whilst her
father had opted for bland porridge. It had always struck
Willie as most extraordinary that her father, ever conservative in his culinary choices and religious views, had married
a Peace Rebel. A Mod. A person from another time. He

must've loved her mother very much indeed, and that made Willie love Michael Goodenough all the more.

A brush of Simon's arm jerked Willie out of her musings. "I would have paid," she whispered as he reached through the trapdoor at the rear of the roof and compensated the coachman. "I received an advance—"

"From the *Informer*."

From Strangelove, but she did not offer the distinction.

"Don't quibble, Canary." He vaulted from the cab and retrieved their luggage. "You look like hell," he said bluntly. "I need you fit and alert and ready to aid me in my quest."

Her vision blurred as he guided her to their lodgings. Her brain pounded and her stomach rebelled. "Tomorrow," she mumbled, losing focus.

"Soon enough." He registered them both in haste, then escorted her up a skinny stairwell. "What can I do for you?" he asked whilst unlocking her door.

He sounded genuinely concerned. Then again, that could be her mind playing tricks, as her thoughts were most fuzzy. Desperate to suffer the migraine in private, Willie procured her valise and hurried into the rented room. "Get some sleep, Darcy," she said, closing the door between them. "Tomorrow the adventure begins."

CHAPTER 7

Patience had never been one of Simon's greater virtues, and retiring early to his room had held no appeal. He would only wallow in somber thoughts—the loss of his project, the death of his father, the betrayal of a long-ago love. He had not wished to brood upon his ill luck, nor to obsess on the Canary's true identity. He'd had no desire to waste one precious minute whilst his brother raced toward Australia to meet with a Mod genius in an extraordinary quest to snatch Briscoe's time machine back from the future. Not that he wished Jules misfortune, but by damn, Simon wanted, *needed*, to win this race.

Leaving the Canary to nurse her headache, he had stowed his bag in his room, intent on initiating the investigation on his own. He had every faith in his ability to mingle with pub regulars and to discreetly ferret out information regarding Jefferson Filmore.

Spirits & Tales had been easy enough to find. Simon had quickly endeared himself to locals, chatting amiably and buying several rounds. He had always been the jovial sort, so consorting with strangers had not proved a hardship. In the course of two hours, he had learned much about Old Town and the haunted underground, but nothing of Filmore. No one knew the name or the man.

He'd returned to the Squire's Inn long after midnight,

foxed on regional whiskey and puzzling the Canary's intent. *Why had she lied about Filmore working at that pub?* Simon had faltered at her door, wanting to question her, wanting to *see* her. If he knocked, would she answer half-asleep and half-naked? Would he recognize the body and flesh beneath the boyish facade? Would he know at once and for certain that she was indeed his Mina? Or would he know without a doubt that she was some other female altogether?

He'd hesitated on the threshold. No, *swayed* on the threshold. Liquor had addled his senses, and most probably his judgment. Confronting the enigmatic Willie G. whilst foxed would be unwise.

Irritated, Simon had returned to his own room. He'd stripped naked and collapsed on the rented bed. Passing out would have been a blessing, but his guilty conscience had prevented such a luxury. Instead, he'd wrestled through the night with insomnia and a maelstrom of regrets and yearnings.

By the time dawn streaked through a crack in the drawn curtains, Simon was unsure as to whether he'd truly ever drifted off. His mind worked and circled as keenly in a dream state as it did whilst fully conscious.

Hung over and exhausted, he pushed out of bed, anxious to attack the day. He hurried through his morning ablutions, determined to rally with a fortifying breakfast before going head-to-head with the Canary. She had looked so sickly the night before. Surely she would sleep until noon. Yet when Simon entered the public dining area, there she was, eating heartily and looking obnoxiously refreshed.

"Mind if I join you?" he asked.

"Do you always sleep so late?" she asked in between bites. "I rang you up, but there was no answer."

"Perhaps I was in the bath."

"Perhaps," she said without looking up.

Simon sat without an invitation. A serving woman greeted him with a smile and a menu, as well as the choice of tea or coffee. He opted for coffee, strong and black. He looked from the menu to the Canary's plate—a colorful mess of assorted fare. "What *are* you inhaling?"

"Eggs, back bacon, bangers, baked beans, fried tomatoes, mushrooms, and . . ." She pushed about the food with her fork. "Ah, yes. Tattie scones, black pudding, and haggis." She furrowed her brow. "Perhaps you are not acquainted—"

"I'm acquainted. Not a fan."

"Of black pudding or haggis? I know sheep's innards are an acquired taste for some but—"

"I'll have porridge," Simon said to the server as his stomach rebelled.

"You look knackered, Darcy," the Canary said as she shoveled more food into her mouth.

He tried not to focus on those mesmerizing lips, smeared and shiny with melted butter. How could greasy lips be so infuriatingly enticing? "Ravenous, are you?"

"Indeed."

"I take it you're feeling better."

"Amazingly better."

"Bully for you." Simon sipped the bracing, strong coffee, then glared. "Why did you mislead me?"

Her actions slowed. "How do you mean?"

"You told me Filmore tends bar at Spirits & Tales."

"Oh. I mean, he does."

"I spent the better part of last night there. He does not."

She glanced up, peering at him through strands of dark, shaggy hair. "Is that the reason for your bloodshot eyes and cranky mood, Darcy?" Smirking, she forked up a bit of bean and mushroom glop. "Hung over?"

He reached for a slice of dry toast. "No one at Spirits & Tales has ever heard of Jefferson Filmore."

"That's because he's utilizing an alias. Few Mods live in the open as themselves. Most are persecuted for instigating the Peace War or hunted and hounded for their advanced knowledge. Filmore's laying low and collecting a living wage under the name Flash. Jim Flash."

Simon frowned. "Why didn't you say so last night?"

"Don't bite my head off because you got pished, Darcy."

The discreet and soft-spoken server set a bowl of porridge in front of Simon. She flitted away and he focused on the face that taunted him. Willie's face. Mina's face. Though, Christ, her complexion seemed even more off today. Darker. Ruddier. "What are you playing at, Canary?"

"I assure you this is not a game." She shoved aside her plate, her appetite appeased or stolen away. "I only hope you didn't tip off Filmore and scare him away with your reckless prodding."

Patience spent, Simon set aside his spoon. "We need to talk."

"No, we don't. We need to work together. I need to secure my job. You need to secure finances for your family." She pushed out of her chair, looking defiant and, to the common eye, like a cocky, gangly young man possessing sensationally bad taste in fashion. "I'll meet you at Spirits & Tales in one hour. Until then, I have private matters to attend. Enjoy your porridge, Darcy."

Porridge.

At once Willie had been charmed and disgusted that Simon would order boiled oats. So unadventurous. So like her father. Although, in truth and in most matters, she knew Simon to be bold to the point of foolhardy. A hundred memories welled, those days long ago when she and Simon had been so hopelessly in love, daring each other to pursue new experiences, to sample life to the fullest. Curious and courageous to the point of being reckless, they'd been the perfect match. He had been willing to do just about anything . . . except marry a Freak.

Refusing to dwell on the betrayal, Willie tucked her hands beneath her armpits in an effort to keep them warm. Her gloves suffered from long wear and they were not well made to begin with. She kept meaning to purchase a new pair, but funds were tight and she had other priorities— such as making sure her father had suitable winter clothing. Winters battered the countryside more than the city. Although Edinburgh was far more raw than London.

Head down against the fierce and frigid wind, Willie stalked from Squire's Inn to St. Giles' Cathedral, also known as the High Kirk of Edinburgh. A short distance, but the freezing weather had made the walkway slick with ice. Her stride was cautious as she crossed the cobbled street. To her right, high upon the volcanic crag of Castle Hill, loomed Edinburgh Castle—an ancient and daunting stone fortress. A more welcoming royal residence sprawled to her left, at the base of the Royal Mile. The Palace of Holyroodhouse. In between, numerous businesses hawked local wares, food, and whiskey. Here the air was crisp and clean, free of the fumes and smoke that marred other parts of the industrialized city.

Few pedestrians were about this cold, dreary morning, and Willie reveled in the relative silence as she stopped short of the paved courtyard and absorbed the majesty of St. Giles'. The glorious stained-glass windows. The famous Crown Spire on the tower. The present incarnation of the church dated back to the fourteenth century, although the Gothic cathedral had recently benefited from a major restoration. The Lord Provost of Edinburgh had charged two acclaimed architects with creating a "Westminster Abbey for Scotland." Hay and Henderson had done well.

"Astonishing," Willie remarked as she hurried toward the cathedral steps.

She did not expect Simon to be on her heels. "Why here?" he asked.

"It's personal," she said whilst spinning to face him. His windblown hair and impeccable clothing triggered the same sense of awe she'd gotten whilst admiring the spire. This six-foot-two, supreme specimen of a man was a glorious sight. Although worn around the edges from too much drink and too little sleep, Simon was strikingly handsome. Sinfully handsome. She blocked several inappropriate thoughts and frowned at the infuriating devil. "I thought you were nursing breakfast."

"You thought wrong. Don't let me stop you," he said as she hesitated on the threshold.

Willie considered fleeing, but she had not been to Edinburgh in ages, and the lure to celebrate her father in his better days was much too strong. Turning her back on Simon, she entered the dimly lit holy place and hustled past monuments, stone pillars, and tucked-away chapels. The interior was massive, comprising several arches and vaulted ceilings. She did not need to look to know that Simon was assessing the magnificent architecture. Intending a thoughtful moment of silence for her father, Willie sat in a simple wooden chair several rows from an unoccupied pulpit. She ignored Simon, hoping he'd continue on, losing himself in one or another engineering aspect of the renovation.

As her dismal luck would have it, he perched on the chair next to her.

"Religious?" he asked, sounding incredulous.

"Not particularly," she whispered. "Although I am tolerant of all religions just as I am tolerant of all nationalities and races."

He slid her a look and she cursed herself for sounding bitter. "You think I am not?" he asked softly.

"I think, like most people, you have boundaries."

"But you do not?"

"I do not."

"You're an arrogant one," Simon said.

Dawson had made the same accusation. She had never thought of herself as thus. The notion rankled. "As are you," she retorted. Although she had made it clear that she did not appreciate the way he encroached on her personal space, he continued to do so.

"You claim we've never met," he said, shifting and staring hard at her profile. "Yet you profess to know my beliefs and practices. Tell me, Canary, are you psychic? Do you possess some sort of mental telepathy or trickery that helps you tap into another person's thoughts? Is that what makes you such a keen interviewer?"

He was being sarcastic, trying to provoke her, but he was also quite close to the mark.

Leaning closer, he whispered in her ear. "Can you read my thoughts?"

"I cannot," she answered honestly, edging away and cursing the rapid pace of her pulse.

"That is good. This moment they would not be to your liking. Or perhaps they would," he added with a wicked smile.

As chilled as she was, Willie heated from head to toe. "You are insufferable, Darcy. Depraved and . . . irreverent," she said, indicating their holy surroundings.

"And you, Canary, are a dichotomy. Dodgy and heartless."

"Heartless?"

Someone shushed them.

Slouching lower in her seat, Willie glared at Simon. "And that harsh assessment is based on what?" Did he think Freaks were without feelings? Without a soul? Many Vics did.

He started to say something, then reconsidered. "*Why* are we here?"

"*I* am here to honor my father."

"Did he pass?"

"Not in body, no. But his mind . . ." She shook her head. "His mind wanders."

"And this disgusts you?" Simon asked, sounding irritated.

"Of course not," she snapped in a hushed voice. "Why would you say that?"

"'Ashford, a distant cousin of the infamous Time Voyager, Briscoe Darcy, was rumored to be obsessed with making his own mark on the world,'" he recited from the *Informer*. "'Fortunately for the realm and unfortunately for his family, Ashford's inventions paled to that of Darcy, earning him ridicule instead of respect, wealth, or fame.'"

Simon glared down at her. "You intimated that my father was a failure and featherbrain when he was indeed quite brilliant, just unfocused. *His* mind wandered as well. On to the next great idea before perfecting the last. Clearly such folly must frustrate or disgust you; otherwise why would you sneer at a good man's efforts?"

She had not sneered. Dawson had sneered, revising her initial words in order to sell more newspapers. Yet, defend-

ing herself was not an option. She could not afford to expose herself by expressing regret over that article. She
could not afford any intimacy whatsoever. She braced her
spine and sniffed. "I do what I must to survive," she said in
a tight voice. "For instance, I am here, with you, on this suspect expedition because I was given no choice. Clearly you
find my company offensive. Trust me, the feeling is mutual."

He blinked.

Willie buttoned her coat. "My time here is ruined." Staying in character, she regarded Simon with irritation whilst
adjusting her scarves in anticipation of the cold. "You, sir, are
a selfish . . . knob. You squandered the power of the Darcy
name, focusing on your own glory, much like your cousin. I
cannot believe I have been saddled with touting the adventure of a Flatliner." With that, she stood and left the cathedral. It was not the confrontation she craved, but it was one
of importance. The Simon Darcy she had known and loved
had evolved into a self-absorbed man. She'd kept tabs on him
over the years. How could she not? He was a Darcy and, by
virtue of his heritage, influential in global matters . . . or at
least he *could* be. On numerous occasions she'd convinced
herself that her obsessive interest in Simon was social and
political, and not of the amorous nature. She did not appreciate the rekindling of her old affections. She did not welcome
the physical attraction or the feminine quirks he inspired.

She had spent far too long this morning lingering in a
bath. Trying to scrub the ever-present ink from her fingers,
soaping the grime and scents of the city and the pressroom
from her person. She'd fussed with her hair in an effort to
soften the boyish style. All because, for the first time in
years, she'd longed to be *pretty*. She'd realized her folly
whilst almost forgetting to bind her breasts. She'd been set
to sabotage her male cover in order to look more appealing,
more feminine.

For *Simon*.

Fortunately, the insanity had quickly passed and she'd
gone out of her way to alter her appearance more than ever.
In doing so, she had applied too much of the tanning agent.

Now her face had an orange tint and the creases of her fingers and palms were stained. Hence she'd brushed her hair forward and kept her hands busy, balled, or gloved. Never had the ruse been so exhausting. Although who was she fooling? Certainly not Simon. At the very least he knew she was a woman.

Just then he appeared at her side and she realized she'd faltered at a lamppost. As if she didn't know which way to turn or where to go. Indeed, she'd been lost in her thoughts.

"Here." He offered her a pair of gloves. An exquisite set of dark blue wool gloves that looked as if they had never been worn.

"Is this where you slap me and challenge me to a duel for attacking your integrity?" she asked with a raised brow.

"Don't be absurd. Last night I noticed that your gloves are quite worn, and I happened to have an extra pair. Actually, Fletcher packed three spare pair in addition to far too many other clothes. I do believe he equates Scotland with the North Pole."

"You employ domestics?" she asked, still staring at the gloves. Given his more-than-comfortable lodgings, she should not have been surprised that his income allowed him the luxury. Still, it only accentuated the social and financial gap between them.

"One. Fletcher acts in the capacity of valet and cook, although I do not think of him as a domestic so much as a pesky caretaker. Of my home. Of me. Take the damned gloves, Canary."

She knew not what to think of the gesture of goodwill, but she had been raised not to snub a kindness. "If you're sure you won't need them."

"I'm sure."

She nodded. "Thank you." She quickly traded her own gloves for his, her eyes widening upon realizing they were lined with . . . cashmere? They must have cost a pretty pence. "I'll return them when—"

"Consider the gloves a gift. Albeit an ill-fitting one," he said.

"I do not mind that they are too large."

"I suspect not," he said, eyeing her baggy, overly long duster. "By the way. I am not a Flatliner. A Flatliner is self-serving and cares nothing about the fate of mankind. Project Monorail was conceived as a way of relieving street and underground congestion as well as pollution. Cost-efficient, fuel-efficient. Utilizing magnets to propel the vehicle forward and . . ." He swiped off his derby, jammed his fingers though his hair. "It doesn't matter."

Dawson had prodded Willie to get the scoop on Project Monorail, and here Simon was dishing. "Magnets? How would that work exactly?"

"It's complicated." Frowning, Simon checked his pocket watch. "Filmore's shift starts at ten o'clock?"

"I do not know precisely, but that's when the pub opens and I know he works during the day. If he starts later, we can at least find out when, and perhaps I can glean information about his lodgings."

"You mean *we*."

Willie cursed the bitter and wistful ache in her gut. There was no *we*. Not in the sense that she had once dreamed.

"Thirty minutes to kill." Simon tugged on his derby and looked up and down High Street. "I received an earful of ghost tales last night, and several originated near or along the Royal Mile—all underground. Mary King's Close. South Bridge Vaults."

"I know them both."

"I'd like to get my bearings." Without warning, he grasped Willie's elbow, inciting a dizzy surge of wanton desire. How preposterous! It was not as if he'd grasped her hand. Nor were they skin to skin in any manner. Several layers of her clothing separated his gloved hand from her flesh and yet . . . she burned.

Clearing her throat, Willie pointed left. "Mary King's is just ahead, but it's been closed to the public for years. In 1645 the plague struck hard and the city bricked up the close and the victims. Grisly business. Hence the ghost tales."

"Grisly business indeed. Anyone with a lick of sense would avoid a place once cursed with the plague. Hence the perfect hiding space."

"Aye, but as I said, it is sealed. It would take magic for the Houdinians to get inside."

"Or," Simon said, rattling her further as he urged her toward the famous haunt, "someone with the imagination and twentieth-century expertise to engineer a secret entrance."

CHAPTER 8

What horrible thing had she done in life to deserve such torture?

For the hundredth time in half an hour, Willie dug deep for calm.

Searching for secret entrances alongside Simon had proved exhilarating and infuriating. For the past three days he'd battered her senses, inciting opposing emotions that left her drained. Confusion, frustration, amusement, *desire*. Vexing, that. Willie was quite certain that the man took advantage of every opportunity to discombobulate her.

Standing too close. Staring too long.

The mere brush of his arm weakened her knees, yet she did not swoon. Not only would giving in to the attraction endanger her family and career, but most assuredly it would damn her heart. Even if they didn't have a past history, no good could come of a Vic and Freak union. Something her parents had preached. Something she'd been averse to believing, but a fact she had long since accepted. The British Empire had outlawed marriage between Vics and Freaks. Just as they'd prohibited Freaks from voting or enrolling in colleges or securing employment in esteemed vocations. Oh, aye. All she had to do was *think* on that, and outrage obliterated lust.

Simon fell into frustrated silence as they abandoned their search and proceeded to Spirits & Tales. He ached, no, *died* to progress in his mission. To advance his goal. Willie sensed it with every fiber of her altered being. This moment, winning the Race for Royal Rejuvenation trumped all else in his life. No matter what he professed, she did not believe he pursued the prize solely for his family. Perhaps he intended the fortune for his mother and sister, but he wanted the glory for himself. There was no denying an aggrandizing "vibe," as her mother would say.

"Did you really think it would be so simple, Darcy?" Willie asked as they walked downhill and against the frosty air. "Few things in life are."

"You see the worst in everything, Canary," he said. "Why is that?"

If she broached that subject full on, she would elaborate for eons. Instead she skirted the issue. "Because I do not trust mankind in general."

"Cynical."

"Realistic." Chilled to the bone, Willie stuffed her gloved hands in her coat pockets, seeking additional warmth. Her knuckles knocked against something hard.

Strangelove's telecommunicator.

The device she would use to betray Simon.

Report to me the moment he's acquired whatever legendary invention he seeks.

Strangelove's instructions had been clear. His intent, however, was shrouded in mystery, as was his true identity. What would a devious, seemingly wealthy and ruthless man like Strangelove do with a working clockwork propulsion engine? The detrimental possibilities cramped her already knotted gut.

Spying the painted sign advertising Spirits & Tales, Willie purposely slowed her stride. "If the Briscoe Bus's engine does, by some wild chance, exist and if we are indeed able to find it, you'll be turning it over to the Jubilee Science Committee posthaste, aye?"

Simon cut her a glance. "Why would I dally when my intention is to win the race?"

"But the prize won't be awarded until the week of the jubilee celebration, and that is several months away. In the meantime hundreds of other participants are in pursuit of a lost invention and who knows what marvel they might find?"

"Nothing is more significant than the Peace Rebels' time-traveling engine," Simon said, although he did not sound wholly convinced.

"I suppose that depends on who determines the importance. Who has the final say? The science committee? The queen? You know how she feels about anything having to do with time travel. If anything, she'd want to diminish the significance of the infamous engine, not celebrate it."

Simon stopped in his tracks, as did Willie. "Are you suggesting I'm chasing another doomed dream?"

"I'm *wondering* if you have alternate grandiose plans for that clockwork propulsion engine. For all I know, Briscoe Darcy shared pertinent information with your father, information passed on to you—a visionary and a gifted engineer. That knowledge, coupled with your intellect and skills, makes you a prime candidate to follow in Briscoe's footsteps. The next Darcy to build a working time-traveling vehicle, hopping dimensions in search of greater glory."

His lip quirked. "Such faith in my abilities."

"So it *has* crossed your mind."

"Why do you care?"

"Because you could make the world worse than it already is."

He studied her hard, causing her to shiver with a chill that had nothing to do with the tundralike weather. "I am intrigued by your cynicism, Canary, but not deterred." He glanced at the pub. "Are you with me or not?"

Given the circumstances, and unwilling to risk the fate of a potentially dangerous discovery, Willie bolstered her shoulders and prepared to trace a Houdinian. "Leave the talking to me."

Simon should have been obsessing on the location of the clockwork propulsion engine or the whereabouts of the Aquarian Cosmology Compendium or the progress of his brother's audacious mission. Any number of personal and global matters of supreme importance deserved his attention, but this moment he had a spectacular case of tunnel

vision. All he saw, all he cared about, was the damnable
Clockwork Canary.

She'd given him a dressing-down at breakfast, then at the
cathedral, and then seconds before in the street. She judged
him. She challenged him. She intrigued the bloody hell out
of him. No matter her gender, he'd thought her a heartless,
glory-seeking pressman. Yet she worried that he'd utilize
the Peace Rebels' engine to jump dimensions? Worried that
he'd somehow damage their already distorted world? And
what of the possibility that he'd disappear in a rainbow of
light, never to be seen again in his own time, much like the
original Time Voyager? Any one of those scenarios would
make for a more sensational story, would it not? One would
think she'd be anxious for Simon to pull the most outrageous and scandalous stunt imaginable, thus providing her
and the *Informer* with the story of the century!

For the life of him Simon could not determine the beliefs, motivations, and goals of this enterprising woman. Old
Worlder? New Worlder? Certainly not a Flatliner. Though
she claimed not to trust mankind, she exhibited passion regarding the fate of the world. Did she support advanced
technology like Simon's fuel-efficient monorail, or like
Queen Victoria and other blinkered conservatives, did she
shun anachronistic marvels?

Crossing the threshold, Simon battled those troubling
musings and focused on their present task. He removed his
derby and pocketed his gloves whilst the Canary pulled off
her cap and glanced about the tavern. He knew without
asking that she was assessing the eerie ambience much as
he had the night before. Mostly Spirits & Tales resembled
any common pub. Cramped confines, crowded seating, dark-
paneled walls and floors. An enormous bar overwhelmed
the small room and a mirrored backbar displayed shelves of
various liquor bottles and filmy glasses.

Unlike most pubs, it did not possess a warm and cheery
atmosphere. The dim lighting cast the room in a sickly
shade of green instead of a warm golden glow. The paintings on the walls depicted scary, even downright ghastly

scenes, and the floorboards creaked with every step. The only difference between last night and now was the quiet. Two, not twenty, people sat at the bar and there was plenty of seating elsewhere. Simon did not recognize the broad-shouldered, older man behind the bar, but it had to be Filmore, aka *Flash*. He sensed it in Willie's demeanor. Yet instead of sitting at the bar, she moved toward a table near the raging hearth.

"It will take more than a hot cup of tea to relieve the chill I sustained whilst poking around Mary King's Close," she said in a grumpy tone. "I could use a whiskey, although I suppose you've yet to recover from last night's bender."

"Your hostility wears thin, Canary."

"As does your impropriety."

He glanced to where she looked and realized he was holding the chair out, waiting for her to sit first—a gentlemanly consideration for a woman. Except she pretended to be a man. Still. His patience on the matter was spent. "Listen, Willie, I—"

"Stay here," she said, barking the order much as she had back at Thimblethumper's Shoppe of Curiosities. *Of all the bleeding cheek,* Simon thought as she strode to the bar in her gangly, boyish manner. *Fine.* Let her buy the drinks. Let her have first crack at the Houdinian. He wanted to make haste with this expedition, and if the Canary could advance their efforts with her extraordinary interviewing skills, Simon would gladly take advantage.

Restless, he eased down in a rickety chair and pretended interest in a menu whilst surreptitiously watching the scene unfold.

The Canary nodded in greeting to the other two patrons, then climbed onto a barstool and motioned to the barkeep. The physically fit, silver-haired man appeared between mid-fifty and sixty years of age, the average age of most living Mods. Other than that, Simon had no way of knowing if the man was indeed Jefferson Filmore. Mods looked like any other Vic. They were wholly normal and human, just from another time. Even so, Simon suspected the man had introduced himself as Jim Flash, since Willie engaged him in animated conversation whilst the man poured two whiskies.

The Canary checked her time cuff as she pulled cash from her ratty wallet. There was something about her posture, her expression. Intense. No, attentive. *Focused.* As if whatever Filmore was saying was of enormous and impressive interest. Was that her trick? Encouraging someone to talk freely by intimating that they were unusually fascinating?

The exchange of payment was quick, and Simon watched as the two shook hands in a friendly farewell gesture. He thought he saw the Canary wince as Filmore pulled back. She checked her time cuff, then a pocket watch. She jammed her hand through her hair, looking somewhat rattled, then downed one of the whiskies.

What the devil?

She ordered another and once again engaged Filmore in talk. Simon could not make out specifics and this moment the Canary lowered her voice even more, causing Filmore to brace his elbows on the bar and lean in as if whatever *she* was saying was now the source of fascination. Simon leaned forward as well, but he couldn't hear a damned thing. He itched to join the Canary at the bar, but by God, she looked to be making some sort of progress.

She checked the time—again. Why did she keep doing that? Then she grasped Filmore's beefy forearm as if saying something of dire importance. Filmore was all ears.

Then the queerest thing happened.

Willie froze.

Literally.

She stopped talking, stopped moving, although she retained a death grip on Filmore. The awkward moment stretched on, and after snapping his fingers in front of her face, Filmore wrenched away his arm and Willie slumped forward on the bar.

Simon pushed to his feet and moved swiftly to the bar. He grasped Willie's shoulder, pulling her upright. Her eyes were open, but unfocused.

"What the hell?" Filmore asked. "We were swapping ghost tales and the kid faded off."

"Afraid my friend's in his cups," Simon said, gesturing at the whiskey. "We've been at it all night. A celebration of sorts. I best see him home."

Unsure as to what was going on and not wanting to raise the Houdinian's suspicions, Simon hoisted Willie over his shoulder like a sack of grain, mumbled an amusing apology to the barkeep and patrons, then whisked the Canary outdoors and into an alley.

"Put me down," she ordered weakly, with an ineffectual punch to Simon's back.

He propped her against a cold brick wall. Held her upright by her shoulders. "What happened in there?"

"What time is it?"

Simon looked on as Willie squinted at her time cuff, then fumbled for her pocket watch.

"That can't be right," she mumbled, sounding more British this moment than Scottish and looking somewhat delirious. "I've never been gone that long."

"Gone where? What are you talking about and why do you keep checking your timepieces?"

She shrugged off his grip, gave herself a shake, then tugged on her cap. "We must hurry. I fear I may have tipped my hand," she said whilst taking off down the alley on shaky legs. "I lingered and meddled. I've never done that before, but when I saw her . ."

"Her, who?" Simon asked, taking a firm hold of the Canary's elbow. Had she gone temporarily bonkers? Had one shot of whiskey addled her mind? "There were two male patrons at the bar, myself, and Filmore—*if* that was Filmore."

Willie nodded. "It was."

"No woman present," Simon said, "other than you."

She cast him a dazed, angry look.

"Keep pretending if you want to," Simon said, "but know that the effort is wasted on me." Vulnerable as she was this moment, he half expected her to throw up her arms, to cry defeat, to admit her true identity and spout some sort of fantastic tale related to her ruse. Wishful thinking on his part. Instead, she bolstered her shoulders and put more starch in her step.

"It's in a vault," she said, leaving the alley and taking a hard left onto a narrow street. "A coffinlike vault with some sort of intricate locking system. I know not the code, but maybe you can crack it. You're good with numbers, right?"

Simon's mind whirled. "Thimblethumper said the Houdinians would kill to protect an object of value, yet Filmore willingly told you the engine is hidden in a locked vault?"

"In a manner of speaking."

"I suppose he gave up the precise location as well."

"He did."

"He said you were swapping ghost stories."

"We were."

Simon tugged his derby down, cursing the frosty wind and this convoluted discussion. He thought back to the interrogation, the way she'd focused intently on her subject, the way she'd gripped Filmore's arm and the way she had frozen.

The kid drifted off.

Indeed, when Simon had pulled her limp body from the bar, she'd looked as though she was in a trance. There was but one explanation. She'd pried into Thimblethumper's and Filmore's thoughts. It would also explain much about her often shocking and candid interviews.

"You lied to me," Simon said as they moved under an arch and then down several stone steps. "You're psychic. Some sort of mind reader."

"Not exactly," she said whilst moving into a musty, darkened corridor.

"What exactly?" Simon persisted.

"I'm a Time Tracer."

CHAPTER 9

Willie had never confessed her supernatural skill aloud. At least not to a Vic. Her mother and father had known of her time-tracing gift—albeit in its infancy. And of course Wesley knew, although since they'd never been close and did not, in fact, converse on a regular basis, he did not know how far her supernatural skills had advanced. Just as she was in the dark as to the progression of his gift.

In a moment of weakness, Willie had once described her powers to a trio of Freaks—fellow members of the Freak Fighters. She was hoping one of them shared the same skill, was hoping to garner some insight or advice and to feel a little less alone. Being one of a kind amongst a minority made her feel even more the outcast rather than special. Amongst her kind she had heard rumors of telepaths and accelerated healers. Of those who could teleport and those with enhanced strength. She had also heard of someone in America who had a modicum of control over the four elements—earth, water, air, and fire. A skill that mirrored her brother's. But to her knowledge, Willie was the only Freak born with the unique skill of reliving other people's memories.

In recent years there had been random abductions, where nefarious agencies had forced Freaks to use their gifts for the agency's greater good, which was ultimately wicked in nature. Some Freaks had gone rogue, offering their services for hefty sums. The majority of Freaks, like Willie, simply longed to integrate their special skills into a normal life and daily job. But unfortunately, until the day they won certain rights, they were forced to live a lie.

Willie had never felt more alone or lost than the moment she'd connected with Filmore. Not once in all the instances where she had traced, and there had been many, had she ever bobbled her objective. In and out. She never lingered. She never interacted. She was the proverbial fly on the wall. Only this time she'd seen something that had caused her to connect with Filmore a second time. Something that had caused her to linger and search. She had seen her mother.

"Bloody hell, woman. Slow down. It's black as night in this corridor. You could walk into wall or fall into a well."

"I see fine."

"How is that possible?" Simon asked. "I can't see a bloody thing."

"Enhanced night vision."

"A Time Tracer, whatever that is, with enhanced night vision. Are you pished or delusional?"

"You know what I am, dammit. It was in the letter." Her voice sounded brittle to her own ears and a little too loud, bouncing off the ancient stone walls. Why had her mother been part of Filmore's memories? Why had they been arguing over whether to hide in the west, north, or south? Willie stopped cold at the junction of two corridors. They looked exactly the same. In his memory, had Filmore gone left or right? Willie had looked away, searching for her mother. She'd even called out her name and in doing so had summoned a whirlwind of memories from another time. Futuristic images from the 1960s, from her mother's past. Filmore's past. Willie had seen them embrace. Had seen them plotting. She'd sensed a deep bond and a strong attraction on Filmore's part. Had Michelle Goodenough had an affair with Jefferson Filmore? Had she been in league with the Houdinians? Had she lied to her family all those years regarding the destruction of the clockwork propulsion engine? If so, how else had she deceived them?

Simon grasped Willie's elbow, startling her out of her musing. "What letter?" he asked in a tight voice.

She whirled, her facade forgotten as years of angst

welled and spewed. "The letter I wrote explaining why I couldn't come. The letter stained with my tears in which I begged you to understand, which apparently you did not. Because instead of meeting me a month later as I asked, you stayed away! Now can we just get the bloody rebel engine and get out of here?"

"Jesus. *Mina?* I *thought* it was you. I sensed . . . Dammit, I can't see you."

But she could see him perfectly. His handsome face contorted in confusion and anger. And she could see the bulk of a man slipping out through a crevice and aiming a weapon directly at Simon's back.

"No!" Willie shoved Simon with all her might, knocking him aside just as something sharp and hot slammed into her shoulder, propelling her backward. The back of her head hit stone and she cried out, pain shooting through her skull and blossoming throughout her shoulder and chest.

"Shite!" Simon scrambled and covered her body with his own just as another shot ricocheted off the walls, inciting sparks and a noxious smell.

Loud voices echoed down the hall and Willie heard their attacker fleeing. "Some sort of gas," she said in a weak voice. "Get out, Simon."

"Not without you."

"Can't move. Can't . . ." Her words trailed off as Simon scooped her off the floor and into his arms.

"Who goes there?" someone yelled. "Police!"

"What's that smell?" another called out. "Look! Smoke!"

Willie coughed as plumes of noxious fog welled.

"Eyes tearing," Simon choked out, "and I'm blind as a bat in this dark. Moving toward the voices—"

"No. No, coppers." She spied a distant splash of light and pointed down a corridor. "That way. Turn left. Walk. Keep walking."

"I see it." He picked up speed, rushing toward a gust of cool air. Moving quickly toward the sliver of light.

"It's a door," Willie said, her vision fading, her voice weak. "Shove."

"I see it, sweetheart. Hush."

She felt him climbing steps and sucked in the fresh cold air even though it hurt like the devil to breathe. Her chest and head hurt and her eyes stung from the gas. Her corneatacts had been contaminated, making the throbbing worse.

Simon's attention was riveted on the seemingly endless and steep stairwell.

Delirious with pain, Willie quickly removed the tinted lenses, letting them fall from her fingertips as she closed her eyes and dropped her head to Simon's shoulder. Light exploded behind her closed lids as they breached the outdoors.

"St. Giles," he said. "We snaked around somehow. We're at the cathedral."

"Secret catacombs," Willie managed.

She felt him opening her duster, heard him curse. "We need a doctor."

"No doctor."

"You've lost a lot of blood."

"Skytown."

"What?"

"Get me to a skytown. Need special care."

"Don't be daft, Mina. There must be a hospital nearby."

"Won't treat my kind." Barely conscious now, she looked up at Simon and for the first time in her life saw him in all his raw brilliance. "And if they do," she whispered just before the brilliance faded to black, "they'll botch it."

It was as if his father had invented and gifted him with winged boots.

Simon fairly flew to the Squire's Inn with the wounded Canary in his arms. A preposterous comparison, but he flashed back on the time his sister had brought home a hideously wounded falcon that had been shot from the sky. She'd believed their inventor father capable of anything and begged him to save the falcon. Indeed, Reginald Darcy had worked night and day and in tandem with a local veterinary to create and apply a false iron beak and talons to "Leo." It had been a grand accomplishment, since the falcon had recovered and adjusted to his prosthetic attachments with astonishing skill. Yet no one, except Jules, Simon, and Amelia, who'd adopted Leo as her faithful companion, had applauded the miracle. Reginald Darcy had never been one to brag, and the world, including the woman in Simon's arms and the newspaper she worked for, had seemed determined to focus on the eccentric man's failures.

As someone who'd suffered his own recent public humiliation, Simon marveled that his father had continually weathered the snub with such grace. Like Amelia, Simon had believed the best in Reginald Darcy, and were the man still alive, Simon would be tempted to enlist his advice concerning the injured and endangered Wilhelmina Goodenough. Instead Simon would have to rely upon his own wits as well as his brother's resources.

Cradling Willie tight in his arms, Simon breezed past the scowling innkeeper. He ascended the stairwell and bypassed Willie's room in favor of his own. He laid her upon his bed and proceeded to peel away the layers. Scarves, duster, sack coat, waistcoat. *Blimey.* Her white shirt was soaked through with crimson blood. *Damn!* He cursed his shaking hands as he gently peeled away the ruined fabric. Briefly he noted her bound breasts and the milky white skin of her stomach, three shades lighter than the ruddy complexion of her face and hands. For the moment, Simon concentrated on the messy wound. He grabbed one of his clean shirts—Fletcher had packed an abundance—and soaked it with water, washing away the blood to examine the severity of the wound. It did not look to be a bullet hole; rather, a goodly portion of her shoulder looked ravaged by several searing and deep cuts. He'd never seen anything like it. Shredding another shirt, Simon devised a compress and bandage. Thank God she was unconscious. He imagined the injury hurt like hell. An injury she'd sustained by shoving Simon from harm's way.

His gut twisted with guilt as he fumbled for the communications device Jules had given him in case of an emergency. The tele-talkie felt like a block of ice in his clammy palm. Perhaps he should have left it in his room instead of carrying it about in the wintry cold. Praying it worked, he thumbed the appropriate button and moved across the small room, whilst composing his thoughts. Since the device operated on limited energy, he was especially cognizant of time.

The tele-talkie squawked and Jules answered. "What's wrong?"

"A mishap with a Houdinian. Why didn't you tell me they were dangerous?"

"Are you hurt?"

"No, but my companion is."

"What companion?"

"You need only know that she is . . . someone I care about and wish to protect."

"Take her to a hospital—"

"She's a Freak." Simon absorbed the thoughtful silence. "Can you help? Do you know of a qualified physician? Someone nearby? Someone you trust?"

"Where are you?"

"Edinburgh, Scotland. High Street. The Squire's Inn."

"Sit tight."

Jules disconnected and Simon glanced over his shoulder at the stricken Canary. He wasn't going anywhere. She'd quite possibly saved his life. He owed her. He *loved* her. Or at least the memory of her.

His mind returned to the catacombs. To the moment before the attack. The revelation. Willie G. and Wilhelmina Goodenough were indeed one and the same. He'd suspected as much, but he had not guessed her a Freak. She thought he knew her race via some letter he'd never received. He had not put the pieces together until he'd looked down into those kaleidoscope eyes. Mesmerizing. Haunting. And filled with such pain.

The tele-talkie squawked. Simon answered.

"Dr. Bella Caro is en route," Jules said. "She's an associate. A friend. You can trust her with your companion's life."

"It looks bad, Jules. When should I expect—"

"Soon. Did you find the engine?"

"Nearly."

"Perhaps you should give up the search. Leave things to me."

Simon bristled. "We agreed to double our efforts. Where are you?"

"Closing in on Australia."

Simon could scarcely believe that the tele-talkies transmitted over thousands of miles. The connection was weak and at times garbled, but by God, it functioned. Then again the device had been influenced by Mod technology and created by a Mechanic. What other wonders did Jules have up his sleeve? More than ever it chafed that his brother had withheld that part of his life. What's more, why hadn't he brought Simon into that world? Surely there was a place for Simon's engineering skills within the agency. Did Jules doubt Simon's talent? His courage? His wherewithal?

Needing to put them on even ground, Simon struck low. "What if Professor Merriweather slips your grip? Or what if he is unable to build a functioning time machine? From where I stand, your chances of winning the contest are no better than mine."

"Since when have we been in direct competition?" Jules asked.

Since always, Simon thought, and Jules had always been ahead. "I'm not giving up on the Briscoe Bus's engine. I was caught unaware. It won't happen again."

"If you need me—"

"Same here. I do have an area of expertise, you know."

"Which is why I pointed you toward the Houdinians."

With that, Jules disconnected and Simon pocketed the fantastic device. His brother's parting words implied confidence, trust. Whereas Simon had been petty. Once again Jules had come out on top.

"Bloody hell."

Someone knocked. Too soon for the doctor, although maybe not. Jules seemed prone to magic these days. Simon cracked open the door. A striking yet enigmatic woman stood on the threshold. Her ghostly pale complexion was offset by bold red-stained lips, dark purple–tinted glasses, and ebony hair sleeked back into a tight bun. Her attire was stark black—from her riding hat fitted with fur-rimmed goggles to her voluminous leather duster to her square-toed boots. She looked more like a mortician than a medical expert, but she did carry a physician's bag. "Dr. Caro?"

Shoulders braced, she pushed her way inside. "Let's get straight to it, shall we?" She swept off her hat, perching it on a table alongside her bag. Glancing toward the patient, she wrenched off her long coat, exposing a formfitting one-piece bodysuit and a utility belt rigged with various devices.

Simon tried not to gawk and failed. Mortician? Try dominatrix.

"Name?"

"Simon Darcy."

"Not you," she said with a raised brow and a tilt of her head. "Her."

"Willie," he blurted, not sure how much information he should share. Though this woman had Jules's trust, Bella Caro was like no doctor Simon had ever seen.

She moved to examine Willie, glaring over her shoulder when Simon leaned in as well. "Stop hovering."

He didn't budge. "She was shot."

"O'blasterated." Caro's hands moved gently and efficiently over Willie's motionless body. "A sinister weapon that works on the same principle as a shotgun. Instead of pellets, the cartridge is packed with razor-sharp metal shards and heated by a core-propulsion blast. Imagine being pierced at a high-velocity impact by hundreds of searing hot blades."

Bugger. "You sound so blasé."

"I've seen worse."

"I haven't."

She glanced over her shoulder. "Why don't you take a walk? Get some air."

"I'm staying."

"Right, then. At least turn whilst I cut away this binding. I need full access to the wound."

As if he would be aroused by the sight of Willie's bare breasts at a time like this. Still, not wanting to anger the curt doctor, he did as she asked.

"From the chopped hair and mannish clothing, I take it Willie's been masquerading as a boy. The dark discoloring of her face and hands suggests use of a tanning agent to further alter her appearance. Astounding what lengths a Freak must go to in order to lead a somewhat normal life."

The bitter tone in her voice caused Simon to peer back around. Caro had already made quick work of the binding, discreetly placing a linen over Willie's torso. She'd also fixed some sort of mask over Willie's nose and mouth.

"To ensure she doesn't awake whilst I work," Caro said, as if reading his mind. "Stop fretting. She won't feel a thing."

Regardless, Simon's shoulders tensed as Caro pulled a weapon from her medical bag—a gleaming pistol with a thick needle protruding from the muzzle. Simon watched, fascinated and wary, as she snapped what looked to be tubes of blood on each side of the barrel. "What the devil is that?"

"She's lost a lot of blood. She needs a transfusion."

He grasped the doctor's wrist as she took aim. "Injecting her with Vic blood could kill her, or sicken her for life."

"Which is why I'm using *Freak* blood," Caro said, sounding vexed. "Step off, Darcy."

His brother's faith in this woman be damned. "How do I know those vials contain Freak blood? Why should I trust you?"

Caro gave a disgusted growl, then raised her tinted spectacles to her forehead.

Simon marveled at her direct and cutting gaze. A gaze that swirled with a rainbow of colors. "You're a Freak."

"I'm a Mechanic. I fix things. Except when waylaid by overbearing oafs. Do you want me to help your friend or not, Darcy?"

He nodded, chagrined. Confused.

Dr. Bella Caro turned back to her work. Injected blood into Willie's arm via the transfusion gun. Simon had never seen anything like it. Then she traded her tinted glasses for bronze goggles that featured three different magnifying loupes and a tubular bulb that shot a fierce beam of direct light. She studied the multiple wounds to Willie's shoulder and upper arm, then procured antiseptic and intricate forceps from her bag of medicinal wonders. "I'll need to extract every piece of shrapnel. Missing one could be dire. Don't worry," she said with a smug smile. "I'm thorough. Although this could take some time. Do sit before your knees give way, Darcy. I've no time to attend to you as well."

He was not, in fact, woozy. Just concerned. For Willie. "Your bedside manner leaves something to be desired, Dr. Caro."

"I don't need to be pleasant, Mr. Darcy. I'm brilliant."

Her arrogance was grating yet inspiring. Though she looked all of twenty summers, surely she had the expertise to mend Willie. Jules would not have enlisted her otherwise. "How do you know my brother?" he couldn't help asking as she pulled slivers of metal from Willie's flesh.

"I fixed him."

"Pardon?"

"When he got his legs blown off, I fixed him. Better than new."

Simon frowned down at the woman. "Jules is in possession of both of his legs. They weren't blown off. Just horribly mangled."

She shrugged. "Figure of speech. Now do leave off. You're a distraction, man. I abhor distractions."

Simon couldn't care less about Bella Caro's comfort level. Damnation. Jules considered this shrew a friend? Mind reeling, Simon dragged a chair to the other side of the bed. Not knowing how else to help, he sat and held Willie's hand. Though limp, her touch was familiar. This moment every bitter thought he'd hurled in her direction melted away until there was nothing left but their pure and youthful love. He chanced a look at the good doctor, who was, thank God, intently focused on Willie's wounds. "Are you and my brother lovers?" he asked directly.

"Rude of you to ask, but no."

"Were you ever—"

"We are associates. Doctor and patient. Acquaintances. Friends. Nothing more."

Never once did she meet his gaze. He did not wholly believe her, but he did not press. He'd been too bold already. His only excuse was that he was now morbidly curious about his twin's life as a Mechanic, as well as the intimate relationships between Freaks and Vics. Simon suppressed further questioning, allowing the doctor to focus on her work. He smoothed his thumbs over Willie's knuckles and allowed his mind to wander. The nostalgic journey was both pleasing and troubling. A hundred questions welled.

"My work here is done."

Simon blinked out of his musings. How much time had passed?

Caro stood abruptly, returned her instruments to her bag, and traded her surgical goggles for her tinted glasses. "Willie will be down and out for a while."

"How long?"

"A week or two. Depends."

"On what?"

"On her." The good and arrogant doctor pulled on her coat and fastened each button with rigid focus. "There could be fever, delirium, but she will survive. Rest is of supreme importance. Do not allow her to move about too soon."

"Anything else?" he asked as she pulled on her riding hat and leather gloves.

"She sustained severe nerve and muscle damage," Caro said with a compassionate glance toward her patient. "Regaining full use of her right arm might prove an arduous and long process. See that she strengthens the muscles and advances flexibility no matter the difficulty or pain."

"What if there are complications?" Simon asked as she marched toward the door. "How can I contact you?"

"You can't. We never met, Mr. Darcy. I was never here."

"Understood. Still." Simon glanced toward Willie's unconscious form. "Have a heart, Dr. Caro."

"How flattering that you find me lacking in compassion," she said with a sniff. "Oh, very well." She slipped a calling card into his hand and glared. "Emergencies only. And that means someone had better be dying."

Simon glanced down at the card as she bolted from the room. He wanted to thank her. He *should* have thanked her. A scant second later he followed the curious doctor into the hallway . . . into the lobby . . . into the street . . . but Dr. Bella Caro was gone.

CHAPTER 10

THREE DAYS LATER
SOMEWHERE OVER THE MEDITERRANEAN SEA

Bingham owned a personal fleet of substantial and impressive dirigibles, but none as grand as his modified zeppelin, a spectacular flying machine dubbed *Mars-a-tron*. Fitted with advanced equipment—steam turbines, rocket blasters, and a state-of-the-art gyrocompass—as well as a luxurious gondola with an ornate private cabin, *Mars-a-tron* would afford Bingham a swift and comfortable journey to the land down under.

Although the day had been pitted with various bumps, Bingham was riding high from a string of good news. On the downside, he'd been visited by the shire constable, who'd been intent on inquiring about the viscount's rocket fuel supply and mentioning the disastrous explosion caused by that buffoon Ashford in his efforts to build a moonship. Bingham had confessed to loaning his poorly neighbor a modicum of fuel, but he was in no way responsible for the regrettable accident.

The constable agreed.

But Bingham's mother doubted the law official's sincerity. *He's sniffing about,* she'd said.

Let him sniff. Bingham would not be outsmarted by some bumpkin constable, nor would he be henpecked by his worrywart mother.

Aside from that minor nuisance, his master plan was progressing.

As of a day ago, the members of Aquarius were indebted to Bingham for handling a potential catastrophe on their behalf, and now, because of his ruthless determination, plans for the royal assassination were once again in motion.

Wilhelmina Goodenough was in league with Simon Darcy, and, if she knew what was good for her, would report to Bingham in due course. Captain Dunkirk, the air pirate he had put on the tail of Amelia, had the youngest Darcy sibling in his sights. The elder brother, Jules, was the only Darcy to elude Bingham, but that would soon change. Bingham paid his spies handsomely for results. He did not reward incompetence. One of them would ferret out the science fiction writer, affording Bingham yet another possibility of stealing away a time-traveling mechanism.

The most promising news had come from one of Bingham's Mod Trackers. After months of chasing their tails, one of his more motivated mercenaries had finally located Professor Maximus Merriweather. The genius recluse had established a small camp in a remote region of the Australian outback. It would take days to make the trek, but Bingham would circumnavigate the globe in order to speak face-to-face with Merriweather. The twentieth-century physicist/cosmologist would be a wealth of information if coerced or bribed. An original Peace Rebel, he'd been instrumental in designing the time-traveling Briscoe Bus. "Time to repeat history."

"Beg your pardon, sir?"

Bingham turned away from the massive map on the wall and regarded his ship's captain with a dour expression. "Set the controls to hover, Northwood, and join the crew topside. Captain Dunkirk should be rendezvousing with us shortly. When he does, send him below."

"Aye, sir." Northwood toggled a switch on the control panel, then left the bridge.

Bingham sank down on his plush throne. The air pirate had been the bearer of encouraging news as well this day.

The fact that Amelia Darcy had joined with the famous and pathetically moral Sky Cowboy in her search for an invention of historical significance had been disconcerting. Tucker Gentry was a worthy opponent, and dammit, Bingham wanted that invention—assuming it had something to do with time travel. If the invention allowed him to pursue a futuristic voyage, well then, no need to journey all the way to the godforsaken outback.

"I am underwhelmed by yer mite crew, but yer dig's damned impressive."

Bingham glanced over at the pirate rogue, known as the Scottish Shark of the Skies, lazing on the threshold of the bridge. Dark, menacing, and arrogant. A mercenary. Dunkirk had served Bingham well on previous occasions. As long as Bingham paid handsomely, the pirate produced. He ignored the man's insolence and gestured him inside. "You intercepted the Sky Cowboy and Miss Darcy?"

"Aye."

"You acquired the artifact?"

"It's what ya hired me to do, yeah?"

Bingham rubbed his hands together in wicked anticipation. "Is it aboard the *Flying Shark*?"

"As I said in the telepage, my ship sustained damages. I commandeered a small transport to meet with ya." Dunkirk produced a brass box from behind his back. "Miss Darcy made quite the fuss when I took this from her. Offered me a percentage of the jubilee prize. Fifty percent of half a million pounds. I confess I was tempted."

"Crossing me would not bode well," Bingham said. "But I guess you know that, as you are here and not in league with the lovely yet vexing Miss Darcy."

Bingham's hands trembled as he rose and reached for the box. So small. What could it be? A component for the clockwork propulsion engine? A diagram of the time machine? A formula or perhaps a document stating the precise location of pertinent wormholes?

He set the box near the gyrocompass and, upon opening the lid, discovered an exquisite model of an ornithopter.

Somewhat fanatical regarding aviation, he'd seen drawings of a similar construction. Flying machines as imagined by the master, Leonardo da Vinci. "Where precisely did you procure this?"

"Tuscany, Italy. Mount Ceceri."

An old stomping ground of da Vinci's.

The great bird will take its first flight on the back of Monte Ceceri....

What, if anything, did this exquisite model of a da Vinci flying machine have to do with time travel?

Bingham donned a pair of magnifying specs and examined the model at great length and with utmost intensity.

"Pay up," Dunkirk said, "and I'll be on me way."

Bingham tempered his disappointment as he inspected the compact, though intricate, model of a da Vinci ornithopter for the third time. He had to be sure. Unfortunately, he was. "This isn't it."

Dunkirk, who'd been lounging in a seat without invitation, leaned forward with a sneer. "It's what Miss Darcy came oot of that cave with, and she was damned well averse to letting it go. I searched the cave for anything else. Empty. Ya told me to steal whatever Amelia Darcy was after, yeah? This is it. A da Vinci ornithopter. An invention of historical significance."

"But it is not significant to me."

"What the fook does that mean?"

Bingham straightened and slid the specialized specs to his forehead. "I don't want it." It did not apply to time travel. It was not even a full-scale working ornithopter. A prized artifact for a museum or a private collector, but nothing but a disappointment to him. "It will not advance my cause."

"Could be worth half a million."

"Ah. The jubilee prize." Bingham refrained from rolling his eyes. Dunkirk was ignorant of his role as anonymous benefactor of the Triple R Tourney, and he intended to keep it that way. He'd learned long ago that the best way to control his "employees" was by controlling what they did and did not know about him and his many ventures.

Bingham rocked back on his heels, anxious to be on his way. He had many irons in the fire, Professor Maximus Merriweather, at this moment, being the hottest. He gestured to the sixteenth-century model. "By all means."

Dunkirk stood. "You're offering me the invention instead of the payment we agreed upon?"

"The ornithopter is worth more than I offered you."

"If it wins the prize."

"Thought you were a gambling man, Captain Dunkirk."

"We had a deal."

"Indeed. You failed to deliver what I anticipated. I am not satisfied with your services and thus shall not pay." He flashed a lethal smile. "Take the ornithopter or leave it. This transaction is over." Bingham had toyed with killing the insolent pirate, but the man was a valuable minion—as long as he stayed in line. Cutting Dunkirk loose for a while, denying him lucrative "work," might inspire the man to treat Bingham with more respect in the future—when next Bingham needed him.

The Scottish bastard eyed him up and down, then smiled. "I be takin' the ornithopter."

Bingham watched as the intimidating man gently scooped up his "prize." "Oh, Dunkirk. You neglected to mention the status of Miss Darcy."

"Dead."

"Pity."

"Aye, it is," he said on his way out.

Bingham sensed true regret in the pirate's voice, when all Bingham mourned was the chance to dominate Miss Darcy in bed. Ah, well. At least her demise would please his mother.

He called for his captain. "Set a course for Australia." He would not dawdle and pine over Miss Darcy's less-than-thrilling discovery. Certainly he would not mourn the outspoken utopian's death. He would seek the expertise of

Merriweather, who had firsthand knowledge of the Briscoe Bus. As backup, he intended to contact Miss Goodenough.

Time to turn up the heat on Simon Darcy.

But first he would deplete some of his frustration by ravaging his sex slave and confidant. He moved toward his private cabin, knowing the automaton was naked and waiting in his bed as ordered. "Renee!" he bellowed. "Get on your hands and knees."

CHAPTER 11

JANUARY 16, 1887
EDINBURGH, SCOTLAND

Heaven.

Willie had died and gone to heaven. Surely that was the only explanation for the bliss flowing through her. No worries. No agony. Unlike before. Before there had been such blinding and weakening pain that she'd felt her mind and body shutting down. But instead of finding peace in a state of unconsciousness, she'd been pummeled with sporadic agitated dreams.

Now, however, there was *bliss*.

Quite certain she would awake to golden archways and fluffy white clouds, Willie smiled a little as she opened her eyes. Disappointment resonated as her gaze fixed upon a cracked blue sky. No, not sky. *Ceiling*.

"That smile was all too brief."

Willie jerked at the sound of a husky voice very close to her ear. She would have bolted upright, but she was pinned down. Fully aware now, she registered the soft mattress beneath her and the hard man wrapped around her like a human vine.

Simon.

She was conscious of his leg draped over her thighs, his arm wrapped around her middle. Heat stole though her body, a heady rush, as she tried to make sense of the moment. Surely this was, at the very least, inappropriate.

In spite of her fuzzy head and a now aching shoulder, Willie tried to shift away whilst looking directly into Simon's intense gaze. "Why are you in bed with me?"

"You invited me."

"I did not."

"True. I was attempting to be a gentleman. You did, in fact, *beg* me to join you."

Willie's cheeks burned hot. She searched her memories, which took her back to the catacombs. A dark corridor. A man. A gun. An excruciating assault to the shoulder. *Her* shoulder.

"You sustained serious injuries and spent the past two days in a feverish delirium," Simon informed her. "This morning you shivered as though subjected to subzero temperatures and cried out for warmth. Demanded it, actually. Curse me if you will—"

"That would be petty," Willie said, forcing her words around a humbling lump in her throat. "Something tells me you saved my life."

"You most assuredly saved mine," Simon said.

For a moment they simply stared into each other's eyes. They'd been intimate in this way before—in bed, entwined—but that had been long ago. The rapid beating of Willie's heart was all too familiar. However, she did not recall Simon's hair color resembling that of a fine cognac, nor his eyes, not just blue, but cobalt blue. How vibrant he looked! Vibrant and intoxicating.

She remembered then that she'd abandoned her corneatacts. Of course, everything would appear less muted. That also meant that Simon was gazing intently into her unshielded eyes, her freakish kaleidoscope eyes.

Self-conscious, she looked away.

Simon trailed a finger down her jawline, then grasped her chin, gently bidding her attention. "Although I was seduced by vivid green and intrigued by brown, there is nothing more enchanting then a rainbow of swirling shades."

Her breath hitched. Could he truly be charmed by an affliction that repelled so many? "Some fear that if they peer into our naked gaze too long, they'll be hypnotized by the swirling effect, and would then be powerless to our whims."

Simon's mouth quirked. "The swirling is very subtle and I am not a gormless twit."

No, indeed. Simon Darcy was most intelligent. It was one of the things, along with his adventurous spirit, that had drawn her to him twelve years prior. That, and his sinfully handsome face. She had not thought it possible, but Simon had grown even more bonny over the years. His chiseled facial features and impeccably, closely groomed beard, which was really more like a sexy whiskered shadow, contrasted with his perpetually disheveled, longish hair.

Had his body matured in a similar fashion? Could time improve upon what she remembered as perfection? Willie could scarcely breathe as her mind took a prurient turn. Even though Simon was fully clothed, she could easily imagine his bare chest, his muscled abdomen, his . . . "How long was I senseless?" she asked, desperate to break the sensual spell.

"Three days, give or take a few hours."

Three days and two nights. Had Simon slept with her throughout? He must have. Glancing about, she noted there was only one bed and this was not her room. He would have no qualms about sharing a bed with a woman, especially one in need of comfort and care. Had he stripped her naked, tended to her wounds? She found it difficult to ask. She felt exposed enough as is. "The Houdinian—"

"Is gone." Simon shifted, resting on one elbow and peering down at her with an enigmatic expression. "I stepped out when you seemed . . . restful," he said. "Filmore, Flash, whatever name he goes by, fled his post at Spirits & Tales. No notice. No explanation. I backtracked our journey through the catacombs and found nothing. I suspect he moved whatever he was protecting."

"Why are you lingering here three days after?" Willie snapped. "You should have followed whilst the trail was hot!"

"And leave you cold?"

Her body stiffened and her heart jerked. "You abandoned me before."

"That would be the other way around, my dear." His tone was harsh and it heightened Willie's sensibilities. He dragged a strong hand through his glorious hair, mussing it even more. "I waited for you that day at Paddington Station. Long past the time you had said you would join me."

"I sent Wesley with a missive of explanation."

"I received no missive."

"Wesley said—"

"He lied."

Willie blinked. Why would he lie? True, they'd never been excessively close, but why would her own brother, her *Freak* brother, betray her? She could not imagine. "I don't believe you."

Simon studied her hard, causing her skin to itch with unease. "What, pray tell, did I ever do to earn your mistrust?" He pushed off the bed, angry now. "You're the one who lied to *me*."

Though weak and stiff, Willie at least pushed up into a sitting position. She did not want to have this discussion whilst flat on her back. If she could stand, she would. But just swinging her legs over the edge of the mattress was an effort. "I wanted to tell you, but . . . the deeper I fell for you, the more I feared you would reject me."

"Based on your *race*?" His expression hardened as he stuffed his shirttails into his trousers.

"You don't understand."

"No, I don't. You agreed to marry me. Did you really think you could hide your race from me for the rest of our lives?"

"Aye! I did! I've fooled the world for ten blasted years. Why not a lifetime? Other than my eyes, which I can camouflage with tinted corneatacts, and my time-tracing abilities, which I can control, there is nothing to differentiate me from any other Vic."

"Except for your blood."

"Oh, aye," she muttered, irritated by her oversight. "There is that."

Hands on hips, he glared down at her. "What if, in those brief torrid weeks that we were together, something had happened to you? Some hideous accident that required my rushing you to a doctor? And what if that doctor had treated you as a Vic, tainting you with a blood transfusion? You could have died. Thank God, you finally confessed your race in the catacombs—otherwise, three days ago, that exact scenario would have played out!"

"Are you saying I required a transfusion?" Using her good arm, Willie untied the strings of her long nightshirt and peeked inside. "So you took me to a skytown?" she asked, noting the bandages applied to the right side of her upper chest, shoulder, and arm. She remembered nothing of a treatment. She remembered nothing at all of the past few days.

"There was no time to arrange for air transport to a skytown."

Her pulse stuttered. "I warned you not to take me to a conventional hospital. Was there a ruckus? Did they refuse to treat me and then relent? Where did they find Freak blood? I can't imagine they had a supply on hand."

"I brought you back here," Simon said. "The physician came to me. A Freak physician. Her skills were quite remarkable, although she did warn that it would be some time before you retained full use of your right arm."

Instead of wondering how in the universe she was going to write her stories with a bum arm, Willie homed in on the curious doctor. "You located a physician who was not only a Freak but a *woman*? Does she practice openly? How can that be? Freaks are denied the right to pursue such positions."

"Which explains your determination to masquerade as a young Vic man. The ruse afforded you the opportunity to flourish as a journalist for a major newspaper. But it does not explain why you failed to confide in me, the man you professed to *love*, twelve years ago. Or at the very least when we initiated this quest!"

Willie's temper flared. "I told you, I thought you would reject me. I was young and impressionable and my parents constantly warned me off mixing with Vics. *You* are not a persecuted minority. *You* are free to work where you will and to marry whom you wish. *I* am not!" Incensed now, she shot to her feet. Unfortunately, her noodly legs crumpled.

Simon caught her in his arms, held her close. "Too much, too soon. The doctor warned me."

Willie looked up at him, her heart in her throat, tears in her eyes. "I explained in the letter that my parents learned of our plans and that they were taking me away. They reminded me that Freaks are forbidden to wed Vics. The marriage would be illegal, and you would be shunned by polite society. Daddy cautioned I could ruin your life, your career. Mother preached that if you knew I was a Freak, you would forsake me. Deep down, I did not believe that part. In the letter I confessed my race and asked you to meet me in a month's time at Gretna Green if you truly loved me." Her chest ached with the betrayal. "I stole away that day, made the journey on my own. I waited two days, but you never showed."

Simon closed his eyes briefly and cursed. "I never saw that letter, Mina."

What had her parents and Wesley done? All these years she'd thought Simon had jilted her, when in truth they'd finessed it so that *she* had jilted *him*. In chagrin and heartbreak, a river of tears flowed.

"Ah, Christ. Don't cry. Don't . . ." Simon cupped the back of her head, then lowered his mouth to hers. The kiss was tender, comforting, and, oh, so magically wondrous. Misunderstanding her moan of delight for one of discomfort, he broke off all too soon and lowered her onto the bed. "I'm going to step out to get you a warm meal. When I return, you can fill me in on the exact skills of a Time Tracer, and then we will formulate a plan for tracking that damned Houdinian."

Poleaxed, Willie gaped as Simon pulled on his coat.

"Knowing who I am, *what* I am ... you still want to work with me?"

Simon paused on the threshold, stealing her breath with his intensity. "Oh, I want much more than that, Canary."

Simon placed a special order with the inn's cook for his sick "friend"; then he stepped out onto the sidewalk, welcoming a gust of frigid wind. Never had he been so aroused by a simple kiss! A damned chaste kiss by his standards. One meant to comfort. Instead, Wilhelmina had moaned, a soft husky moan that betrayed her pleasure. Raging lust had steeled his shaft, warring and meshing with stirring compassion. Laying her on the bed, seeing her stark black hair fall away from her now naturally pale face, he'd ached to rid her of that nightshirt and to caress her every curve. He longed to make her damaged body soar. To incite pleasure that would override any pain. Simon had watched her suffer, and although he still had issues with their past as well as her recent journalistic antics, his guilt regarding her injury trumped all else. Severe muscle and nerve damage, Dr. Caro had said. What if the Canary's ability to pen or type her tales had been forever compromised as a result of her pushing Simon out of harm's way?

In addition to that troubling scenario, he was also now saddled with the knowledge that her family had conspired to keep them apart. If only her brother had delivered that damned letter. Simon would not have waited an entire month. Impetuous and madly in love, he would have tracked down Mina and whisked her away. Learning she was a Freak would not have diminished his love. Although ... if such an alliance would have truly hindered his career, perhaps he would have hesitated. He could not imagine not being able to provide handsomely for his wife or lover.

Of course, if he won that jubilee prize, they could both thumb their noses at society and settle comfortably in a more tolerant or remote setting. The least he could do for Wilhelmina Goodenough in gratitude for saving his life was to ensure her well-being. He could protect and provide for her best by claiming her as his own. *For once and for always. You and no other.*

Daunting, but doable.

The biggest hurdle, he imagined, would be getting Wilhelmina to agree to the alliance. She had grown headstrong and independent over the years. Obstinate, even. And she was proud. She would not appreciate a proposal based on his gratitude and guilty conscience. He would have to be most calculated in his wording.

With that in mind, Simon poked his head into a sundry shop where he purchased a fragrant bar of soap, fresh bandages, and the latest issue of the *Informer*. He preferred to read more reputable broadsheets, but this was for Mina. Willie. What the devil should he call her?

Heading back toward the inn, Simon glanced at several window displays, thinking, once she'd convalesced, he'd have to take the Canary shopping for more feminine attire. He wasn't keen on people mistaking his future wife for a bloke. As to her race, or rather the restrictions and prejudices regarding Freaks, he'd have to ponder that vexing problem at greater length.

"Baltic oot there, yeah?" The Squire's cook, known as McLaughlin, greeted him with a tray of aromatic food. "Ye might consider a cap and mitts fer the future."

No doubt his hair was wind tossed and his fingers ice-cold as he relieved her of the tray.

"A bowl of hearty cock-a-leekie soup, a wedge of warm brown bread, and a pot of hot tea." McLaughlin gave a curt nod, then waddled off. "Hope yer friend is up and aboot soon," she tossed over her shoulder.

As in, *hurry up and get the bloody hell out of here*? Simon was aware he'd courted gossip by refusing to let the chambermaid into his room, taking the fresh linens and saying he'd fend for himself. The staff knew he'd moved Willie into his room, and they knew the kid was injured or sickly. The owner had seen Simon carrying her upstairs the day she'd been o'blasterated.

Had they been up to some criminal shenanigans?

Were they homosexual lovers?
Was Willie contagious?

Let them ponder and talk. The Darcys had been at the root of gossip for decades. Simon couldn't care less. What he cared about was seeing Willie fit and under his protection. What he cared about was catching up to that Houdinian, making him pay for his odious attack, confiscating the clockwork propulsion engine, and winning the jubilee prize. Providing for his family and future wife and restoring honor to the Darcy name and his father's memory. Grabbing a bit of glory and respect for himself. *That* was what Simon cared about.

Juggling his purchases and the food tray, Simon opened the door to his rented room and froze. What the . . . ? The bed was rumpled and empty, with Wilhelmina nowhere in sight. Heart thudding, he set the tray on a table, then noticed the closed door of the loo. Knocking instead of pounding—or, hell, bursting in—was an effort. "Willie?"

"One moment."

Her voice sounded weak, but at least she was all right. Relatively speaking.

Simon shrugged out of his coat. He rubbed warmth back into his icy hands whilst keeping an eye on that bloody door and listening for an ominous crash or thud. He heard nothing. One moment stretched to three or four. "Willie?" No answer. "Mina?" Dammit!

The door creaked open. "Sorry." She cradled her injured arm as she moved gingerly toward a chair. "I wanted to wash up a bit."

"You couldn't wait until I got back? What if you'd tripped? Passed out?"

"I managed," she said, fumbling to tighten the sash of the robe she'd pulled on—a hideous, oversized dressing gown, manly like the rest of the Canary's wardrobe.

Brow raised, Simon procured the newly purchased soap from his bag. "For what it's worth, I brought you a fresh bar of soap."

She sniffed and frowned. "It smells girly."

"You *are* a girl, Mina."

"Not outside of this room. And I prefer *Willie*. *Mina* . . . she's not cut out for this world."

What the devil?

She nodded toward the food. "Is this for me?"

"It is. Hungry?"

"Famished."

"I'll take that as a good sign." Simon abandoned the soap, and eased into a seat across from hers, wondering at her distant tone and manner. "Something happen whilst I was out?"

"No."

He didn't believe her. He wanted to pry, but he also wanted her to fill her belly. The faster she regained full strength and health, the sooner they could move on and resume their expedition. "Need help?" he asked as she tried buttering the bread, one-handed, left-handed.

"I'll manage."

That phrase was beginning to grate. Without asking, he poured them both a cup of tea, then sat back as she peppered her soup. She'd scrubbed her face and combed her hair, tucking the shaggy locks behind her ears and exposing creamy earlobes that he found quite lovely. He remembered suckling those soft lobes—teasing, seducing, making her squirm with desire.

Simon's own desire flared and he stifled a colorful curse. There was nothing provocative about her attire, nothing overtly alluring about her fresh face and unfashionable hair, yet he burned to make love to this woman. Shifting, he sought distraction via the tabloid he abhorred.

"You purchased the *London Informer*?" she asked.

"I did."

"But you favor the *Victorian Times*."

"I bought this for you." He peered around the news-sheet, noting her look of surprise and the blush of her cheeks.

"Any news regarding the Triple R Tourney?" she asked, dipping a hunk of bread in her soup.

"Front page."

"Headline?"

" 'Royal Rejuvenation or Royal Mistake?' "

"Titillating," she said around a mouthful. "Dawson's work."

"Who's Dawson?"

"Artemis Dawson. Managing editor. My boss. The one who insisted I get the scoop on you and your quest, the manipulative sod."

"Ah."

"What else?" she asked.

Curious himself, Simon read the article aloud. " 'According to an inside source, Her Majesty Queen Victoria has embraced the Triple R Tourney sponsored by an anonymous benefactor via the British Science Museum. Celebrating inventions of historical significance not only honors Prince Albert's passion for science, but maintains the queen's conviction to focus on past accomplishments rather than encourage the pursuit and development of anachronistic marvels beyond our natural scope. Old Worlders celebrate any cause for the reclusive queen's enthusiasm and therefore rejoice in the mounting excitement of the Triple R. Outspoken New Worlders continue to condemn the suppression of technological knowledge and ideological preachings of the twentieth-century Peace Rebels. Rumblings of an underground rebellion have jubilee coordinators on their proverbial toes, although they have assured our source that the threat of violence will not dampen the festivities. Voice your opinion to the editor. The Triple R Tourney—Royal Rejuvenation or Royal Mistake?' "

Simon furrowed his brow and skimmed the article a second time. "I don't like the sound of this."

"Which part?"

"The underground rebellion part." Simon eyed Willie closely. Since his return, she'd yet to meet his gaze. "Are you part of the Freak Fighter movement?"

"What do you know of the Freak Fighters?"

"Very little. Rumors. News bits."

"I do not advocate violent measures."

"But you are a part of the movement."

That earned her full attention. "What if I am?"

"Just want to know where I stand. What I'm in for."

"My social and political convictions have nothing to do with you, Simon Darcy."

"Oh, but they do, sweetheart." Simon leaned forward, his gaze intense. "You are going to marry me, Wilhelmina Goodenough."

CHAPTER 12

So little rattled Willie anymore and yet these past few days she'd been shaken about like a rag doll and spun like a top. But nothing had shocked her more than Simon's matrimonial bombshell. Appetite obliterated, she set aside her flatware and palmed the table. She would not, under any circumstance, betray the trembling of her hands. "Perhaps my senses are addled from the catacombs mishap, but was that a proposal?"

"It was not. I proposed twelve years ago. On bended knee, heart in hand, if memory serves. You accepted. I'm merely asking you make good on your promise."

Willie gaped. Her heart hammered against her ribs as she sought to make sense of the moment. Was she still unconscious? Hallucinating? Was this a dream or some subconscious manifestation of a buried yearning? "Why?"

"I want to gift you with a certain amount of freedom. As my wife you could tell that manipulative sod, Artemis Dawson, to go to hell. As my wife you would not need to ensure your job at the *Informer*. You would not need to work."

"Never mind that I *want* to work. I have a family to support."

"The family that betrayed you?" He shook his head, held up an apologetic hand. "Not for me to judge. I'm sure they had your best interest at heart."

Willie was, in fact, unsure of her family's motivation. Especially Wesley's. Her father, however ... She could not imagine that his agenda was anything but well-intentioned. "Let us backtrack. You want to *gift* me? With marriage?

How is that a gift? It would bind me to you, make me accountable to you."

"A limited perception."

"An accurate perception."

"You twist my intent."

"You assume I need saving."

"Truly?" Simon narrowed his eyes. "Is it truly an assumption, Willie? Or an obvious conclusion? Your modest and worn wardrobe suggests there is little left over from your salary once you provide for your father. I would wager you live on a shoestring. In addition, in order to maintain your position at the *Informer*, you are forced to deny your gender and alter your physical appearance. Do you not tire of slathering your beautiful pale skin with that noxious tanning agent? Do you not miss your natural, luxurious red hair? I recall you delighted in fashioning your long tresses into imaginative styles. And I'm quite certain you were keen on pretty gowns."

Her heart ached, remembering how she'd once looked, how she'd once felt. But that free-spirited innocence, that girlish indulgence, was long gone. "I told you. Mina is dead."

"Not dead. Hiding."

Left hand planted on the table for support, Willie pushed out of her chair. Perhaps it was the fortifying meal. Perhaps it was the panicked adrenaline coursing through her veins, but her legs felt strong enough to carry her away from the table. Away from Simon. She leaned against the window sash and gazed through the frosty pane. The chill icing down her spine had nothing to do with the wintry scene and everything to do with the telecoded message she'd received whilst Simon had been out. That infernal device had blipped from her duster pocket and she'd hobbled across the room in a panicked sweat. Had it blipped in the two days she'd been in a state of delirium? Had Simon heard it? Had he deciphered the code? Did he know she was in league with Strangelove, a man intent on seizing Simon's targeted invention? Mind racing, guilt churning, she had checked the small screen, mentally altering the numbers to letters.

Betray me, Goodenough, and I will crush your family.

She did not need to be reminded of Strangelove's initial threat, but the message had indeed introduced a sense of urgency to her recuperation. Someway, somehow, she needed to thwart that wicked man. She doubted Strangelove had put all of his eggs in one basket. Surely he had other spies nosing about. And now, because of her, Jefferson Filmore was on the run with an invention that could cause great harm in the wrong hands. What if the Houdinian was careless and fell prey to one of Strangelove's cohorts? What if Strangelove intended to use the Peace Rebels' engine for devious means? What if it landed on the black market?

Willie's stomach churned with a sense of dread. She couldn't shake the memory, *Filmore's* memory, of her mother. In modern times, Michelle Goodenough had been a security specialist. How was it that she'd ended up in league with Filmore, a fanatical peace activist? Why had they conspired to keep the clockwork propulsion engine in deep hiding as opposed to destroying it?

Willie felt the weight of the world, indeed the *fate* of the world, upon her injured shoulder. In tandem Simon was meddling with her heart. She braced as he moved in behind her, wrapped strong arms around her middle, and held her in a gentle embrace. The scent of faded soap had never been so tantalizing. The feel of his stubbled jaw brushing against her smooth cheek never so seductive.

"Marry me," he persisted in a low, sensual voice. "We were good together once. It could be so again."

He said nothing of love, but of course they were very different people now. The love of their youth was but a bittersweet memory. Even so, a fierce longing scraped Willie's soul. "Marriage is not permitted between Vics and Freaks."

"Anything can be bought in Skytown," he said calmly. "Even a marriage certificate."

Skytowns operated "above the law." Most flew the flag of the Peace Rebels, welcoming Mods and Freaks to socialize openly on the floating pleasure meccas. The meccas also appealed to adventurous Vics seeking a scandalous good time, as well as assorted corrupt and dubious scoundrels. Oh, aye, anything could be purchased in Skytown, but that did not mean that, once upon the ground, the marriage would be legal.

As if sensing her apprehension, Simon nipped her earlobe, inciting a delicious shiver. "How far did you take the ruse, Willie?"

Her breath caught as she fought off a knee-buckling wave of desire. "What do you mean?"

"In denying your gender, did you also deny yourself the company of men?"

"Intimacy would not have been wise," she said. And honestly, she had not deemed any man enticing enough to risk her anonymity.

"Ten years is a long time."

Twelve, she wanted to correct. She had not been with any man since Simon. But she would not admit that, as it would afford him too much power, and she was already bending to his will. She did not resist when he gently turned her in his arms. Nor did she protest when he cradled the side of her face, his fingers threading through her hair. She relished the headiness of the moment, the anticipation of a kiss. Her heart nearly stopped when his lips brushed over hers, then stuttered back to glorious life as his mouth laid claim. This kiss was not meant to comfort, she thought hazily. It was designed to seduce.

Willie gave over, reaching up with her good hand and grasping the back of Simon's neck. She pulled him closer, opened her mouth, and took the kiss deeper. Oh, aye, she remembered how it was done, what Simon liked. Eyes closed, her mind regressed. At once, she was sixteen and consumed with heart-pounding, stomach-fluttering love for the young rogue who'd stolen her heart. Fearless and curious, eager to please and to be pleasured, she saw no shame in exploring the sexual universe with the man who'd pledged deep affection until his dying day.

Lost in passionate euphoria, Willie pressed against her

lover, feeling the evidence of his arousal, which only intensified her fierce and consuming hunger.

Groaning low, Simon unknotted her sash, reached beneath her robe, and palmed her breast through her thin nightshirt.

Blimey.

She could scarcely breathe. Yet she needed more. She straddled his thigh and continued to rock her hips, giving over to the sensual pressure building in her core as the kiss turned wilder, his touch more brazen. It had been so long and never this riotous.

Willie exploded—an earthshaking climax that left her breathless and weak in the knees.

"Good God," Simon said, holding her close. "Did you—"

"Aye." She rested her cheek against his chest, entranced by the rapid, heavy thud of his heart. Once she recovered, she was most certain she would be embarrassed by this brazen display, but for now, she simply marveled in the magic. It was as if the years had faded away. Willie's defenses floundered as did her energy.

Shoulder throbbing and her right arm queerly numb, she did not protest when Simon lifted her into his arms and laid her upon the bed.

Raw desire sparked in his eyes. "If it weren't for your shoulder—"

"My shoulder need not factor in." She ached far more in other places. Rusty in the art of flirting, she quirked what she hoped was a saucy grin. "I'll just lay here and enjoy."

"Sweet Christ." Simon blew out a breath, then pulled his shirt over his head. "I'll be gentle."

"I was hoping for spectacular," she said whilst ogling his magnificent bare torso.

He grinned at that, tripping her pulse further as he peeled off his trousers. They had never made love in the light of day. She had not realized the thrill she'd missed out upon. Simon Darcy's body was a work of art much like the engineering marvels he designed.

"I'll save spectacular until you are fully healed. For now," he said whilst skimming his hands up her thighs and hiking her nightshirt to her waist, "you'll have to settle for skilled."

She parted her legs, expecting him to enter, to ease her ache, but instead he lowered his head between her thighs and pressed his mouth to her intimate juncture. Oh, aye, this was new. This was scandalous. Yet she had no wish to stop him as his lips and tongue worked astonishing magic.

His palms branded her quivering thighs. His mouth drove her to distraction. She scaled passionate heights she'd yet to experience. She felt positively dizzy. Deliciously wanton. Clutching his broad shoulder, she cried out his name as her body trembled, then shattered with glorious, heart-pounding release.

Bleary-eyed, Willie stared up at the cracked ceiling. "Oh, aye. Most skilled," she managed, her chest and lungs burning, her body sated.

Simon moved over her, on top of her, his gorgeous face looking down at her. "There's more. If you deem yourself able."

She would not have thought it possible, as she was fully satisfied, but she experienced a desirous pang. Living in the moment, she held his gaze, trailed her left hand down his strong back, and wiggled her hips. "Do not disappoint, Mr. Darcy."

"Challenge accepted, Miss Goodenough."

She was slick with want, delirious with need, and yet he hesitated when he breached her womanly walls. She surmised he was surprised by the tight fit, but then he kissed her wantonly and plunged deep.

Willie's emotions danced as Simon reawakened the woman she'd abandoned long ago. So beautiful, so exciting . . . so *troubling*. She pushed the latter thought aside. She would live in the moment because this moment might not come again.

"Willie," he bade as he rocked her to orgasm. "Open your eyes."

But he would then see her as a Freak. She ignored his command until he stilled.

He smoothed his thumb across her cheek, nipped her lower lip. "I want to see you when I come. The real you," he emphasized.

That caught her off guard and her lids flew open.

Simon cradled her face and held her gaze as he resumed his skilled and sensual mating.

Mesmerized, enchanted, and seduced, Willie climaxed in tandem with the love of her youth.

"Sweet Christ," he whispered as he collapsed upon her.

Indeed, was her only coherent thought.

CHAPTER 13

Simon had enjoyed many a tryst. Numerous alliances far more risqué than this recent dalliance with Willie. Yet his mind and body reeled in the aftermath. Never had he felt so focused, so driven, so *lost*.

Lost in the moment. Lost in her beauty. Lost in the passion.

Mystifying.

Terrifying.

Was it possible that he'd never fallen out of love with Wilhelmina Goodenough? Even though she'd broken his heart? Even though twelve years had passed and she was nothing like the young girl he remembered?

She was, in fact, more. Vastly complicated and assured trouble. Life with this woman would not be easy. Or boring.

Simon stared up into the darkening room, contemplating the future. Typically his mind churned with visions and calculations. Advanced designs that were not only functional but impressive. He had goals, monumental goals, and though he felt compelled to marry Willie—indeed, he *would* marry her, even if only in spirit—he could not yet imagine how she would fit into his life. The fact that she was a Freak was challenging enough, but her involvement in an underground movement, a movement ripe for radical upheaval should their cause go unrecognized, could prove inconvenient, if not detrimental to his career. On that score, her parents had been spot-on. In order to construct his more inspired creations, Simon needed the support of various government agencies and, upon occasion, assorted officials.

This meant walking a fine line politically and not ruffling feathers. Willie's association with the Freak Fighters would most definitely ruffle stodgy and fearful Old Worlders. If protests and demonstrations turned ugly, if Freaks and their supporters turned to more extreme measures resulting in violence and mayhem, New Worlders would be wary as well. A rebellion such as this would too greatly resemble the civil rights movements of the twentieth century. Movements that sought equality for Negroes and Indians in the United States, Catholics in Northern Ireland, and blacks and women in the United Kingdom, to name but a few. All cited in the Book of Mods and many resulting in bloody conflict.

Simon thought about Willie engaged in a heated protest and frowned. Just because she didn't advocate violence, that didn't mean she wouldn't get caught up in a ruckus and hurt. Or worse. *Killed.*

"What troubles you?" Willie asked in a scratchy voice.

Simon turned his face into the pillow, toward the woman who'd been sleeping in his arms. "You're awake."

She looked at her wrist, then frowned. "I feel at odds without my timepieces. What hour is it?"

"Close to dinnertime."

"I can't believe I slept into the evening," she said, pushing upright with her good arm. "My stamina is lacking. How frustrating."

"In light of the severity of your injury," he said, smoothing a comforting hand down her back, "I'd venture exhaustion is natural. Look at it this way, the more you rest, the faster your recovery. Perhaps we should not have—"

"I'm glad we did." She looked over her shoulder at him and smiled. "You did not disappoint, Mr. Darcy. Indeed, I can't imagine spectacular."

"Rest and recover," he said with a wicked grin, "and you will not have to imagine."

She instantly sobered. "I'm not sure it is wise for us to persist as lovers."

"Nor am I. What I'm sure of is an attraction, a connection

that has gone unbroken in spite of the years. In spite of the misunderstandings. I've no intention of running from this. From you."

Cheeks flushed, she looked away. "I've changed, Simon. I am not the carefree girl you fell in love with. In fact, I don't know how to behave like a proper lady anymore. I don't know how to live life as a woman whilst maintaining my career—a career that allows me to support, not only my father, but a cause I deeply believe in."

"Ah. The Freak Fighters." Simon sat up and swung his bare feet to the chilly floor. "Just how involved are you?"

She dragged a hand through her rumpled hair, shrugged. "Only as an anonymous voice to date. I pen articles under pseudonyms, draft pamphlets to distribute to the masses in an effort to properly educate Vics regarding our race. Old Worlders tend to circulate ignorant propaganda in hopes of suppressing our rights as a way of keeping us down. What they don't seem to understand is that suppression and intolerance are fueling discontent amongst Freaks. Causing some to branch out as mercenaries—using their supernatural gifts for dubious gain. Whilst others—like the Freak Fighters—band together to instigate change for the better. The remainder simply try to blend, to be invisible, denying who they are even to themselves. It is for those intimidated few that I fight the hardest."

Her passion and intent stirred his blood and indeed left him humbled. Aside from designing assorted contraptions and conveniences, what had he really done to make a difference in this unstable world?

"I do not oppose your cause," Simon said. "Indeed I am moved by your plight and passion, but know this, Willie. Change is often perceived as chaos and not always won peacefully. As was evidenced by the Peace Rebels."

She cut him an injured glance. "They came here, to this century, with good intentions. Were it not for a few bad apples—"

"You don't have to defend your father—or was it your

mother?—to me." Sensing he was entering dangerous territory, Simon grasped her hand in reassurance. "Which of your parents was the Mod?"

Not breaking his grasp, she swung around so that they were sitting side by side. "My mother." She licked her lips, then swallowed. "I think she was involved somehow with Jefferson Filmore. I saw her in his memories. They were arguing and—"

"Back up." Simon angled his head. "You read Filmore's mind?"

She shook her head. "Traced his memories. Went back in time and . . ." She furrowed her brow. "I have only explained this to a couple of people, and never to a Vic."

He smiled. "Happy to be your first."

She smiled back but averted her gaze, studying the toes of her pretty, bare feet. "In order for me to time-trace, there must be some sort of physical contact and I must be focused. It helps if I prompt the transmitter—the person who'll be sharing his memories—with a subject or event that will trigger memories of the experience that is of interest to me."

Simon recalled the way she'd shaken hands with Thimblethumper and the grip she'd had on Filmore's arm. He remembered her intense focus. "Regarding your work with the *London Informer*, I assume this is how you obtain such in-depth information on the people you interview."

"No doubt you think it is an invasion of privacy, but I view it as a means of survival. And I assure you I have never publicly reported anything I learned via a memory unless the transmitter willingly, *verbally* offered the information."

"After you *prompted* them, asking a question or swinging the conversation toward something you witnessed in the memory." In other words, not information granted entirely of the transmitter's accord. "Not that I'm judging," Simon said. "Just assessing the whole picture."

She gave a small shrug. "That is one way to look at it."

"So you mentioned Edinburgh or the Houdinian, connected physically with Thimblethumper, then focused and *traced* his memory." Simon pressed on. "How does that work? What is it like?"

"It's like . . . being an invisible voyeur. I dwell in the shadows, in the recesses, of the memory and simply watch it play out. I see everything, hear everything, as if I were there, living the moment, only I'm not. I'm just . . . visiting. I never stay long and I never interact. Except . . ." She shifted, frowned. "When I traced Filmore's memory and saw my mother, I was caught off guard. They were arguing about the clockwork propulsion engine. About where to hide it." She looked over and held Simon's gaze. "This made no sense to me. From the time I can first remember, any tale my mother shared with our family regarding her arrival to this century, she swore the Peace Rebels destroyed the Briscoe Bus. She described the explosion in great detail. The destruction of the exterior and interior portions of the vehicle, including the engine. Why would she lie to us?"

Simon registered the betrayal in Willie's mesmerizing eyes, knowing he was about to intensify her confusion and possibly her pain. "The list I showed Thimblethumper. There were three names." He smoothed a thumb over her knuckles. "One of them was Mickey Goodenough."

She blinked.

"You never told me your mother's first name," he went on, "but I knew your father's was Michael. It occurred that his nickname might be Mickey. But then Thimblethumper declared that Houdinian dead, and you said your father lives."

"My mother's name was Michelle," Willie said, looking impossibly pale. "In Filmore's memories, he called her Mickey. All those years . . . I thought . . ." She shook her head. "In the twentieth century, she had been a security specialist for a British firm and before that NASA."

"National Aeronautics and Space Administration. An American venture," Simon said. "I read about it in the Book of Mods. Or what little there was pertaining to the space race." Indeed, his father and sister, both avid fans of aviation, had always mourned the fact that there had not been more information regarding NASA nor the competing space program in Russia. To them it was all so fantastical and inspiring.

"In this century, she claimed she was doing vital, top secret work pertaining to world security," Willie continued. "Wesley and I assumed she worked for an elite agency that policed the development of advanced weaponry or transportation. We even fantasized that she was working undercover for Her Majesty's Mechanics." She barked a humorless laugh. "How naive we were. How wretchedly duped."

"Not really," Simon pointed out, steering clear of the Mechanics and defending Michelle—Mickey—Goodenough, if only to make Willie feel better. "If, as a Houdinian, she'd been charged to keep the clockwork propulsion engine well hidden in order to ensure it didn't fall into unscrupulous hands, then her job did indeed pertain to world security."

Willie smirked. "Yes, but what if their motives were not so pure? A few days ago you suggested that perhaps the PRs had decided to steal away and sequester the engine on the chance that, at some point, Mods wished to rejoin and return home to their own time. If *that* was the objective, then her job was not only selfish but based on cowardice. If you travel back in time with the express intent of altering the future," she said, her face growing red and her voice loud. "If a portion of your team defects and shares technological knowledge in order to build a fortune. If you muck things up so badly that you trigger a transcontinental *war*. Then you should have the gumption to stick around and monitor your mess!"

Although he did not want Willie to overtax herself, he did not want to stifle her either. From everything she'd said over the last day, he assumed she did not confide in too many people, if any. So, not only did she conceal her gender and race, but she denied herself friendship and free expression? Simon could not imagine. True, he was a diplomat whilst dealing with people and matters affecting his work. But amongst friends, and certainly with his family, he expressed himself often and loudly on a good many subjects. He could not conceive of stifling his thoughts and opinions on a daily, *hourly* basis. How extraordinarily tiresome.

"How is it you did not learn about your mother's role as a Houdinian via her memories?" Simon asked. "I assume as mother and daughter there must have been an abundance of physical contact."

"There was a goodly amount when I was quite little," Willie said. "But as a young child I did not fully recognize or understand my gift. One thing that Freaks have in common aside from our kaleidoscope eyes and unique blood type, whatever our given supernatural gift, it strengthens and intensifies with age. When I realized my ability to peek into people's memories and mentioned as such to my mother . . . henceforth she kept a modicum of distance. Caresses and hugs were saved for Wesley. Logically, I presumed her intent was to protect her top secret assignment. Regardless, to be shunned by one's own mother . . ." She shook her head, and pulled her hand from Simon's grasp. "I detest the bitter tone of my voice. I have no patience for self-pity. Life is what you make it and I have made a good life, for a Freak."

She met his gaze and torched him with a fiery conviction. "I do not wish to be rescued, but I would appreciate your assistance in preserving the career that enables me to care for my father and surreptitiously and peacefully advance the cause of my race."

Simon was not keen on her choice of words. Nor her subtle refusal to marry him. But he would not argue the point now.

Later. When she'd more fully recovered. At that time he would not take no for an answer. "The primary objective, then, is to locate the Briscoe Bus's engine." He lifted a challenging brow. "Are we in accord, Canary?"

She narrowed her eyes. Obviously she did not wholly trust him. Smart. But then he did not wholly trust *her*. "Aye," she said.

"I have no clue as to where the Houdinian might have taken the engine."

"Nor do I," Willie said, then smiled. "But I do know of someone who might have the past knowledge to point us in the right direction."

CHAPTER 14

Three days came and went. With every sunrise, Willie had deemed herself fit enough to proceed with their expedition. Yet each day she physically faltered.

Until day four.

Upon that day, *this* day, mind conquered body. No, she did not have full use of her right arm. Far from it. Her shoulder pained her like the devil. Her arm and therefore her hand did not respond as it should. Indeed her hand felt nearly numb. Although she could not hide the fumbling of pencils and utensils, hair combs, and such from Simon, she did conceal her intense discomfort. She would conquer this inconvenience or she would, at the least, manage the pain.

Willie shoved the last of her belongings into her valise. She was becoming most proficient with her left hand, although what little writing she'd done in her journal resembled a child's. No matter, she assured herself, at least it was somewhat legible. Though she tried her best not to entertain the notion, the realist in her warned that she might never recover normal use of her right arm. In which case, she needed to adapt.

Clasping the latch of her valise, she moved to the window and looked down upon High Street. Another blustery snowy day. She did not care. She would relish every biting chill. Aside from a brief daily walk in order to garner fresh air and exercise, Willie had been cooped up in this small rented room for seven days! Simon had done his best to distract and entertain her, ensuring she had at least three daily newspapers. Plenty of fodder for discussion and debate and several word games to occupy her mind. They'd also pored over her BOM, searching for more clues regarding the Houdinians, speculating about the true capabilities of assorted modern marvels, and bemoaning various global atrocities. Part of Willie wished that her mother and the rest of the brilliant and innovative Peace Rebels would have stayed in their own time, working harder to overcome the crises of the twentieth century rather than fleeing what they perceived as a doomed world in order to rewrite history.

Then again, had that been the case, Willie would not have been born. She would not have met Simon. It would seem as if they were indeed destined for togetherness in some form or fashion. Blessedly there'd been no further talk of marriage—a notion that vexed Willie on multiple levels. They had, however, been intimate nightly. Willie had taken her heart out of the equation, fully focusing on the physical pleasures of lovemaking. She was the daughter of a Mod, after all. A generation who had preached, *Make love, not war.* Indeed, she was fairly open-minded about sex. At least sex with Simon.

She smiled a little, thinking how he continued to be tender and somewhat cautious in deference to her injuries. Spectacular was still on the horizon. Not that there was anything wrong with skilled. A sensuous ache coiled Willie's stomach as she reflected on just *how* skilled Simon was.

Gads.

Indeed, the nights and random portions of the days had been spent most pleasurably. Simon had proved a most stimulating constant companion. She would even go so far as to say she enjoyed his company—except for when he scolded her for overtaxing her shoulder or lectured her regarding yo-yo techniques. Two days ago, out of boredom, Willie had snagged the yo-yo from her case. Apparently the Freak doctor had emphasized the importance of gently exercising her damaged muscles. Finessing a yo-yo as it twirled and glided up and down a string attached to her middle finger seemed like an inspired bit of therapy to Willie. Simon agreed. Unfortunately, he was determined to give her lessons when it came to specialty tricks. It's not that he was an impatient teacher. *She* was an impatient student. In her heart she knew she had the intellect and talent to learn; what she lacked was strength and flexibility. One impulsive act had quite possibly cost her the full mobility of her right arm for life. Not that she would take back that terrifying moment in the catacombs. Searching her own memories, she was certain Simon would have taken a direct hit between his shoulder blades had she not pushed him aside. He could have been killed or at the very least crippled, his spine o'blasterated.

No, she did not regret her actions. Just her slow and frustrating recovery.

Anxious to be on their way, Willie turned from the window and paced the small room. She checked her time cuff, then her pocket watch. The timepieces concurred. Simon had been gone for four hours, thirty-five minutes, and eleven seconds. He'd promised they would leave for England as soon as he returned from an important errand. He'd been running "errands" for the past three days, each time returning with a few *girly* purchases. He seemed most earnest in reacquainting Willie with her feminine side, and very much to her surprise, she could not resist the decadent temptation of silk unmentionables and French perfume. Much like their lovemaking, it had seemed a wicked boon whilst locked away from the harsh realities of the maddening world.

That moment, Simon walked through the door and her heart fluttered like an infatuated schoolgirl's. As always, he was windblown yet impeccably dressed. So dashing. So tempting. She could kiss this man for hours. Annoyed by her shallow thoughts, she tore her gaze from his gorgeous face and noted the large leather bag slung over his shoulder.

"Sorry to be so long," he said whilst laying his goods gently upon the bed. "Complications. But I do believe I mastered that infernal glitch."

Willie's pulse skipped as Simon tugged off his gloves, then flipped the latches of the case.

"What *have* you purchased now?"

"I didn't buy it. Well, not as is. I built it."

What the . . . She'd expected a fur-lined greatcoat or perhaps a flowered or feathered top hat. Never in her wildest dreams had she imagined . . . "An arm." She gaped at the jointed contraption. "You built me an artificial arm?"

"A Thera-Steam-Atic Brace. A steam-powered prosthesis that will enhance your strength and mobility. Temporarily," he added with an encouraging smile. "Just until your arm is functioning properly. I've devised a shoulder guard as well. Armor, if you will. Added protection for your most damaged and sensitive area. The brace and guard attach to this combination waistcoat–cutaway skirt. A garment inspired by my sister, who also favors trousers. Functional and fashionable. At least that was my intention." He angled his head, frowned. "You hate it."

The hardware was intricate and fascinating. The garment— feminine but not overly frilly and made to be worn over trousers or a long skirt. What touched her most was the thought behind the gift. "On the contrary, I am most impressed and humbled." Stunned, she shoved her good hand through her hair. "This is what you've been doing for the past few days? Designing and engineering a therapeutic brace?"

"I worked on the sketches and calculations whilst you read or wrote in your journal, mentally cataloged my supplies, then located a tinkerer in New Town who could accommodate my needs. His workshop was top-notch, as were his skills. Mr. Standish proved a most competent assistant and his wife, a talented seamstress. She helped devise the augmented waistcoat. It took a few days, some trial and error, but I was highly motivated." Simon vibrated with excitement. "Ditch your sack coat. The baggy vest as well."

Which left her in striped trousers, a flouncy-sleeved blouse . . . and her new silky unmentionables. Exposed, by Willie's standards. "Whatever inspired this creation?" she asked, entranced by Simon's infectious energy.

"I'd been thinking about Leo."

"Who?"

"My sister's enhanced falcon." Simon told her a story about how his father had created and fitted an injured bird with an artificial beak and talons whilst he suited Willie up in his own fantastic design. "Then, whilst reading the Book of Mods the other night, I came to that passage on robotics and something clicked." He secured the last strap and cinched the corseted waistcoat tight. "How does it feel?"

"Foreign. Snug." She glanced down at the gleaming brass rods, cylinders, and gears. The etched shoulder guard and brocaded black and gold corset. The fitted bodice cinched her waist and provided lift to her small breasts, affording a hint of cleavage. She lifted a suspicious brow. "Surprisingly seductive."

"Because of the woman wearing it."

Willie's heart pounded beneath her customized garment. Partly because of the heat in Simon's gaze. Mostly because of a deep and crushing fear. "Within the privacy of these walls, I acquiesced to my feminine self, but out there . . . in the real world I am Willie G. The Clockwork Canary. I navigate life with the confidence and ease of a male. I do not . . . I cannot . . ." She swallowed hard, panic stirring in her blood. "Blast you for twisting me up, Simon Darcy."

He tucked her shaggy hair behind her ears, framed her face with his hands. "I understand your motivation in terms of concealing your race. But your gender? You ask too much of yourself, Willie. And of me. I have no intention of losing you again. And, by damn, I will not see you struggling with circumstances on your own. I know," he said, cutting her off when she tried to interject. "You'd manage. I have no doubt. You have managed for a good long time. If anyone is impressed and humbled, it is me. Now please do me the favor of allowing me to assist."

Poleaxed by his fervid plea, she fairly swooned. Instead, she gestured to the Thera-Steam-Atic Brace. "How does this inspired gadget work?"

His eyes lit up and torched her heart. "Engineering the device was a bit of a challenge, but it is, in fact, quite simple to manipulate."

Willie listened intently as he walked her through the procedure. A toggle here. A button there. She did as Simon instructed and, upon second try, grasped a pen in her augmented right hand and wrote upon a page most beautifully. "You're a genius," she said in honest, unabashed awe.

"I am my father's son," he said with a twinge of melancholy. "That is, I inherited his passion for tinkering with inventions. I do not believe I ever told him how much I admired his tenacity."

Willie swallowed hard, feeling guilty about that wretched article regarding Reginald Darcy. For someone who composed sentences for a living, this moment she struggled with a proper response. "I wager he was aware of your regard."

"Perhaps. At any rate," Simon said, shrugging off the dark moment, "I do think Papa would have been particularly impressed and flattered by this invention."

"Because you were inspired by his modifications for Leo?"

"A remarkable accomplishment."

"As is this." Willie manipulated her Thera-Steam-Atic Brace, grasping the whiskey bottle Simon had purchased two nights prior, and steadily pouring them a drink. She could feel the brace supporting yet manipulating her muscles. Her spirits soared, as did her confidence. "Astonishing," she said. "Truly, Simon." She lifted her glass in a toast. "To your innovative brilliance."

He dipped his chin in quiet gratitude, but she caught the flash of excitement in his eyes as he clinked his glass to hers. "To your good health."

Willie thought about his brother, Jules, and how Simon had always felt a bit inferior to his glorified twin. And she knew most certainly that his famous cousin Briscoe cast a wide shadow. Simon was most inspired and gifted in his own right. How frustrating it must be trying to excel above and beyond the Time Voyager. To make one's mark.

Project Monorail.

A most wondrous concept that would have indeed been a celebrated contribution to society. Why exactly had it been stonewalled? The pressman in Willie itched to know.

"There's something I've been meaning to ask you," Simon said as he recalibrated a portion of her brace. "This time-tracing ability. Does it work on everyone?"

She smiled down at the top of his head. "You mean, can I trace, *have* I traced, your memories? I'm surprised it took you this long to ask."

He caught her gaze briefly. "So can you?" he asked, then went back to tinkering.

"I cannot. It is a conundrum, I confess. It did not happen of its own accord upon the many times we touched nor when I intentionally 'focused' out of curiosity. Your memories are closed to me, Simon. I cannot say I am sorry."

"Nor I."

"You have secrets?"

"I have a history."

"With the ladies." She snorted in jest, but her jealous heart squeezed. "Your affairs are fodder for many a man's fantasy. At least those men working at the *Informer*."

Once again his gaze flicked to hers, only this time he held it. "My affairs are but dalliances and have nothing to do with here and now. With us. From here on out there will be but one woman in my bed."

Willie's heart hammered against her chest with joy. With dread. She did not play coy. "You're suggesting forever with a Freak, Simon."

"I am."

"I'm the first generation of my kind. Anything is possible."

"How thrilling."

"My life span could be short or it could be eternal. My supernatural skills could spiral out of control and overtake me or . . . or disappear altogether."

"I could get hit by an automocoach tomorrow," Simon said. "Or develop some horrific lingering disease. Nothing is a given."

"There has been no documentation of a second generation. Yes, we are young, but not too young to engage in affairs and, hypothetically, produce children. What if we are infertile? Or what if those born of a Freak and Freak or a Freak and Vic are so hideous that—"

Simon kissed her. Deeply and with great passion. At once her anxiety melted away, and when at last he broke off, Willie swayed. Holding her steady, he quirked an arrogant, heart-stopping smile. "Concern noted and rejected. Here's what's going to happen, sweetheart. We're going to do as you suggested and visit your father in hopes that he can, through his memories, lead us to the Houdinian and the clockwork propulsion engine. But first, we're going to wed. I don't give a good damn if it's legal in the eyes of the queen. It will be significant to me and for once, I'm going to get what I want. That would be you." He brushed his thumb along her lower lip. "Are we in accord, Canary?"

Their marriage would never last for a dozen reasons, starting with Strangelove, but, this moment, she could not deny Simon . . . or her heart. "Aye."

CHAPTER 15

Simon couldn't decide which thrilled him more: Willie's re-action to his Thera-Steam-Atic Brace or his insistence that they wed. Although he assumed she would be amenable to anything that would accelerate her healing, he did not think she would adjust so easily to the brace. Nor did he expect such praise for his mechanical creation. His chest had swelled with pride. An adrenaline rush had rendered him dizzy. A preposterous, overblown reaction to her professing him brilliant. But by God, it had felt good.

Building one therapeutic brace for one woman paled in comparison with building a fuel-efficient monorail system for an entire city and yet it had felt equally important. Was this how his father had felt when fitting Leo with his artifi-cial parts? Was this why he hadn't bragged to the press or dragged Leo off to some scientific exhibition? Were Leo's ability to adapt and Amelia's undying gratitude satisfaction enough?

"I shall miss this city," Willie said as their hansom cab rolled over the cobblestone of High Street.

"We must return at some point," Simon said. "A leisure trip as opposed to business."

She smiled but looked away and Simon knew she did not believe that they would be together long enough to enjoy a future holiday. Although she'd agreed to marry him, her lack of faith in a long and successful union was monstrously clear. Aside from the concerns she'd stated, she did not be-lieve their marriage would be legal and binding. She as-sumed, the moment it was known she was a Freak, they would be no more than illicit lovers in the eyes of society as well as the British government. Which might have been the case, except Simon was of the mind that every law had a loophole, and he was confident he'd determined two whilst perusing assorted resources he'd found at a library within a few blocks of Squire's Inn.

The British law that pertained to legal religious marriages of Vics and Freaks had never been enforced in Scotland. Hence if they married in Scotland . . . Loophole number one.

"The coachman missed our turn," Willie said as they rolled past Cockburn Road.

"No, he didn't."

"But Waverley Station—"

"We're not taking the train. And we're not leaving for Canterbury until tomorrow morning."

"But—"

"It's dusk and I have other plans for the evening."

Although her eyes were shielded behind the deep amber–tinted spectacles she'd insisted upon wearing, Simon knew her rainbow gaze was narrowed. "Where are we going, Simon?"

"To the nearest skytown." Loophole number two. Transient pleasure meccas floating above major cities and therefore "above the law," skytowns welcomed Freaks, Mods, and Vics with open gangways. He anticipated little difficulty in locating a certified clergyman, or, hell, even one of those love gurus, to perform a civil wedding ceremony between a Freak and a Vic. By night's end, Miss Goodenough would be a Darcy.

For better, for worse.

Willie held silent as Simon escorted her onto the compact steam-powered dirigible that would transport them from the lush fields of Arthur's Seat to the pleasure mecca floating amongst the stars. Her mind, however, raced aplenty.

Her Thera-Steam-Atic Brace was packed safely away and stowed with their luggage; thus, she found it difficult to manipulate the buckle of the seat harness. Between her weak arm and the thick gloves she'd donned against the frigid weather, the task proved impossible. In her mind, she swore most vigorously. Her pride warred with gratitude as Simon completed the task for her, initiating another stream of colorful mental curses.

Rather than consoling her, Simon passed the grungy pilot several banknotes. "Make haste, good man." He then settled next to Willie on the cramped bench, wrapping his arm about her as the air transport lunged forward and picked up speed, rolling across the grass, bouncing toward a precipice, lifting and lifting, until the vehicle at last took flight.

Willie let out a breath she wasn't aware she'd been holding. It wasn't as if she were unaccustomed to flying. But this night vibrated with a plethora of unknowns.

"As luck would have it," Simon said close to her ear, "a skytown hovers just past the northern boundaries of the city. This won't take long."

She merely nodded, keeping her gaze lowered as she tried to tame her riotous emotions. Simon intended for them to wed this very evening. He had not said specifically as such, but she was a savvy sort and he was none too subtle. She had not anticipated this moment so soon. *"This moment is long overdue,"* she could imagine him saying. However, it would not be as she had imagined her dream ceremony. No family. No pretty bustled gown with yards of silk and lace.

Upon leaving Squire's Inn, Willie had bundled up in her normal boyish layers, including her oversized duster, three colorful scarves, and the man-sized, cashmere-lined gloves given to her by Simon. Even her floppy newsboy cap was firmly in place. With the exception of her fair, tanning-agent-free complexion, Willie looked much as she had every day of the past ten years. Only she didn't *feel* the same. Beneath the mannish ensemble beat the heart of a woman on the verge of what should be the most memorable and beautiful event of her life.

This would not be a traditional wedding, which logically

was to be expected given her extraordinary circumstances. And true, they had initially planned to elope all those years ago, which would have entailed a quick and simple ceremony. Still, she harbored fanciful thoughts of silk, lace, and flowers.

"You're shivering." Simon huddled closer, holding her tighter, assuming she was cold.

Again she said nothing, just snuggled into his embrace. She was not shivering so much as trembling. *Excitement. Anxiety. Anticipation.* Numerous afflictions rattled her senses.

Willie gazed ahead through the transparent shield that afforded protection from the forceful winds. Given her enhanced night vision, she easily spotted their destination in the not-so-far distance.

Though insanely popular, skytowns were considered an eyesore and outrage amongst polite society. By their very nature they courted scandal and trouble, and as a way of avoiding hassle by ALE (Air Law Enforcement), they rarely hovered in one place for more than a couple of days. Composed of four to five airships with connecting gangways, skytowns were interchangeable and mobile.

And highly decadent.

Gambling halls, opium dens, brothels. Coffeehouses featured outlawed folk and rock music inspired by twentieth-century Mods and served liquor and weed on the side. Transformation centers afforded visitors the chance to live out a night's fetish or fantasy via elaborate temporary makeovers. Merchants and artisans peddled wares of the Love Generation—bongs, herbs, incense, flower patches, bell-bottoms, peasant dresses, and love beads. Simon had been correct in saying anything could be bought in Skytown. Anything was possible and anything went.

One would think such freedom would spur much trouble, but for the most part, brutal violence was rare on these fleets of fancy. Even though Willie had always boarded a skytown in disguise, she never felt more at ease then when navigating the aerial bazaars that flew under the Peace

Rebel flag. Even though she was half-Vic, there was something about the circle with a stick and two legs—the sign of "peace"—that soothed and invigorated Willie's soul.

Some things were worth fighting for.

She stole a glance at Simon, pondered the kindness he'd shown her over the last few days, and reflected on his charm and affections at the onset of their youthful affair. Perhaps she'd given up on him and their love far too easily. She knew not what to make of this second chance, could not yet see her way around a biracial union . . . or Strangelove's threat. But, by damn, she would at least rise to the challenge. She would live in the moment and tackle the future day by day. She would manage.

Willie's pulse raced as their air transport drifted toward the massive dirigibles joined and silhouetted against the darkened sky. All manner of lighting twinkled in the airships' windows and the decks were awash in the soft glow of moonlight and assorted illuminated carnival rides. Although she knew much of the nocturnal activities on board to be bawdy, this moment Willie viewed the spectacle as delightfully romantic. Her heart danced and her stomach fluttered with nervous anticipation.

Was this how a Vic or Mod woman, a normal woman, felt on her way to a conventional church? On the way to her wedding? "Are you sure about this?" she asked as their air dinghy docked.

"Think of it as Gretna Green," Simon said. "In the air." He tipped the transport captain and issued orders regarding the delivery of their luggage.

Willie took a calming breath as Simon lifted her upon a swinging gangway and guided her toward the sounds of rollicking fun.

Dressed in the flamboyant *threads* of a hippie, a professional long-haired greeter approached as they crossed to the deck of a magnificent airship advertised as the *Love Bug*. Willie glanced heavenward, smiling at the ship's attached bally. The steam-air balloon was painted a rainbow of bright swirling colors. Psychedelic, her mother would say. *Cool.*

"Welcome to Skytown," the greeter said. "Name's Woodstock, but you can call me Bear."

Simon raised a brow at that and Amelia sniffed. She knew that scent. "Bear" was *stoned*. He was also American. She knew not why, but young Americans seemed most drawn to the "Peace, man" and "free love" messages of the Mods.

"Right, then. *Bear,*" Simon said. "Anyone on this dirigible perform marriages?"

"Not this dig, but two digs over, the *Flying Flower*. Reverend Karma. Hitches anyone who declares their love." He looked from Simon to Willie and smirked. "Though *this* might be a first."

Willie realized then that Bear saw her as a man. Although her objective for a decade, it was the last thing she wanted this eve. Irritated, she swept off her cap and shoved her hair out of her face. "I'm a woman."

"My mistake," Bear said. "And a pretty one at that. Dig the shades, by the way."

Willie was tempted to dispense with her tinted spectacles as well, but it had been jolting enough confessing her gender, never mind her race. "Where would I find the transformation center?" she asked Bear.

"Why would you want to go there?" Simon asked.

"I'd rather look like a bride than a groom," she answered honestly.

"I don't care—"

"I do."

"I'll come with you."

"Bad luck for the groom to see the bride before the ceremony," she said.

"Kind of square," Bear said. "But hey, whatever the lady says should go."

Simon shot the longhair a lethal look, then turned back to Willie. "I'm not keen on letting you out of my sight. Not in this wild territory. Not after—"

"I can take care of myself, Simon. I've been doing so a very long time." She reached out and grasped his hand. "Do not deny me this pleasure."

He met her gaze and Willie felt the force of his passion to her toes. The intensity shook her soul.

"Meanwhile back at the ranch . . ." Bear shoved his hair behind his pierced ears, then eyed Simon with a disapproving frown. "Listen, dude, in Skytown, everyone's equal. Mods, Vics, Freaks, Orientals, blacks, fairies, men, women. Playin' the heavy ain't cool. Let the chick do her thing and meet up with you later."

Simon held her gaze, her hand. "The *Flying Flower* in one hour."

"Two," Willie amended.

Frowning, he pressed a kiss to her palm. "I'll be waiting."

The hardest thing about letting Willie go was having faith that she'd show up at the appointed rendezvous. That she wouldn't stand him up. *Again.* That she wouldn't give over to doubts and fears and flee. *Again.*

Simon spent the next two hours wrestling with dread whilst making arrangements for his wedding. *By God,* he'd thought more than once, *I'm getting married.*

His mother would be horrified that she hadn't been invited. Although he couldn't imagine a staunch Old Worlder like Anne Darcy ever setting a pristine boot on a skytown deck. Nor could he imagine her reaction to the news that he'd married a Freak. Jules and Amelia would be accepting of Willie. This Simon knew in his heart. But his mother? It did not settle well, knowing intolerance existed within his family. Like many people, Anne Darcy feared what she did not understand.

Simon thought about Willie's mission to educate the skeptical world regarding her race. He could not dismiss the importance of her contribution to "the cause" and wondered briefly how he could support her efforts whilst keeping her safe. It didn't help that, whilst bracing for the evening with a snifter of brandy, he'd overheard other patrons discussing reported skirmishes between Freak Fighters and International ALE over the Atlantic Ocean. How long until those skirmishes reached shore?

Downing the brandy, Simon left the cannabis-hazed bar and immersed himself in the here and now. He tracked down Reverend Karma, bought a ring, secured overnight lodgings, and tried to transform the opulent, harem-looking room into a tasteful honeymoon suite. Simon had always enjoyed lavishing attention upon women, sweeping them off their feet with gifts and special outings, showering them with compliments, flowers, and champagne. He rarely questioned himself when it came to romance and yet on this night he questioned everything.

Blast.

By the time Simon returned to Karma's Chapel of Love, he was quite miserably a nervous wreck. He stood next to the reverend as the seconds ticked by. He combed his fingers through his hair in an effort to tame the perpetual wildness, checked the time, then smoothed the lapels of his burgundy velvet frock coat. He stared down at his shiny boots, willing his toe to stop tapping; then he glanced at the musicians who would double as "witnesses." A long-haired guitarist sat cross-legged on a plump velvet pillow playing a love song Simon did not recognize. A slight young woman wearing a billowy peasant gown and a flowery wreath upon her head looked blissfully serene as she rang her finger bells.

Simon envied their calm.

"Natural to be anxious," Reverend Karma said when Simon glanced at his pocket watch for the umpteenth time.

"She's ten minutes late."

"Also natural. Chicks tend to lose track of time when preparing for their nuptials. Chill out, my friend."

Simon eyed the Nehru-suited preacher man with his long, wiry hair and layers of wooden love beads, and, again, second-guessed himself. "You're quite certain this will be legal."

The old man spread his arms wide and looked serenely skyward. "To anyone who truly matters. Yes."

Mmm. Simon checked his watch again, surprised when Woodstock-you-can-call-me-Bear peeked in through a flowered archway.

"Dude," Bear said. "Your lady wants a word."

So Willie hadn't jumped ship. That was something, although Simon still sensed a problem. He followed Bear out of the chapel and into a dimly lit reception area ... and nearly tripped over his feet at the vision of loveliness stirring up the petal and herb rushes as she paced the flower-strewn floor.

"Blew my mind too," Bear said in a low voice. "Saw her comin' out of Fuddrucker's Fantasy Farm and thought, *Whoa. Some dog's gonna jump this fox before she ever gets to her man.* So I walked her over but then ..." He dragged a hand over his scraggly beard. "Don't freak, dude, but I think she got cold feet."

"Thank you for ensuring her safety."

Bear looked at Simon's proffered hand as though it were a stick of dynamite. Instead of clasping palms, he raised two fingers. "Peace, man. And good luck."

The stoner slipped away and Simon moved toward the woman in white. She'd had her hair color restored to its natural, vibrant red. Curled and fashioned into a soft updo, the stylish hairstyle accentuated her long neck and exquisite bone structure. The gown, with its corseted bodice and voluminous skirts, was somehow sensual and angelic at the same time. Simon had never seen a more beautiful bride. He knew not if she'd made this spectacular transformation for him or for herself. What he knew was that she'd made a solid and courageous decision to shed her male persona. It was an extraordinary step.

Simon was grappling for a worthy compliment when she whirled to face him, her expression troubled if not tortured.

"I apologize for the delay, but I had a most difficult time settling on a gown. It has been a long time since I've dallied over fripperies."

"I'm glad you dallied," Simon said, mouth dry. "You look stunning, Wilhelmina." He found it difficult to think of her as Willie when she looked so utterly feminine, and even though she'd returned her hair to her natural hue, *Mina* did not fit either. Mina had been a young girl. The angel before him was all woman.

"I thought the long lace sleeves to be most brilliant as they disguise my bandages, but do you think the décolletage too revealing?"

Simon admired her slender neck, her smooth, pale skin, and the swell of her small but exquisite breasts. He quirked an appreciative smile. "I think it perfect."

"The skirts? Too frilly?"

"You look like a princess." He angled his head. "Except perhaps for the tinted spectacles."

"I did purchase new corneatacts, as I'm not yet ready to reveal my race to the masses, but for tonight, I'd prefer no illusions."

"I appreciate that." He reached up and slid off the glasses, smiled into her rainbow eyes. "I'm entranced. Truly."

She glanced away, blew out a nervous breath.

Interesting that whilst shedding her mannish clothes, she'd also been stripped of her brazen confidence. "What troubles you?"

"The vows."

"Pardon?"

"I don't practice any one faith."

He thought about Reverend Karma and his love beads. "Trust me. The ceremony won't be religious as much as spiritual."

"Still, we shouldn't promise things we do not mean."

To love and cherish? Honor and obey? He didn't ask which part, because he didn't want to broach a subject that might veer them off course. In truth, he wasn't all too keen on pledging his love when, this moment, he wasn't sure love entered into it. Passion, yes. Gratitude, yes. Affection, yes. Bone-deep love? As in delirious, all-consuming, I'll-die-if-I-can't-have-you-forever-and-always *love*?

Perhaps that notion, that happy illusion, was reserved for the naive. For the very young. He had felt it once—for

Mina. But life's experiences had molded him into a more pragmatic man. He was wary in matters of the heart. Particularly when they pertained to Wilhelmina Goodenough. "I'll tell the reverend to keep it simple."

She narrowed her mesmerizing eyes. "I do not wish to be difficult, but I feel compelled, to be fair, to reiterate the obvious. Life with a Freak will not be easy."

Simon nodded. "In the same spirit of goodwill, might I say, life with a Darcy will not be a walk in the proverbial park."

She blinked.

"More than thirty years ago, my distant cousin Briscoe Darcy, the Time Voyager, jumped dimensions in his time machine. As you well know, that journey had dire repercussions. Whilst half the world damns Briscoe and any family associated with him, the other half views us, all of us, each and every Darcy, no matter if we ever met the man, as a ticket to . . . something more. Something extraordinary. As if every Darcy ever born possesses the knowledge or the ability to time travel at any moment. As such we are often scrutinized and sometimes hunted. Definitely ill judged." Simon framed his intended's lovely face and swept a gentle kiss over her subtly tinted lips. "Let us be curiosities together."

"You make an intriguing case."

"I can upon occasion be most persuasive." If she still balked, he would be forced to play dirty. To threaten her job at the *Informer* by cutting all ties with her and thereby robbing her of the sensational story she'd been assigned to report. He did not wish to go that course, but he would. He refused to go through life wondering how she fared, worrying about her safety and finances, obsessing on whether she'd fallen prey to another man's charms. Although he might not love her, dammit to hell, she was in his blood.

She glanced over his shoulder at the flowered archway leading into the Chapel of Love. Rustic and whimsical. "I fear I have overdressed for the occasion. What was I thinking?"

Blessed acquiescence.

Simon smiled. "That you wanted to look like a bride." He smoothed his thumbs over her cheeks. "Although I can't promise you a storybook wedding, I promise you an unforgettable night."

She quirked a teasing grin. "I'll settle for spectacular."

Kissing her neck, just below her ear, Simon whispered, "Challenge accepted."

CHAPTER 16

"I now pronounce you man and wife."

Willie stared at the simple band Simon had placed on her left ring finger, tears pricking her eyes. How ridiculous. Reverend Karma had kept the ceremony not only temporal but amazingly brief. She'd forgone her timepieces, but she would swear less than two minutes had elapsed between "Welcome" and "Blessings on your union." If anything, she should feel slighted, not overwhelmed, yet her heart had blossomed so, squeezing against her lungs, she could scarcely breathe.

She glanced up at Simon. "Did I say, 'I do'?" She could not recall. How woefully insane.

"You did." His intense gaze sparked in a new and perplexing way. Smiling, he leaned in and brushed a tender kiss across her lips. "Hello, Mrs. Darcy."

Mrs. Simon Darcy.

Wilhelmina Darcy.

Her senses whirled. What had she done? This would never work out. Although maybe it would. Maybe they could indeed be curiosities together. First and foremost, she needed to find the clockwork propulsion engine and ensure its safety and then she needed to somehow thwart or appease Strangelove. She needed to protect her family. And that family now included Simon. Good God.

Willie gathered her wits as Simon led her to a table where Reverend Karma now stood with a pen and certificate. Whilst waiting for them to sign their names, the hippie preacher man described various amusements to be found upon this skytown, suitable romantic entertainment, unless of course they preferred something more decadent. She barely heard a word. She was too busy trying to properly grasp the pen. Frustration bubbled and she almost wished she'd worn the Thera-Steam-Atic Brace.

But then Simon closed in, wrapping his hand around her forearm and lending support as she managed a signature. His palm burned through the thin lace of her sleeve, ignited her blood, and tripled her determination to overcome this physical setback. After tonight she would work most avidly to strengthen her muscles. She would become wholly self-reliant and this troubling sense of inferiority would forever vanish.

Willie watched as, after signing his own name, Simon thanked Reverend Karma, then pocketed the marriage certificate. A keepsake, a token of their personal commitment, but surely not a legal and binding document. All the same, Willie felt different, *transformed*. Her mother had been wrong. Simon had not rejected her because of her race. He had embraced her diversity and all the mystery attached. He had made her battle his own.

How extraordinarily courageous. How remarkably rebellious.

"I now pronounce you man and wife."

Vic and Freak.

A fire stirred within. A flicker of purpose. If every person was afforded one chance to make a significant change for the betterment of this world, perhaps this banned marriage was her unique opportunity. She had never taken a public stand for her race. She had always operated behind false identities and names. Perhaps it was time to fight in the open. Something inside of her snapped and burned and for the first time in her life, Wilhelmina-formerly-Goodenough understood the true meaning of *rebel*.

"I thought we could dine first, something exotic," Simon said as he ushered her toward the petal-strewn exit. "Then perhaps you would fancy dancing to outlawed music, or a bit of radical theater, or a starry ride aboard the Ferris wheel."

"I would fancy a sampling of all of those things." She would enjoy the tolerance and freedom of Skytown as never before and then she would top off her wedding night with "spectacular."

Pausing on the threshold, Simon pulled Willie's tinted spectacles from his inner pocket.

She waved them off, cupped the back of his neck, and pulled him down for a highly inappropriate kiss, given they were not alone. She heard the celebratory tinkling of finger bells and Reverend Karma saying, "Far out." Willie welcomed the passionate heat, a surge of confidence, and the rebellious spark stoking her blood. Heart pounding, she eased away and met Simon's curious gaze. "No more hiding."

He framed her face and scorched her soul with a proud and seductive smile. "Tonight is ours, Mrs. Darcy. Tomorrow, we take on the world."

Willie could not have imagined a more perfect honeymoon. Dinner, perfect. Dancing, perfect. Everything, *perfect*.

Perfect because she'd been with Simon.

This night she found it most difficult to separate the girl who'd fallen in love with the college boy from the woman who'd been seduced by the brilliant engineer. She found it most difficult to focus period. Which was why they had not lingered long at any one festivity.

Had they been anywhere but in a skytown, they would have been a source of fascination or ridicule. First, because she had spent the evening dressed in her princess bridal gown. Second, because anyone who peered close enough and got a glimpse of her eyes knew she was a Freak. But this was Skytown. Her bridal gown was not nearly as fascinating as the couple who'd donned the full medieval regalia of a knight and his winged fairy enchantress. Nor the geared and hissing, iron and bronzed, half-man, half-mechanical cigar-puffing robber baron from America who had a predilection for ballerinas.

As for being a Freak, Willie was one of a few like souls and several pretenders. Aye, there were those who reveled in being mistaken for a supernatural freak of cross-dimensions. They dressed in the colorful and bizarre fashion known as ModVic. They preened and paraded about as if being a Freak was akin to being a celebrated artist, someone who was revered or admired for being extraordinarily special.

Their hero worship would be flattering if it weren't so naive. Obviously they did not understand the true plight of Freaks. However, Willie did not dwell on the notion overly long as she might have done another time.

Everything Willie saw, heard, or experienced this night was overshadowed by the intense passion burning between her and her new husband. There was a possessive and protective quality about Simon that she had not noticed before. The way he placed his hand at the small of her back whilst guiding her though a crowd, the frown he bestowed upon any man who stared too long at her cleavage, his pithy reply to a Vic who'd made an off-color remark about her supernatural *skills*. Had the man not been so roaring drunk and ready to pitch over, she was quite certain Simon would have called him out. She could well imagine growing irritated with Simon's sudden commitment to sheltering her from ridicule or harm. But tonight, she was merely charmed and soundly seduced off her time-tracing feet.

Moments ago Simon had obliterated the last of her composure by besting a game of chance and winning her a prize just as he had on one magical night of their youthful courtship. Only this time, instead of a china doll, he'd chosen a mechanical bird. A clockwork canary. She'd pocketed the tiny toy, marveling at how something so chintzy could mean so much.

"I suggest we make haste to our lodgings," Willie said as Simon purchased tickets for a starry carnival ride.

"Are you ill? Faint? Chilled?" He stuffed the tickets in

his jacket with a curse, then readjusted the white fur coat that had come with her ensemble. "But of course you're exhausted. It has been a long and eventful day and no doubt your shoulder is paining you. Dammit, Willie, why didn't you speak up earlier?"

"I am neither ill nor faint, but I do have a tremendous ache and unless you wish me to tear off your clothes right here on this deck, in front of these multitudes of visitors—"

Simon scooped her off her feet, causing her to gasp whilst others around them whistled and applauded as he whisked her across one deck, a gangway, and three-quarters of another crowded deck before entering a magnificent canvas and steel structure marked as SULTAN'S SUITES. The colorful fabrics hanging from the walls and draped from the ceiling stole away her breath, as did the shockingly explicit paintings. Her heart pounded as Simon carried her one deck below and down a vibrant purple hallway, bypassing several rooms until he came to a gilded door at the end of the corridor.

Somehow he finessed the lock without bungling his hold on her, although once he'd pushed into the room and kicked shut the door, he set Willie swiftly to her feet. "You were saying?"

His intense gaze fueled her already raging desire, as did the sensual surroundings. The flickering golden lanterns, the draped bold fabrics, the rose petals strewn over the thick Persian rug. The intoxicating scent of musk and jasmine filled the small room, as did a large round bed piled high with satin pillows. That bed was just behind Simon and that bed was where she wanted them both to be.

Lustful cravings eviscerated any semblance of decorum. Willie shrugged off her coat and made quick work of Simon's jacket. Her left arm did most of the work, but her injured arm managed keenly enough to aid her in her frenzied mission to rid her husband of his damnable clothes. Perhaps it was the adrenaline. Or perhaps he was helping her along. Oh, aye, he was most anxious to indulge her wishes. They kissed whilst attacking his buttons and snaps, a frenzied affair that only heightened her excitement as one by one his fashionable garments fell to the floor.

Breaking away, Simon stood before her wearing nothing but a wicked grin. "You got me naked," he said. "Now what?"

Emboldened, Willie raised a cocky brow. "I could allow you to undress me. Or," she said, planting a hand on his muscled chest and pushing him back until he fell upon the pillow-laden bed. "I could make you watch."

The heat in his gaze nearly set her gown afire, burning the silk and lace into oblivion.

Willie relished the heady feeling of power as she ever so slowly loosened the front lacing of her corseted bodice. She reveled in Simon's frustrated groan as her fingers glided over the satin ribbons, as the décolletage slipped lower, revealing more of her breasts. When he rose up and reached out, she knocked away his hands. "No touching."

His raunchy muttered curse worked like an aphrodisiac. Never had she been so wanton, so scandalous. She had feared she would feel chained by marriage when somehow it had set her free.

"You're killing me, wife."

Why did that endearment drive her so deliciously mad? Ready to reach the tipping point herself, Willie fingered the customized release clasp, a trick sewn into the bodice by the wardrobe mistress at the Fantasy Farm. In a heartbeat, the corset loosened completely and with a mere roll of her shoulders the wedding gown slid from her body and pooled around her feet. Now she too was naked—all but her silky unmentionables and her embroidered pointy-toed mules.

"There is something that I have been longing to try," she said as she kicked off the shoes.

"Far be it from me to stop you." Simon watched intently as she shimmied out of the last wisp of silk.

Admiring his impeccable body, she climbed onto the bed, knocking aside pillows as she kissed a hot trail down his chest, his stomach. . . . "It requires you to relinquish control."

He managed a not-so-pithy grunt, which only spurred her on.

She smoothed her hands over his chiseled abdomen. All she wanted was a taste, a sampling. Living under the guise of a man, she had heard things not meant for a woman's ears. Things men enjoyed. *Sexually.*

Heart pounding, Willie kissed the tip of Simon's erection, then flicked her tongue over the ridge and, in a supreme leap of curiosity, took him into her mouth. A sensual thrill surged through her blood, but he hissed and flinched, reaching down and easing her away. "Did I do something wrong?" she asked.

"You did everything right. Therein lies the problem, sweetheart. I would not last beyond a minute if you continued to pleasure me thusly. My restraint is unusually taxed this night."

He appeared this side of miserable and her confidence soared at the knowledge she could so easily drive him to the brink. Quirking a teasing smile, Willie indulged in another fantasy. "I have faith that you will allow a bride her pleasure."

She straddled his impressive arousal, moaning with sinful bliss as she slid over him, as he filled her deeply, completely. Gripping his shoulder, she closed her eyes and rocked her hips. The motion. The friction. The erotic thrill of being in control. He gripped her waist, aiding her in her quest, urging her to soar. Apparently her restraint was as taxed as her husband's, for she felt her body tensing, quivering. Her senses spiraled higher and higher and then . . . she soared. "Sweet heaven," she whispered whilst collapsing upon his chest.

"Indeed," he said, stroking his hands over her bare back.

She smiled against his neck. "That was . . ."

"Spectacular." Simon framed her face and kissed her deeply, finessing her body beneath his own. He nipped her lower lip, kissed her cheek, her chin, her neck. . . . His hands caressed and teased as did the gleam in his eye. "I wonder," he said, whilst taking delicious control, "if I can invent something *beyond* spectacular?"

She gasped as he touched her most intimately, most scandalously. Was such naughty delight a boon to marriage? Aching to explore ecstasy beyond her known realms, Willie trusted in the moment and the man and opened to wondrous possibilities.

CHAPTER 17

The land of the kangaroo. Or as the Mods called it: Oz.

Why anyone would choose to hide in this mosquito-infested, abysmally hot and humid, godforsaken land was beyond Bingham. Along with his sparse yet top-notch crew, he had navigated the skies over Europe, the Mediterranean Sea, Arabia, and the seemingly never-ending Indian Ocean. Due to volatile weather and mechanical malfunctions, the journey had taken two days more than Bingham had anticipated. Worse, a horrendous storm had blown them off course, pushing them south of their appointed mark and assaulting *Mars-a-Tron* so viciously that Captain Northwood had been forced to ground the enhanced zeppelin in order to facilitate vital repairs. Another delay, although as Northwood had pointed out, it could have been worse. At least Perth, a coastal city in Western Australia, had resources.

"How long?" Bingham had asked.

Northwood stood hat in hand, shoulders bolstered, as if bracing for an assault of the personal nature. "Five to six days. Maybe longer."

"Unacceptable."

"Unavoidable."

"Money is no object."

"Naturally," Northwood said. "Locating and obtaining

all of the required components is the issue. Then as you heard from our chief engineer, the repairs are of a laborious nature."

Bingham held his temper. The damages were not Northwood's or Judd's fault and Bingham had no desire to cross the Great Victoria Desert in an unreliable airship. As abominable as a summer down under was here on the coast, the conditions would be far worse in the isolated dunes and plains of the expansive desert named after Queen Victoria herself. How ironic if Her Majesty the Queen proved the death of Viscount Bingham when he conspired to be the death of *her*. The notion of his demise did not amuse.

Instead of risking his neck, Bingham sanctioned the repairs on *Mars-a-Tron*. Meanwhile he arranged ground transport across the city to a worldwide establishment known as the Adventurer's Club. Bingham had frequented the London branch upon occasion and had deemed it worthwhile to purchase an annual membership. Familiar with the sort who haunted the enterprising social club, he knew this would be the place to acquire suitable transport and guidance over the Great Victoria Desert, into South Australia, and beyond to the southwestern corner of Queensland—where Professor Merriweather had been spotted by his Mod Tracker, Crag.

Upon entering the rustic building, Bingham noted the swashbuckling decor. Paintings and photographs of heroic feats and remote terrains. Brilliant examples of taxidermy as practiced on varied exotic creatures. Assorted displays of archaic and progressive instruments pertaining to navigation and weaponry. This society championed the perseverance and ingenuity of fearless adventurers. Scouts, pilots, navigators, scientists—those willing to brave uncharted or dangerous territories in the name of exploration and discovery. It also attracted adventurers with less noble intent. Soldiers of fortune. Bingham's preferred recruit.

A uniformed steward approached, his expression wary. "Be of service, mate?"

Bingham flashed his membership card. "I require access

to your Reception Room, a cool drink, and swift and reliable transport to Queensland."

"An expedition?"

"Private mission. No questions asked," he added with a meaningful look.

"Sounds like a job for the Rocketeer."

The name meant nothing to Bingham. "Is he the best you've got?"

"He's the best there is." The steward jerked his thumb toward a room to the right. "Teletype, telephone, telegraph, and, as with all of our worldwide branches, worldwide reception. I'll see to your other two requests, Lord Bingham. Welcome to the Adventurer's Club."

The man left and Bingham strode toward the Reception Room, ignoring the curious looks of the few members seated at an ornate bar and swilling beer. He was not here to socialize or to exchange tall tales. He was here on business and with luck would soon be on his way.

His vision acclimating to the shaded and dark-paneled ambience, Bingham welcomed the cooler air as afforded by numerous brass and mahogany ceiling fans. He'd dressed down by his standards and yet the oppressive humidity had caused his shirt to stick and his brow to perspire. The damnable insects worsened his discomfort and mood, as did the disruption of his telecommunications device. He was unaccustomed to being uninformed. After clearing the worst of the bad weather, he'd noted several incoming messages on his telecommunicator. Too many to retrieve in their entirety.

Alone in the small Reception Room, Bingham utilized a custom-made wire enabling him to connect his portable device to the club's teleprinter, an ingenious machine developed via modern technology. According to his sources, this form of communications had originally been developed in the early 1900s. A few short decades from now. Bingham fairly salivated imagining the communication wonders he would discover once he traveled forward to the 1960s. Satellites, computers, televisions. He'd read about them in the

Book of Mods. Heard them gossiped about within the scientific realm as well as the black market, where old stories regarding the future ran rampant via corrupt Peace Rebels. Gossip and conjecture be damned. Bingham would acquire the knowledge enabling him to manufacture those marvels. He would be ahead of his time. A miracle man. A technological kingpin.

Heady with thoughts of colossal wealth and power, Bingham stared at the stream of coded messages now transferring onto paper and mentally translated the numbers to letters.

His mother wondering how he fared.

P. B. Waddington reporting an increase of Triple R entrants. Two new inventions submitted to the committee. An electric battery from biblical times and a functioning steam engine from the first century.

Not caring a whit about either discovery, Bingham moved on.

A trusted snitch claiming Amelia Darcy had been spotted in London.

Bingham frowned at that one. Dunkirk had declared Miss Darcy dead. If Dunkirk lied about that, had he lied about Amelia's unearthed treasure? Had the Scottish Shark of the Skies double-crossed Bingham, instead striking a deal with Amelia Darcy and the Sky Cowboy? His temper surged.

But wait.

Waddington had said nothing of a time-traveling device being submitted to the committee. Perhaps da Vinci's ornithopter had indeed been Amelia's booty. Knowing her obsession with flying, he could well imagine an obsession with flying machines. Bingham would not overthink this. However, he would be questioning that lying bastard Captain Colin Dunkirk.

Hearing booted heels striding in his direction, Bingham quickly decoded the last message. At first he smiled. One of his sources with International ALE had news of Jules Darcy. Finally. A lead on the elusive science fiction writer. But then he swore.

J. Darcy over Gulf of Carpentaria.

An inlet of the Arafura Sea. The northern coast of Australia. Damnation! Was Darcy en route to Professor Merriweather? How did he learn of the Peace Rebel's whereabouts? Bingham had the wealth and resources to track the brilliant recluse. Darcy did not. Regardless, the man could well foil Bingham's plans. Darcy was exactly where he would have been if that damned storm hadn't blown *Mars-a-Tron* so wretchedly off track!

"Your grog, *Lord* Bingham. No chance of gettin' spiffed on this spiked Lolly Water, but it's a cool one. As requested."

The man's sarcasm grated, but Bingham held his tongue. His back to the cretin with a thick Aussie accent and the scent of grease and tobacco upon his person, Bingham disconnected and pocketed his telecommunicator, tore the coded page from the teleprinter, and stuffed that as well. Shoulders squared, expression calm, Bingham turned and faced a giant of a man resembling a down-under cowboy. "You don't look like a server," he said. More like an outlaw. A heavily armed outlaw wearing a sweat-stained slouch hat and smoking a hand-rolled cigarette that dangled from his lower lip.

"Just deliverin' the goods and offerin' my services," he said as smoke curled into the air and into Bingham's eyes. "That's if the price is right."

"I require safe and speedy passage to the southwestern corner of Queensland."

"Can you be more specific?"

"I can but I won't. Not as of yet. Are you my man?"

"Let me put it this way, mate. You wouldn't want to make this trek with any scout *but* me."

"You're merely a scout?"

"I'm not merely anything. They call me the Rocketeer."

Bingham looked down his nose at the man. "What should *I* call you?"

The Aussie's mouth twitched. "Name's Austin Steele. I answer to Austin or Steele or Rock." He tugged at the brim of his hat by way of a handshake. "Own and pilot my own transport. The *Iron Tarantula*."

"A rocket-fueled airship?"

"A monster. No one screws with the *Tarantula*." He squashed his cigarette beneath his mud-caked bootheel. "Or me. You're lookin' to cover wild territory, Bingham. The harsh elements, ballsy bushrangers, a few hostile aboriginals, not to mention the starving dingoes and poisonous reptiles." He scribbled on a piece of paper. "This is my price. Half now. Half on arrival."

A hefty price that reeked of arrogance and instilled confidence. Bingham withdrew his wallet from his inner pocket, obsessing on the fact that he hadn't heard from Crag in days. Was Merriweather still on the fringes of the rain forest? Or had he been spooked and moved on? Did Crag have the professor in his sights or had the brilliant Mod, once again, fallen off the proverbial map? Had Crag sighted Jules Darcy? Crazed now, Bingham thumbed through several banknotes with multiple zeros. "I answer to 'Lord Bingham' or 'sir' or 'Kingpin of the Universe.'" He slapped a juicy stack of bills into the reprobate's beefy hand. "You're hired."

CHAPTER 18

"Rise and shine, lover boy."

Simon's eyes flew open at the sound of a gruff baritone voice. "What the hell, Phin?" Shrugging off a sleepy haze, Simon dragged his hair off his face and focused on Phineas Bourdain, pilot and machinist extraordinaire. "How did you get in here?"

The cocky airman quirked a teasing brow. "Your pretty lady friend let me in on her way out."

Head clearing, Simon pushed up into a sitting position. "That was no lady—not in the sense you're suggesting. That was my wife."

"The devil you say."

"Where was she going?"

"Didn't ask. But, ah . . ." He leaned over Simon and plucked a folded paper from Willie's empty pillow. "A clue perhaps."

Simon snatched the note from the man's hand and squinted to decipher the wretched scrawl, obviously penned with her bad hand.

Returning bridal gown to Fantasy Farm. Back soon with breakfast.

Though enormously pleased that his wife was indeed returning and not bolting—he'd fully braced himself for marriage remorse—Simon still felt a pang of disappointment. Her note lacked the fiery passion of the night before. No endearments. No poetic pledge. Not that there'd been any mention of or reference to love whilst they'd singed the satin linens with their honeymoon sex-capades. Still, this morning, he felt different. At the very least he'd expected to be awakened by Willie's sweet kisses, not Phin's cocky mug.

"Trouble in paradise?"

"What?" Simon frowned at his brother's closest friend. "No." He rolled out of bed and stabbed his legs into a pair of trousers. "Thought we agreed to rendezvous at eight."

"We did. It's half past."

"What?" Reeling, Simon checked his pocket watch. "Damnation." Granted, he'd slept very little. Willie had been most keen on exploring the sensual realm and Simon had been more than thrilled to comply. And yes, they'd indulged in champagne. Two bottles, in fact, but damn. Never had he felt so foggy. Was there such a thing as a sexual hangover?

"Time factor aside," Phin said. "Bring me up to speed, man. You're bloody truly matched for life?"

"Yes."

"Were you tricked? Coerced? Blackmailed?"

"No."

"Drunk?"

"Not until after vows had been exchanged."

"You're a hound, Simon. A rake."

"Not anymore."

"Are you saying you're in love?"

Was he? He paused in his frantic dressing and absorbed. He was deeply affected. Entranced and seduced. Love surely circled in his emotional realm, but so did mistrust. "I'm obliged."

Phin crossed his arms and raised a dark brow.

"As I stated in our communication, I entered the Triple R Tourney. In my quest, I encountered a dangerous man. There was an incident. Wilhelmina saved my life."

"So you forfeited your freedom in exchange?"

"It's complicated." Simon poured cool water into a basin

and splashed his face. "Did the upgrades go smoothly on the *Flying Cloud*?"

"She won't plummet from the sky midjourney, but she won't break any speed records either. Only so much I could do with that boat given your restricted budget. I'm a machinist, not a miracle worker."

Simon had contacted Phin four days prior, enlisting his mechanical and piloting skills. From this point on in his efforts to retrieve the clockwork propulsion engine, Simon preferred to dodge any complications or dicey encounters via public transportation. Utilizing private transport would also afford Willie a chance to adjust to living as a woman and enable Simon to distance her from harm. He couldn't banish the image of her being o'blasterated in the catacombs. Even now he worried about her being accosted on her trek from the Fantasy Farm back to this suite. Another glance at his watch. Too soon to be alarmed. Even so . . .

"I appreciate your efforts, Phin, and your willingness to pilot the *Cloud*," Simon said as he shoved the last of his belongings into his valise. "Flying is not my forte and in this instance I prefer to focus my attention elsewhere."

"I can imagine. She's quite lovely."

Simon glanced over his shoulder. Just as he thought, Phin was grinning. Phin, who was every bit the rake Simon used to be. The compliment was simply that. No need to take offense. Still, Simon bristled from a bite of the green-eyed monster. "In saving my life, Willie was badly injured. Her right arm . . . there was severe nerve and muscle damage. Until it heals, *if* it heals, I feel she is at a disadvantage. Better for me to stick close."

"Feeling protective. I understand that: And guilty. I understand that too," Phin said. "What I don't fathom is marrying a woman you just met. A woman you know nothing about. And then dragging her along on an expedition you now deem dangerous. Why put her in harm's way? Let's drop her in London at your town house. Fletcher will look after her. Or at Ashford, under the watchful eye of your mother and sister."

"First of all," Simon said as he shrugged into his frock coat, "we are not newly acquainted. We have a history. Second, she possesses the . . . *expertise* to acquire the information needed to track the historical invention that slipped my possession."

"The plot thickens."

"Fair warning, Phin. The man who absconded with the coveted device is the man who shot Willie. When we cross paths again—"

"I might find myself in the line of fire?"

"I might well kill him."

"What? With your drafting compass? Your bare hands?" Phin grunted, then reached under his coat. "Ever shot a gun?"

"Only at a carnival," Simon said, eyeing the augmented pistol in Phin's hand. "Nick the cast-iron bird and win a trinket for your lady."

"Did you?"

"What?"

"Win a trinket for your lady?"

"Several." Indeed, he had won a china doll for Willie the first week they'd met and then last night, a mechanical bird. She had admired the novelties as if they were diamonds. Simon's heart jerked just thinking about it.

"Must have decent aim, then," Phin said. "That's something. *This*," he said, "is a Disrupter 29. The latest black market version of a McCabe Derringer as enhanced by me. Listen and learn, brainiac."

Simon focused as Phin pointed out the working parts of the ominous-looking pistol. Unlike Phin and Jules, Simon had not been in the military. Nor had he been drawn to hunting. Beastly business, that. He was an academic. A man of math and science, not war. Regardless, when he thought about the blood that had poured out of Willie's wounds, murder raged in his soul.

"Got it?" Phin asked.

"It's not rocket science," Simon said as he engaged the safety mechanism and slid the weapon into his pocket. "Not leaving you defenseless, am I?"

Phin opened his coat and flashed a shoulder harness and a much bigger gun. "I have more of an arsenal on board the *Flying Cloud*. You told me to come armed. I did."

Just then the door to the colorful suite opened and Willie walked in and stole away Simon's breath. For some reason, he'd expected her to revert to her baggy trousers, but she had purchased a fetching traveling ensemble. An ebony long-sleeved bodice cinched with a leather under-bust corset. A full skirt with tassels rimming its hem stopped just shy of her black ankle boots. Simple yet feminine and accentuated by a whimsical chain looped twice around her waist. It reminded him of a charm bracelet with its multitude of dangling fobs. The only evidence of the former Clockwork Canary was the time cuff upon her wrist and the chain of her pocket watch dangling from a skirt pocket. Her vibrant red hair was tucked behind her ears, exposing her lovely face and slender neck. Instead of a floppy cap, she wore a flattop derby accented with a quirky combination of clockwork, lace, and feathers, and, by jiminy, Simon's mechanical bird. Charming.

Noting Simon's appreciative gaze, she flushed and focused on Phin. "I apologize for rushing away without a proper introduction, Mr. Bourdain. Last night Simon had mentioned we were to meet you promptly at eight and I fear we overslept. Most unsettling, as I am always cognizant of the time. At any rate I had to return a dress and . . . and now I'm rambling, delaying our departure even more. Gads." She set aside a small basket and offered her left hand in greeting. "Willie G. Or rather Wilhelmina Goodenough."

"Darcy," Simon corrected, moving to her side just as Phin pressed a kiss to the back of her hand. He could tell by Willie's expression that the intimacy had caught her off guard. Masquerading as a man, she'd been accustomed to shaking hands. Simon put his arm around her waist and gave a supportive squeeze.

"Willie G.," Phin said, taking a step back and regarding her with interest. "The Clockwork Canary?"

Her shoulders tensed. "Does that present a problem?"

Phin cut Simon a glance. "Curiouser and curiouser."

"She's chronicling the expedition for a serial in the *London Informer*."

"Ah." The aviator angled his head. "Rumor portrayed the Clockwork Canary as a cocky young lad."

"A necessary ruse," Willie said. "At the time."

Phin said nothing, but Simon could hear the man's wheels turning. "We should get going," Simon said, then glanced into the basket Willie had set aside. "Are those fresh croissants?"

"And Danish. I thought warm pastries might make up for our tardiness." She focused on Phin. "Are you fond of pastries, Mr. Bourdain?"

"Indeed, Mrs. Darcy. I can provide coffee or tea once we're aboard the *Flying Cloud*."

Anxious to break the tension and advance their cause, Simon helped Willie into her old oversized coat, then gathered their bags.

"Have you no reservations about flying with my kind, Mr. Bourdain?" she asked whilst looping scarves around her neck.

"Why would I be spooked by a journalist?"

"Simon didn't tell you."

"Tell me what?"

Oh, hell, Simon thought. Not knowing Phin's views regarding Freaks, he'd decided to allow the man time to warm to Willie before breaking the news. He watched as she took off her tinted spectacles and established unflinching eye contact with Phin.

To his credit, the man didn't react. He simply nabbed the basket of fragrant pastries and held open the door, initiating their exit.

Willie crossed the threshold. Simon followed and Phin spoke at a volume for Simon's ears only. "Curiouser and curiouser."

Willie leaned into Simon as they crossed the deck of the *Flying Flower*. "He does not approve. Of me. *Us.* I warned you, Simon. And Mr. Bourdain is your friend."

"Technically he's my friend by way of Jules. Those two share a long and complicated past. And it's not that he disapproves. He's intrigued. Skeptical, maybe. Doubting my sanity, definitely. Who marries on a whim?"

"Us apparently."

"Twelve years in the making is not a whim. Phin doesn't know our history. You look beautiful, by the way."

She harrumphed. It was rude. But she was in no mood to be seduced. She hated that she'd overslept, that she'd lost track of time in a haze of blissful exhaustion. She hated that she felt so fiercely out of sync. Still connected to her old ways, whilst inspired to strike out in a bold new way. As a woman. As a Freak. As the wife of a Vic. One thing was clear. She could not dredge up an iota of motivation to bind her breasts or to hide her shape. Nor did she wish to alter her complexion or to remind herself incessantly to slouch and to speak in a lowered, gruff pitch. She'd woken up resenting the fact that she'd lived a lie for so long. That she'd suppressed her femininity, that she'd denied her race. She resented having to pretend she was a male Vic simply to work in a profession she excelled at. And she regretted her penchant to operate on the fringes, hiding behind costumes and pen names rather than fighting out in the open for her cause. She preached equality, yet she did not present herself as an equal.

A troubling realization.

Indeed, the dawn had introduced a maelstrom of conflict. It was as if thwarting the law and marrying Simon had jarred every rebellious bone in her body. And yet she felt . . . unfocused. Restless. She'd known how to contribute to the cause whilst incognito, but could she truly make a positive difference regarding intolerance and equality operating as a female Freak? Aye, she'd been accepted on Skytown, but the real world would judge her most harshly, limiting her freedom and rights. Making it harder to achieve her goals. This morning, in the light of day, with reality looming, she questioned her brave new agenda. At the same time she would not, *could* not, revert to living a lie.

"At the risk of appearing vapid," Simon said as they crossed the gangway to the *Love Bug*, "what happened between last night and this morning? Why are you angry with me?"

She stopped cold. "I'm not angry with you. I'm angry with the world."

"Then let's change the world."

"You say that as if we can do so with the snap of our fingers."

"Change is rarely easy. Historically you know this to be true." Simon moved in and grasped her hands. "I don't believe Phin rattled you so. You're stronger than that. What troubles you truly?"

She glanced around Skytown, looking everywhere but at Simon. What troubled her? How about everything? So much on her mind. Too much to share. She'd been a lone wolf for so long. Unburdening herself, speaking her opinions and thoughts, her hopes and fears, did not come easily. Flustered, she homed in on one concern. *One* she could manage. "Do you remember the moment I time-traced Filmore?"

"The Houdinian?" He nodded, frowned. "Like it was yesterday."

"I faltered in his memories. I stayed too long. Interfered. I've never done that before. There was a moment when I felt . . . lost. As if I'd never find my way out."

"Go on."

"It was terrifying. Exhausting. My father . . . I need to trace his memories in order to search for clues regarding the Houdinians and any knowledge of their process regarding the protection of the clockwork propulsion engine, but Daddy is not mentally stable. What if . . . what if I get lost and can't come back?"

"Then don't go. Ask him your questions straight out."

"I can try that, but I'm afraid he'll be evasive. He's loyal to my mother and if she swore him to certain secrets . . . Also some details might be lost to his conscious mind yet available via ingrained memories. I need to know, Simon. Not just for you and the salvation of your family. I need to know for *me*. My mother ... what was her true mission? Where did her allegiance lie? Did she truly love my father or was their marriage part of a necessary ruse? Everything she ever told us ... it feels like a lie. I feel ... misguided. Like I'm floundering. I don't want to flounder. I need to know where I came from, what I'm meant for. I need to know who I am."

"You're Wilhelmina Darcy. The Clockwork Canary. My wife."

"I need more. I'm sorry if that sounds cruel but—"

"I understand." Simon dropped their bags and wrapped her in a strong embrace. "You want to make your mark on the world," he said close to her ear. "You want to make a notable difference. I have wanted the same thing all my life. Perhaps if we work together."

He sounded so strong, so sure of their alliance, and yet, as much as she wanted to spend the rest of her days with this man, Willie harbored no illusions. The queen and her sovereign would declare their marriage illegal. Null and void. As a couple of mixed dimensions they would be shunned, perhaps mocked. Simon's reputation would suffer. Her own career might well be doomed.

And then there was Strangelove.

His telecommunicator burned a hole in her pocket as well as her conscience. The man had hired her to betray Simon. She'd taken his money. She'd buckled under his threats. She'd reconnected with Simon in order to cheat him of a technological invention of historical significance. Nothing personal. But now it was. On many and monumental levels.

"I have to make this right," she blurted.

"Make what right?" Simon asked. "Us?"

"Everything." Willie stepped back and bolstered her spine. Fretting would get her nowhere. Time-tracing would give them direction.

A shrill whistle seized their attention. Phineas Bourdain standing a few feet away, the pastry basket looped over his arm and a small clipper ship—the *Flying Cloud*, she assumed— hovering just beyond his shoulder.

"Anytime, lovebirds," he called.

"You'll get used to him," Simon said to Willie whilst retrieving their bags.

Willie just smiled. Mr. Bourdain was the least of her problems. "When I trace my father's memories," she said as they made haste, "I'll need your help."

"Anything."

Heart racing, she checked the hour on her time cuff, then her pocket watch. Synchronized to the second. Swallowing hard, she put her life in Simon's hands by slipping her pocket watch into his coat. "I'll need you to be my lifeline."

CHAPTER 19

Bundled up against the freezing temperature and strong winds, goggles firmly in place, Simon stood on the port side of the *Flying Cloud*, gripping the gunwale and staring down at the passing landscape.

Phin was a spectacular pilot and the few upgrades he'd managed on this boat had made a world of difference. Their flight out of Scotland and over northern England had, thus far, been as smooth as glass. Not once had they taken a sudden and heart-stopping dip. Eleven days ago, Simon had wrestled with a malfunctioning turbine and the steering mechanism had jammed. Piloting his father's creation had been a bit of a harrowing experience. More than once he'd contemplated his own demise. Is that how Willie had felt when she'd gotten distracted in Filmore's memories? A wisp or tremor of fear? The notion that she might not pull through the experience unscathed? That she was quite possibly flirting with death?

Could time-tracing kill her? Simon had mulled over the possibility as he'd helped Willie settle into a small but comfortable cabin. Whilst Phin had set a course for Canterbury, Willie had talked Simon through the upcoming time-trace with her father.

"Typically the transmitter is unaware that I am tracing," she'd said. "But I think it would be best to be honest with my father. I want to stay longer, to probe deeper. If he knows what I'm doing, and if I'm in a safe and sequestered environment, it won't matter that I appear to be daydreaming and unresponsive."

"What's the longest you've been in?" Simon asked.

"Up until Filmore, five to ten seconds. The first time with Filmore—thirty seconds. That was shocking, but not so unsettling as the second time I went in. By the time I broke free of the trance . . . I'd been gone two minutes." She blew out a tense breath. "Mind you, two minutes in reality rivals two hours to two days in someone's memories."

"Fascinating," Simon said, "and utterly fantastic. It's hard to imagine."

"It can be wondrous but also disturbing. Some of the people I've interviewed . . . well, they were not all the most reputable of citizens. Where's the sensation in that?" She laughed, though the sound was rusty and forced. "Point being, in all those instances, and there have been many, I have never felt panicked or emotionally engaged. That's where things went wrong. Not that I was gone for so long, but that I lost control. I reacted emotionally to something I saw. I interacted. As long as I stay focused and in the shadows, all should be well."

In that moment, Simon questioned the woman's judgment, if not sanity. "Willie," he'd said calmly and gently, "you're going to trace your father's memories. A man you adore. A man who is mentally unstable. You're going to summon memories of your mother and of her past as a Peace Rebel. A woman who misled you. Do you honestly think you can remain emotionally detached?"

"Aye."

He shoved a hand through his hair, frowned. He didn't buy it.

"I'm a professional, Simon. A journalist. A Time Tracer. Objective. Resourceful."

"This is different."

"Do you want to find the clockwork propulsion engine? Do you want to submit it to the Jubilee Science Committee? Do you want to make your mark on this world, Simon?"

"More than anything." *But not at the cost of losing you.* He wasn't sure why he hadn't said those words aloud. He felt them, but damnation, they stuck in his throat. Maybe because they made him feel vulnerable. Willie had given herself to him in name and in bed, but in the light of day, she maintained an emotional distance that set his nerves on edge. He understood her discontent with the world. At least he thought he did. And he sympathized with her concerns regarding her mother. What vexed him was the sense that she was keeping secrets. What did he have to do to earn this woman's trust? He could only shake his head in wonder, for surely she was as complex and mystifying as the Egyptian pyramids.

Frustrated, Simon pushed on. "So how will it work? Me being your lifeline?

"We'll agree upon an increment of time. If I don't come out on my own before then, you will pull me out."

"How?"

"Physical contact. Tug my hand, grip my shoulders. Something firm. And call me home. To you."

His heart pounded with the unexpected sentiment. The responsibility. "Have you tried this before?"

"No."

"How do you know it will work?"

"A calculated guess."

"Not good enough." Yes, Simon projected and took chances whilst drafting many a project. His mobile staircase, for instance. Others had patented a design to transport pedestrians up and down several stories via mechanically moving steps, but no one had engineered a working model. Simon had been distracted by Project Monorail, but lately he'd been tinkering with his designs for a mobile staircase, a device composed of motorized chain-linked steps, and projected his new version would absolutely work.

In theory.

Theory and execution were two different animals.

"I'd feel better if we took a test run," he said. "Experiment on someone of sound mind. What about Phin?"

She snorted. "As if he'd agree."

"He'll agree."

She didn't look convinced, but she didn't say no. Instead

she asked his assistance with the Thera-Steam-Atic Brace. "It's only been a day and I already feel as though I am slacking on my therapy," she said whilst unlacing her under-bust corset.

Simon tried blocking images of her striptease the night before, but that didn't work. Cursing an untimely erection, he helped her into the brace and the attached customized corset. "How do you plan to exercise your arm?"

"I thought I would practice some yo-yo tricks and then concentrate on penning some notes of our expedition thus far. Whilst details are fresh in my mind."

The adventures most keen in Simon's mind were of the intimate nature. He caught her gaze, noted the flush of her cheeks.

"Don't worry. I'll be discreet."

"So in other words you'll leave out the best parts," he teased, although his humor was somewhat taxed. As far as he was concerned, they had shared several moments of intimacy that extended beyond the bedroom. Their first encounter on the streets of Notting Hill, the exchanged looks within the private compartment of the Flying Scotsman. "What about the risqué romance element?"

"Pardon?"

"The *Informer* promised its readers tales of risqué romance, high drama, and nail-biting intrigue."

Gaze averted, she rooted the yo-yo and journal from her valise. "Ah, well, you'd be surprised at how I can spin a tale."

"That's what I'm afraid of."

She shot him a sharp look, her color high. "I've apologized regarding that article on your father and I explained—"

"I'm speaking in general." Although, damn, that insulting death announcement still rankled. Rather than expanding on a personal level, he tried an objective approach. "You've made a career out of writing titillating, sometimes scandalous pieces. I don't fancy seeing a cheapened, sensationalized account of our unexpected and, may I say, emotionally charged reunion in a national tabloid."

"Are you mocking my body of work? Judging my morals? Questioning my integrity?"

"No. A little. Maybe. *Christ.* How did we get to this?"

"It's been festering in the back of your mind," she snapped. "Obviously."

Maybe she was right. The explosion that had ripped Simon's father from his life had happened almost three weeks ago and yet he still carried that damnable article on his person. Folded and tucked into his inner coat pocket, it was a grim reminder of the part he'd played in his father's death, and because the Canary's name was attached to the piece, he couldn't disentangle her from his feelings of guilt and grief. "I should get some fresh air."

"Good idea."

She was furious with him, but in that moment he hadn't cared. He'd left her to her therapy, to her creative spinning of their alliance. He'd sought calm on the main deck. Twenty minutes later, he still struggled.

Simon turned away from the wintry landscape and focused on the *Flying Cloud.* A creation of his father's. Far from perfect, but brimming with passion. He closed his eyes, remembering how hard Papa had worked, utilizing used parts and his imagination to give this abandoned clipper ship wings. Part of him wished Willie *could* time-trace his memories; then she'd see for herself what a great man Reginald Darcy had been. Then again, she'd also see how Simon had been too busy with his own projects to stay on at Ashford and offer his father a hand. Simon had always thought the design of the *Flying Cloud* faulty. He could have helped, had it not been for his selfish ambition. He'd had bigger fish to fry in London.

Shame washed over him now. Willie had been right back at St. Giles' Cathedral when she'd charged him self-involved. It would seem they both had their faults. Breathing deep and finding his air legs, Simon made his way across the deck to the altered cockpit.

"Done brooding?" Phin asked.

Simon didn't bother arguing the obvious. "You banished the wooden walls in favor of a thermoplastic shield."

"Better visibility," Phin said, his hands at ease on the controls, the wheel.

"Agreed." Looking skyward Simon added, "And the whirling arms are a brilliant addition."

"I thought so. Swiped the blades from a junked monoplane. The rotation maximizes lift and thrust."

"Amelia will be impressed."

Phin shot him a concerned look before focusing back on the skies. "How is your sister?"

"Mourning my father."

"I regret missing the funeral. If I could have—"

"We know." Simon rolled back his shoulders and eyed the heavens. "Dismal turnout, not counting the curious, morbid few who showed up simply because of Papa's ties to the Time Voyager."

"As brought to light by the Clockwork Canary. Surprised you were able to get past that," Phin said.

"I wasn't. A recent realization and most vexing."

"I take it that's why you're up here with me and she's down there alone?"

"I need to ask you a favor," Simon said by way of an answer. "You know Willie's a Freak."

"The swirling rainbow eyes? Dead giveaway, my friend."

"She's a Time Tracer," he said, anxious to make her normal by speaking frankly and casually.

"Meaning?"

"If she connects with a person, physically, and focuses, mentally, she can experience a portion of the transmitter's past via their memories."

"Fascinating, I guess. What does that have to do with me?"

"She needs to probe her father's memories for some vital information, but his mind is unstable and I might need to pull her out."

"Sounds tricky."

"Exactly. Which is why I'd prefer to test this 'lifeline' plan of hers on a transmitter of stable mind."

Phin raised a eyebrow. "You're asking me to allow your woman to tread through my mind?"

"Your memories."

"Bugger off."

"Don't make me resort to threats, Phin."

It was almost imperceptible, but not quite. Phin's right eye ticked. "You wouldn't."

"I would." As close as Phin and Jules were, there was something Simon knew about Phin that Jules didn't. Even though he'd been several years older, Phin had been smitten with their sister and had stolen a kiss. An inappropriate advance that Amelia had rebuffed, Simon had witnessed, and Jules knew nothing about. He held Phin's gaze.

"Wanker."

"Is that a yes?"

"Never knew you had a vicious streak." Phin regarded Simon with a hint of anger and a dash of respect. "I like it."

CHAPTER 20

"Will I feel you?" Phin asked, looking uncomfortable. "In my head, I mean?"

Willie suppressed an eye roll. "You won't even know I'm there."

"Actually, I will."

"He's right," Simon said. "Past transmitters were unaware that you were time-tracing. Phin knows that you're going to trace his memories. Won't that make a difference?"

"I don't think so. It's not as if I'm invading his present thoughts. As I said, I'm not psychic. Nor am I a hypnotist. I can't manipulate your thoughts or bend your will. Time-tracing deals solely in established memories. It's a wholly different process and unique to me, as far as I know. I can liken it to watching a play. I'm in the audience, watching scenes unfold, absorbing the dialogue and action. But I am not a part of the show."

Willie sensed Phin's lingering skepticism and wondered why he'd agreed to this at all. She'd been belowdecks, exercising her arm and trying to rid herself of the seething resentment and anger inspired by Simon's attack on her past articles. His lowly assessment of her style, of her integrity, cut to the core. Aye, she'd pushed the limits regarding good taste in some instances, and aye, she consistently went for titillating. That's what the public wanted. That's what sold newspapers. That's what earned her a living and supported her father. She'd never falsified facts. She'd never caused malicious harm. In fact, most of the people she interviewed or featured within an article benefited from the press. Most of them reveled in the exposure. The exception had been the write-up on Reginald Darcy's death and that had been somewhat out of her hands. Although . . . she could have relinquished the byline. That thought had been humbling enough to cool her temper. She still resented Simon's snobbish generalization of her work, but she also realized he'd spoken from an extremely personal point of hurt. By the time he'd joined her below, announcing Phin had agreed to a time-tracing experiment, she'd calmed herself to civil. The tension between them, however, lingered on both sides.

"If you'd rather not do this," Willie said to Phin.

"What? And miss the thrill of being a crucible?" He shot Simon an enigmatic look. "I wouldn't dream of it. One caveat, however. I choose the memory."

"Nothing to do with war," Simon said. "I don't want her subjected to those images."

"I appreciate your concern," Willie said, touched and piqued at the same time. "But I am not faint of heart."

"And for God's sake no reminiscing about an intimate liaison," Simon said as if she hadn't spoken.

Phin started to say something, then thought better of it. There was however a contrary spark in his eyes. "Give me some credit, Darcy."

Suddenly Willie itched to take charge and to move this experiment along. The flight had been uneventful and swift. The *Flying Cloud* hovered just outside the limits of Canterbury. They'd delayed landing until after Willie time-traced Phin. Now the three of them stood on deck, protected from the brunt of the frigid wind by the cockpit's transparent shield. Beyond and below, the cathedral city glistened from a fresh snowfall. Just outside those city walls, her father lived in a small brownstone cottage, a home cluttered with his manic collections. Willie ached to see him, to make sure Strangelove hadn't intruded on his life in some nefarious way. That new and troubling concern had occurred whilst Willie had been jotting notes in her journal. Provided her father was in good health and amenable to her request, she itched to probe his memories posthaste, to solve several mysteries concerning her mother and to advance their search for the Briscoe Bus engine. A clock ticked in her head as sure and loud as her cuff and pocket watch. Time had never seemed of more dire importance. It was as if by setting off the Houdinian, she'd ignited some sort of fuse.

"Right, then," she said. "Let's do this." She met Simon's gaze, ignored her skipping heart. It would seem that their tiff had done nothing to quell her intense attraction to the man. Time-tracing as a team would only deepen their connection. Even though he'd remain on the outside, in the real world, as her timekeeper and lifeline, he would be privy to a portion of her like no one else. She shivered with the relevance.

"You sure about this?" Simon asked.

"Absolutely." She took off her gloves and stuffed them in her pocket, then ordered Phin to do the same.

He complained about the *bloody freezing cold*, but did as she asked. "Now what?"

"I need to touch you."

"Good God, but I'm biting my tongue," Phin said with a glance at Simon.

"Just give me your bloody hands," Willie said. Her grip on his right hand was weak, but she squeezed hard with her left. "When I tell you, I want you to take a walk down memory lane. Any lane. It doesn't matter if you deviate. I'll trace wherever you go."

Simon palmed her pocket watch, looking anxious. Phin held her hands, looking suspicious. As if he was plotting. What road did he aim to take her down? What experience did he wish her to see? She suspected he meant to shock her in some way. The man had no clue as to what she had witnessed in the course of her lifetime via time-tracing. Although she had not witnessed much of a sexual nature. Would Phin ignore Simon's warning and expose her to some decadent liaison? A sex game? An orgy? She hoped not, but braced all the same.

"Remember what we discussed, Simon. Allow me two minutes. If I'm not out by then, pull me out." She was determined to linger as long as possible, no matter what Phin had in store. Otherwise the experiment would be for naught. She glanced at her time cuff. "Do try not to bore me, Mr. Bourdain." With that cheeky challenge, Willie looked to both men, signaling they commence. She held tight to Phin's hands, focused and . . .

"Are you sure you don't mind me intruding upon your holiday, Lord Ashford?"

The older man gripped his shoulder and squeezed. "Of course not, Phineas. You are like family. Closer to us than most of our blood. As such, I insist you call me Reggie. Or Reginald, if you must. We are most informal here." He leaned in and winked. "Much to Mrs. Darcy's dismay."

"Jules and Simon are right behind me. Amelia waylaid them, gushing about some new project."

"Ah, yes," the older man said. "The moonship."

Willie caught her breath as she acclimated to Phin's vivid memory. They'd just been welcomed into a small estate, a humble home decorated with boughs of holly, glitter-dusted angels, images of Father Christmas, beautiful wreaths, and an exquisite tree bedecked with candles and homemade decorations. The furnishings were modest but pleasant. The rooms tidy and warm. Ashford. *Simon's childhood home.*

But what mesmerized her most was the skinny older man with the longish, disheveled silver hair. *Simon's father.* His cheeks were rosy, his eyes bright, his smile infectious. Rectangular gold-wired spectacles perched on the end of his slender nose. His clothing was rumpled but festive. In the next instant, two other men pushed over the threshold. Both handsome. One dark. One fair. Jules and Simon. Willie's pulse kicked as she backed into the shadows. Was this a memory from this past Christmas? Reginald Darcy's *last* Christmas? It could not have been too long ago. Simon and Phin looked exactly the same.

"Sorry we're late, Papa," Simon said, embracing the man in an affectionate hug. "We missed the train we'd intended to catch and ended up twisting Phin's arm for an airlift."

"Didn't take much twisting," Phin said. "It's not like I had anything better to do."

"*Don't let him fool you, Papa,*" Jules said, embracing his father as well. "*Phin always paints London red on Christmas Eve. The life of many a party.*"

"*Drinking, dancing, the ladies,*" Phin said. "*It's the same every year. Happy for the change of pace.*"

Simon snorted. "*He's happy for the chance to avoid a certain smitten lady and her jealous husband.*"

"*Don't listen to them, sir. I'm looking forward to dinner with you and the family.*"

The older man smiled. "*I believe you, Phineas.*"

And so did Willie. Phin was thinking about how he didn't have a family anymore and how the one he'd once had paled to the Darcys. How he'd grown up in squalor, how his mum had been addicted to laudanum and his pa addicted to gambling. Memories within a memory, intensified by raw emotion. Willie trembled under the tremendous impact, but she did not break.

"*Where's Mother?*" Simon asked whilst removing his gloves.

"*In the kitchen with Concetta and Eliza preparing the most delicious feast.*" Mr. Darcy leaned in to Phin. "*Wait until you taste the plum pudding. Oh, and don't take off your coats. This may be the only chance we get to steal away for my secret gifts. Come on, boys. You too, Phineas.*"

The man shot out the door without his own coat or hat and scurried across the snow-dusted lawn toward his workshop.

"*Secret gifts?*" Phin asked Jules. "*Secret from your mother?*"

"*Mother wouldn't approve.*"

Simon called to Amelia, who was draping a tarp over an exposed portion of metal and gears.

"*The moonship?*" Phin asked.

"*Apollo Zero Two,*" Jules said. "*Father's second attempt at affording Amelia a ride amongst the stars. She's thinks he's onto something this time, although she worries he's overly obsessed.*"

"*He's always overly obsessed with his inventions until*

he's distracted by the next one. If he would just slow down and spend more time in the planning stages but—"

"He's a tinkerer, not a thinker." Jules lowered his voice as they entered the magnificently cluttered work shed. *"As with all of Papa's creations, his secret Christmas gifts tend not to work properly."*

"Or for long," Simon said.

"But it's the thought that counts," Amelia said as she pushed in behind them. She hurried toward her father, a curious-looking falcon perched soundly on her iron-mesh wrist cuff.

The metal-enhanced bird flapped away and settled on a massive celestial globe.

Phin hung back, allowing the family privacy as Reginald Darcy pulled a Father Christmas hat over his wild and wind-blown hair.

Willie dwelled in the shadows, watching the same scene and wrestling with Phin's emotions as well as her own. They watched as one by one the eccentric tinkerer gifted his children with a modified version of some twentieth-century gadget.

To Jules—a handheld Dicta-player that operated with some sort of "cassette." Something he could carry in his pocket and speak into at any time recording spontaneous ideas for his fantastical novels.

To Simon—an electric shaver. Since he seemed to have an aversion to conventional razors, Mr. Darcy said with a good-humored wink.

Then he'd presented Amelia with night-vision goggles accentuated with a telescope loupe so she could better study the skies for her someday flight to the moon.

The Darcy siblings accepted their secret gifts with the same enthusiasm as they were given and Phin was reveling in their good fortune and remembering his bad luck when it came to family. More memories within a memory. Willie reeled. Her knees felt weak and she'd swear someone gripped her shoulder to hold her steady.

Then Mr. Darcy called Phin forward and she could feel

his embarrassment and excitement as Mr. Darcy presented him with a brightly painted box.

Willie leaned out of the shadows, wanting to see, but someone held her back. No, someone *pulled* her back. She heard her name, Simon calling her home. She didn't want to leave, not yet, but therein lay the test. And she was detached just enough to know it.

The memory faded and her heart cracked at her last sight of Mr. Darcy, his mischievous smile wide as Phin reached for the present. . . .

"Willie!"

Reality flooded her senses. Simon stood behind her, gripping her shoulders, and she thanked God for his presence as she wilted back against him. "It's okay. I'm back. I'm good." She looked at Phin, embarrassed that she was still holding his hands. "What did he give you?"

Phin broke contact, reached into his inner coat pocket, and pulled out what looked to be a complex version of a set of brass knuckles. "Knuckle Shocker Stun Gun with an attached distress whistle. Supposed to help protect me from sky pirates," he said with a wink to Simon.

"Does it work?"

"Not properly. Not since the day after he gave it to me."

But Phin kept the faulty weapon with him anyway. Because it had been a gift from a kind and caring man, a man so unlike his own neglectful father. A man who presented his children with customized secret gifts every year and that Christmas had extended the same kindness to Phin. Somehow Reginald Darcy had understood Phin's secret misery.

Tears blurred Willie's eyes as she turned to Simon, heart in throat. "I'm so sorry," she choked out. "For the loss of your father. For that wretched article." Emotionally spent, she buried her face against Simon's chest and wept.

Holding her tight, Simon turned his frustration on Phin. "What the hell did you do? What did you show her?"

Phin cleared his throat, clearly choked up by his own emotions. "A great man."

CHAPTER 21

By the time Phin had landed the *Flying Cloud* in a small meadow, night had fallen. It was cold and dark and the walk from the field into town was plagued with tension and melancholy.

Simon had been on pins and needles whilst Willie had traced Phin's memories. He'd glance over every few seconds, happy that he saw no distress, just two people daydreaming. Or at least that's how it appeared. For the most part, Simon's attention had been riveted on Willie's pocket watch, his heart thudding with every tick of the second hand. His own thoughts had whirled as seconds ticked to a minute and then to a minute and a half. Upon the two-minute mark, he had gripped Willie's shoulder and called her home. His pulse had stuttered when she'd remained deep in her trance. *Where was she? What was she witnessing?* It had taken immense restraint not to tear her hands from Phin's and to shake her to reality. But they hadn't discussed breaking the physical connection. If the connection was broken whilst she was still deeply tracing, would that leave her stuck in Phin's memory? Simon had hesitated, gripped her shoulders tighter, and commanded a more fervent return. His relief had been intense when she blinked back and announced herself "good," but it was also short-lived. Phin had reduced her to tears with a cherished memory of Simon's father. The notion left Simon rattled as well. He had not known how deeply affected his friend had been by the secret gift—an impulsive gift from his father, as the man had not known well in advance that Phin was joining them for the Christmas holiday. But of course he wouldn't leave Phin out of the joyous tradition. That wasn't Reginald Darcy's way.

Simon was also touched that Phin had taken it upon himself to show the Clockwork Canary her misstep in presenting Reginald Darcy to the world as an inept kook rather than the gentle and inspired spirit that he was. That one deed coupled with Willie's tearful apology had somehow washed the hurt of that ugly article from his soul. Simon had taken the folded paper from his inner pocket and ripped it to shreds, declaring that grudge obliterated. He couldn't quite forgive his own contribution to his father's demise, but he could indeed forgive Willie for her insensitive transgression.

"This is it," Willie said, stopping and pointing to a narrow two-story brick cottage wedged in between several other homes of the same ilk. This residential road ran just outside the ancient city walls on the fringes of the more bustling areas of the City of Canterbury.

"It's lit up like Piccadilly Circus," Phin said.

"They recently wired this section with electricity," Willie said, rubbing her gloved hands together whilst studying the multiple illuminated windows of her father's two-story home. "Father is a bit obsessed with technology and trinkets that harken of the twentieth century. You'll see what I mean as soon as we step inside."

"If you don't mind," Phin said, "I'll skip the family reunion."

Simon watched as Phin and Willie exchanged an awkward yet meaningful look before Phin focused on the city gate. "I have business I can attend to in town. Figure I'll grab a meal and inquire about overnight lodgings."

"I'd suggest the Hawthorne Inn," Willie said, hugging herself against the night wind. "It's on Dunstan's Street. Just over—"

"I know where it is," Phin said. He glanced to Simon. "Shall I secure two rooms?"

"Yes, please," Willie said before Simon could answer.

"I'm not leaving you alone for the night," he said.

"I won't be alone. I'll be with my father."

"Then I'll stay here with the two of you. We're man and wife, Willie. I'm not going to keep that from your father."

"I'm not asking you to, although I'm not sure how he will react to the news. Regardless," she said with another glance at the cottage, "I'm not sure Father could accommodate us both. It gets worse every time I visit."

Simon wanted to know what she meant by that, but didn't ask. It seemed too personal and Phin lingered.

"Right, then," the man said. "Two rooms at the Hawthorne Inn." Bowler shading his eyes, hands stuffed deep in his pockets, Phin swiveled away on booted heel. "Good luck in there."

Simon nodded and Willie scrambled up the steps ahead of him. She knocked on the old wooden door and seconds later the door swung open and a fit-looking man of perfect posture greeted Willie with a dazed look.

"Michelle?" he asked in a croaky voice.

Willie visibly trembled with emotion as she took off her tinted spectacles and pinned the man with her raw swirling gaze. "It's me, Daddy. Wilhelmina."

Michael Goodenough pushed his spectacles to the top of his head and rubbed his eyes. "But of course. You couldn't be Michelle. She is gone to me. Your red hair threw me. You look so much like your mother."

She blew out a tense breath. "Would you mind inviting us inside?"

"Us?"

Simon stepped forward and into the wash of light flickering from the entryway. He offered his hand in greeting. "Simon Darcy, sir."

Goodenough gripped Simon's hand, stared hard. "Name's familiar."

It should be, Simon wanted to say, but tempered his resentment. He reminded himself that this man had done what he thought best for his Freak daughter by thwarting their plans to elope. What perplexed Simon this minute was how young and physically fit this man appeared, and yet Willie supported him financially? Was there no job he could manage? Yes, he seemed a bit off, but not bonkers by any means.

Still squeezing Simon's hand, Goodenough looked to Willie, who'd just unbuttoned her duster. Noting a glimpse of her gown, he frowned. "Why are you dressed as a woman?"

"Because I *am* a woman," she said with a twinge of defiance. "I am through hiding, Daddy."

"I don't think I like the sound of that."

"It gets worse," she said, as Goodenough backed inside, allowing them passage. "I'm married."

Not the most flattering announcement, Simon thought as he followed her over the threshold. But at least she'd addressed their new status head-on. He hadn't expected that.

Goodenough gawked from Willie to Simon. "To this man? But he doesn't look like a Freak."

"That's because he's a Vic, Daddy. The same Vic I was set to elope with twelve years ago. Only you and Mother put an end to that. Remember?"

"Of course, I remember." He rubbed his temples. "Ah. That is why the name is familiar. I told Michelle love would find a way. I'm surprised it took this long."

"But it wouldn't have taken this long if you had not stopped Wesley from giving Simon my letter," Willie said, red-faced.

"Letter? I know of no letter."

The man looked truly perplexed and Simon wondered at Willie's direct attack. It was as if she'd been harboring resentment for days only to explode the moment she confronted her father.

"But how can you be married?" Goodenough asked. "It is against the law."

"Aye, well, call us rebels."

The man paled at that term, probably thinking of his wife. The most famous of rebels. A Peace Rebel. Simon's attention bounced between father and daughter and the man's cramped living quarters. Indeed the entryway and parlor were crammed wall to wall, floor to shoulder, with so much stuff it was hard to determine useful items from bobbins.

"Why is it so cold in here?" Willie asked.

"Conserving energy," Goodenough mumbled.

"Meaning instead of replenishing your firewood supply, you instead purchased what? This pop-up toaster? Don't you have four of these already?"

"Five. But this is a new model. Four slices of bread as opposed to two."

"But the four you had would make eight pieces of toast," she pointed out logically. "And this tube thing ... what is it?"

"A lava lamp." His face lit up. "Remember how your mother used to talk about these? I purchased it from a traveling Mod-Tech peddler last week. Now that I have electricity ..." He made certain the cylindrical object was plugged into a socket and then flipped a switch. A light shone from within the glass tube and colorful globs of goo rose to the top, breaking apart, then reshaping. "Magnificent, yes?" Goodenough asked.

"Groovy," Simon said because in this instance a Mod term truly applied. He smiled a little, intrigued and saddened by the whimsical sight. His own father would have been entranced.

"Aye, but it won't keep you warm, Daddy," Willie said.

"I have your mother's memory to keep me warm."

Willie frowned at that and Simon placed a calming hand at the base of her spine. "Perhaps I could make us all some hot tea. Just point me to the kitchen."

She met his gaze and nodded, seemingly understanding that he wanted to afford them some time alone and that perhaps she should relax. "I'm certain you'll find a conventional teakettle hiding amongst all the infernal contraptions," she said whilst indicating the next room over. "Most of which do not work and never did."

Simon gave her good arm a reassuring squeeze, then took off his hat and gloves whilst serpentining through the barrage of collectibles. On the surface, Simon understood Willie's frustration. She worked hard to help support her father and yet he squandered money on modern bits and bobs. Much of what he saw must've been purchased on the black market. Some items looked like fantastical hybrid reproductions of pictures he'd seen in the Book of Mods. In many instances, copycat tinkerers constructed superficial look-alikes. Superficial, because all thought went into the exterior design, whilst the inner workings were either completely ignored or faulty. Many guessed at how a *television* or a *computer* might work, but no Vic had mastered the engineering. At least these were not things available to the common man. Not yet anyway. With the introduction and leaking of so much technological knowledge since the arrival of the Peace Rebels, the timetable for certain innovations was well ahead of its original course.

Simon was sorting through the mechanical chaos of the small kitchen, remembering with fondness the chaos of his own father's workshop, when he caught wind of another kind of mayhem altogether. Angry voices booming from the parlor. Willie and her father fighting. He tried to ignore it. None of his affair. Yet, dammit, it was. Setting a kettle of water upon the stove, he adjusted the flame of the burner, then braved the verbal row

"I won't hear of it," Goodenough blasted whilst wearing a path in the narrow space between the parlor and staircase. "Every memory regarding your mother is precious to me and there are many that I and I alone are privy to. Intimate moments. Private yearnings and dreams. Cherished reminiscences of her life in the future. I won't have them tainted—"

"I won't meddle in any way. The memories will go unchanged. I will be in and out. A fly on the wall—"

"No. Absolutely not. Discussion over," he snapped, then stomped up the stairs like a petulant child.

Willie stood ramrod straight, watching his retreating back. Her eyes were wide, her voice wobbly as she commented on the man's exit. "I did not anticipate a refusal," she said as Simon wrapped his arm around her waist. "I am his only daughter and I ask so little. I thought . . . I thought he would want to help."

"He obviously loved your mother very much. Some memories are sacred, Willie."

"But I need to know. She lied about the clockwork propulsion engine. She lied about her job. What else did she keep from us?"

"Does it really matter?"

She turned to him then, fists clenched at her sides. "It matters to me. What if I've set a terrible course of events into play by rooting out a Houdinian, Simon? What if that engine falls into the hands of someone who means to use it for selfish and nefarious means?"

"The Houdinians have kept the engine safe and hidden for thirty-some years now."

"But that's when there were three of them. Now there is only one. Filmore. Thimblethumper said the third was missing, remember?"

"Perhaps that only means that Ollie Rollins eluded Thimblethumper. I've been thinking about that day in the catacombs, Willie. Are you certain that it was Filmore who attacked us? He did not seem suspicious when we left him at the pub. Why would he leave in the midst of his shift? Why would he follow us?"

She closed her eyes as if thinking back, envisioning the moment. "It happened so fast," she said. "A tall man, a big man, sliding out of the shadows. An enormous gun." She opened her eyes, locked gazes with Simon. "I focused on the weapon. Not his face. I did not see his face plainly. I cannot swear it was Filmore."

"If they patrol the vault, it would make sense to work as a pair. Maybe the shooter was Rollins."

"I saw Rollins in Filmore's memories. Just a glance. A memory from just before they arrived in this time. He was a shorter man and Filmore's senior by at least ten years. That would make him quite old now. Although I confess there was something familiar about Rollins, I do not believe he was the shooter."

"All right, then maybe Filmore enlisted two other Peace Rebels to act in Rollins's place as well as your mother's."

"I don't think so," she said, with a glance at the empty stairway. "Something I saw, *sensed*, within Filmore's memories. A sworn pact. I think this was a rogue act. Between my mother, Filmore, and Rollins. I don't think he'd seek out another Mod. A Vic mercenary, maybe? At any rate, something is terribly amiss. I feel it."

Simon guided her into the kitchen. "Let's have some tea. Perhaps your father needs a moment to absorb your request. Maybe he'll change his mind."

"Maybe," she said, whilst locating two teacups.

Simon took the hissing kettle from the stove and soon after, they were sitting at a cluttered table, drinking hot tea and wrestling with inner thoughts. Simon was thinking about how he should leave and procure chopped wood for the hearths.

Willie chimed in with something altogether different. "I live like this too," she said softly.

He raised a brow. "You collect things you don't need? Hoard?"

"No. But my belongings are typically scattered. Although I always know where everything is. Organized chaos, I call it. Dawson typically refers to my desk as a disaster area." She shrugged without meeting his gaze. "I just thought you should know."

Meaning she was thinking about them living together. He'd been too wary to bring it up, knowing she was already skittish about their union. Her train of thought warmed him much more than the damnable tea. He suppressed a smile. "Have I mentioned Fletcher is a meticulous sod?"

"Your valet." She nodded. "I'm thinking we'll butt heads."

"Most assuredly." Now he did smile, even if only a little. "I'm looking forward to it."

She didn't respond and he knew she was still torn. At least they were making progress.

They sipped more tea. A clock on the mantel ticked. No sign of Mr. Goodenough. "Your father's much younger than I imagined," Simon ventured in a low voice. "And in fine health. A little thin but . . . Does his mind really wander so wretchedly that he's unable to hold a job?"

"Oh, he works," Willie said. "There's a merchant in town, a kind and patient man. He owns a sundry shop. My father works there four days a week, helping with stock and chores. I think he'd go simply mad if he had nothing to occupy his time other than thoughts of my mother."

Simon dragged a hand down his face. "But you send him money—"

She motioned him to lower his voice. "Not directly. His pride would not stand for it. I made arrangements with his landlord to pay the bulk of his rent and I struck a deal with the woman who lives next door to cook for him at least a few times a week. When he needs new clothes, I try to finagle something through the merchant he works for. As you see, my father is obsessed with anything that reminds him of my mother or her century. He spends his money unwisely, but as my mother handled the finances in our house . . . he no longer understands the concept of budget."

"So you take care of the essentials for him?" Simon bristled. "Blimey, Willie. Would it not be better to have a talk with him?"

Her eyes brimmed with tears. "I've tried, but to no avail. He would let himself starve before passing up the opportunity to surround himself with another 'piece' of my mother. He is beyond obsessed, Simon. You don't understand. When she died . . ."

He reached across the table and grasped her hand. "It's okay. Truly. Please don't—"

"I have come to a decision," Mr. Goodenough announced whilst bursting into the kitchen. He'd already changed into his nightclothes and a tattered robe. A nightcap sat askew upon his head.

The rumpled sight made Simon think of his own father. He hadn't been there for Reggie as much as he could have been. Maybe he could make small amends by helping another distracted soul. Simon stood. "Would you like some tea, Mr. Goodenough?"

"What? No. Too late for tea. I always have a snort of brandy before bed. But never mind that. I've come to make peace with my daughter."

Now Willie stood as well. "You're going to allow me to time-trace?"

"I can't do that, Wilhelmina. But I will grant you this. Make a list of questions regarding your mother and I will answer them to the best of my ability."

Simon saw that Willie was torn between disappointment and euphoria. He could also see that she was emotionally spent. "That would be most helpful, Mr. Goodenough."

"Aye," Willie managed. "Thank you, Daddy."

He gave a stiff nod. "I'm afraid it will have to wait until tomorrow. I find I am most distracted tonight," he said whilst rooting through a box. "Ah, yes. Here it is. They call this an electric blanket." He showed them the electrical cord dangling from one edge. "Most ingenious. Well worth the cost." Then he glanced from Willie to Simon, looking chagrined. "I'm afraid I only have one."

"That's all right, Daddy. We've arranged for lodgings this evening at a bed-and-breakfast."

"Very good, then," he said, breaking into an awkward smile. "On the morrow." He turned and left, the blanket around his shoulders, cord dragging.

Simon knew Willie wanted to hug her father and he knew the man wouldn't let her. "Wife," he said softly, opening his arms as she turned and, teary-eyed, sought comfort in her husband's embrace.

Chapter 22

Upon reaching their room at the Hawthorne, Willie had been so weary she'd fallen upon the bed fully clothed. All she wanted to do was sleep and recover from the emotionally exhausting day. Simon had removed her spectacles and her boots and then he'd prodded her to sit up whilst he'd helped her out of her gown and stockings. Still wearing her chemise, she'd crawled under the covers with a weary sigh.

Next thing she knew, the lamps were doused and Simon had climbed into bed, pulling her into his arms. He was gloriously naked and she was so very tired. "I fear I am not up to spectacular," she whispered.

"I am not even capable of mildly wonderful." He kissed her forehead, then tucked her face into his chest. "We shall make up for it another time," he said with a smile in his voice.

Her heart had fluttered with tender regard, but then she'd drifted off and her dreams had carried her into the next morning. She did not think she had slept overly long and was alarmed to find Simon gone. Dawn's light had yet to fully break through the partially drawn curtains. She checked her time cuff. Half past six in the morning. What the devil?

Just then he walked in the door, handsome and wind-blown, shaking off a chill.

"Where have you been?" she asked, pushing up to her elbows.

"Taking care of a few errands. Checked in on my mother and sister via Teletype. Heard back from Harry, Ashford's groundskeeper. He said they are in London visiting a friend. I find it curious that they traveled to the city alone. It's certainly not like Mama, but at least they are together, and I confess I am relieved that they are finding comfort in each other's company. They have never been of like mind."

"Perhaps your father's passing has brought them closer. I wish my father would have sought comfort in my company after my mother's death, but instead his mind and attentions drifted."

"Speaking of your father," Simon said whilst hanging his greatcoat on a wall peg. "I arranged to have a supply of chopped wood sent to his cottage and hired someone to examine the heating system. I spied a radiator in each room. There must be access to steam heat at least."

"There is," she said, chest tight. "It's forever malfunctioning, but as long as there are fires in the hearth . . ." She choked up as her heart pounded with the same fierce flutter as the night before. "Such kindness, Simon. How can I thank you?"

He grinned whilst shedding more layers and raking his gaze over her scantily clothed body. "I can think of a thing or two."

"Lucky you, I am feeling most refreshed this morning," she said with a coy smile.

He dropped onto the bed and smothered her with an achingly sweet kiss that soon turned torrid. "Lucky indeed."

Their lovemaking had been passionate and frenzied, both in need but both anxious to start the day. An unspoken physical and emotional symmetry that had been exhilarating in its own right. Their ablutions had been equally rushed, although Simon had slowed the process enough to change her bandages.

"A couple more days," he'd said. "To be on the safe side."

He had made no mention of the small but numerous and ugly puckered ridges marring her shoulder and the region of her chest just above her breast, but Willie knew he felt guilty. She saw it in his eyes, sensed it in his touch. He'd once noted that she'd saved his life and she wondered fleetingly if that hadn't influenced his determination in marrying her. A debt of gratitude paid by offering his support and protection for life? The notion rankled, but she pushed it away, choosing to focus on their immediate mission. Their interrogation of her father and the confiscation of the clockwork propulsion engine.

Once dressed, they'd rushed down to the dining area and found Phin seated and waiting at a table, drinking coffee and reading the *Victorian Times*. He stood whilst Simon seated Willie, then poured them each a cup of coffee from the steaming pot in the center of the table. "How did it go with your father?" he asked Willie.

"Not well," she answered, stirring sugar into the black brew. "He won't let me trace," she said in a soft voice, "but he did agree to answer some questions this morning. Any news of the Triple R Tourney in the *Times*?"

"Not that I saw," Phin said, passing her the newspaper. "Although you may find another article of interest."

Intrigued, Willie focused on the front page whilst Phin updated Simon on the weather and flying conditions. She was vaguely aware of the multiple conversations buzzing around her via other breakfast patrons as she zeroed in on the top headline: FREAKS ATTEMPT POLITICAL KIDNAPPING OVER ATLANTIC!

Stomach turning, disbelieving, she pushed her tinted spectacles to the top of her head and squinted at the short but damning article.

Last night, in a brash and disastrous kidnapping attempt, a rogue faction of the increasingly dangerous Freak Fighters attacked a transcontinental airship transporting several dignitaries, including staunch Old Worlder Prime Minister Avery Madstone. Although the prime minister escaped abduction, lives were lost and severe injuries sustained in the overseas skirmish. The British Naval Service and International ALE have been placed on full alert. Details are unknown at this time but forthcoming.

Heart thudding in her ears, Willie reread each sentence, not wanting to believe, but knowing that a more aggressive faction of the FF did exist.

Lives were lost, severe injuries sustained. . . .

No.

"Willie."

She blinked out of her daze when Simon touched her forearm.

"The waitress was asking if you'd like to see a menu," he said as she passed the newspaper back to Phin.

"My appetite is suddenly lacking, but I . . . I suppose I should have something." Horribly distracted, she tried to focus on the young girl's smiling face, her stomach flopping when the smile flattened and the girl's cheeks flushed. It was then that Willie realized her spectacles were still on top of her head, and thus her rainbow eyes on full display.

"I'm sorry," the waitress said in a hushed voice. "We don't serve your kind."

"What kind would that be?" Simon asked with a steely edge.

The girl swallowed and nodded toward Willie. "Her kind. There's a sign posted outside." She lowered her voice even more. "'No Freaks Allowed.'"

"I saw no sign," Phin said, his own voice hard.

"Nor did we," Willie said, her heart beating so frantically she feared her chest might explode. "But we all came in after dark last night. Since when?" she asked the anxious server. "I've passed by several times before." She'd even eaten here, although disguised as a male Vic. "I recall no such restriction."

"New management, new rules."

"I'd like to speak to that management," Simon said, starting to stand.

Willie grasped his hand. "No, wait." She was all too aware that she'd become the focal point and that the whispered conversations throughout the room were now directed at her. How many had read this morning's headline? How many thought her dangerous and aligned with the alleged Freak Fighters who'd attacked the prime minister's dirigible?

"This is absurd," Phin said to the visibly flustered waitress. "Her money is as good as any Vic in this room."

"The money is acceptable," the woman fairly whispered, "but she is not. Please don't make a fuss. This is my first week on the job and I am desperate for the wages."

Because she had always hidden her race from the public, Willie had never withstood a direct and personal attack of prejudice. It set her blood and temper afire like nothing else, and the fact that Simon looked ready to challenge the manager to a duel only intensified her emotions. As much as she wanted to take a stand, that damnable headline prompted her to proceed with caution. Drawing on her acting skills, she mustered extreme restraint and calmly stood. "We were just leaving."

"The hell we were," Simon said.

Willie squeezed his hand. "Please."

Stone-faced, Phin stood and reached into his wallet.

"Coffee's on the house," the waitress said as if desperate for them to leave.

"The hell it is." Phin paid, then looked to Simon. "I'll gather your possessions from upstairs and settle the room accounts. Meet you outside," he added as Simon slipped him their room key. "Your wife looks as if she could use some fresh air."

The use of the term *wife* instigated several gasps and murmurs and outright gawking.

In a show of defiance, Simon gently grasped her waist. "Come on, sweetheart."

"You're not going to shift me into a toad or conjure a perpetual rain cloud over my head, are you?" the waitress asked in their wake.

"If only she could," Simon said as he guided Willie outside.

Willie welcomed the bracing air as well as her husband's avid support. Her heart pounded and fluttered with mixed emotions as she fought for a calm and clear thought. "I appreciate your outrage on my behalf," she said honestly. Indeed, she was most certain she loved him for it. "But now wasn't the time to take a stand."

"You can't change the world if you ignore the problems."

"I'm not ignoring, just choosing my battles, as it were. We would not have initiated positive change on the behalf of Freaks," she said, hugging herself against a chill. "Not today. There was an attack last night. An attempted kidnapping over the Atlantic Ocean. A rogue faction of Freak Fighters attacked Avery Madstone's air transport."

Simon gawked. "The prime minister?"

"It would seem he escaped but that others were harmed and killed in the attack. At least as reported by the *Times*. It's possible facts have been twisted. God, I hope they're twisted."

Phin joined them, their bags and coats in tow. "That was fun."

Though his mind was obviously racing, Simon said nothing as he helped Willie into her duster and then donned his own outerwear.

Phin passed a valise to Simon, saying, "One moment," then ripped the NO FREAKS ALLOWED sign from the storefront and winged it into the alley. "Right, then," he said as he and Simon flanked Willie. "Did I mention I'm a bloody good cook? How does your father feel about eggs, beans, and bangers?"

As someone who'd navigated life on her own these last several years, as someone who had no friends, the allegiance of these two men filled a void in Willie's soul that she hadn't fully acknowledged until now. "As long as you allow Daddy to make the toast," she said with an affectionate glance at Simon, "I'm sure he'll be thrilled."

CHAPTER 23

Willie would not have believed herself capable of a single bite. Between the troubling article in the *Times*, her ugly bout with prejudice, and her anxiety regarding her father's "interview," her appetite had taken a severe thrashing. Yet there had been something soothing about Simon and Phin's purchasing food and making themselves at home in her father's cluttered kitchen. They'd even charmed Michael Goodenough by inquiring about his collection of modern cookware, allowing him to demonstrate his pop-up toaster, and indulging him by drinking the fruits and vegetables he'd whipped into a disgusting liquid via his electrified blenderizer.

Their natural curiosity regarding his futuristic collection had fed into her father's obsession with his wife's birth century and therefore had naturally led to talk about Michelle Goodenough herself. Soon Willie realized that there was no need to fret over posing formal questions. If she simply went with the flow, she could no doubt learn much about her mother in casual conversation. It had been years since she'd seen her father so at ease and engaged. And she had Simon and Phin to thank for it.

"I find it utterly fascinating that your wife worked for NASA," Simon said as he bit off a corner of burned toast. "My family has a long history of tinkering with fantastical flight. In fact my father started building a moonship several months ago. Named it *Apollo* in honor of the Mod rockets. To think Mrs. Goodenough worked for the team that put a man on the moon."

"Ah, yes," Michael said. "An amazing feat and one that Michelle was ultimately proud of. That was in 1969 just before the Peace Rebels came back in time. Michelle left NASA in 1967 after a beastly accident that took the lives of three spacemen. She never got over that horrifying fire. *If only they had been Houdini,* she once said. Then they would have escaped in time."

"Houdini?" Willie's fork paused midair. She remembered her mother saying an accident had caused her to leave NASA, but there had been no mention of Houdini.

"Harry Houdini," he expanded whilst scooping up the last of his scrambled eggs. "You know. The famous escape artist. Although, wait. I don't believe he's famous yet." He chewed his eggs, brow scrunched in thought. "No. That's right. He was born of our century, but gained global fame after the turn of the century, so of course you don't know of him yet. Not to mention *Houdini* was his stage name. He goes by another name now. I think. What year is this?"

"It's 1887, sir," Simon said.

"More eggs?" Phin asked, trying to keep the conversation light and rolling.

"No, thank you . . . What was your name?"

"Phin, sir. Phineas Bourdain."

"That's right." He pointed his fork at Simon. "And you?"

Willie cringed. It was happening. Confusing days and years. Forgetting names and places.

However, Simon stayed calm, sipped his god-awful drip-o-matic coffee, and reminded her father of his name.

"Ah, yes. The chap who married my daughter. Could I have some more eggs?" he asked Phin, then turned back to Simon. "It's not legal, you know."

"It's binding to us," Simon said, and Willie felt her heart glow.

"Bully for you!" Michael banged a fist to the table. "Bully, I say. You know, in Michelle's time a lot of couples lived in sin. Make love, not war. You'll be happier for it."

Phin coughed into his hand.

Willie's cheeks burned.

"Your eggs, sir," Phin said, frying pan at the ready.

Michael waved him off. "I'm full, thank you. Darcy, eh?" He narrowed his eyes on Simon. "I say, you aren't related to Briscoe Darcy, are you?"

"Distant cousin."

"Michelle met him, you know. She was in charge of security."

"Of the time machine?" Simon asked.

"No," Willie said. "Of the Time Voyager himself. Right, Daddy?" She caught Simon's gaze and noted his surprise. She realized suddenly that they'd never discussed any ties between her mother and his cousin. Their focus had been on the Briscoe Bus clockwork propulsion engine.

"You mustn't hold that against your mother-in-law," Michael said to Simon. "She was only doing her job. She was in charge of security and Briscoe was a national treasure, of sorts. He traveled through time, jumped dimensions. Gadzooks! No wonder they wanted to pick the man's brain."

"Who?" Simon asked.

"The agency Michelle worked for."

"And what agency was that?" Willie asked. "I don't recall." In fact she never knew. Only that it was a British firm.

Michael held a shushing finger to his lips. "Top secret, that."

"More coffee?" Phin asked, filling Michael's cup before the man could decide. "I'm thinking a secret branch of the Metropolitan Police," Phin prompted.

"No," Simon said. "Mrs. Goodenough was at the top of her craft. National level, I'd wager. There was mention of an elite agency in the Book of Mods. MI5?"

"She went by Agent Price then," Michael said, looking off as though somewhere else. "And she worked for the best."

"The Mechanics," Willie whispered.

Michael held up another shushing finger, then looked to Phin. "Are there any more eggs?"

Willie's pulse raced with a surge of relief and excitement. She and Wesley had been right. Their mother *had* worked for Her Majesty's Mechanics. Although in the twentieth century, not this century. Not everything had been a lie. Her mind scrambled, trying to connect the dots of her father's scattered disclosures. She glanced across the table at Simon. He looked almost as far away as her father. Gads.

"According to the preachings of the Peace Rebels," Simon ventured whilst Phin dished out more scrambled eggs, "the time machine was secured and locked away by the British government whilst Briscoe escaped and disappeared."

"Quite the opposite, dear boy. That was the brilliance of my Michelle. What did you add to these eggs, Phineas? The flavor is most pleasing. I must know."

Rigid now, Simon pushed out of his chair. "Excuse me."

Phin traded a look with Willie, then tried to distract her father with his secret recipe whilst she hurried after Simon. By the time she caught up to him, he was outside in the rear garden. "What is it? What's wrong?"

"I have to contact my brother."

Her mouth went dry as he pulled some sort of palm-sized device from his pocket, much like the one Strangelove had given her. Had he found her telecommunicator? But no. This device was different. "What is that?" she asked as he toggled a switch.

He warded her off with a raised hand and turned his back. "Jules?"

She heard a squeal and then static. Then Simon calling his brother again, followed by more static.

"Damnation." His shoulders slumped as he slid the device back into his pocket. He jammed a hand through his hair, making it stand every which way. "He couldn't have made the leap already. It's too soon."

"What leap? What..." Heart pounding, she moved around and faced him. "What are you talking about, Simon?"

"My brother traveled to Australia to meet with Professor Merriweather."

"Maximus Merriweather? The Peace Rebels' genius scientist?"

He nodded. "Jules was convinced that Merriweather has the knowledge and expertise to build him a time machine, a machine that would transport him into the future. To 1969, to be exact."

Time travel. Exactly what the Peace Rebels had meant to prevent by destroying the Briscoe Bus. At least that's what they'd preached. Meanwhile the Houdinians had absconded with the most vital mechanism. Willie's brain hurt trying to make sense of it all. Jules seriously intended to breach 1969? "For what purpose?"

"To obtain the Time Voyager's original clockwork propulsion engine and to bring it back to our time."

"But why?"

"In order to win the jubilee prize. To restore honor to the Darcy name. To secure our family's future and fortune. *Christ.*"

Unsettled by his panic, she reached up and palmed the sides of his face. Even though her right shoulder screamed, she ignored the pain. "Talk to me, Simon."

"My brother is risking his life to leap into the future, to retrieve something that isn't there. Don't you understand, Willie? The Peace Rebels didn't re-create Briscoe's design. They stole the original clockwork propulsion engine. The engine that your mother and the other two Houdinians pinched from the Briscoe Bus, the engine they hid and protected all these years, is *the* engine. The Time Voyager's engine. There is only one."

Willie held Simon's gaze, though her mind raced in several directions. "The depth of intrigue is beyond my immediate comprehension. But we'll sort this out. It would seem destiny brought us together for some grand purpose, Mr. Darcy."

He smiled at that, a pained smile, but at least she'd chased away some of the tension. He placed his hands over hers, saying, "How romantic, Mrs. Darcy," then leaned in for a kiss.

Probably her imagination, but she'd swear she'd felt a merging of souls and purpose as their lips parted and their tongues met. Aye. Surely her cross-dimensional, love-struck imagination.

To think that he'd once thought his life in London exhilarating. Simon had felt more alive in the past two days—more challenged, more aware, more emotionally invested—than in any given moment in the last ten years. For once, the world did not revolve around his problems, his projects, his race for glory. In the last three hours alone his eyes had been opened and his focus turned outward.

The outrageous and unacceptable treatment of his wife by an establishment that barred *her kind* had seeped into his brain, forever changing his status as a passive bystander. Not that he had ever approved of intolerance or prejudice in any form, but, to date, he'd done nothing viable to advocate the rights of Freaks. That would change.

He had felt good about warming Mr. Goodenough's house by stocking his hearths and for establishing a friendly relationship even though he wasn't convinced the man would remember him upon their next visit. Indeed, Michael Goodenough's mind worked in mysterious ways. His inability to accept his wife's absence chained him to the past. Her past, their past. Making sense of his ramblings was like reading every other chapter of a book. The overall story was pitted with holes, leaving it to the reader to puzzle the missing parts. As it happened, Simon was a fan of working puzzles. Part of what had drawn him to being an engineer. In kind, Willie's journalistic experience spoke of an inquisitive and analytic mind. Between the two of them and Phin, bolstered by Simon's suspicion that Willie had time-traced her father on the sly, Simon was confident they would conquer the mystery of the Houdinians and the clockwork propulsion engine. Somehow Simon would make things right for his family and Willie's family whilst acting in the best interest of mankind. He could think of no finer tribute to his father.

As for his brother . . . not wanting to unnecessarily compromise Jules's position in HMM, Simon had decided to give it until the next morning before taking extreme measures. If he had not reached his brother by then, he would consider the situation an emergency and contact the only other Mechanic he knew. He'd ferret out the secret headquarters and storm the doors if he had to, whatever it took to cover his brother's arse.

Simon hadn't realized how intensely quiet the walk from Goodenough's cottage back to the *Flying Cloud* had been until Phin broke the silence.

"A most invigorating day," the aviator said as they boarded the grounded ship. "I can only imagine what lies ahead."

"I feel as though we've been given all or most of the pieces," Willie said. "Working together, perhaps we can solve the puzzle."

"Although some of us possess more pieces than others." Simon grasped Willie's elbow and brought her to a stop just shy of the cockpit. "You time-traced your father."

Phin turned, brows raised in surprise. "She did?"

"When she hugged him good-bye."

"But the embrace lasted no longer than seconds," Phin said.

"A few seconds in reality can equate to a few hours in one's memory," Simon said. "Right, sweetheart?"

Even though her cheeks were flushed, her eyes sparked with defiance. "Don't look at me like that. It wasn't calculated. Upon leaving, I was so overcome. . . . You don't understand. He hasn't been that warm and engaged in years. Even though he mostly talked about Mother and her century, he was connecting with me. With us. The hug was spontaneous and when he didn't push me away . . ." Her throat caught. "Because of my tracing quirk, it's been so very long since he allowed any sort of physical contact."

"So you hugged," Phin said, "and it just happened? Suddenly you were in a memory? I thought you had to focus."

"I'd been focused," she said. "For over two hours. Intently focused. On my father and his every word and expression. I suppose I was primed." She looked now to

Simon. "How did you know? When it happens that fast, no one's the wiser."

"I'm not sure. Sensed it, I suppose." Torn between curious and perturbed, Simon shook his head. "He didn't want that, Willie. You in his memories."

Her cheeks flushed brighter. "I know. But as I said, it wasn't on purpose and he didn't feel me in there. He doesn't know. So no harm done, aye?"

Something ugly stirred within Simon. "If you truly believe that, then you and I have very different views on trust."

She hugged herself and looked away. "You're trying to make me feel guilty for something I didn't intend."

"You could have pulled away the moment you realized what was happening."

"Except it happened too fast and then I was stunned for a moment. Stunned by what I saw, heard. For what it's worth, I *did* break the connection sooner than I wanted. I did, *do* feel remorse for invading Daddy's privacy." She chewed her lower lip, met his gaze. "Are you happy now?"

"Not precisely." But her tormented gaze somewhat cooled his temper. It had been a trying day, a volatile day. As a gesture of peace, he brushed a thumb over her cheek and stated another concern that had set him off. "You didn't have a lifeline, Willie. If you'd gotten lost in there, distracted—"

"But she didn't," Phin said reasonably, reminding them of his presence. "At the risk of stirring things up more, since the deed is done, as it were, I'd like to know if she learned anything of consequence."

Phin was being a diplomat and a pragmatist and Simon had to admit he, too, was curious. He felt hypocritical, but tried to focus on the greater good. "Did you?"

Her eyes widened. "There's a traitor amongst them."

"Who? The Houdinians?"

"I think so. I need to rethink the memory. Sort things out. My father's memories were like a twisted collage."

"I can imagine." And the thought of her getting lost in

those memories, any memories, caught up in some sort of psychic limbo, chilled Simon to the bone.

"Right, then," Phin said. "Let's go below. Work the puzzle until we can determine our next move. I don't know about you, but I could use some *real* coffee. Protect me from that drip-o-matic swill of the future." Mumbling on, he took the lead, expecting them to follow.

"You go on," Simon said to Willie. "I want to try Jules one more time."

Willie slipped into his arms, eviscerating the lingering tension between them. "Being his twin, don't you think you would feel something in your stomach, in your spirit, if something was terribly wrong?"

"Yes. I do believe I would. I felt it when he was horribly injured in the war, even though we were miles apart." Simon was feeling several things just now, but no ominous portent. He hooked her hair behind her ears. "Thank you for reminding me of that."

She smiled up at him, though the smile was troubled. "I do believe we've stepped into a monumental mess, Simon."

He couldn't argue that, and though this was monumental, being steeped in larger-than-life drama was all too familiar. "All part of being a Darcy."

CHAPTER 24

Although Bingham had insisted upon a swift journey to Queensland, after being cooped up within the foul bowels of the *Iron Tarantula* for almost twenty-four hours, he was desperate for fresh air and steady ground.

The gigantic metal arachnid was an impressive terrain vehicle merely for its size, durability, and innovative design. The iron cephalothorax housed the cockpit, sleeping quarters, and galley, whilst the abdomen boasted a sophisticated engine room and cavernous storage area. The eight towering legs crawled easily if not evenly over sand and rock and did indeed carry them safely over treacherous landscapes at a goodly speed. But the constant and jolting rocking motion coupled with the questionable ventilation system and high temperatures had taxed Bingham's titled being. He always traveled in style and the *Iron Tarantula* was not even remotely comfortable. However, the most distressing aspect of this trek was Bingham's inability to communicate with the outside world. He knew not whether to attribute the vexing phenomenon to the remote setting or the thick iron walls of the beastly steam-powered spider.

Stomach rolling, Bingham made his way to the cockpit on shaky legs. He did not knock upon the closed door. He slid it open with a vengeance and braced his hands on the iron frame so as not to pitch forward. "I insist you divert to the nearest town."

"The nearest town's not so near, mate. Not on this course."

"Then plot a new course."

The Rocketeer swiveled in his leather captain's chair, cigarette clamped between his teeth, jaw bristled by two days' growth of beard. He pushed up the brim of his slouch hat and regarded Bingham with boredom. "You hired me to deliver you to Queensland as quickly as possible, mate, and now you not only want me to veer off course, but to stop?"

"I'm not your mate. I'm your employer. And yes, I am requesting just that, Mr. Steele."

"Your money, Lord Bingham. My mistake. I thought time was of the essence."

Bingham gritted his teeth. "Most assuredly. But because of my inability to communicate with the outside world, I have no way of knowing if I am already too late."

Steele waved him inside, then swiveled back around. "Who do you need to contact and how?" he asked, flicking switches on a complex console. "What do you need to know? I can access various communication devices as well as the latest global news. Take a load off, mate."

Bingham ignored the insolence and dropped into the seat next to Steele's. He stared at the instrumental panel before him, entranced, impressed, and vexed as hell that not one of his transports had anything like this. "Where did you acquire all of this advanced technology?"

Steele quirked an infuriating grin. "If I told you, I'd have to kill you."

"Your humor is unwelcome."

"Who's joking?" The ash on Steele's cigarette glowed like a taunting beacon of disrespect. "What do you need to know? Who do you need to contact?"

His list was long, but he homed in on his most fervent concern. "I need to contact a Mod Tracker by the name of Crag. I need coordinates on a man by the name of Jules

Darcy. But mostly I want to make sure Professor Maximus Merriweather is exactly where I've been told he would be." At that moment, Bingham shared his most detailed coordinates.

"You're a demanding but direct bloke, Lord Bingham. Let's see what we can do," Steele said whilst pushing multiple buttons. "Meanwhile, a word of advice. Your traveling companion, Renee? I'd treat her more kindly, mate. Hell hath no wrath like an automaton scorned."

Bingham barked a humorless laugh. "Renee has no feelings." In addition to enlisting one of his *Mars-a-tron* crewmen as a bodyguard, he'd brought Renee along as a way of amusing himself should he grow bored. He had, in fact, been most bored last night. Her stamina and inability to register pain or fear was both a boon and an annoyance. "Renee is a machine."

"When abused or neglected, machines tend to malfunction. Just a friendly observance, mate. Oh, crikey," he added, leaning forward to peer out the transparent shield overlooking the landscape. *"Damn."*

Bingham leaned forward as well, spying a cloud of dust a few meters off. "What is it? A sandstorm?"

"Bushrangers. Runaway convicts who thrive in these parts due to their impeccable survival skills. Robbers. Highwaymen."

The hair on the back of Bingham's neck prickled as Steele utilized an intercom system to inform his crew of an imminent attack. Out of the voluminous dust broke a pack of armored vehicles. He'd expected horses. Not steaming, belching weapons on wheels. Was that a bloody cannon rocket?

"Looks like the Musquito Gang. Thievin' cutthroats."

Bingham wiped his moist palms over the trousers he had ordered Renee to steam press just that morning. Indeed, he was not dressed for a skirmish. "What do they want?"

"Whatever I've got." Steele chucked his cigarette, then jerked his thumb. "Best take cover in your cabin, oh, Kingpin of the Universe. It's gonna be a rough one."

Bingham pushed out of the chair, heart pounding. "You promised me safe passage, Mr. Steele."

"Yup." But his attention was on the controls and the incoming cutthroats.

Bingham heard the first explosion and hurried toward his cabin. He weaved and stumbled as the *Iron Tarantula* swerved, then vibrated as though taking a hit. He heard the crew shouting and bellowed for his own bodyguard. But when Bingham breached his cabin door, he only found Renee. She was sitting stiff-backed in a chair, darning his socks.

Bingham hurried to the window, saw one of Steele's men arming a rapid-firing cannon from a balcony on one of the *Tarantula*'s legs. Good. They were fighting back. Still, Musquito's gang comprised at least seven armed vehicles. No telling how many men. What if they got on board? Where the devil was his bodyguard?

"Put down the bloody socks, Renee, and get my Peabody 382. We're under attack."

"Attack. To set upon forcefully."

"Yes, I know what it means. Just get my bloody gun. I have not come this far to be felled by a band of bloody bushrangers. We must fight back. Kill the enemy."

"Enemy," she said in that monotone voice that grated. "A hostile force that seeks to injure."

Furious for the delay, Bingham spun around. "What the . . . Don't point the gun at me, you brainless, worthless bob of junk. The *enemy*! Shoot the — " He saw the flash, felt the blow, the pain and the astonishment. His knees buckled and Bingham pitched forward. His thoughts blurred as he spied his blood pooling. The pain was excruciating, then numbing. His lids fluttered, then started to close. His last vision: Renee sitting stiff-backed darning his socks, a smoking gun at her feet.

CHAPTER 25

"One more time," Simon said. "From the beginning."

"Maybe we should sleep on this," Phin said, elbows on the table, his head in his hands. "We've been at it for hours. Swear to God, my brain hurts."

"I agree with Simon," Willie said.

"Of course you do," Phin said.

"We're close to making some sense of all this," Willie said. "I feel it. Each time we create a scenario, it jogs another detail of one of the memories I experienced via Filmore or my father." Willie's cheeks burned. Her gut twinged. She did indeed feel guilty about time-tracing her father, but she couldn't focus on that regret just now. Nor could she meet Simon's gaze. She'd disappointed him. Even though the tracing had been accidental, the fact that she'd willingly gone along for the ride made her question her morals. A new and wretched feeling.

"Right, then," Phin said. "Another round. But not on an empty stomach. I can only go on coffee for so long and we already missed a midday meal. Go on," he said as he moved toward a bank of cabinets. "I'm listening."

Willie straightened in her chair as she gathered her thoughts. Her shoulder felt stiff and her back ached. After this round, she vowed a bracing walk on the main deck. Phin was right. They'd been cooped up in this small, rustic galley for hours. Even so, she wasn't ready for a break. Not just yet. "Starting with what we know of 1969," she prompted. "My mother—"

"Agent Mickey Price," Simon clarified.

"—was a security specialist with Her Majesty's Mechanics."

"Formerly with NASA," Phin said whilst slicing a loaf of bread. "Hence she'd been exposed to advanced aeronautics and the concept of exploring new worlds in the quest to benefit mankind."

"Logical that she would be assigned to the 'voyager' who traveled through time," Willie said. "A phenomenal endeavor not yet accomplished by the American, British, or Soviet space programs."

"National treasure, indeed," Simon said. "Briscoe Darcy was not only the most famous man on the planet at that moment, but also the most wanted. Every national intelligence agency in the world would be keen on unlocking his mind in order to learn his secrets. If the 'Space Race' was intense, imagine the motivation to possess the knowledge enabling men to travel into the past and future. Could jumping cosmic dimensions be much farther behind?"

"So Briscoe's under lock and key," Phin said, attacking a block of cheese. "And the time machine's under lock and key. Maybe someone in the Mechanics tried to take it for a test run, but it didn't work. Maybe Briscoe alone knew how to activate the clockwork propulsion engine."

"Which brings us to the assumption that my mother, who'd had unlimited access to Briscoe, tricked, coerced, or convinced the Time Voyager to impart her with that vital information."

"She then helped to coordinate the theft of the engine with the Peace Rebels. We know from things she told you," Simon said to Willie, "that she had been involved with the underground organization for almost a year."

"I'm almost certain it was Jefferson Filmore who drew her in," Willie said. "I think he was some sort of professor and I know he was a fierce peace activist. I'm convinced they were acquainted on an intimate level. I saw them embrace. I felt his affection. In a memory, that is." That specific knowledge cramped her stomach, made her ache for her father, but at the same time, she sensed the affair had been short-lived.

"Soured on her life in America, she pursued a new existence in the UK," Simon said, "but things weren't much better there. The world was careening toward self-destruction and she was desperate to make a difference."

"Desperate enough to betray Her Majesty's Mechanics, the British government, and the wrath of every nation who had their eye on Briscoe and his time machine." Phin set a large platter on the wooden table in between Simon and Willie. "Bread, cheese, dried pork, fruit, and biscuits. It will have to do, as the pantry and icebox are minimally stocked."

"Difficult to conjure an appetite," Willie said, "when you've just reminded me my mother was a thief and a traitor."

"Whose objective was to save the world," Simon said, reaching across the table to give her hand a supportive squeeze.

"So we're surmising," she said.

"We're surmising everything," Phin said. "Spiced wine," he announced, pouring them each a generous mug. "Now eat or you'll hurt my feelings."

Simon snorted, but even though Phin was being glib, Willie knew deep down that he was indeed a sensitive soul. She helped herself to a small portion of bread and cheese whilst striving to keep the conversation on track. "You're right, of course, Phin. Nothing we've read in the Book of Mods, nothing my mother told me, and, to an extent, not even what I learned whilst time-tracing is a given. Indeed it is most difficult to sort fact from fiction, reality from illusion. I must strive to keep my personal feelings at bay."

Simon looked at her with pride and affection whilst sipping his wine. "Let's jump ahead. However the vital missing knowledge was obtained, however the theft was arranged, the end result was that the PRs installed Briscoe's clockwork propulsion engine into their psychedelic painted bus and sixty-nine, give or take, twentieth-century radical peace activists—"

"Of various brilliance and professions within the realm of arts and science," Phin added.

"—successfully hopped dimensions," Simon said. "Departing in 1969 and traveling in reverse, arriving in 1856, five years after Briscoe made his great escape from Prince Albert's Great Exhibition in 1851."

"Houdini," Willie said, whilst nibbling on cheese. "Daddy said Harry Houdini was, or will be, a famous escape artist. A magician. A showman. According to tales, Briscoe made a show out of his time-traveling launch."

"It's true," Simon said. "My father witnessed the event. Although Briscoe was a distant cousin and several years my father's senior, they did have an acquaintance and a shared passion for science. My father was but eighteen when he attended Prince Albert's tribute to technological achievements. Briscoe chose his platform well. He had an audience of thousands. And, after much bloated pomp and circumstance, the man strapped himself into his gleaming self-professed 'time machine' and disappeared in a rainbow of brilliant light. At the time many thought it was an optical illusion. A magician's trick."

"By a flamboyant showman," Phin said. "Escaping to another time. An unparalleled stunt of magnificent proportions."

"A stunt that would have made Houdini proud." Willie closed her eyes and thought back. Back to Filmore's memories. "Something about Houdini," she said.

"We've already determined that the Houdinians took their name from Harry Houdini," Phin said. "Like Houdini and like Briscoe, the Peace Rebels performed a magnificent stunt, escaping back in time."

"Then we *surmise*," Simon said, "that at some point your mother, Filmore, and Rollins conspired to pinch the clockwork propulsion engine—"

"Again," Phin said.

"—and to secure it somewhere safe in case it became necessary to escape even this century."

"In order to spread their cautionary tales even earlier in time, say the eighteenth century," Phin ventured. "Or perhaps to return to their own time. Or, hell, to take a spontaneous holiday. Who knows? Well, aside from Jefferson Filmore and Ollie Rollins. Wherever they are."

"London." Willie's eyes flew open as she slammed her palms to the table. "I think they, or at least Filmore, might be in London."

Simon and Phin traded a look. "Why?"

"The revolving safe house."

Brow raised, Simon abandoned his cold pork sandwich. "We've been over this several times and that is the first mention of a *revolving safe house*. Am I right, Phin?" Simon asked without breaking eye contact with Willie.

"Right you are. What does it mean? Where did it come from?"

"One of Filmore's memories." Willie sipped her wine, tried to temper her excitement. "When I saw my mother, I was so stunned, I called out. *Mother*, first. Then *Michelle*. At once Filmore flashed back to the future. What I saw and heard was so unfamiliar and then all at once he reverted to the past. He was arguing with my mother and Rollins about whether to hide in the west, north, or south. In one of the future memories, my mother made mention of a revolving safe house. It was just one of a few phrases I did not understand and it only came back to me just now as I was trying to slow those memories."

"Yes, but what is it?" Phin asked. "Is it to be taken literally? A house that is safe?"

"Or perhaps a house where you keep something safe," Simon said.

Willie's journalistic mind chugged as she fueled it with more and more conjecture. "In my lifetime, my family lived in three cities. New York City, Edinburgh, and London."

"West, north, and south," Simon said.

"In that order?" Phin asked.

"No. London, Edinburgh, America, then back to London. My mother claimed to work for a global security firm, so it would make sense that she would live near whatever she was protecting, aye? She was killed seven years ago whilst living in London—a victim of a hit-and-run accident. We found Filmore in Edinburgh."

"The revolving safe house," Phin said. "Three cities. Every so often or whenever they felt threatened, they revolved the engine to one of those three cities."

"If you follow the pattern as you stated it, Willie, the next safe house would be New York City," Simon said.

"If you followed the pattern, aye. But there are no longer three Houdinians. Only Filmore and Rollins or Filmore and a mercenary. And they have been protecting that engine for more than thirty years now. You saw Filmore. He had to be close to sixty years old, which would make Rollins seventy or more." She paused as his younger face flashed in her mind, shivered with a wave of déjà vu.

Simon touched her forearm. "What is it?"

She shook off the strangeness. "Nothing. Sorry. Just that feeling that I've seen Rollins before, but damn, I cannot seem to place him."

"It'll come to you," Phin said, drinking the last of his wine. "Meanwhile we have a vague location. London is a hell of a lot closer than New York City. It would make sense to look there first regardless. But where to start?"

"Underground," Willie said.

Simon angled his head. "Another vault?"

Willie gulped her own wine now. "Whilst tracing my father, the most vivid and tumultuous memory was one of my mother looking wide-eyed and spooked. My father held her, saying, *You spend too much time with the dead.*"

"Catacombs," Simon said. "The coffinlike vault. That is the actual 'safe house.' And they shuffle it between the three cities."

"Three cities with extensive underground passages." Phin scratched his head. "Good God. London Bridge alone harbors a veritable subterranean city of passages, crypts, and vaults. There's an entire lattice of catacombs beneath Waterloo. Those are just two possibilities. And what about all of the churches and abbeys? How do we know what we're dealing with? Where to look?"

"I have a friend," Simon said. "Montague Lambert. He owns a literary antiquities shop. His map collection is quite extensive. I say we fly back to London tonight, get a good night's sleep, and meet at Lambert's tomorrow morning."

"Right, then," Phin said, pushing to his feet. "London it is. God, but I love a good adventure," he added whilst rushing toward the main deck.

Willie tried to stand but couldn't find the energy. "I must confess, I'm feeling overwhelmed. It's all somewhat fantastical."

"Quite the story," Simon said, shifting to sit beside her. "And we still don't know the whole of it yet. I have a feeling your editor, Dawson, will sing your praises, indeed kiss your feet, when you submit your serialized account of our adventure."

Willie's mouth went dry. "Indeed, this is the sort of sensational reporting that would put the *London Informer* back on top."

"And to catapult the Clockwork Canary to celebrity status."

She cast him a hurt look. "Are you testing me, Simon?"

"No." He put his arm around her and pulled her close. "Truly I'm not. It is a conundrum even for me. A story like this, it's bigger than one newspaper. It alters history books. Depending on how things unfold, we could be sitting on a damned fortune."

"Fortune enough to save your family."

"And yours."

She rubbed her temples. "If only it weren't so personal."

He kissed the top of her head. "The conundrum."

She glanced up at him then. "My pressman's nose smells more trouble. Something foul, Simon. I worry that we're going to discover something . . . ugly. Remember when I relayed the memory of my mother telling my father, *There's a traitor among us*?"

Simon nodded.

"I think . . . I believe it was just days, maybe even hours, before she was killed. Maybe the hit-and-run was not an accident as reported, but a calculated means of making sure every secret she knew died with her. Or perhaps she was distressed and distracted by what she'd learned and that had caused her to unwittingly step in a coach's path. Either way, I think she died because of that traitor. Someone she knew. Someone close."

"Do you have someone specific in mind?"

She shook her head. She did not. But she did have a bad feeling.

Simon tucked her shaggy hair behind her ears. "What say you we deal with the mystery as it unfolds? One revelation at a time."

"Patience has never been one of my better qualities."

He laughed at that. "Nor mine." Smiling, he held her close as the *Flying Cloud* rumbled to life and took to a bumpy flight.

Willie grasped his forearm, licked her lips. "It will be strange returning to London as a woman, let alone a Freak. I'm grappling with the notion of revealing my Freak nature just now. I do not wish to deny my race, Simon. I am beyond that. But I fear it would hinder the progress of this investigation, so to speak. Once my true race is known to Dawson, to my coworkers, to anyone who looks me in my kaleidoscope eyes, I will become a source of fascination and ridicule. I will lose certain freedoms, which will hinder my ability to interact or converse with Vics on an effective level. And," she said, meeting his gaze with her heart in her eyes, "our existence as a married couple will be under fervent fire."

Simon smiled a little. "Are you saying you'd appreciate a few days of anonymity in order to fully enjoy our union as man and wife?"

Overwhelmed by their daunting expedition and future, Willie rested her head against Simon's strong shoulder. "And to acclimate to the challenges of resuming my life in London as a woman."

"So be it," Simon said, smoothing his fingers over her cheek. "One revelation at a time."

CHAPTER 26

The flight from Canterbury to the outskirts of London did not take long; however, given the winter season, they were already well under the cloak of night. The moon sat full and bright in the sky and the city of London glittered on the horizon almost as keenly as the stars above.

Although Queen Victoria was not a fan of the twentieth century and thereby anachronistic technology, she could not ignore, dismiss, or halt the natural progress of science. Candles had given way to oil lamps and then to gas lighting, and now, because Peace Rebels had inspired (or infected—the distinction depending on whether you were a New or Old Worlder) and educated nineteenth-century innovators, electricity was "ahead of its time" and fast becoming the most popular source of lighting in the home.

Simon's own town house was wired for the modern convenience, although Fletcher still seemed inclined to fall back on old ways. How Simon, a forward thinker, had ended up with a valet who deplored change had always been a source of amusement and frustration on both sides. This morning, after Teletyping Ashford, Simon had placed a long-distance telephone call to Fletcher. The connection had been poor, but Simon had been able to prepare the man for a change of monumental proportions.

"I do not know precisely when I'll be returning home," he'd said. *"But when I do, it will be with a wife."*

To which Fletcher replied, *"Whose wife would that be, sir? Should I start preparing for the invasion of an angry husband?"*

"My previous indiscretions are just that, Fletcher. In the past. I refer to my own wife."

"Are you snockered, Master Simon?"

"No, Fletcher. I am not snockered. I am married."

"Were you forced by gunpoint, sir? An irate father or brother perhaps? I could alert your solicitor. Perhaps he could find a loophole."

"This marriage is of my design, Fletcher, and I expect you to welcome Mrs. Darcy with an open mind and heart."

"I see, sir."

"No, you don't."

"No, I don't. Should I prepare a bedchamber for Mrs. Darcy?"

"We won't be sleeping in separate rooms."

"Ah. It is quite serious, then."

"Most serious," Simon had said, his chest aching as he'd fought against the notion of love. A fruitless effort, it would seem. As the day had played out, he was most certain he was unequivocally in love with Wilhelmina Darcy. The realization was as invigorating and chilling as the frigid night air.

Restless, Simon joined Phin in the cockpit as the superb aviator began their descent into Pickford Field. "When I last made this trek two weeks ago, I was at the wheel, and the *Flying Cloud* handled like a flying death trap."

"She was in dire need of upgrades and fine-tuning, true," Phin said. "Although I'm sure it didn't help that you're a shite pilot," he said with a teasing grin.

"Be that as it may," Simon said, adjusting his goggles. "Thank you for all you've done. And thank you for being so kind to Willie."

"Not a hardship. Trust me." He glanced toward the stair-well. "She still below?"

"Putting the galley to rights and resting her eyes."

"And lovely eyes they are," Phin said. "A man could get lost in those swirls of color."

"Yes, well, I'll thank you to keep your wits."

Phin laughed. "Good God, man. You are arse over teakettle in love. In the words of Mr. Goodenough," he said with a wink, "bully for you."

Simon shook off the green-eyed monster and smiled a bit. "You don't need to meet us at Lambert's tomorrow."

"And miss out on the rest of the adventure?"

"Surely you must have duties here at Pickford. Unfinished repairs. Booked charters."

"Nothing I can't put off or reschedule."

Simon braced for landing and narrowed his eyes on the former militiaman. "Did Jules ask you to look after me?"

"I'm no man's keeper, Simon."

"He knew about my run-in with a Houdinian. Knew that Willie had been injured and that I was determined to pursue the engine, no matter the danger. It's no secret that I'm inexperienced when it comes to facing a deadly opponent. You, however, are a professional."

Phin spared him a glance as he steered the airship toward the moonlit landing strip. "Don't get all pissy about it."

"I'm not," Simon said honestly. He appreciated Phin's multiple areas of expertise and he'd be a fool to turn away a man who could help in protecting Willie from harm. Especially since Phin was a man both he and Jules trusted implicitly. "That means Jules has been in communication with you since he left for Australia. Have you heard from him recently?"

"Not since last week." The *Flying Cloud* skimmed over the snow-dusted field, the whirling blades slowing, the engines quieting. "Considering his expedition," Phin said, "I did not anticipate hearing from Jules anytime soon."

"So you know what he's after."

"Same as you. The jubilee prize."

"Yes, but are you aware of his destination?"

"I am."

"Then you must understand my concern."

"You think he's risking a journey into the future for nothing." Phin cast him an enigmatic glance. "What if he's not after the clockwork propulsion engine?"

"What else?" Simon frowned. "Briscoe?"

"He *is* family and he is in quite the pickle," Phin said as he finessed the airship to a smooth and full stop.

"But that was thirty-six years ago. Given my infamous cousin's *pickle*, he's probably dead by now."

Phin shrugged. "Not if Jules arrives in the future close to the same day Briscoe did."

"You mean before the Peace Rebels even left there?" Simon massaged his temples. "I cannot begin to fathom the effect and impact that could have on *our* time. Surely Jules is aware."

"Of course he's aware. He writes science fiction, for God's sake. I'm sure he's considered the paradoxes and ramifications. Look, good man. Jules didn't inform me of specifics and I didn't ask. I know my boundaries and I know his limitations."

Meaning his brother's mission was top secret? An official assignment? Who better to infiltrate and pinch something or someone from Her Majesty's Mechanics than another Mechanic? "What do you know of Jules's ... extracurricular activities?" he asked as Phin cut the engines.

"Probably as much as you do."

"I only know that he is a Mechanic," Simon admitted, trusting he wasn't betraying Jules's confidence.

"Then we're on even ground." Phin pushed his goggles to the top of his head. "Here comes your lovely bride," he said with a nod toward Willie, who'd just breached the upper deck. "Listen, Simon," he continued in a low voice. "Jules trusted you with a covert tip about the Houdinians. Let us trust that he knows what he's doing. Aside from being quite brilliant, he's the most cunning bastard I've ever known."

"But his bum leg—"

"Won't slow him down." Phin rapped Simon on the shoulder. "See you at Lambert's on the morrow," he said, then moved forward to bid Willie a temporary farewell.

*   *   *

By the time they took the short train ride into London and then an automocab to Covent Garden, Willie felt as though she had been awake for three days. Her brain was as exhausted as her body and she was emotionally drained. She wanted to fall into bed and to sleep for a week. But first she had to get past Simon's valet and cook, the meticulous caretaker who had been in Simon's employ for five years—Fletcher.

"You're sure he is expecting us," Willie whispered as Simon guided her from the automocab to the stone steps of his Georgian townhome.

"As I said before, I not only spoke with Fletcher this morning, but I telephoned again from Phin's office. Yes, he is expecting us." Simon paid and tipped the driver, who'd carried their bags to the stoop just as the front door swung open, and they were greeted by a stiff-backed gentleman with slicked-back salt-and-pepper hair and astonishingly kind brown eyes.

"Welcome home, Master Simon. I assume the lovely woman upon your arm is Mrs. Darcy," he said whilst retrieving their bags.

"Please call me Willie," she managed, feeling more flustered than she had anticipated. She had never employed a domestic and felt extraordinarily uncomfortable at the thought of someone attending to her needs.

"As you wish, Mrs. Darcy."

Simon just smiled as they followed Fletcher into the entryway and Willie got her first peek inside Simon's home. The interior, for all its spaciousness, was not overly extravagant. Whilst moving toward the stairway that would take them to the first floor, Willie peeked into the ground-level drawing room, adjacent dining area, and a small parlor. The decor and furnishings were simple and quaint, and even though this residence was far grander than her rented rooms, she did not feel overly intimidated. On the other hand, she did not feel entirely at home either. Each room was extraordinarily tidy and free of clutter. And for that matter was absent of anything that spoke of Simon's adventurous and technology-savvy persona.

"I've never been much of a homebody," Simon said as if reading her mind. "When I am here, I spend most of my time in the library. I'll give you the grand tour later."

"Please, sir, allow me to tidy up in there before—"

"Move one pencil and I shall have to sack you, Fletcher."

"You should be ashamed, sir."

"Of threatening you?"

"Of that library," the valet said with a sniff, then continued up the steps.

Willie blinked.

Simon squeezed her waist and spoke close to her ear. "I told you he was a fussbudget and a stick-in-the-mud. I did not say he was conventional."

"I heard that," Fletcher said, halfway up the stairs.

"He also has excellent hearing."

Now Willie smiled. She found the casual relationship between this particular employer and domestic most endearing. Perhaps it would not be as difficult to acclimate to this new environment as she had feared. Breaching the landing, she noted the first floor seemed to be composed of two large rooms. Since the door was open, it was clear that the room at the front of the house was the principal bedchamber. She glanced over her shoulder at the closed double doors to the rear. "The library?"

"In all its mortifying disarray," Fletcher said. "Do have you have a headache, Mrs. Darcy? Should I fetch some medicine?"

"What? Oh. Oh, no," she said, realizing she was wearing her sunshades in order to conceal her race.

"Willie's sensitive to bright light," Simon said as Fletcher carried their valises into his bedchamber.

"I see," Fletcher said.

"No, you don't," Simon said.

"No, I don't." Probably because it had been dark outside and Fletcher had illuminated each room with only minimal lighting. *Bright* did not apply. "However, it is not my place to question."

"But you will."

"Not at this precise moment, sir. Would you like some tea, Mrs. Darcy?"

"I don't want to be any trouble."

"No trouble," he said as he glided toward the hallway. "Dinner?"

"It's been a long day," Simon said. "We'll be retiring early."

"Very well. Welcome to our humble home, Mrs. Darcy," he said, turning on the threshold and affording her a slight bow. "I warn you, Master Simon is most incorrigible to live with, although he does have a good heart. Should you need anything at all, do not hesitate to ring."

Simon rolled his eyes.

"I like him," Willie said when the door closed.

"I heard that," Fletcher called even though it sounded as though he had already reached the landing.

She laughed then, a welcome feeling after being so tense and anxious throughout the day.

"Music to my ears. You should laugh more often, Willie. We'll have to do something about that." Simon smiled whilst dragging off his paisley scarf. "What do you think of this room? Will it do? I know the decor is quite masculine but—"

"You forget I lived as a male for the past ten years," she said whilst shedding her sunshades and outerwear. "I'm not accustomed to frilly things."

"Not even in the privacy of your flat?"

"I couldn't afford the slightest chance of giving myself away." She swept off her derby, admiring the whimsical mechanical bird and lace as well as the charmed chain around her waist. Small considerations, yet they made her heart swell with immense pleasure. They made her feel pretty. "It's astonishing to me that I denied my true self for so long."

"Yes, well that's over now."

She shook her head. "I cannot move on entirely until we have solved the mystery. Until I understand what happened to my mother. Until we have—"

"Hush now." Simon moved forward and took her into his arms. "We've been at this all day. Time to rest our minds. We'll have another brain buster in front of us tomorrow whilst we try to narrow down and pinpoint which underground passages to explore. Good thing the Golden Jubilee and hence the announcement for the Triple R prize is a few months away. Realistically it could take a while to locate that vault. Especially if Filmore opted for the New York City rather than the London safe house."

Willie stiffened in his arms. "We cannot afford months, Simon. We need to find the engine before it falls into dangerous hands."

"The Houdinians have successfully protected the time-traveling engine for over thirty years."

"Aye, but the Houdinians are quite possibly down to one, and the Triple R Tourney has inspired thousands of adventurers and explorers to set off in search of a technological invention of historical significance."

Including Strangelove. Her stomach turned just thinking about that man. Now that she was back in London, she felt that his eyes were upon her, his spies everywhere. Imagined or not, the notion rankled.

"I cannot believe that in all these years news did not leak of the survival of the clockwork propulsion engine. Remember my mother's words regarding a traitor? We cannot be the only ones searching for it." Willie palmed her brow. "Gadzooks! Maybe the man who shot me was looking for it! Why did *that* never occur to us?"

Simon shushed her mounting hysteria with a demanding kiss. She struggled but a moment before giving in, giving over. She parted her lips and welcomed his tongue, reveled in the feel of his hands smoothing down her back and squeezing her bottom. Her panic ebbed and her passion flowed. Indeed, her heart was beating most frantically, her desires flaring most earnestly. "Take me, Simon," she begged whilst tugging his shirttails from his trousers. "Take me now and completely. Ravish me. Make me forget my name."

One night of oblivion. She was desperate to rest her mind.

He looked down at her with such fire, she was certain she felt flames licking her most intimate places. "My dear Willie, do you know what you're asking for?"

"Everything you have."

In a blur of a second he had doused the wall sconces and locked the door. She was fumbling with the front laces of her new corset, her actions slowed by her weak hand. Simon accomplished the task with quick and nimble fingers, kissing her all the while. Her neck, her chin, her cheeks, her eyelids. His mouth skimmed over her face with butterfly kisses, so soft, so teasing. Astonishing that those barely there kisses invoked such an aggressive response. She fairly ripped Simon's shirt from his body. She most assuredly heard fabric tearing.

"So that's the way of it, pet."

A statement. Not a question. The breath whooshed from Willie's lungs as Simon backed her against the wall and yanked up her skirt. She felt his fingers stroking her bare inner thighs. She tensed, shocked when he homed in on her most sensitive and sensual region, his fingers teasing, rubbing. *Good Lord.* Her back arched as an erotic ache coiled tighter and tighter. Whilst one hand worked wicked magic on her nether region, the other hand caressed her breast whilst he kissed her senseless. Still mostly dressed, her clothes askew, Willie felt almost as exposed and brazen as if she were fully nude.

"Come for me, pet."

He had never called her that. He had never been this forceful. It drove Willie deliciously mad. Her body quivered and clenched as she acquiesced to her husband's bidding.

"Tell me your name," he ordered as she shuddered with a colossal climax. "Your name, dammit."

"Willie."

"So we are not finished, then. Marvelous."

Her mind grappled to make sense of his words as he swooped her off her feet.

A knock on the door. "Tea is served."

"Leave it!" Simon bellowed over his shoulder.

"That was rude," Willie whispered, half-dazed.

"He'll get over it." Simon bent her over the side of his massive bed. "Don't move," he ordered whilst ridding her of her boots, her stockings, her petticoats, her skirt.

Willie shivered with anticipation as he peeled each article of clothing from her body, and none too gently. At once she was completely naked, bare feet on the floor, torso plastered to his feathery soft mattress, her bottom scandalously exposed.

Simon trailed featherlight fingers over her shoulder blades, her spine. "Your name?"

"Willie," she whispered.

"Yes, well, remember you asked for this."

One palm at the small of her back, the other brazenly gripping her bottom, Simon slid into her from behind. The intrusion was shocking and welcome. She was slick with desire. Delirious with need. She groaned low with the initial thrust, then moaned, mewled, begging for harder and faster when his fingers twisted in her hair.

Scandalous.

Wicked.

She cried out in ecstasy, embarrassed by the vehemence but unable to temper her response to Simon's fervent and imaginative lovemaking. This was not the young, reckless man she'd fallen in love with twelve years past, but the experienced, confident man she'd fallen in love with all over again.

"Name?" he asked as she shuddered with yet another orgasm.

"Wilhelmina Darcy."

"Christ."

He lifted her and suddenly she was on her back, in the center of a wondrously masculine bed. Simon's bed. She realized in a far-off way that in all the frantic lovemaking he had been most careful not to harm her shoulder. That, in itself, heightened her senses. Along with the glorious feel of his tongue, lips, and hands honoring every inch of her body, pleasuring her in ways that made her cheeks flush and her pulse skitter. Just when she thought she would expire from the erotic sensations, Simon ceased his avid ministrations.

Her breath caught and her mind reeled. It was as though she was perched on a precipice, teetering on the brink of a breathtaking fall. The anticipation consumed her being, obliterated the outside world.

There was only Simon.

"Open your eyes," he demanded in a measured voice. "Do not deviate from my gaze."

She nodded, incapable of words. And then ... he did nothing. He held his magnificent body above hers, poised, promising wondrous pleasure yet not delivering. Her breath stalled in her chest, his gaze ... so intent, so unsettling.

And then she felt the tip of his shaft. The breach. The friction. She felt him moving inside of her—so slow, so controlled—and suddenly time ceased. She felt his hand moving over her mound, his fingers teasing her folds. He increased the pressure, making her crazy *there* as he drove into her with hard, unrelenting strokes in the other *there*. The orgasm was twofold. Earthshaking. Mind-bending.

"Name?" Simon asked in a gruff voice.

"Sorry?" Willie grappled to make sense of the query as her husband plunged deep and shuddered.

His release was fierce and loud. "Good Christ," he rasped.

A heartbeat later—or was it a lifetime?—Simon rolled to his side and pulled her into his arms. "Willie," he beckoned softly.

Body tingling, chest heaving, she struggled to engage her brain.

"Have you forgotten your name, pet?"

"Sorry?"

She thought she felt him smile as he pressed a kiss to her forehead. "Sleep well, wife."

CHAPTER 27

Bingham blinked up at a white ceiling, smelled antiseptic, and heard the steady thwacking of a ceiling fan. He'd expected to wake up in purgatory or hell, but a quick glance about confirmed that he was lying in a small, although private—thank God—hospital room.

"Doctor said you'd rouse sooner or later this morning. Glad it was sooner," Austin Steele said as he pushed through the door. "Don't fancy cooling my heels in Cunnamulla a third day."

Bingham tried to push himself up into a sitting position and almost passed out in the process.

"Easy, mate. You were gutshot. Lost a lot of blood. Lucky you're alive. If your bodyguard hadn't found you when he did—"

"That bitch shot me." Bingham palmed his sweaty brow and tempered his labored breathing as his last memories cleared. They'd been under attack. He'd commanded Renee to shoot at the enemy and she'd bloody well shot *him*. "She'll pay for this."

"Something tells me she paid in spades up front." Steele was hovering bedside now and scowling down at Bingham. "You hired me to deliver you to Queensland and I did. Even more so, I saved your sorry life. No need to thank me, mate, just pay me the other half of what we agreed on and I'll be on my way."

Bingham fisted clammy hands at his sides. "You can't abandon me in this godforsaken place."

"Cunnamulla's not as civilized as, say, Perth or Brisbane, but it is on the map and as close as I could get you to the last coordinates you gave me without forgoing professional medical aid. Your bodyguard, for all the good he is, alerted your captain of your location and situation. Northwood, I believe his name was, said to assure you he will be here within forty-eight hours. Don't rush recovery, do as the doctor instructs, and you may be up and around by then."

Bingham gritted his teeth. "My personal possessions."

Steele opened the drawer of the tall table next to the bed, handed Bingham his thick wallet.

"I'm surprised you didn't help yourself," Bingham said upon noting his booty was still intact.

"Not my way." Steele pushed his sweat-stained hat to the back of his head as Bingham counted out several large banknotes. "Just so you know, as a bonus for saving your life, I'll be taking Renee off your hands."

Bingham shot him a look. "She's a menace and you're a fool."

"I don't see it that way," the insolent man said whilst he tucked away the money. "Then again, I don't intend to bugger Renee. I like my women warm and willing and I sure as hell don't abuse them."

Bingham made a mental note to eviscerate this man at some point in time. Just now he simply wanted him out of his sight. "I don't suppose you garnered the information I asked for."

"Did better than that," Steele said as he strode to the door. "Found your Mod Tracker and roped him in. Job complete. Wish I could say it was nice knowin' you, Bingham."

He blew out the door and a second later another man crossed the threshold. "Lord Bingham."

"Crag." Finally something was going right. Maybe.

"Can you adjust this bed, these pillows? Something to elevate me."

"Certainly, sir."

Crag was every bit as rugged, weather-beaten, and common as Steele, but he, at least, was respectful. After cranking the top portion of the bed so that Bingham was no longer lying flat out, he poured Bingham a glass of water from the pitcher on the table.

Bingham took the glass, vexed that his hand was shaking and rattled by the severe pain in his abdomen. Fortunately Renee hadn't aimed higher or, God help him, lower. Considering, he supposed he was lucky she hadn't shot off his manhood. "What of Professor Merriweather?"

Crag swiped off his hat and sleeved sweat from his brow. "Sure you're up to hearing this?"

Bingham braced and soothed his parched throat with the cool water. "I take it you've lost him."

"More like someone stole him."

"Excuse me?"

Crag fingered the brim of his hat. "Merriweather was holed up in a makeshift compound with his daughter. That compound sits in the middle of a barren tract of land. Man nor beast could approach from any direction without being seen. Using a high-powered telescope, I kept watch from a secluded copse of trees. Traded shifts with my partner, Boyd. No one got past that fence without the gate being magically opened from the inside of the house. Merriweather must be some sort of technological wizard."

"Go on," Bingham said, fairly salivating at the thought of picking Merriweather's genius brain.

"Day before yesterday, a dark-haired man limped up to the gate."

Jules Darcy.

"I don't know where he came from. No land or air transport that I could see. He just appeared at the gate. Then . . ." Crag scratched his jaw, gave a nervous chuckle. "This will sound crazy. Next thing I knew . . . he disappeared before my very eyes."

"You're right," Bingham said, palming his bandaged stomach. In addition to the pain he was beginning to feel ill. "That is a preposterous statement."

"I scanned the area with my telescope, with my naked eye, and then with my binoculars. Know where I found the cripple? In the house. Speaking with Merriweather. Have no idea how he got in there. But I can tell you one thing. He never left."

"But you insinuated Merriweather is missing."

"He is. Along with the professor's daughter and the cripple. They were all in that compound. Now they're not. Boyd and I kept watch. Never saw them leave the grounds. But then as of yesterday, there wasn't a lick of activity within the house. Boyd and I even approached the fence, skirted the grounds, used our optical scopes to spy in every window. Either those three are dead on the floor or they're gone."

"Why didn't you go inside?"

"Can't get past that electrified fencing."

"Find a way," Bingham said. "Either they're in there or they got past you in the dead of night. Secure Merriweather, Crag. If you've lost him, find him. At the very least secure the contents of that compound. I intend to inspect that house for myself as soon as I'm on my feet."

Crag tugged his hat back on. "Whatever you say, Lord Bingham."

"Open that drawer," Bingham told the man, pointing to the table where Steele had procured his wallet. "Do you see my telecommunicator?"

Crag handed him the device, then moved to leave. "I'll be in touch."

"See that you are." He waited until Crag was gone, then thumbed a threatening coded message. He hadn't flown halfway around the world and survived a deadly storm, cutthroat bushrangers, and a gunshot wound to lose this race. If Jules Darcy had indeed absconded with Professor Merriweather, then it was time to light a fire under Wilhelmina Goodenough's sweet arse.

CHAPTER 28

Willie had been astounded by the enormous number of underground passages they'd discovered whilst scouring Montague Lambert's vast collection of maps. Phin had been right. London teemed with tunnels—ancient and new—as well as viaducts, catacombs, and subterranean crypts and vaults. Simon had been acquainted with random locations and specifics, and she'd soon realized it was because of former research and surveys he'd done in relation to his work as a civil engineer. One could not design and construct a building, bridge, road, canal, or railway without knowing the lay of the land. She had gotten a strong sense of his passion and experience when she'd first entered his library the morning after he'd pleasured her into forgetting her name.

"It's magnificent."

"It's a mess," Simon countered. "According to Fletcher."

"That is because he's so painfully neat," Willie said as she moved inside. "He does not understand the comfort of chaos. I do." Wide-eyed and charmed, she slowly toured about the dark-paneled library. A massive room with massive clutter. The floor-to-ceiling shelves were so crammed with books that many volumes were stacked on their sides. There were also piles of books on his ornate desk as well as on the floor. One wall boasted a huge and extensive map of the city, whilst another wall was covered in sketches and paintings of famed

global architecture such as St. Paul's Cathedral, the Vatican, and Notre-Dame. Willie also recognized several international engineering marvels—the Great Pyramid of Giza, the Great Wall of China, the Roman Colosseum, Stonehenge.

Along with multiple pencils and drafting tools, Simon's own sketchbooks were strewn everywhere—the desk, the chaise, two tables. Some journals were wide open, some closed, and a few lone sketches stood on easels. One in particular caught her eye. "Project Monorail?" she asked.

"Mmm."

She angled her head and studied the detailed sketch. An elevated railway system running through the heart of Westminster. Aside from the futuristic aspect of a smooth-nosed, streamlined train practically floating over the streets and gardens below, the attention to detail regarding Parliament, Clock Tower, and Westminster Abbey was quite astonishing. She'd never known Simon had such a flair for art.

He moved in behind her, the scent of fresh soap as potent as an aphrodisiac. Willie tried her best to ward off wanton thoughts. Most difficult considering their recent bout of love-making. All she could think was, More shocking variations, please, *and* How can I pleasure you, husband? *Simon had unwittingly unleashed a wild streak within her that she had no wish to tame.*

"What do you think?"

"Sorry?" Willie flushed and blinked out of her naughty musings.

"My design," he said. "Do you think it ridiculous? Intriguing? An eyesore?"

"Intriguing, to be sure." The train possessed no wheels and seemed to glide over a single track. "How does it operate?"

"A complex system based on magnetic levitation. I'll explain it someday if you like. When we're not rushed for time."

"I would like that very much." She turned in his arms and peered up at him with awe. "You are quite the visionary, Simon Darcy."

"My father thought so."

"Your father was right. Hang the Old Worlders who sabotaged this project. You must not give up."

"Yes, well, one challenge at a time, eh?"

And hence they'd spent several hours at Lambert's Literary Antiquities studying maps and making notes and thereafter almost two full days trudging through dank underground passages. Aside from several claustrophobic encounters, they had withstood everything from mud to cobwebs to spiders to rats. And of course dead people. Hordes and hordes of dead people. Not for the faint of heart. Fortunately, Phin and Simon were not easily spooked. Nor was Willie, for that matter. She was, however, discouraged.

"I don't see it," she said, studying another iron gate as well as peeking through the bars at the four coffins stacked on the shelves of two walls.

"Perhaps if you'd use the battery-charged torchlight I offered you," Phin said.

"I told you, I can see fine."

"Night vision," he said irritably. "Right, then. And how does that work exactly?"

"She told you before," Simon snapped. "She doesn't know exactly."

"We need to change tactics," Willie said, slumping back against a cold brick wall. "We need to narrow our focus. We're only two days into this search and we're already sniping at one another."

"I don't snipe," Phin said.

"The hell you don't," Simon countered.

"What? You think you're a ball of sunshine, Darcy?"

"It's the constant anticipation of being attacked like we were in Edinburgh," Willie said. "That's what has us on edge. Plus the constant dark and gloom. The tight spaces and odious smells. It's oppressive. Suffocating. Not to mention being surrounded by so much death. How did they stand it?"

"Who?" Simon asked.

"The Houdinians. *This* was my mother's life? Patrolling

a dank catacomb? Trading shifts with Filmore and Rollins? Hiding in the shadows and staring at a bloody coffin for hours, primed to o'blasterate any person who ventured too close?" Willie heard the hitch in her voice and cursed her lack of control. But by *God*. "How wretchedly pathetic."

"Or noble," Simon said, giving her shoulder a sympathetic squeeze. "And perhaps they did not and do not guard the engine around the clock, sweetheart. Perhaps that is precisely why they chose underground crypts as their *safe house*. Few people venture into these places."

Phin slouched against the wall next to her, flashed his torchlight on another gated vault. "You're quite sure you'd recognize it. The conveyance housing the clockwork propulsion engine," he clarified in a calmer tone.

"Aye," Willie said. "Filmore's memory was most vivid. Perhaps they utilize a different-looking conveyance in each city—whether it be a lone crypt or a coffin stacked into the walls like these—but the locking mechanism is constant and quite specific."

This moment they were in South London, exploring the catacombs beneath West Norwood Cemetery. They'd already tackled another catacomb this morning and had another two ahead of them. Willie's stomach cramped with the projected futility. Deep in thought, she gasped when she felt a strong vibration. Her coat pocket. The telecommunicator. Strangelove.

"What is it?" Simon asked.

"Nothing. I just . . . I need fresh air."

"We'll come with you," Simon said.

"No!" Willie instantly regretted the outburst. "Please," she added in a softer voice. "I need but a moment and there are still several vaults along this corridor. I've described the lock to you and Phin. Continue on. I'll rejoin you as soon as I catch my breath."

Simon balked.

Phin nudged him. "She's safer up there than down here." He looked to Willie then. "Are you wearing the stun cuff I gave you?"

She flashed her left wrist.

"Don't hesitate to use it," Simon said.

Indeed, she would not. Willie left without another word and hurriedly backtracked until her lungs filled with fresh air and her eyes gazed upon blue skies. She grappled with the telecommunicator, the code, her pulse revving when she deciphered the message.

LEST YOU DOUBT MY SINCERITY, CONTACT YOUR EDITOR.

Willie collapsed against the cool stone of an aboveground crypt. So. Strangelove had done something to prove he could and would crush her should she fail him. She didn't need to telephone Dawson to establish the damage, but she would. Eventually. For now she accepted on faith that Strangelove was a motivated bastard. Motivated and perplexing. Astonishing that the man had such unflinching faith that Simon would indeed locate and procure an invention of historical significance. The mystery hoodlum was fast becoming a source of intense vexation. Had he conspired against other Triple R entrants in this manner? Was he a rabid and slightly mad appropriator of rare antiquities? Did he mean to steal away famous artifacts for a private collection or perhaps to sell them upon the black market? Or was he simply after the monumental prize money and global glory? Surely he had not set his sights upon Simon alone. Surely he could not know for certain what invention Simon sought.

Or could he?

Willie massaged her aching heart, wishing she'd never buckled under Strangelove's threats. Yearning to come clean with Simon, but fearing he would never forgive her for setting out to betray him, no matter the reason. One thing was certain. He would never trust her again. Whatever it was between them that burned so bright would be forever dimmed.

She could not bear it.

At sea with her quandary, she caressed the wings of a stone angel. In a desperate plea for guidance, Willie prayed to someone, anyone, for direction.

One word, one name, flashed in her brain, a divine intervention. Heavenly direction.

Thimblethumper.

Stiffening her spine, Willie typed her coded reply into Strangelove's telecommunicator.

EXPEDITION FRAUGHT WITH MYSTERY. ATTEMPTING TO SOLVE.

A message meant to intrigue and pacify, affording her precious leeway. Strangelove had demanded an invention of historical significance. And that's what he would get. Somehow. Some way. But *not* the time-traveling engine.

A heartbeat later, Phin and Simon joined her aboveground. Their coats were smudged with grime and they smelled of dirt. Their dour expression spoke of yet another failed venture into yet another catacomb.

"Willie," Simon said.

She grasped and squeezed his hand. "I have a plan."

"I don't like it."

"So you said." Phin dropped a sugar cube into his coffee, looking annoyingly relaxed now that they'd emerged from the dank crypts and rejoined the living.

Simon, on the other hand, still bristled with ill humor. His own chipped crockery sat before him, the steaming bitter swill untouched. When they'd entered McSteam's Coffeehouse, Simon had requested a table near the window, where he could have a clear view of Thimblethumper's Shoppe of Curiosities. Willie was just now entering the cluttered store and Simon hated that he wasn't with her.

"Listen, good man, feeling protective of your wife is natural, but this need to be at her side twenty-four hours a day borders on obsession."

"Less than two weeks ago," Simon said, his gaze intent on the storefront across the street, "someone o'blasterated Willie."

"Yes, well, we're not down in the tunnels now."

"Two days ago she was mocked for being a Freak."

"Today she's wearing corneatacts," Phin reminded him whilst lighting a cigar. "She looks like any other Vic woman strolling the streets of London. If anyone bothers her, it will be to ask for the time. I've never seen so many bloody timepieces on one person."

"She'll need those if she time-traces Thimblethumper."

"I personally hope that she does," Phin said. "If she can glean more intelligence on Filmore and his habits, anything at all having to do with the Houdinians, then it could increase our chance of locating the man and the engine in a timelier fashion."

"I agree with the intent and goal," Simon said, ruffling his hair in agitation. "I simply wish I was with her."

Phin blew out a heady stream of smoke, whilst skimming a complimentary newspaper. "We're only across the street and she is armed with a stun cuff. Willie's a resourceful sort and damned smart. Give her some credit. I think her assessment of the situation was bang-on. From what you both said, Thimblethumper associates you with your brother and for whatever reason he feels hassled by the Mechanics. She stands a better chance of garnering information on her own using her tried-and-true methods."

"Maybe," Simon said, finally indulging in the piquant brew. But he couldn't shake the feeling that something was off with Willie. Something beyond her anxiety regarding her mother and the Houdinians. It made him question her judgment. Made him suspicious and restless.

"What a pungent and appallingly frowsy establishment," came a pinched, feminine voice.

Simon glanced up, saying, "Dr. Caro," at the same time Phin said, "Bella."

Never mind that Simon was surprised by the Freak doctor's personal visit, the informality of Phin's greeting was doubly intriguing. "You know one another?" Simon asked as he stood to greet the woman.

"Unfortunately," Caro said with a tight expression.

She looked exactly as she had when she'd visited Simon's room in Edinburgh. Ghostly complexion, bold red lip stain, glossy ebony hair twisted into a severe and complex knot. Purple-tinted spectacles shielded her kaleidoscope eyes, her riding hat sat a jaunty tilt, and she was buttoned neck to ankle in that black leather duster with the gleaming brass fasteners. Hauntingly beautiful, Simon thought, in a severe and repressed way.

Although with a delay, Phin stood out of respect as well. "Should have known you were Simon's contact within the agency."

"Indeed," the young woman said. "Then again, you were always slow at putting together two and two, Phineas. May I join you, Mr. Darcy? My time is limited."

Since Phin was Jules's closest friend and since Caro had been Jules's personal surgeon, it made sense that they'd met at some point, Simon supposed. The white-hot tension between them, however, was baffling. Although Phin offered her a seat, she instead chose to sit on the same side of the table as Simon.

Whilst those two traded steely glares, Simon glanced over to Thimblethumper's, his mind on Willie even though he was anxious for news of his brother. "I didn't expect a personal report," Simon said honestly as he moved in beside the stiff-backed woman. Much as Phin had advised Simon to trust that Jules was in control of his situation, he'd been unsettled by his inability to contact his twin via the tele-talkie. Yesterday Simon had buckled under an intensifying discomfort and had, after consulting the calling card she'd given him, telephoned Dr. Bella Caro.

She'd answered on first ring. *"Dr. Caro."*

"It's Simon Darcy."

"Who's dying?"

"I'm worried about Jules."

The woman's tone had been as cold as ice, but the mention of his brother's name had snagged her interest. Simon had asked whether she'd heard from Jules. If she knew where he was and if he was on official business. Simon had mentioned the tele-talkie and the fact that there'd been no response to his emergency calls in close to ten days. She'd said she'd be in touch. He'd expected a call, a telegram, or a Teletype. Now here she was in all her chilling arrogance.

"Would you like some coffee?" Simon asked.

"And risk contracting gastroenteritis or hepatitis?" she asked whilst frowning at the bare-armed, stained-aproned attendants and the dingy, battered surroundings. "No, thank you."

Simon noticed then that she was still wearing her gloves and seemed averse to touching even the tabletop.

"We're here for the location, not the ambience," Phin said, obnoxiously blowing cigar smoke in her direction.

"Willie's attending to some business in that shop across the way," Simon said, leaving it at that.

"I was sorry to hear that her recovery's been slow, but I did warn you," she said, sounding somewhat defensive.

"We're grateful for all you did," Simon said. "What have you learned of Jules?"

"Conflicting conjecture. I'm leaving for Australia within the hour."

Simon blinked.

"Did the agency sanction this jaunt?" Phin asked. "Or is this a personal mission?"

"I'm acting in Jules's best interest."

"Meaning?" Simon asked.

"If he is broken or malfunctioning, I am the only one who can fix him."

Simon frowned. "What the devil does that mean?"

"Never mind her," Phin said. "Bella has an unusual way with words and ofttimes speaks in a language all her own." He extinguished his cigar, narrowed his gaze on the pale-faced woman with the bloodred lips. "I'll fly you."

"Your piloting services are not required, nor your company wanted. I'm warning you, Phineas, stay out of this."

Even though Simon kept stealing glances at Thimblethumper's storefront, he was more than aware of the war raging between Phin and Bella Caro. He was also more concerned than ever about his brother's welfare. "Do you have reason to believe Jules has been injured?" he asked the doctor.

"I do not."

"But you implied—"

"I merely intend to ascertain Jules's situation and to make myself available should he need assistance."

Phin snorted.

"I must go," she said, gesturing for Simon to move out of her way. "Contrary to popular belief, I do have a heart. I did not wish to leave you wondering and worrying, hence this visit."

"You could have called," Phin said.

"That would have been unwise," she said, rising.

"What is the speculation?" Simon asked. "Within the Mechanics?"

Posture ramrod straight, expression enigmatic, she lowered her voice to a near whisper. "Some say his mission is known only to the director of HMM and the queen herself. Some say he has gone rogue." Her sensual lips flattened. "I'll contact you as soon as I know anything," she said to Simon, then turned on her booted heel.

For a moment he sat there stunned. "How can I know so little about my twin? What the hell is he about? What is *she* about?"

"Bella and I have our differences," Phin said, "but I can tell you this. She'd walk through fire for Jules. He's her greatest accomplishment."

"She loves him."

"Like Dr. Frankenstein loved his monster."

Simon shook off a chill, watching as Bella Caro glided past the window and disappeared into the throng of pedestrians. "What exactly is her supernatural skill?"

"Superhuman mentality. An intelligence quotient far above that of a genius."

He thought back to Edinburgh when she'd said Jules's legs had been blown off and just now, her concern that he could be broken or malfunctioning. Both she and Phin had waved off her odd word choices, but Simon suspected now that she meant exactly what she'd said. He met his friend's gaze, demanding an honest answer. "What is Dr. Caro's area of expertise? Specifically?"

Phin blew out a ragged breath. "Something called *bionics*."

CHAPTER 29

Upon leaving West Norwood Cemetery, the grave-poking threesome (as Willie had begun to think of herself, Simon, and Phin) had returned to the Covent Garden town house in order to wash away the odor and grime of the underground before setting off for Notting Hill. Fletcher had fussed over their "deplorable" outerwear, determined to pound away patches of dirt. Simon and Phin had ducked into the library to consult the city map, and Willie had slipped into another room to ring Dawson. Simon hadn't flinched when she'd said she needed to touch base with her editor. She was, after all, officially on the job.

"How are you faring?" Dawson had asked. "Please tell me you're in the midst of a rollicking adventure."

"You have no idea."

"Intrigue? Peril?"

"A brush with death and forbidden love."

"Brilliant!" Dawson had bellowed, no doubt punching his fist to his desk to emphasize his exuberance. "Readers will be enthralled. The *Informer* will flourish. I knew I could count on you, Willie. The Clockwork Canary at his best."

"Yes, well . . ." Adopting her former and feigned manner of speaking had proved surprisingly difficult. At some point she would have to come clean with Dawson about her true self, but for now, one challenge at a time. "I read about the attempted kidnapping of Prime Minister Madstone. Who did you put on the story?"

"Bloomenboyd."

"Bloo is a narrow-minded ninnyhammer."

"Everyone is a ninnyhammer in your book, Canary. Just carry on with Darcy and the Triple R Tourney and leave the delicious rest to me. There's a reason I'm managing editor."

Willie had been thrown by her extraordinarily ordinary discussion with Dawson. Had Strangelove's taunt been a red herring? "On the run," she'd said in her affected boyish tone. "What's the blether around the pressroom?"

Dawson had spewed a dizzying amount of gossip before ending with "But the latest kerfuffle revolves around an anonymous tip that there's an impostor on staff. Someone who's leading a double life. Naturally there is much speculation and imaginations are running rampant. Abbernathy started a betting pool. And before you interrupt," Dawson said, "yes, I know and quite agree that Abbernathy is a ninnyhammer. Still and all, a bit of intrigue and fun is jolly good for the spirits. Speaking of, you must be flying high with this Darcy assignment. Any scuttlebutt on Project Monorail?"

"Working on it. Speaking of, I best be off." Willie had ended the conversation quickly, her pulse pounding with dread. Strangelove *had* flexed his browbeating muscles. Since she intended to come clean with her identity the moment she'd completed this mission, she couldn't care less if anyone at the *Informer* pegged the Clockwork Canary as the impostor. She did worry, however, that Strangelove would step up his game and threaten the well-being of her family, which now included Simon.

Intensely motivated to manipulate the bastard toff and to bring this exasperating chapter of her life to a close, Willie had procured a secret keepsake from her cherished copy of the Book of Mods. Something with which to snag Thimblethumper's attention. As a bonus maybe she'd finally learn the name and purpose of the thingamabob she'd found tucked into a secret crevice when she'd painstakingly re-covered the book years ago in an attempt to disguise its true content.

Now, less than an hour later, Willie entered Thimblethumper's Shoppe of Curiosities with a dual sense of anticipation and dread. Call it a revelation, an epiphany, or divine intervention. Whatever the reason, she was most certain she would glean valuable information pertaining to the Houdinians from the former Mod Tracker. She'd bet her wedding ring, her most valued possession aside from her BOM, that Thimblethumper knew far more than he'd first shared. Considering he'd been guarded and crotchety after learning Simon had gotten his name from a Mechanic, Willie thought it best to start with a clean slate, as a new acquaintance.

Upon her last visit, she'd been introduced as Willie G. She'd been dressed as a boy. Her hair had been dyed black. She had slouched her shoulders and spoken in a lower tone, using a more brash vocabulary.

This moment her hair was a brilliant red and she wore a fashionable and shapely ModVic greatcoat and a feminine, accessorized derby. Instead of brown corneatacts, she'd opted for the color of her youth, the same vivid green shade as her mother's, and she planned to introduce herself as Mina. Her goal was to engage Thimblethumper in casual conversation and then to segue into a subject that would set her up to time-trace specific memories.

Her pulse skittered as she crossed the threshold. A bell tinkled as she shut the door behind her.

"With you in a moment," Thimblethumper called from the till.

"Just browsing," Willie called back.

He was speaking with another shopper and she preferred to have the merchant to herself. She'd wait until this customer left and pray for a slow period.

Willie pulled off her gloves and stuffed them in her pocket. She skirted a few tables, examining collectibles past and present, as well as a few reproductions of futuristic devices. Merchandise as described by the Peace Rebels or portrayed in the Book of Mods. She recognized a bong and a model of a moonship. Her mother had owned a similar model, a reminder of her time at NASA.

Intrigued, Willie skimmed more items—a jar of marbles, a

telephone with buttons instead of a dial, and a mug sporting the sign of peace—but spied nothing similar to the thingamabob in her purse. The thin black square was a little over twenty centimeters in diameter, near the size of the front cover of the Book of Mods, and had a hole in the center. When she'd first discovered it, soon after her mother's death, Willie had shown it to a few Mod enthusiasts, but no one recognized the article. Someone had likened it to a futuristic beverage coaster. Someone else, a durable page keeper or perhaps a portion of a modern ringtoss game. Willie had ended up tucking the black square back into its secret pocket, cherishing it simply because it had belonged to her mother— whatever it was. Perhaps Thimblethumper would have an inkling.

The sole customer, aside from her, brushed past Willie and out the door. Intent on taking advantage of the privacy, she pulled the plastic square from her sizable drawstring purse, turning just as the old Mod Tracker approached.

Thimblethumper winced as though slapped, stumbled back, and knocked into a table. "Mickey?"

Willie blinked at the sound of her mother's modern nickname. She grasped Thimblethumper's arm as he tripped over his own feet, connecting not only physically, but mentally.

"There was too much information for one disk. This is but one of three."

"So the Aquarian Cosmology Compendium is in fact a trilogy?" Mickey said. *"Where are the other two volumes?"*

"As far as I know, Professor Merriweather is still in possession of one disk. The other he entrusted to Dickey Everest."

"Dickey was killed last month."

"I know."

"So where is that disk?"

"I don't know. Maybe someone stole it. Maybe he hid it. All I know is that I don't want the responsibility anymore. As if protecting the clockwork propulsion engine isn't enough. I've been saddled with this additional enterprise for twenty

*years. I'm too old for this cloak-and-dagger bullshit. My eye-
sight is going and my reflexes are poor. I want out, Mickey."*

"But you're a pledged Houdinian."

Willie broke contact and blinked out of the memory, her
chest tight, her heart racing. Out of habit she glanced at her
time cuff, but since she hadn't checked the time before tracing, she could only guess how long she'd been in this man's
memory. Three seconds? Five? He was staring at her now
as if in shock. She was more than a little stunned herself.
"Ollie Rollins," she choked out. She'd seen him in Filmore's
memories, but as a much younger man. The years had not
been kind.

He licked his thin, chapped lips. "How . . . how is this
possible? You're dead."

She realized then that Thimblethumper, *Rollins*, still
thought she was her mother. Michelle Goodenough had
had red hair and green eyes and she was probably around
Willie's age when she and Rollins first met in the future.
Worried the man was on the brink of having a heart attack,
Willie corrected his misassumption. "My name is Wilhelmina Goodenough, Mr. Rollins. I'm Michelle . . .
Mickey's daughter." Her previous plan of how to handle
this situation had been blown to smithereens. Like any
good journalist, she would now operate on the fly.

Rollins pushed his thick spectacles to the top of his balding head, shut his milky eyes, and rubbed his wrinkled lids
as if trying to dispel a hallucination. "Lock the door."

Willie rushed over and turned a locking mechanism. She
also flipped the WELCOME sign to CLOSED.

"How did you find me?" he asked, his weight propped
against a table. "Where did you get the memory disk?"

So that was what it was called. "My mother bequeathed
me her copy of the Book of Mods. The . . . *disk* was hidden
in a pocket devised into the inner cover."

"I can't decide if that was a brilliant or hideous place to
conceal such dangerous and valuable information. And it's
been in your possession these past seven years?"

"It has." One-third of the legendary Aquarian Cosmology Compendium. Willie was beyond incredulous. "I have some questions, Mr. Rollins. Some concerns."

He winced, looked over his shoulders in a cautious and worried manner. "Please. I am known as Thimblethumper now."

She nodded. "You are retired. No longer an active Houdinian and afraid of being publicly branded a Mod. I understand."

"No you don't. No one understands. No one is capable of understanding what I have seen. What I have done. I want only to live out what is left of my life in anonymity. But I will answer your questions, Wilhelmina Goodenough," he said whilst pushing off the table and gesturing her to follow. "Out of respect to your mother and because I sympathize with your dismal and colossal responsibility."

She did not understand how an innocuous black square translated to a collection of scientific designs from the twentieth century. She could not believe her mother, a woman who had been so emotionally and physically distant, had entrusted her daughter to keep something so valuable and volatile safe. As Willie followed the retired Houdinian, an original Peace Rebel, to the back of his shop, her heart swelled even as her knees quaked.

"Willie just turned the 'Welcome' sign to 'Closed,'" Simon said, whilst peering across the street. "Why?"

"To assure privacy?" Phin ventured.

"I don't like it."

"Of course you don't." His friend gestured for an attendant. "Something stronger," he ordered.

"I'm sorry," the female server said with a tight smile, "but we don't—"

"Of course you do," Phin said, flashing a banknote.

"One moment," she said, then scurried off.

"I'm going over," Simon said.

"Don't be a mug," Phin said. "Give Willie a chance."

Being likened to a half-wit chafed, but Simon recognized the good intention behind the cocky slur. *Relax and show trust in your wife's abilities.* Simon tried but to no avail. He'd allow Willie ten more minutes and then he was busting in. "Tell me about Dr. Caro."

"What about her?"

"Jules's lover?"

"For a time."

"Your lover?"

"No. Although I was tempted."

Intrigued, Simon raised a brow.

"When Jules backed off from the affair, Bella turned to me. For a cool and aloof woman, she's extremely . . . passionate. I almost succumbed to her wiles, but then I realized she was only using me to make Jules jealous."

"Did it work?"

Phin shook his head. "Jules cares about Bella, but he doesn't love her. Although, damn her obsessed heart, she believes otherwise."

"What led up to this?" Simon asked, an ancient and buried question flaring back to life. "Why was Jules declared a war hero? What did he do and why is he living a double life?"

Phin rolled back his shoulders, obviously relieved when the server returned with their heavily spiked coffee. Simon could smell the whiskey fumes even before raising the cup to his lips.

"Not within my power to reveal details pertaining to the mission that led to Jules's injuries nor his affiliation with the Mechanics," Phin replied. "However, I will say this. A lesser man would not have survived or fought as fiercely as he did to live. The only time his spirits flagged dismally was after the reconstructive surgery."

Simon and his family had been barred from visiting Jules for several weeks. The extent of his injuries too severe, they'd been told. The risk of infection via outside sources too great. Early on they'd seen Jules only through a window and at a distance and only from the chest up. Their visitation rights during rehabilitation had been rigidly restricted as well, but part of that had been due to Jules's determination to push through the ordeal in private. It had been a trying time for the Darcys. Most especially for Simon, who'd felt literally severed from his twin. Respecting Jules's *privacy* had proved one of Simon's greatest challenges in life. Knowing Jules had chosen a friend as a confidant over his own brother stung Simon to the core. But he didn't blame Phin. "What can you tell me of the reconstruction?"

"Bella . . . Dr. Caro exacted drastic measures to save Jules's life and, as it were, to make him whole again. After spearheading a mind-boggling surgical procedure, Bella pushed forth therapeutic measures. She made it her personal mission to convince Jules that although he was not wholly normal, he was fully functioning by normal standards."

"Are you saying he feared he'd lost the ability to make love to a woman?"

"More like he'd lost the desire. He felt like a monster."

"I don't understand."

Phin downed the rest of his whiskey-laden coffee, then leaned forward, gaze intent. "For the most part, Simon, Jules's legs are not his own."

Simon struggled with the sickening revelation. What the devil would it feel like to lose part of oneself? No wonder Jules had been adamant about his privacy. Simon would have reacted in the same exact fashion. Yet the man did in fact *have* legs. Or rather some extraordinary facsimile. "Artificial limbs?"

"Highly advanced prosthetics."

Simon thought about his Thera-Steam-Atic Brace. Although the device wasn't *highly* advanced, it had proved astoundingly advantageous in Willie's efforts to regain strength and mobility in her arm. Simon wished he would have been the one to devise prosthetics for his brother, to enable Jules to walk again. Although he acknowledged that his engineering skills were not as honed then as they were now. And, no matter how advanced his creation, it would not compare with prosthetic limbs as engineered by someone with superhuman intelligence. "Bionics," he said, repeating the word Phin had mentioned before, a term that meant nothing to Simon.

"I don't profess to understand it," Phin said. "I don't think anyone does. Or can. Aside from Bella. And, much to the disappointment of the Mechanics, she has yet been able to duplicate the process."

"So Jules is one of a kind."

"And extremely valuable to the agency. I find it hard to believe they'd send him on a mission they didn't believe he could return from."

"Why are you telling me this, Phin? Why now?"

"Because *Jules* has doubts regarding his return, and if the subject regarding his surgery came up, he wanted you to know. At least as much as I know. Which is, quite frankly, only basics."

Simon dragged a hand down his face. "Swear to God this is like something out of one of Jules's science fiction novels. Damned hard to believe. I assume these bionic prosthetics are what make Jules so invaluable to the agency." He frowned. "Yet he walks with a limp."

"A glitch Bella has yet to modify. A glitch that disappears when the prosthetics are fully engaged."

Simon wondered if he could vanquish that glitch. He'd die for a chance to try. Senses buzzing, he leaned forward and lowered his voice even more. "How does bionics enhance Jules's worth, Phin? What is he capable of?"

"Superhuman speed. Brace yourself, brainiac. He can move from here to there so fast, it renders him invisible."

Hence Jules's ability to disappear before Simon's very eyes. "Bloody hell."

CHAPTER 30

By the time Ollie Rollins, former Houdinian, former Mod Tracker, current rueful *traitor*, slipped out the back door, leaving Willie alone in his Shoppe of Curiosities, her brain was overloaded and reeling. She'd committed everything the frazzled Peace Rebel had said to memory. *Her* memory. She intended to share everything she'd learned from Rollins, aka Thimblethumper, with Simon and Phin.

All but the existence and purpose of the memory disk.

Willie still could not fathom how detailed scientific data had been transferred to the black square in her purse. What she did understand was that one needed a specific kind of computer to read the stored memories, and such a complex machine, capable of processing arithmetic and logic operations and comparable to those of the mid-twentieth century, had yet to be devised. That said, a breakthrough was imminent. The scientific community had been dabbling with the technology as inspired by the brilliant Vic Charles Babbage and influenced by a corrupt few Mods for several years. Were it not for the oppressive restrictions and nonexistent funding of key Old Worlders, advanced computers could well be a wonder of *now* instead of the *future*.

As it stood, according to Rollins, the memory disk was like a cylinder or record disc without a Graphophone—useless. He had also emphasized the possibility that the disk had corroded and thereby been corrupted by time and elements, making the information *unreadable*. Quite possibly, most possibly, the plastic square within her possession was defective. However, there was a slight chance, an off chance, a small percent chance, that the memory disk was in perfect order—even after thirty-one years.

Willie preferred the former scenario. She preferred to believe the disk within her possession was faulty because her intention was to present this artifact to Strangelove as the technological historical invention of significance. The Aquarian Cosmology Compendium was legendary and, according to rumor, existed, whereas the clockwork propulsion engine had been destroyed. *Supposedly.* But of course Strangelove would be pleased to possess the ACC, which contained a gold mine of information regarding the construction of technological wonders. She could well imagine that arrogant and ruthless man having delusions of grandeur, imagining himself as some sort of technological lord of the universe. Oh, aye, the memory disk was indeed her ticket to freedom. As soon as she met Strangelove's demand, she would be out from under his thumb. Her family would be safe and she could sort out her new life with Simon.

Simon.

As a brilliant engineer, surely he would be most keen on studying the legendary compendium. Without a doubt he would resent Willie for robbing him of the chance. She quelled her bucking conscience by reminding herself that there was no way to *access* that data. Simon wasn't missing out and Strangelove would not benefit.

On the wild chance Strangelove *did* procure access to a futuristic computer at some point, and if by a long shot the memory disk *was* functional, chances were still one in three that the data compiled and entered regarding studies on Briscoe Darcy's time machine were not stored on *this* particular disk, but on one of the other two volumes. Worst-case scenario, she thought as she left the shop, Strangelove would access information that would enable him to build a rocket ship, thereby shooting him to the moon or beyond. That did not seem a bad thing.

"I hope the information you gleaned was worth the several heart attacks I suffered whilst you were lollygagging with Thimblethumper," Simon said, sweeping in beside Willie as she walked briskly to the corner.

"Leave off, Darcy," Phin said good-naturedly as he took up pace along her opposite side. "Can't you see she's bursting with news?"

"Of course I have news," Willie said as they hurried toward the station for the underground that would take them to Simon's town house. "I am the Clockwork Canary."

She wasn't sure why she'd felt compelled to tout her famous moniker. Perhaps because Simon's admonishment rubbed her the wrong way. Lollygagging, her arse. She'd been working.

Simon started to say something, then thought better of it.

"Right, then," Phin said. "A subject best discussed behind closed doors."

Securing seats on the underground transit, they fell into a charged silence and Willie pondered Simon's sour mood. No, not sour. Anxious. Restless. Intense. Deep down she understood that he'd been worried about her, but Willie couldn't abide someone breathing down her neck, questioning her judgment. She'd been operating on her own for years. She was smart. She was savvy. And, damnation, she was skilled. True, time-tracing gave her an advantage and, aye, an unfair edge, but regardless, she was quite good at procuring sensitive information utilizing her brain and wit.

By the time they reached Covent Garden, Willie had worked herself up to a frightful huff. Part of her wanted to blast Simon and his possessive tendencies, whilst the other part itched to share a goodly portion of what she'd learned from Thimblethumper. She was still debating her choices when Simon prodded her over the threshold of his home, blast him.

Fletcher took their coats and announced a forthcoming evening meal. Simon begged Phin's pardon, then whisked Willie upstairs and into the library. "Too long." ·

"What?"

"The suspense. The waiting. You took too bloody long with Thimblethumper. Don't do that to me again, Willie."

"I cannot promise."

He backed her against the wall displaying the ancient wonders of Egypt, China, and Rome. "Is this what I have to look forward to?" he asked. "Standing by whilst you indulge in your unique interviews? Worrying that you might get distracted, that you might interact and somehow lose yourself in another person's mind?"

"In all the years I have been time-tracing, in all the thousands of instances," Willie said, "only once was I distracted and that was by my mother. I know what I'm doing, Simon."

"Maybe now. But what about two years from now? Ten years from now? You said it yourself. A Freak's supernatural gift strengthens and intensifies with age. Your ability to time-trace could spiral out of control."

"And you could contract some hideous disease. That is what *you* said." Fists clenched at her side, chest heaving, she gave her obnoxiously controlling husband what-for. "How dare you manipulate me into marriage with sweet words of support and understanding regarding my gift only to snatch them back days later!"

Hands braced on the wall on either side of her head, Simon leaned in, eyes sparking. "I did not manipulate you."

"I beg to differ." She ignored the sensual ache coiling in her stomach. Being stimulated by his intimidating manner was beyond perverse. Disgusted with herself, she rallied. "You discombobulated me beyond measure, Simon Darcy. Turned my head with sensual kisses, seduced my soul by pretending you accepted me for who I am."

"I do accept you, dammit."

"Yet you're asking me to ignore a vital part of who I am. I am a Time Tracer. You knew this when you married me. Not that the marriage is binding."

"One tiff and you're ready to forsake our vows?"

"I'm not forsaking anything," she said as her heart cracked. "I am merely pointing out the disgusting reality of our circumstance."

"Do tell."

"I am a Freak and you are a Vic and an official union is forbidden."

"Yes, well. Some of us color outside the lines."

"Meaning?"

"I am not willing to live my life as ordered by someone else. Are you?"

"No. No, I am not. That is why I am telling you to bugger off." Before he could respond, Willie ducked under Simon's arm and out the door. Never could she recall being this angry, this hurt. Except for that day twelve years past when she thought Simon had jilted her. She resented the power he had over her. The way he could make her feel. The things he could make her do.

She'd been confident attacking life as a male Vic. Simon had tempted her to embrace her true gender and race. She'd fallen for his utopian views. She'd put him on a pedestal above all other Vics. Her heart had proclaimed Simon Darcy different, but her heart had been blinded by love. Aye, *love*. There was no skirting her situation. She loved Simon Darcy. She was in love with Simon Darcy. Blast and damnation, she had always and always would love Simon Thomas Darcy.

But that didn't mean she had to like him.

The infuriating sod caught up to her before she descended the stairs. He touched her arm. "Willie. Wilhelmina," he amended in a gentler tone.

"Phin is waiting," she said without turning. Just now she wanted nothing more than to distance herself from Simon and the emotions ravaging her soul. Between the enlightening discussion with Ollie Rollins and the volatile confrontation with her husband, her mind and heart were spectacularly overtaxed.

"Whatever you learned from Thimblethumper, is there anything to be done about it today?"

"No," she said, spine stiff. "Still—"

"Phin!" Holding Willie steady, Simon glanced to the bottom of the stairs, casting his friend a meaningful look when he appeared at the landing. "We'll be picking up on this tomorrow."

"Right, then," Phin said with a nod. "I'll be on my way as soon as I wrangle my coat from Fletcher. On the morrow, then." The man flashed Willie a sympathetic smile, then disappeared around the corner.

Willie whirled on Simon, eyes narrowed.

"Before you accuse me of being rude," he said, "let me assure you Phin understood. We need to be alone, Willie. We need to work through our differences instead of walking away or counting on Phin to act as a buffer."

Another reproach? Her temper sizzled and snapped. "Had you not attacked me the moment I emerged from Thimblethumper's—"

"I apologize. I did indeed initiate this argument, albeit unwittingly."

Frowning, she shook her head. "Why . . ." She looked over her shoulder just as Fletcher let Phin out the door.

The caretaker cast a disapproving glance Simon's way, prompting Simon to hustle Willie back into the library. "The longer you kept me waiting at McSteam's," he said in a measured tone, "the longer I had to envision a time-tracing venture gone wrong. Not just with Thimblethumper, but with future transmitters. My imagination got the best of me, as did my frustration. When you emerged from the shop unscathed . . ." He closed the door behind them, visibly tempering his emotions. "I cannot explain the fathom of my relief."

"Yet you admonished me! In front of Phin, no less!" Willie paced, hoping to walk off her animosity. Indeed, she felt like a walking powder keg with a short lit fuse. "Then once home—"

"I know. Apparently love has a way of skewing one's senses."

Willie stopped in her tracks. She slowly turned to face the man who consistently charmed her with amorous words and kind gestures, only to disappoint on a whim.

He held her gaze, looking somewhat tortured yet sincere.

"I love you, Wilhelmina. I fell in love with you twelve years ago and that love never died. Nothing can crush it. Not even, as you say, our disgusting circumstance."

Heart pounding, she balled her fists at her sides. How she'd longed to hear a declaration such as this, but just now the sentiment rang false. "Sugar words to dilute the bitter *tiff*? Your timing is appalling bad, Simon."

"It is," he conceded, "the bane of my existence. Nevertheless . . ."

Willie ached to stalk past her husband and out of the room. Or to back away and to pace to the window. But her traitorous body stood its ground as Simon closed the distance and took her into his arms. Her smitten heart skipped as she melted under his touch and rested her cheek against his chest. "I'm still angry," she said in a weary voice.

"I'm still wrestling with volatile opinions regarding our future."

"I cannot repress my gift."

"I cannot help but worry."

"I will not sever my ties with the Freak Fighters, nor ease off our fight for equality."

"Again, I cannot help but worry."

"I will not bend to your every demand."

"I only ask that you bend now and then to my concerns." He gently gripped her chin and bade her attention. His expressive gaze locked with hers and her knees fairly buckled under the intensity of his regard. "I am and have always been a spontaneous sort, ofttimes speaking without thinking. As Fletcher pointed out, I am not easy to live with, Willie. Then again, neither are you."

Her damnable heart fluttered. "Are you suggesting a compromise?"

"I'm asking that you trust my good intentions."

His heartfelt request summoned a twinge of guilt and obliterated the last of her ire. Initially she had succumbed to Strangelove's threats in order to protect loved ones, and now she schemed to pay off that wretched man with the legendary compendium in order to protect loved ones. She schemed behind Simon's back in order to procure the clock-work propulsion engine, to protect mankind, and to champion Simon, his family, and her father.

Good intentions.

Heart and mind reeling, Willie rose up on her toes and brushed her lips across Simon's tantalizing mouth. "As you must trust in mine."

Suddenly she wanted nothing more than to seal the love he'd professed. To steer Simon's thoughts beyond their disagreement, beyond their challenging future and her present deception. She could think of but one way to distract her husband beyond measure.

Determined, Willie deepened the kiss, anxious to soothe her soul and to addle Simon's senses.

Chapter 31

Deceit.

As Willie leaned into Simon, as she intensified the kiss she'd initiated, he swore he tasted deceit. Absurd that her fervid affection should leave an unpleasant tang in his mouth, yet he could not dismiss the feeling that this was a calculated seduction. That she wished to distract him with sex, to turn his thoughts away from . . . *what*?

This was not the first time that Simon sensed Willie was keeping secrets, but it was the first time he sensed a deliberate and colossal betrayal. What he did not sense was malevolence.

Wary, curious, he disentangled her hands from his hair and eased away with a raised brow. "Should we proceed down this path, I'll end up taking you on that Oriental rug," he said with a nod, "or perhaps over the back of the sofa. It would seem my passion where you are concerned runs unchecked."

"If you meant to dissuade me with that threat, you should rethink your tactics, Simon."

"Simply warning you that at this rate I cannot promise we'll make it to the bedroom."

"Why delay what burns between us now?" She gripped his lapel with one hand whilst using the other to palm his arousal through his trousers. "I have heard it said in the pressroom that some of the most astonishing . . . *alliances* occur after a heated row."

Stirred by her boldness, Simon nipped her earlobe and palmed her rear. "I shudder to think of all you heard from other men whilst masquerading as a man yourself."

"Consider it an education."

"I strive not to consider it at all," he said whilst leaning into her brazen touch. It still chafed that she had felt compelled to deny her gender and race all those years. Nor did he enjoy contemplating the rows she'd no doubt encountered whilst incognito. A man did not dwell in London or circulate in skytowns without engaging in confrontations of some form or fashion. But of course she would have developed a fierce independent streak as a layer of protection. Even now, when she no longer needed to go it alone, the Canary persisted in flying solo. How the devil could he earn her confidence? Her unadulterated trust? Bad enough that his brother had kept him in the dark regarding intimate details of his life. By God, he would not be shut out or misled by his enigmatic wife.

As her seduction grew more bold, Simon embraced his own calculated agenda. How better to weaken her defenses than to pleasure her senseless? She thought to distract or somehow manipulate him with sex? "Fair warning, pet," he said as she loosened the buttons of his trousers. "You're playing with fire."

"Warning noted and rejected."

Simon escaped her touch and, after locking the double doors, plucked her off her feet and backed her against the massive wall of books. Their kiss was wild, their actions frenzied. There would be no foreplay this moment, no lingering or teasing caresses. Simon pushed up her skirts as she struggled with his trousers.

Her hand around his rock-hard shaft.

His hand up her silky drawers.

She wrapped her legs around his waist, and cupping her backside, Simon plunged deep. One swift stroke and then another. He made love to Willie with primal urgency, his thoughts ash as his blood burned. He felt her clenching around him, felt her body trembling as he stroked her to orgasm.

Harder.

Faster.

Novels and scientific journals tumbled about them as he nailed his beautiful and perplexing wife against the over-crowded literary shelves.

Deeper.

Slower.

One last thrust . . .

She cried out and he held still. Held back as she shuddered with a tremendous and lingering climax.

Heart pounding, Simon nuzzled her ear. He'd only just begun. He would unravel this woman. He would know her secrets. Motivated by love, driven by passion, he would strip away years of deception and cynicism and lay bare her heart and mind. "I suggest we retire to the bedchamber."

"I have no need of a bed."

At once she slid from his body and to the floor, to her knees. Sweet Christ, she took him in hand, working magic on his throbbing member. Adjusting pressure as she stroked, fingers gliding, lips . . . "Ah." His knackers tightened and his heart stilled when he felt the warmth of her sweet, sassy mouth. At this rate, she would have the best of him in three seconds. "No."

Simon swept her up and laid her back on the rug, shoved her skirt and petticoats to her waist, and buried his head between her legs. "This." He ravished her with his mouth. His tongue, his teeth, his lips. He savored. He tortured. He endured as her fingers bit into his shoulders, as they clutched at his hair and pulled, as she bucked wildly beneath his erotic ministrations. When she peaked, his pulse raced and the need to possess her completely, to find his own release, burned with a vengeance. He thought to take her again here, now, sprawled on the floor or perhaps on her knees, but then it would be over much too soon. Where lovemaking was concerned, Willie had made her adventurous streak clear. Her curiosity and ravenous appetite challenged his normally versed control.

"I want you naked," Simon said, tugging her skirts down and his trousers closed. "Now."

Chest heaving, she blinked up at him in confusion and he

wrestled with a moment of self-recrimination, knowing he was halfway to pleasuring his wife into mental and emotional submission. Believing he had her best interest at heart and prompted by bone-deep passion, Simon snuffed the flames of guilt licking at his conscience.

Sweeping Willie off the floor and into his arms, he stalked out of the library and across the hall, locking them in his master bedchamber. Setting her to her feet, he lazed against the wall with a cocky grin and a lustful gleam in his eye. She'd started this game, but he was the master. If she thought to take charge, she best think again. "Strip."

Muted golden light seeped through a crack in Simon's drawn curtains. Light from the newfangled electric lanterns lining the street in front of his town house.

Willie blinked into the darkened room. When they'd tumbled into this bed, it had been early evening—predusk. Their lovemaking had been shockingly intense, each vying for control. Simon's stamina had been absurdly and wonderfully impressive. No matter her efforts to unhinge him completely, he had rallied and turned the tables, pleasuring her again and again. When she'd been too sated, too weak in the limbs and mind, to counter with her own passionate assault, only then did he surrender to his own need.

She did not remember drifting off. She knew not how long they'd been asleep. It was all she could do to remember her name.

Wilhelmina Darcy

Her eyes burned with sudden emotion, her heart squeezed.

She had taken Simon's name without pledging her love, and even now, even after he'd declared his affections, even now as she lay in his bed, in his arms, a dazzled and dazed recipient of his spectacular lovemaking, Willie had not spoken her heart. She had never considered herself a coward, but in this instance she could not deny her bone-deep fear. She was too unsure of the future to commit her feelings aloud. Speaking her heart would be opening her heart to possible obliteration. Staying silent afforded her a chance to live in denial, should the worst happen. As a writer she could imagine endless scenarios that would involve being ripped or thrown from Simon's life. Her chest ached at just the thought of it.

"What's wrong?" Simon tightened his hold and stroked a hand down her bare back.

How could he know her misery? Her head was tucked beneath his chin and although her mind had raced, her body had been most still. "How long have you been awake?" she asked, without looking up.

"A while."

"Why did you not stir?"

"Given our extreme alliance," he said with a teasing smile in his voice, "I am not sure that I can."

She snorted lightly against his chest. "I'm certain you have exerted similar energies in similar circumstances."

"There have been no similar circumstances."

That brought her head up. "Knowing what I have heard, what much of London gossips about, do you really expect me to believe you've led a chaste life?"

"Certainly not. But there has been no one like you. No interludes that can compare."

Willie's heart fluttered as she gazed upon his handsome face, into his earnest eyes. Her night vision ensured that his expression was indeed sincere. "In our long yet spotty association, you have said some wonderfully sweet things, Simon Darcy, but that is by far the most romantic."

His brow furrowed. "More romantic than my declaration of love?"

"Let us not speak of love."

"I know you care for me, Willie. I know you desire me. And I know, once upon a time, you loved me."

"Travel down this road if you wish," she said, pushing off his hard, warm body, "but I shall not join you."

Simon caught her hand. "What are you afraid of?"

"Losing you," she said honestly, then broke free and rolled out of bed. She pulled on a shift and dressing gown just as Simon flicked on an incandescent lamp. She felt even more vulnerable, knowing he could now read her expressions clearly. She felt unhinged by their lovemaking and by his emotional commitment. She felt like a despicable rat for not telling him about the portion of the Aquarian Cosmology Compendium within her possession or about her plan to surrender the memory disk to the horrible man who'd threatened her loved ones and livelihood. However, she did not trust Simon not to intercede. He would want to protect her and he would want the ACC. Meanwhile the clockwork propulsion engine would be at risk.

Surely she was right to proceed as planned. Appease Strangelove with the compendium, locate and surrender the clockwork propulsion engine to the Jubilee Science Committee. Queen Victoria would order the engine hidden away, under lock and key. Simon would claim the Triple R Tourney prize, ensuring the financial welfare of their families and restoring glory to the Darcy name. Aye, she would do well to focus on the greater good.

She realized then that Simon had pulled on loose silk trousers and a robe as well. He knotted the sash whilst stepping into a pair of slippers. Was he walking out on their argument? On her? "Where are you going?"

"I don't know about you, but I worked up an appetite and we missed dinner. I can promise you Fletcher set something aside." Simon moved closer and pulled her into his arms. "I say we raid the kitchen and discuss whatever you learned from Thimblethumper. The sooner we submit the engine to the science committee, the sooner we can get on with our life. The sooner you'll realize I'm not going anywhere."

She wanted to believe, was desperate to believe. She'd been living on her own for so long—her mother gone, her father distant, her brother estranged. She'd trusted no one with her true identity or race—no Freak, no Vic—and therefore no friends. Phin had become her friend and Simon . . . She smiled up into his eyes. "I find I am indeed most famished."

"It's settled, then." He gave her waist a squeeze, guided her into the hallway . . . and straight into Fletcher.

Willie yelped and Fletcher, who balanced an oil lantern in his hands, gasped.

"For God's sake," Simon said to the man whilst flicking on an electric wall sconce. "Step into the new age, man, and stop skulking about like a character in a gothic novel."

"I do not skulk," Fletcher said. "And I do not see the need in lighting up the house like a Christmas tree when a lone lantern will illuminate my way."

"Very practical," Willie said in the man's defense. She realized then that Fletcher was staring at her. Self-conscious, she smoothed a hand over her bed-mussed hair, but then realized her eyes held his attention. She'd forgone her corneatacts.

"Ah," was all he said.

"I hope this won't present a problem," Willie said outright.

"No problem," Simon said. "Right, Fletcher?"

The stiff-postured man raised one brow. "You won't make it rain inside the house when you're feeling melancholy, will you, ma'am?"

Willie's lip twitched. "That would be within my brother's power," she said. "But not mine."

"You're not one of those shape-shifters I heard about, are you? I would not be keen on cleaning up the shedding fur of a wolf or some such."

Smiling now, Willie hugged herself, feeling somewhat exposed in her morning gown. "I promise you, I do not shed, Fletcher."

"Then I foresee no problem, Mrs. Darcy. I'll see to your dinner now," he said with a curt nod.

"No need," Simon said. "We're on our way to raid the pantry."

"I see."

"But you don't approve," Simon said with a grin. "Go back to whatever you were doing, Fletcher. I thank you, but we're fine."

Willie admired Simon for not taking advantage of hired help. She liked not having to hold to strict conventions. The undercurrents of true friendship between these two very different men bolstered her outlook on a more utopian state where Old Worlders and New Worlders, Vics, Freaks, and Mods could coexist equally.

Fletcher stopped midway to the servants' stairs that led to an upper level. "I say, Mrs. Darcy, are you able to move objects with your mind?"

"Telekinesis?" She shook her head. "Definitely not."

"Pity. It would have been a boon in helping to clean up the mess Mr. Darcy will no doubt make of my kitchen." With that, he disappeared up the stairs in a haunting wash of flickering flames and shadows.

With the distinct impression that she'd been officially welcomed into this household and accepted by yet another Vic, Willie's spirit soared.

"Fletcher may be mired in old ways," Simon said as he guided Willie to the landing, "but that vexatious coot has a big heart."

"He heard that," Willie said with a slight smile.

"I heard that," Fletcher echoed.

CHAPTER 32

"So what did you learn from Thimblethumper?" Simon asked as he seated Willie at a small table in the kitchen.

"My findings were quite astonishing and somewhat complex. Would you like me to help you?" she asked as he rooted through cabinets.

"You concentrate on expediting our expedition; I'll manage dinner." No matter his good intentions, using sex to ply Willie's secrets had been a rather seedy affair. In the end he had not been able to take advantage of the moment. Instead of questioning her in the aftermath of their mind-bending alliance, he'd held his curiosity at bay whilst she'd drifted to sleep in his arms. At this point he was sailing on a wing and a prayer that she would come clean of her own accord. "Go on, then. Astonish me."

Willie blew out a breath. "Let me preface this by saying most of what I learned resulted from a live interaction prompted by minimal time-tracing."

Simon glanced over his shoulder. "In other words, your interviewing skills are as honed and beneficial as your supernatural gift. Noted and acknowledged."

She smiled a little and his heart skipped. Christ.

"Bear with me," she said, "whilst I try to report my findings in a succinct manner. There was much to absorb, and dare I say, I believe you will be as shocked as I was by this revelation."

Simon couldn't think of anything more shocking than learning his brother was some sort of bionic man, but he held his tongue and set out plates and flatware.

"I'll start with the most surprising discovery," Willie said. "Thimblethumper is in fact Ollie Rollins."

Simon nearly fumbled a fork. "The missing Houdinian?"

"Indeed. If you recall, I had mentioned that I had seen Ollie Rollins in Filmore's memories and that he looked familiar. That is because I'd met his much older self in person only a couple of weeks prior. He's been living under the alias of Thimblethumper for the last several years."

Simon frowned. "Why didn't Jules tell me this straight out?"

"He did not know. Thimblethumper shared a plethora of information with the Mechanics, including names and descriptions of prominent Peace Rebels—such as Professor Maximus Merriweather—in exchange for being set up with a false Vic identity and business. He also spilled the beans regarding the existence of the Houdinians, but he never admitted to *being* a Houdinian. Like Filmore, he'd been utilizing aliases for years. Hence, he dangled a carrot in front of the Mechanics whilst leading them on a bit of a merry chase."

So, Simon thought, she finally knew for certain the agency Jules worked for. If she was vexed with Simon for withholding that detail, she did not show it. Indeed, Willie seemed fully focused on her unfolding tale. He raided the icebox—chicken, cheese. "If Thimblethumper, that is, Rollins, set the Mechanics on the trails of his own people, then he must be the traitor your mother referred to in your father's memory."

"A logical assumption," Willie said as she worried the edges of a linen napkin. "Except Rollins didn't seek the protection of the Mechanics until *after* my mother's death. It was then that he felt most vulnerable. Then that he saw the world as he knew it crumbling around him. Her death is what drove him into informing on other Mods—although he swore he never put another PR in harm's way. He cooperated with the Mechanics because he was desperate to live out his remaining days in peace. The same reason he resigned his post with the Houdinians in the first place."

"He resigned?" Simon asked. "Whilst your mother was still alive?"

"Aye."

"Perhaps that was enough for her to label him a traitor. After all those years, to suddenly break their sworn pact. To leave the protection of the engine to her and Filmore alone. Surely she felt pressured and betrayed."

"Probably." Brow furrowed, Willie reached for a slice of fresh bed and slathered it with butter.

Simon didn't comment when her right hand fumbled a bit, but damn, he worried that her injury still caused her difficulty.

"So much information and still so many holes," she said. "My mind is awash with summations and theories. And Rollins was only helpful in certain aspects. He seems to be teetering on the edge of a breakdown."

"All the more reason not to be alone with the man again," Simon said earnestly. "If he snaps—"

"Warning noted," Willie said, his eyes narrowed.

"Easy."

"Sorry." She shook off her irritation whilst Simon poured them each a glass of red wine.

"Perhaps we can fill in some of the gaps together." He took his seat and together they sampled bits of Fletcher's delicious fare. "We have our three Houdinians. Your mother, a security specialist. Filmorc, a pcace activist—"

"A radical peace activist," Willie said, whilst picking at her cold chicken. "A professor who specialized in political science, most specifically sociology. Quite brilliant, according to Rollins. Definitely paranoid and, at this point, dangerously unstable. Driven to compulsive, obsessive behavior due to the extraordinary failure of the Peace Rebels and his solitary focus upon protecting the clockwork propulsion engine. Believing he is a vital force in nurturing mankind, he has now taken the role of protector to the extreme—the sole guardian with the aid of an occasional mercenary."

"Sounds like a bloody lunatic. Although that's often the case with fanatics." Simon staved off thoughts of pulverizing the man who'd been responsible for Willie's near-fatal injuries. Instead he focused on everything Willie had learned. Impressive that she'd convinced Thimblethumper/ Rollins, the tight-lipped curmudgeon, to be so damned forthcoming. "How does Ollie Rollins fit into this?"

"He was one of the several Americans who'd united with the Brit faction of the Peace Rebels. A mechanical engineer and a fierce and loyal supporter of Professor Jefferson Filmore and his high-profile lectures regarding the end of the world. Filmore was a most passionate and persuasive man. Again, according to Rollins.

"On the day the Peace Rebels voted to destroy the Briscoe Bus," she went on, "Filmore convinced my mother and Rollins that it was in the best interest of mankind to preserve the engine that had catapulted them through time. As you had pondered, Filmore foresaw the need for a backup plan. An escape pod, should things not work according to plan. A way to travel even further back in time—in the name of global peace. Filmore, who had indeed had an intimate liaison with my mother," Willie said, cheeks flushing, "and who continued to command her devotion and allegiance even after they were no longer intimate, knew he could trust Mickey to devise a security plan to keep the engine safe. At the time Rollins had also been under Filmore's charismatic and idealistic spell and had fallen hook, line, and sinker for the professor's backup plan. When and if the time came that the trio felt compelled to activate their emergency exit, Rollins would build the vehicle and install the engine."

"Yes, well, things did go wrong," Simon said. "Abominably wrong. Instead of changing the world for the better, the Peace Rebels instigated a global political divide as well as a transcontinental war." He sipped his wine, marveling as always at the mayhem. "Why didn't the Houdinians jump dimensions in an effort to right that wrong? That *was* the motivation behind their pact, yes?"

"Aye." Willie nibbled on bread and cheese, then lingered over a long drink of wine.

Simon could tell she was fighting to mask her emotions,

to remain objective. Her journalistic training at play, no doubt. Or perhaps her pride. However, he sensed a hint of melancholy, as if all this knowledge weighed heavily upon her heart. "Perhaps we should leave the rest of this story until morning."

"No. Let us press on. I'm fine. Truly. Just sorting through my memories. Thimblethumper—*Rollins*—rambled most vigorously as though confessing a lifetime of sins to a priest."

Simon topped off her wine, noting that in the midst of the upset and intrigue, he had never felt more settled. Yes, he was worried about Jules. He worried about the financial fate of his mother and sister. He worried about Willie and her father, and his own future as a professional engineer. On a grander scale, he harbored anxiety regarding the intolerance of Freaks as well the fate of the world should the clockwork propulsion engine fall into unscrupulous hands. So much unrest, and yet this moment, in this small, warm kitchen partaking in a cold meal with his intelligent, beautiful wife, Simon felt very much at peace.

"Rollins said the Houdinians were essentially paralyzed by the Peace War," Willie went on as if garnering a second wind. "They wanted to stay and help their fellow Mods. Those who had not been corrupted and remained true to the cause. Those who still thought they could make a positive difference. Those who refused to abandon this time even if they had the chance.

"But then when the dust settled," she plowed on, "and it became apparent that the Peace Rebels had perpetuated everything they stood against—civil intolerance, political corruption—and had perhaps set the future on an even more abysmal course . . . when Mods and their Freak offspring became the focus of derision instead of curiosity, those that had survived the war went into hiding. Some continued on a corrupt course, selling advance knowledge and expertise. Some merely tried to integrate into society, living under false identities. Others, like Professor Merriweather, went on the run and continue to run. Filmore deemed it time to utilize the Houdinian backup plan. To escape and start over in another time, but Rollins declared himself too old and too weary and my mother . . ." Willie licked her lips. "Rollins said she refused to abandon her children, nor would she risk hopping dimensions with them, fearing they, Wesley and I, might not survive or that time travel would somehow mutate our already altered genes even more."

"So she chose you and your brother over the cause," Simon said, knowing that must have touched her deeply.

She nodded, eyes bright. "Apparently so."

Simon had never once questioned his own father's love and support. And though his mother was somewhat aloof in nature, he trusted in her affections. Never had he been so aware of his good fortune. Humbled, Simon reached across the table and clasped Willie's hand. Because of her time-tracing gift, her parents had held her at bay. Was it any wonder she guarded her heart so fiercely? "Why didn't Filmore make the jump himself?"

She sighed a little. *Exasperated? Weary?* Another sip of wine and then she rallied on. "Rollins thinks it boiled down to a few factors," she said. "First of all, he wouldn't get far without a vehicle that was compatible with the clockwork propulsion engine, and Rollins refused to construct one."

"Surely another twentieth-century engineer could have performed the task. More than one arrived here on the Briscoe Bus," Simon said whilst stroking her knuckles.

"Aye, but Filmore trusted no PR outside of the Houdinians. Rollins said as the years progressed, Filmore became more and more paranoid, always spouting one or another conspiracy theory. He also believes that Filmore was secretly afraid of landing in an unfamiliar time on his own. When you think about it," Willie said, "that is a daunting adventure indeed."

"Briscoe did it. And Jules is about to do it," Simon said, gut cramping. "If he hasn't already."

"Aye, but Filmore strikes me as someone who cannot operate without minions, so to speak. Rabid followers. Devoted admirers. People who hang on his every word. Even living undercover he chose a job where he could talk people's ears off, the pub bartender who enraptured patrons with passionate, exaggerated ghost tales."

"Must have knocked him off-balance," Simon said, "losing Rollins, and then your mother."

"According to Rollins, Filmore went a bit batty after my mother died. Even though he'd respected my mother's marriage to my father, he'd harbored . . . affections. It seems to me a most complex and muddled relationship," Willie said. "I don't need to make sense of it, I just want to ensure that the clockwork propulsion engine doesn't fall into dangerous hands. Neither I nor Rollins deem Filmore the best person for the job anymore."

"So you're stepping into your mother's shoes as guardian of the engine?" Simon asked.

"Not forever," Willie said, catching and holding his gaze. "Just until the engine is safe. As far as I'm concerned, this Triple R Tourney is a godsend. The Jubilee Science Committee will guard that engine as keenly as the Tower's yeomen guard the crown jewels. Once it is presented to Queen Victoria during the jubilee, given Her Majesty's disdain for modern technology, she will no doubt have it locked away. Aye. That will be the way of it," Willie said. "The engine will be as protected as a royal secret."

Either that, Simon thought, *or the queen would order someone to destroy the engine.* That notion vexed on multiple levels. Mind reeling with his brother's predicament as well as Willie's latest findings, Simon downed the last of his wine. "So we're back to scouring a plethora of catacombs in search of the engine."

"No." Willie squeezed his hand. "There is a spot of good news in all of this. Rollins promised to intercede."

"The revolving safe house." Simon all but thunked his own forehead. "But of course, Thimblethumper—hell, *Rollins*—would know the precise London location."

"*If* Filmore maintained protocol. Rollins ventures he has not. What he is certain of is his ability to track Filmore."

"So we wait."

"Hopefully not for long. Perhaps even as soon as tomorrow."

"Then by all means we should get some rest," Simon said, noting the weary set of his wife's shoulders. "I'm eager to leave this particular adventure in the dust."

"As am I," she said with a smile that did not reach her eyes.

Simon reached for the platter of half-eaten chicken, then paused upon noting Willie's queer intensity as she stared at their dirty plates. "What are you doing?"

"Testing my supernatural ability on the off chance that it has manifested in a way that would please Fletcher."

"Telekinesis." Simon's lip twitched. "In which case these plates would now be flying across the room and into the sink." He raised a brow. "Doesn't seem to be working."

"No," she said, her kaleidoscope eyes sparking with a hint of humor. "Pity."

CHAPTER 33

An entire day and night had passed since that bastard mercenary guide, Austin Steele, had abandoned Bingham in Cunnamulla. Since "the Rocketeer" had taken Renee with him, Bingham had been left without a confidant. He wasn't about to engage the bodyguard who'd failed to protect him from getting "gutshot" in conversation regarding sensitive information. Nor could he discuss his thoughts and concerns with the doctor or nurses who'd been attending to his god-awful wound. He'd dispatched his Mod Tracker, Crag, to infiltrate Merriweather's compound and to determine the status of the professor and his daughter as well as the damnable meddling Jules Darcy.

Crag's findings had been disappointing, not to mention perplexing. The compound had been deserted. No sign of a living soul. Nothing of value left behind, yet no trace of evidence explaining how or when the trio had escaped. It made no sense and Crag's ineptitude only enraged Bingham more.

We'll just have to wait until one of them slips up and shows his face, Crag had said. *I tracked Merriweather before, I'll track him again.*

Meanwhile time was ticking, and for all Bingham knew, Jules Darcy had already coerced Merriweather into re-creating a working time machine. Question was, what did Darcy intend to do with the outlawed vehicle?

"Damnation!"

Impatience ripped through Bingham like a firestorm. He had not traveled this far, nor taken such risks, to be outfoxed by one of Reginald Darcy's offspring. How was it possible that the dotty old inventor had sired three highly industrious and intelligent spawns? Yes, Bingham had hoped one of the three would ferret out pertinent information or an actual device as created by their distant cousin, but he had also counted on snatching that data or device from their clutches. Thus far, events were unfolding in a most displeasing way.

Amelia Darcy had failed to produce an invention that would further Bingham's cause. Jules Darcy had quite possibly stolen Merriweather's knowledge and intellect from beneath Bingham's nose. The unknown variable this moment was the other son, Simon. Desperate to know the civil engineer's progress, he tried his telecommunicator for the hundredth time this day.

Still dead.

Blast!

He knew not whether the device was malfunctioning, or the area was simply too remote to support the requisite signal. Just as he was ready to throw the blasted gadget against the wall, someone knocked, then stepped inside.

"Captain Northwood," Bingham said. "Thank God."

Within the hour Bingham had left that wretchedly primitive hospital in the dust and had boarded his beloved *Mars-a-Tron*. Once in the air and back in charge, his mind cleared, as did radio transmissions. He waded through several coded messages, adrenaline surging when he spied news from Wilhelmina Goodenough.

Bingham smiled. He should have known the engineer would have sought out the Aquarian Cosmology Compendium. No doubt Miss Goodenough had played a major role in the recovery of the elusive journal. After all her mother had been an original Peace Rebel, a specialist in matters of security.

"Good news?" Northwood asked from his console.

"Excellent news from London."

"Should I set a course for home, sir?"

"Continue as instructed." Bingham could not leave without inspecting Professor Merriweather's compound first. There was, after all, a possibility that Crag had missed some clue. Meanwhile, England was several days away and Bingham worried that Goodenough might bobble the deed, allowing Simon Darcy to submit the ACC to the Jubilee Science Committee. As the anonymous benefactor, Bingham had commanded a first look at all submissions, but he was out of the country and he did not trust the committee's director to sit on such a momentous discovery. P. B. Waddington had proved to be a competent subordinate thus far, but he was also a man of science and a loyal subject to the Crown. At this point, Bingham trusted no one. But there was someone he could count on to procure the ACC from Miss Goodenough and to keep it hidden and safe until Bingham's return.

A mercenary Freak ruled by greed and vengeance. A young man who'd been manipulating the weather to advance the plundering exploits of the Scottish Shark of the Skies—compliments of Bingham. Considering Captain Dunkirk had failed Bingham in a monumental way and knowing the man would welcome a chance to benefit again from Bingham's power and wealth, Bingham sent a tantalizing directive, engaging the infamous sky pirate and his secret weapon—the *Stormerator*.

GREATER LONDON

Willie had spent the last day and a half on pins and needles awaiting word from Rollins. Oh, how she wanted to revisit Thimblethumper's Shoppe of Curiosities, but Simon had thought it best not to pressure the old man.

He promised to intercede, Simon had said, *on behalf of his fellow Houdinian and old friend's daughter. He said it could take a couple of days. Patience, sweetheart.*

Yet Simon had been equally tense, poring over various sketches of his inspired designs in order to distract himself from thoughts of the Triple R Tourney as well as his brother's mysterious circumstances. To Willie's dismay, he had shut away his sketches of Project Monorail, deeming that idea dead in the water. A failure. She did not agree, but she did not press. Not now. Not when he was so worried about his brother. In addition, though he'd been told his sister and mother were in London, he had not been able to locate them, nor had they phoned or stopped by. Aye, they thought he was aboard the *Flying Cloud* and in pursuit of a legendary invention. Still . . . not to check in with Fletcher in hopes of obtaining news of Simon's progress and safety? Unfortunately, Willie understood her husband's concern.

Meanwhile Phin kept in touch, also awaiting the news from Rollins that would alert them as to their next step.

Willie relied on her acting skills to present a strong and confident front, although she was most certain Simon and perhaps even Phin saw through her facade. In truth, she was scared spitless. She had sent a message to Strangelove informing him that she was in possession of the ACC. She had not heard back. Did he not believe her? Had the transmission failed? Was he at this moment en route to meet her face-to-face? Surely he would not do so without warning. He would not want a confrontation with Simon. He would simply want the priceless, legendary compendium.

This moment, she had taken sanctuary in Simon's library . . . along with Simon. Fletcher had made his opinion known regarding Willie's "organized chaos" and was in the process of putting the master bedchamber to rights.

Let us keep the chaos to the library, shall we? he'd said with a sniff.

Whilst Simon sat at his desk tinkering with her Thera-Steam-Atic Brace in an attempt to make it even more effective, Willie pored over her journal trying to pen an exhilarating yet tasteful version of their adventure thus far. If they did not win the Triple R Tourney prize, she wished to contribute to their financial standing in her own way.

Chronicling a tale that would captivate the whole of Great Britain might well ensure her job with the *Informer*, even after she disclosed her true gender and race. A long shot, but as a way of advancing a more utopian future, she had made a personal pledge to adopt a more optimistic outlook.

The telephone rang and Willie nearly catapulted from the pillow-laden sofa. She had provided Rollins with Simon's telephone number as well as his address, although she had not mentioned Simon by name.

"Hello?" Simon said into the mouthpiece—ambiguous as they had discussed. "Miss Goodenough? Yes. Hold on." Brow raised, he passed the receiver to Willie.

Holding Simon's supportive gaze, she willed her hand not to tremble. "Miss Goodenough here."

"Thimblethumper calling."

"I'm glad. Good news?"

"There's a skytown hovering southeast of London. Ask around for specific coordinates. Meet me at nine p.m. in the Vulcan Grogshop aboard the USS *Enterprise*."

"Aye, but—"

"Don't be late."

"Eight oh five," Phin said as he steered the *Flying Cloud* toward a pier floating alongside their appointed destination. "Unfashionably early."

"Better safe than sorry," Willie said, noting her dual timepieces. "Rollins sounded nervous and he was most adamant about punctuality."

"Feeling anxious myself." Simon squinted through his goggles at the transient skytown and the banner that declared this airborne mecca as *The Milky Way*. "I'm not crazy about you going into that pub alone."

"The USS *Enterprise* is famous for its international captain and crew," Willie said as she studied the collection of rigged airships. "Somewhat like the crew of the American courier ship the *Maverick*."

"Captained by the Sky Cowboy," Phin said as he docked. "Didn't you interview him once?"

"I did," Willie said, hugging herself against the frigid air.

"Tucker Gentry is a fugitive from justice," Simon said, cringing at the thought of Willie mixing with a murderer.

"He's an innocent man wrongly accused of a hideous crime."

"How can you be certain of his virtue?" Phin asked.

"I traced his memories."

"Bloody hell," Simon mumbled. Gentry had been a former US air marshal. He'd wrangled with heinous outlaws. The man was no stranger to mayhem and bloodshed. Surely his memories mirrored a gruesome battlefield.

"I merely meant that the USS *Enterprise* fosters a mixed clientele even more so than other digs in various skytowns. The Vulcan Grogshop is a popular watering hole for Freaks. I'll be amongst my own kind."

"Some of which could be the more dangerous faction of the Freak Fighters," Simon pointed out.

"No more dangerous than the rabble-rousing Vics who board these skytowns looking for a hell-raising good time," Phin said. "Don't flash that piece I gave you, brainiac, but remember what it's for."

Willie frowned up at Simon. "You're carrying a gun?"

"A Disrupter 29," Phin answered for him. "A peashooter compared to what I've got holstered beneath my coat, but it'll make a point. Give me your wrist," he said to Willie.

"I see no need for a stun cuff," she said.

"I do," Simon said.

"You're not going into that pub unarmed," Phin said.

"Wear the cuff," Simon said, "or I'm coming in with you."

"In which case Rollins might spot you." Scowling, she offered her left wrist to Phin. "I won't have the two of you scaring him off."

"Rollins has never met me," Phin said. "I'd just be another face in the crowd."

"Phin's right," Simon said. "Change of plan. I'll lurk outside as agreed, but Phin's going inside." He raised a hand to cut off Willie's counter. "Bend to reason, I beg you, or we're shoving off here and now."

She huffed but nodded and Simon breathed easier. "Thank you."

Together they disembarked and navigated the swinging gangway that led to the largest of the five dirigibles—*Jupiter 2*. As usual on any skytown, they were met by a costumed greeter.

"Peace and love, dudes and dudette. Welcome to the Milky Way."

Simon swiped off his goggles and squinted at the long-haired, cannabis-reeking hippie. "Woodstock?"

"Gadzooks," Willie said, pushing her sunshades to her forehead. "You're right. What are you doing here, Bear?"

"Which is it?" Phin asked. "Woodstock or Bear?"

"Both," Simon and Willie chorused.

"Ohhhh . . . woooow . . ." Bear drew out each word as though operating in slow motion. "The skittish fox and the uptight hound. Cooooool." He pushed his tinted glasses up his nose. "Edinburgh was a drag, so I thumbed a ride down to London. Hooked up a job in this skytown for a spell. What are *you* doing here?" He looked from Simon and Willie to Phin. "Bored with the fidelity thing and broadening your horizons?" He waggled his brows. "The more the merrier. That's my motto."

Phin coughed.

Willie dipped her chin.

"Good God, man," Simon said. "Could you just point us to the nearest coffeehouse. Preferably one on this ship."

"Sure thing, dude. Java Jupiter. One deck down. Fab bean juice. Bitchin' band."

"Right, then," Phin said with an eye roll. "Off we go."

"Which way to the USS *Enterprise*?" Willie asked.

"Three digs over, chick-a-doodle." He gave them the two-finger salute. "Peace out."

"Every time I step foot in a bloody skytown," Phin said as they hastened belowdecks, "I feel as though I've ventured into another world."

"That's because you have," Willie said. "I rather like it."

Simon tried not to fixate on all the times Willie had visited skytowns on her own to mix freely with other Freaks. It wasn't *her kind* that worried him, although he wasn't happy about her scheming with Freak Fighters. His deepest concern regarded the reprobates and outlaws that typically sought refuge and recreation amongst these floating pleasure meccas. Outlaws like the Sky Cowboy, to name one. Amelia used to hoard penny dreadfuls exploiting the adventures of that Wild West air marshal before and after his fall from grace. He'd never understood glorifying dubious personages—although that *had* been a specialty of the Clockwork Canary.

The smell of coffee grounds, whiskey, and marijuana wafted down the dimly lit corridor, as did the blaring sounds of an electrified band. A style of music perpetuated by the Mods—something called psychedelic or *acid* rock. As it happened, Simon was a fan. The complex song structures, artful rhythms, and emotional lyrics were preferable to the other Mod genre—folk music. Growing up, Amelia had latched on to that oddly cheerful antiwar tune, "If I Had a Hammer," and Simon and Jules had thought they'd go mad from their sister's incessant singing.

With his hand at the small of her back, Simon guided Willie into Java Jupiter, surprised at how crowded the coffee house was for this relatively early hour. The intimate room was packed with men and women alike. Half dressed in traditional Vic clothing, whereas the other half leaned toward moderate to extreme ModVic with a few costumed oddities thrown into the mix. The *bitchin' band* was but a trio, although their musical equipment took up a good portion of the raised stage. A small area had been cleared in front of the stage and a few ModVics engaged in free-form dancing, jerking and gyrating in scandalous manners that would shock Her Majesty the Queen into heart palpitations.

"Have you ever danced like that?" Willie shouted over the musical chaos.

"I was roaring drunk at the time, but yes."

"Was it fun?"

Simon smiled down at her. "Yes."

She smiled back as they wove through the crowd, finally locating an empty table close to the stage.

Phin swept off his bowler and stuffed a ripped paper serviette into his ears.

Simon didn't blame him—the volume of the music was deafening—but he refrained from making a visual spectacle of himself. He offered to help Willie off with her coat, but she politely refused. Nor did she remove her decorative derby. He knew her mind. She was anxious to be off to the Vulcan Grogshop. He preferred she wait here, with him, until closer to the appointed meeting time with Rollins.

"Coffee, please," Willie said when their server appeared.

"Side of weed?" the young woman asked. "Absinthe? Opium-laced cigarette?"

"Just coffee."

"Same here," Simon said.

"Make that three," Phin shouted.

"You'd enjoy the music more if you accentuated your bean juice with a mind-bending substance."

"Enjoying the music just fine," Simon said. He'd indulged in the past, along with a rather rowdy pack of friends. The effects were not displeasing; they were, however, compromising. A state he could ill afford this night. Or any other, now that he had a wife to look after.

"Squaresville, but whatever." Dressed in a gauzy shapeless dress, the doe-eyed girl disappeared into the crowd.

The rock trio segued into a ballad, a beautifully haunting piece, and the bodies on the dance floor doubled.

"I say," Phin shouted over the drone of the bass guitar and the screeching organ. "That young chit looks exactly like Amelia."

Simon looked to where Phin pointed. Short in stature, her normally coiled blond curls cascading down her back, a corseted tail-vest worn over trousers... By God, it *was* Amelia. In the middle of the dance floor canoodling with some man. Simon's temper flared as the cheeky bloke smoothed a hand down her back, his palm resting a scant inch from her backside.

"Bloody hell!" Enraged, Simon catapulted out of his chair and, in the blur of a second, separated the pair, slamming his fist into the lecher's hard jaw.

The stranger plowed into a slew of hippie impersonators and landed on his arse.

Amelia screamed.

The music faltered.

And Simon was instantly surrounded by several men pointing nasty-looking weapons in his personal direction. Drawing his *peashooter* in retaliation seemed absurd. Hopefully Phin had his back.

"Simon?" Amelia gawked at him, her eyes wide in shock and sparking with, of all things, *indignity.* "What's *wrong* with you?"

"You know this scalawag, Flygirl?" This from the stranger rising from the floor and working his offended jaw.

"My brother," she huffed, cheeks blazing. "Simon Darcy."

"In that case," the man said, his American accent grating, "holster your weapons, boys."

"Who the devil is this man?" Simon asked his sister.

"My husband."

Simon's blood boiled. "Since when? I don't even know this bloke. For Christ's sake, Amelia!"

"Don't be swearin' at Mrs. Gentry." This from a broad-shouldered, ill-tempered-looking man with a cigar clamped between his teeth. A man who'd yet to lower his enormous gun.

"Gentry?" Simon's stomach knotted as he took a second look at the man he'd coldcocked. The American accent. The Western boots and the cowboy hat. "Oh, hell, no, Amelia."

"I warned you, fancy pants," cigar-man said.

Out of nowhere Willie moved in, rainbow eyes swirling with fury. "Step off, you overbearing sod."

"And if I don't?"

Willie clipped him with her stun cuff and the big man wilted like a rain-deprived flower.

Amelia squealed, outraged. "What the . . . who the devil are *you*?"

Willie squared her shoulders. "Your brother's wife."

Simon appreciated Willie's staunch proclamation, although her penchant to save him in risky circumstances battered his male pride.

Amelia whirled and nailed Simon with a look of astonishment.

Gentry studied Willie, then rubbed his jaw whilst peering down at his odious cohort. "Zapped by a Freak. Axel's gonna be fit to be tied when he rouses."

"In that case," Phin said, calmly stepping in, "perhaps we should sort this out in private."

Amelia whirled again. "Phin?"

Gentry's eyes narrowed. "Phineas Bourdain?"

Phin raised one brow. "You know of me?"

Gentry responded by knocking Phin off his feet with a wicked roundhouse.

"Bloody hell," Simon said to his sister. "You told your husband Phin stole a kiss?"

She gave an innocent shrug. "He wasn't my husband at the time."

CHAPTER 34

After much hullabaloo, the proprietor of Java Jupiter had shown the vexatious rabble-rousers, as he called them, to a private salon at the rear of the small coffeehouse. Though Willie longed to sort through this family mess, she was immensely concerned with the time. According to her time cuff it was half past eight. Shouldn't she be making her way to the USS *Enterprise*?

Tucker Gentry's crew—StarMan, Eli Boone, and Birdman Chang—had remained in the main room trying to rouse their boneheaded mate, the ship's engineer, Axel O'Donnell. Phin had been shut out of this meeting as well and was currently nursing his bruised jaw and pride with a shot of whiskey.

Seated across from Amelia in an upholstered booth, Willie tried to focus on her sister-in-law's (good God, she had never thought to have a *sister*) animated rambling regarding her exploits over the last two weeks. Against her brothers' wishes she had joined the Triple R Tourney, taking off on something called a kitecycle and nearly crashing into the *Maverick* midair. She'd lassoed the Sky Cowboy into her search for a legendary invention, their adventure had taken them to France, then on to Italy and then, following an international *incident*, back to England—their penance doled out by none other than Queen Victoria.

"And that is how we came to be wed," Amelia said matter-of-factly.

"By royal decree." Simon drummed his fingers on the

table, his expression somewhere between astounded and explosive.

"She would have married me regardless, Darcy. Eventually," Gentry said. "We're very much in love."

"Astonishing, but true," Amelia said with a smitten smile. She leaned into her husband and the handsome crack aviator wrapped his arm about her in a possessive manner that warmed Willie's heart.

Simon, on the other hand, looked as if he wanted to strangle the both of them. Bad enough his little sister had married a notorious rake and purported outlaw, but they'd embarked on a spectacular adventure that dazzled and shocked far more than anything Simon and Willie had experienced in their venture thus far. At least in Willie's eyes. It was just the kind of story that would rivet the readers of the *Informer*, and indeed, Willie was considering asking the Gentrys' permission to weave their adventure into her chronicled serial. Although she'd probably opt to temper the portion about the *Maverick*'s physician, a Freak named Doc Blue, who'd betrayed them in support of his brother, a volatile Freak Fighter. As if the Freaks needed more bad press.

She glanced at her time cuff, deeming the serial a subject best approached later. She shifted in her seat, eyed the door.

"Are we keeping you from something?" Amelia asked, brow raised.

"As it happens, I have an appointment."

Simon consulted his own watch. "Willie's right. We should go."

Amelia gawked. "Surely you jest! I explained my circumstances and now you think to leave me dangling regarding yours? You claim to be married, yet how can this be, Simon? Marriage between Vics and Freaks is forbidden!"

"Yes, well, sometimes one is inclined to thwart the law," he said, looking directly at Gentry.

"I told you," Amelia said. "Tucker is innocent. Queen Victoria believes him."

"As do I," Willie said as she slid from her seat.

"You seem familiar to me, Mrs. Darcy," Gentry said as he, too, stood. "Have we met before?"

"Please call me Willie. And, aye, we have met. I interviewed you once." Her cheeks burned with the past deception. Her male guise, her probing of the cowboy's memories without his permission. "You knew me as the Clockwork Canary."

Gentry merely angled his head as though absorbing and reconciling the Freak woman he saw before him with the so-called Vic male who'd written a story about him months before.

Amelia, however, took a menacing step forward, fists balled at her side. "*The* Clockwork Canary? Lead journalist for the *Informer*? The insensitive sensationalist who maligned my *father*?"

"I can explain."

Amelia launched forward like a human cannonball.

Willie swore she felt the brush of the woman's knuckles as her fist swung past her nose. The only reason the blow didn't land was that Gentry had caught her by the waist and hauled her back in the nick of time.

"Easy, Flygirl."

"Dammit, Amelia." Finessing Willie behind him, Simon dragged his hands through his already disheveled hair. "I can explain. *We* can explain all of this. But not now. Willie has an appointment with a man who's going to relay the location of the clockwork propulsion engine."

Still holding tight to his wife, Gentry tipped back his hat. "The time-traveling engine from the Briscoe Bus? It was destroyed—"

"No, it wasn't," Willie said. "That was a ruse concocted by a renegade trio of Peace Rebels. One of them being my mother. As Simon said, we can explain, but . . ." She glanced at her time cuff.

Simon checked the safety mechanism on his derringer.

Amelia palmed her forehead. "What in the devil are you doing with a Disrupter 29?"

"Making a point if need be," Simon said.

"But that's an advanced weapon and you've never even used a slingshot!"

"Aim. Fire. Think I can handle it."

"Why do you need a gun?" Gentry asked as Simon pocketed the pistol.

"Because twelve days ago the people we're dealing with didn't think twice about o'blasterating my wife. Willie was severely wounded trying to protect me," Simon said specifically to his sister. "I'll be damned if I'll let anyone harm her again."

Amelia blinked at Willie with shock and perhaps a smidgen of gratitude.

"I promise, we'll explain at length later," Willie said, pushing out of the salon and into the crush of the rollicking coffeehouse.

"Where are you meeting this yahoo?" Gentry asked.

"USS *Enterprise*," Simon said. "The Vulcan Grogshop. The contact is wary of me, so I can't be seen. Phin's going inside with Willie. That's if his wits are about him."

Phin pushed away from the bar and a bottle of whiskey. "My jaw's sore," Phin said, whilst scowling at Gentry. "But my wits are fine." He checked his holstered weapon. "Let's do this."

"I know the *Enterprise* and the Vulcan," Gentry said over the ear-blistering music. "I'll come with you."

Amelia pushed forward. "Me too."

"Like hell," Gentry said. "Stay here with Eli. Get Axel back on his feet and talk him down from his all-fired fury. StarMan, Chang, you're with me."

Willie's nerves jangled. "Too many people."

"He won't even know we're there," Gentry said, then doubled back to kiss his wife and whisper something in her ear. She didn't look happy, but she didn't follow.

"I don't want Amelia to come," Simon said as Gentry rejoined them. "But I don't want to leave her here."

"Eli will kick the ass of any man who looks sideways at

her. Axel will do worse. That's if he regains consciousness anytime soon. You pack a hell of a wallop, Mrs. Darcy."

"Stun cuff," Willie said, flashing her wrist as they hit topside. "Phin's idea."

Gentry nodded. "Long as Mr. Bourdain keeps his hands and lips off Amelia, guess we'll get along just fine."

Simon shot his new brother-in-law a look as they crossed over to the next dig. "I could say the same thing about you, cowboy."

The Vulcan Grogshop was twice the size of Java Jupiter and easily as crowded. A blessing, as it meant Phin, Gentry, Star-Man, and Chang were difficult to spot. Even Willie was unsure as to the exact location of each man. As discussed on the walk over, they'd entered in intervals, dispersing to different areas of the smoky, chaotic pub.

There were several raucous gaming tables and the stage at the far end featured a burlesque show of sorts. Lively music and boisterous conversation filled the air, as did the clinking of glasses and the hissing and clanking of steam-powered metallic robots serving up smokes and snacks.

Willie was not the only woman in attendance, but she was certainly in the minority. She felt a twinge of unease as a few men at the bar looked her way. She wished Simon were with her, even though he couldn't be. She wished Rollins would have declared a more specific place to meet. She glanced at her time cuff. Nine p.m. sharp.

"Miss Goodenough." Rollins stepped in beside her. "You're alone?"

"Not precisely. Skytowns are notoriously wild. I thought it best to have an escort." She did not wish him to think her foolhardy or vulnerable. She did not fully trust the man. He had, after all, ratted out his own people in a bid for personal peace. "He's waiting outside whilst we conduct our business, so you need not worry."

"Do I look worried?"

"Indeed you do, Mr. Thimblethumper." The old man looked as if he'd aged ten years in two days.

"My world draws to an end. It is . . . unsettling."

"What do you mean—"

"I don't have much time. Please." He grasped her forearm and guided her to an empty table in the thick of the crowd. "You must act quickly," he said as they sat side by side at a table littered with empty glasses and smoking butts. "Tonight. The engine is unprotected this moment, but the mercenary will show for his shift sometime before dawn."

"Why is it unprotected?" Willie asked. "Where is Filmore?"

"The engine is hidden within a vault," he plowed on in a brittle tone. "It is marked *H. Houdini* and you will find it the catacombs near Westminster Abbey."

"Beneath the Abbey?" Willie scrunched her brow. She had pored over maps along with Simon and Phin. She did not recall tunnels under Westminster.

"The tunnels are ancient and dangerous. You must not linger. Get the engine and get out." He shoved a piece of paper in her hand, then rattled off directions.

The collective noise was such that Willie found herself focusing intently on Rollins's every word and expression. His milky eyes were somewhat dazed behind his thick spectacles. His wrinkled skin was ashen and clammy, his urgent manner troublesome.

"There is a lock on the vault," he said. "A special lock. I'm providing you with the code and entrusting you with the engine. Follow through for your mother. She was the best of us. Protect the world from further mayhem, Wilhelmina. The Houdinians are no more."

"What do you mean? What about Filmore?" Willie grasped the old man's hands when he tried to leave. "Why are you spooked? What have you done?"

"What had to be done."

"I knew you would come to your senses, Ollie," Filmore said. *"Although it took far longer than I anticipated."*

"I had thought to live out my life in peace. But now a Freak rebellion is rising. There was an incident over the Atlantic. Surely you read about it. Freaks are dangerous, Jefferson, and they exist because of us. We must right our wrongs and save the world from further mutation and destruction. Think of the atrocities those supernatural beings could commit upon Vics if they all band together as we once did."

"You are once again in league with my thinking. I'm encouraged by the timing. This past week I had decided to take extreme measures. I've been researching engineers, a man suited to my purpose. Ingenious, fearless, a fellow Utopian. And now here you are. We must go back in time," Filmore said as he paced amongst marble and granite tombstones. "Perhaps to the day we first arrived. Before Mods mated with Vics. We could alert the other Peace Rebels, caution them against having sex with anyone other than another Mod. Mickey would help us to instill the importance of remaining faithful to our fellow Peace Rebels." He stopped and caressed the sculpted angel marking one particular grave. "Mickey would still be alive."

"Yes. Yes, she would, Jefferson." Rollins latched on to the glazed look in Filmore's eyes. "And you and Mickey could be together again. But this time forever. I've already begun the construction of a compatible vehicle for the clockwork propulsion engine. We must make haste. This Race for Royal Rejuvenation has ignited interest in extraordinary inventions. I worry the engine is at risk now more than ever."

"It is. There was an incident, Ollie. A thwarted robbery."

Filmore looked frazzled and Rollins moved in for the kill. "Where is the safe house, Jefferson?"

"Where do you think?"

"You stuck to Mickey's original plan?"

"Why would I deviate? The woman was brilliant."

"Yes. Yes, she was." Rollins swallowed bile. "I can safely say she would not have advised repeating past mistakes."

"What are you saying? What are you . . ." Filmore blanched as Rollins pulled a black-market weapon, a *modern weapon, and aimed it at Filmore's heart. "Traitor!"*

Rollins's hand shook. "Yes. Yes, I am. A traitor to our fellow PRs who voted to destroy the engine. A traitor to our century. We should have stayed and fought for peace in our own time. We never should have played God. And yet you are willing to do it all again. To wreck more havoc."

Filmore lunged for the gun.

A loud blast.

A painful cry.

Filmore crumpled and blood pooled next to the grave marked MICHELLE GOODENOUGH.

Rollins stumbled back.

Panic. Remorse. Exhilaration.

"What have you done?" Willie cried. She was a mere shadow. A fly on the wall. Even so, Rollins flinched. The memory glitched, shifted, and suddenly she was catapulted back to Rollins's childhood. Back to the future where she was overwhelmed by foreign innovations and bizarre references. She was out of her element. Out of her time.

She was lost.

The moment Willie had grasped Rollins's hands, Simon had started pushing through the crowd. Unbeknownst to her, Gentry had offered Simon his American duster and cowboy hat so that he could lurk inside the grogshop incognito. Brim pulled low, chin dipped, he reached their table just as Willie slumped forward in a catatonic state.

Rollins gasped when she wilted into him, her derby tumbling to the floor. Before he could wrench away, Simon and Phin took action.

"Don't break contact, Thimblethumper." Simon exuded calm even as his heart bucked.

Phin grasped the old man's shoulder and held him steady whilst Gentry and his men circled, affording a modicum of privacy and protection from prying eyes.

"Chit can't hold her liquor," Simon heard someone joke as he stooped down and wrapped his arms around his wife.

"Is that it?" Rollins asked, wild-eyed. "Is she gassed? High?"

"Tracing. She's lost in your memories, old man." Simon swallowed hard, racking his brain for a way to pull her out. "Willie, sweetheart," he said close to her ear. "Come back. Come home."

She did not respond and Rollins fidgeted. "What's going on? Leave me be. Let me go."

Phin squeezed the man's shoulders. "What were you thinking about? Before Willie passed out?"

The man blanched. "I cannot say."

"Jesus," Simon said as Willie's glazed eyes rolled shut and her breathing grew shallow. This was different from before when she'd "gotten lost" whilst searching for her mother in Filmore's memories. She was deeper in, farther away. The seconds ticked on, and swear to God, Simon could feel Willie slipping away, languishing in a stranger's memories. A man from another time. Was she disoriented? Scared? Resigned? He swept off his borrowed hat, wrapped his hands over hers to reinforce her hold on Rollins and to strengthen his own physical connection.

"I know you," Rollins said in a scratchy voice.

Adrenaline surged.

Prompt the transmitter. . . .

Holding Willie close, Simon caught and held the old man's panicked gaze. "Simon Darcy. I came into your shop a couple of weeks ago with a young lad. Remember?" *Please, God, remember.*

Rollins drifted. "Ah, yes. The lad who bought the yo-yo."

"That's right." Simon then prompted Willie. "Do you see me, kid? I'm right there. Right beside you. We're in Thimblethumper's shop. He's tinkering with some toys behind his desk. I'm tugging on your scarf. Feel that? Come on. Take my hand, Canary. That's it." His pulse tripped as he felt her fingers tighten around his own. "Hold tight. We're done here. Time to leave." Her grip eased and his stomach knotted. Desperate, he gave her a squeeze and a shake. "I love you, Willie. Yield to me, dammit. Let me help."

He glanced at her time cuff. The second hand ticked and ticked . . . and he realized that the pub had fallen silent and the ticking sounded like a death knell.

Dear God. Had he failed his wife as he'd failed his father? "Don't leave me, Wilhelmina Darcy," he pleaded in a thick voice. "I can't change the world without you."

She gasped. Once. Twice. Her eyes flew open and she flinched, sucking air like a drowning woman pulled from the sea. "Simon?"

Relief blew through him with the ferocity of a summer storm. Heart pounding, he pulled her away from Rollins and crushed her to his chest. "Right here, sweetheart."

"Thank God," Phin said.

"Drawin' a boodle of attention," Gentry said. "We should go."

"Who are you?" Rollins asked. "Are you with the Mechanics?"

"No," Simon said. "We're with Willie."

Still the old man looked frantic to escape.

"Let him go," Willie said in a weak voice. Holding tight to Simon, she shifted her gaze to Rollins. "You have to go. Someplace far away."

The man nodded. "The . . . device."

"Will be safe. I promise."

Rollins gave a jerky nod, then pushed out of the chair, hastening away without a single look back.

"Should I follow him?" Gentry asked.

"No," Willie said. "I have what we need and he has paid for any transgressions with his soul." She looked up at Simon, tears clouding her rainbow eyes. "You came for me. How—"

"A mystery and a miracle." Heart overflowing with relief, Simon swept Willie up into his arms. Phin and the other men surrounded him as he carried her from the grogshop, away from curious onlookers.

"Just when I thought I'd seen everything," StarMan said.

Birdman Chang scratched his head. "And Doc thinks he's got it bad."

"What now?" Gentry asked as they breached the main deck of the *Enterprise*.

"I'm taking Willie home," Simon said.

"No." She pushed against his shoulder. "We have to go after the engine. Now. Timing is crucial."

Simon shook off a sense of foreboding as he eased Willie to her feet. "Shite."

"What's wrong?" Gentry asked whilst tugging on his hat.

Simon looked to Phin, who knew his history well. "Where timing is concerned, I've been cursed since birth."

CHAPTER 35

Although she'd physically recovered from her time-tracing fiasco with Rollins, Willie's heart and mind remained shell-shocked even two hours later. Pride somewhat battered, she accepted that Simon had been right and that she could not continue tracing as she had in the past. There'd been a shift in her powers and she did not understand the new parameters. Perhaps it was merely a matter of honing her skills even more. To intensify her ability to resist interacting or to explore new ways of pulling free of a transmitter's memory. The matter required thorough consideration. She could not imagine shunning her gift forever. She was not sure that she could. She would, however, strive not to time-trace again until they'd managed this crisis with the clockwork propulsion engine. Until she'd cleaned up the Houdinians' mess and bested that bastard blackmailer Strangelove. Surely she would hear from him tomorrow, but by then at least, the engine would be under royal protection.

Tucker Gentry had *guaran-damn-teed* he could secure a private audience with Queen Victoria. According to her new sister-in-law, the sovereign of the British Empire had taken a shine to the transcontinental tabloid hero. So much so, the queen had promised to intercede with the president of the United States, securing a pardon for the ill-accused Sky Cowboy and his crew, as well as providing safe passage to England for his younger sister, Lily.

Amelia also had hopes that this "discovery and donation" on behalf of the Darcys would help to appease the queen for the trouble she had caused in Italy. As it was, she and Gentry were still on shaky ground and had, in fact, been dispatched to retrieve an invaluable artifact they'd stolen from Leonardo da Vinci's secret vault (an *Italian* treasure) and then lost to the Scottish Shark of the Skies.

Willie's mind reeled with the Gentrys' ongoing adventure. They'd been married just earlier today, a quiet ceremony in London. They'd docked at the Milky Way for a brief celebration before setting off in search of the dreaded Captain Dunkirk. And now they'd interrupted not only their honeymoon but their royal mission in order to aid Willie and Simon on their quest.

Two weeks ago, Willie had been fairly alone in this world. Now she had family *and* friends. She had a husband who had somehow saved her from the chaos of another man's mind and a sister-in-law who, although leery regarding the Canary's report on her father, hadn't flinched at accepting a Freak as a Darcy. As her brother-in-law navigated the *Maverick*'s air dinghy over the Thames, past Clock Tower, and toward the narrow road running between Parliament and Westminster Abbey, Willie's entire being buzzed with optimism. It was an unfamiliar and wondrous feeling and infected her with a sense of invincibility.

"What are you smiling at?" Simon asked as they came in for a landing.

"I'm envisioning your monorail," she whispered back. "The draft in your library. The Abbey, Parliament. It looks exactly as you sketched it. All that is missing is your magnificent monorail. Promise me you won't give up on your dream."

Simon squeezed her waist. "I have other dreams now."

Moments later, they disembarked and hid the small transport behind a copse of manicured bushes. After analyzing the situation, Willie, Simon, and Phin had joined forces with Amelia, Gentry, and his crew in order to procure the infamous engine. They'd chosen the *Maverick*, the fastest airship in Europe and far and away more reliable than the *Flying Cloud*, as their main transport. Gentry's crew, with the exception of Eli Boone—a master tinker, according to Gentry—had stayed aboard, watching for trouble from above and preparing for a fast escape. Amelia had refused to stay behind and as Simon wouldn't think of barring Willie from this recovery, Gentry had been forced to acquiesce to his wife's demand. But not until after he and Axel had armed her with a stun cuff and a Remington Blaster.

"Are you sure you know where you're going?" Amelia whispered to Willie as the motley crew of five proceeded down St. Margaret Street.

"Rollins's directions were quite specific," Willie said as she pushed on. "And I am well acquainted with London."

"As am I," Simon said.

Because of the late hour and because this was a business district, there was nary a pedestrian to be found and road traffic was scant. A rolling fog added to the already eerie ambience, and although Willie did not celebrate Jefferson Filmore's death, she was most grateful that friends and family would not be subjected to his deranged presence nor that of his hired mercenary.

Her shoulder twinged just thinking about the hired thug who'd shot her in Edinburgh. Indeed, her arm had been paining her most of this day. After the time-tracing debacle with Rollins she had felt the need for as much fortification as possible and was glad she had stowed her Thera-Steam-Atic Brace aboard the *Flying Cloud*. She wore it now with pride and confidence. She stole a glance at Simon, in awe of his ingenuity and the depth of her admiration. At one point, she'd accused him of arrogance. Now that she knew him better, she was most certain his success was hindered by a streak of humbleness and a dash of insecurity, which only deepened her regard.

"Can't see a thing," Eli complained as they veered away from the streetlamps.

"Just follow me." Utilizing her night vision and Rollins's landmarks, Willie guided her team to Jewel Tower, a surviving section of a royal palace built in the fourteenth century. A three-story limestone structure that sat across the road from Parliament and upon the same grounds as Westminster Abbey. "Here," she said, pointing to an entry point as described by Rollins. "Remember," she said as Simon pushed open a vine-covered gate, "we must trudge through a sewage duct to gain entrance to this particular catacomb. There could be rats and snakes and such, not to mention filth," she said for Amelia's benefit.

The blond woman snorted and adjusted her shoulder harness.

Phin groaned. "I hate snakes."

"Don't worry, Bourdain," Gentry said in a condescending tone. "I've got your back."

"Leave him be," Amelia whispered to her husband. "It was just a kiss and not even a good one at that."

"Bloody hell," Phin said.

Gentry chuckled and Simon looked to Willie and rolled his eyes. "Once inside," he said to everyone, "it should be safe to use your torchlights."

Battery-operated tubes of light. A most ingenious alternative to a kerosene lantern, Willie thought. She would have to purchase one for Fletcher.

Ignoring the putrid smell and the feel of squishy clay beneath her boots, Willie slogged through the sewage tunnel. She ignored the scurrying rats, as did everyone else, including Amelia. Indeed, she was most impressed with her sister-in-law. Senses keen, Willie felt her heart skip when she spied the entrance to the catacombs as described by Rollins. "This way." No one, including Simon, countered, although once inside the musty labyrinth, Simon, Phin, and Gentry took the lead whilst Eli protected the rear.

As they were all armed with torchlights, golden beams swept over every wall and crevice. Every coffin, every vault. Every disgusting pile of exposed skulls and bones. On pins and needles, Willie almost yelped when she felt a vibration against her ribs.

The telecommunicator.

Strangelove.

She fell back behind Amelia and, whilst pretending to

examine a vault, shone her light upon the device. Upon decoding the message, panic ensued.

BRING ACC. WESTMINSTER BRIDGE. SECOND LAMP. MIDNIGHT. SENDING COURIER. YOUR BROTHER. FAIL ME. HE DIES.

How had Strangelove located Wesley? Aye, she and her brother were estranged, but the thought of him dying, let alone because of *her*, was crushing. The time factor only intensified her angst. By midnight *tonight*? Willie pocketed the device and noted the time. Eleven oh five. Surely Strangelove would not have given her such short notice. Had there been a glitch in the transmission? Had the message been delayed? Did he perhaps mean tomorrow? She could not take that chance. If she did not show . . .

"Here!" Phin shouted, his voice echoing down the tunnel and prompting Willie to join the others.

Five torchlights shone upon one vault, illuminating the safe house like a divine entity.

"H. Houdini," she said, noting the inscription and marveling once again that her mother had dedicated so much of her life to protecting a device that committed her to the bowels of the earth. She did not understand her mother. But she respected her. "We must hurry."

"You said the mercenary would not show for his shift until predawn," Simon said.

"Sometime around predawn," Willie said, reaching into her pocket for the secret code. "Rollins was not specific about the time, and who knows what other means of security Filmore might have initiated? Rollins was adamant that we enter and exit posthaste." Whilst they were depositing the engine in the air dinghy, she would somehow slip away. Simon would be worried, furious. Gadzooks. How had it come to this?

"In addition to the locking box at the bottom of the gate," Simon said, whilst examining the vault, "there's a padlock. Did Rollins give you a key, sweetheart?"

Her upper lip beaded with sweat. "No."

"I can break that lock," Eli said. The big black man pulled tools from the arsenal belt beneath his voluminous coat.

"Make sure it's not rigged," Phin said.

"A bomb?" Amelia groaned. "The queen would never forgive us if we blew up another artifact of importance."

"If we're blown to smithereens, darlin'," Gentry said, "won't be nothin' left of us to forgive."

"I don't see any wires," Simon said.

"Me neither," Eli said.

"Just that combination lock contraption," Gentry said.

"An astonishing amount of dials," Amelia noted. "You don't suppose that's booby-trapped, do you? Dial the wrong number and *kaplooey*?"

Simon shot his sister a look and Willie wondered if they were thinking of their father, who'd gone *kaplooey* along with his moonship. Indeed, the image was most unsettling. Heart pounding, she knelt beside her husband amongst dirt and cobwebs and studied the locking mechanism. "The combination is quite lengthy," she said. "Let me read it to you, and that way you can concentrate solely on the dials."

He flashed her an encouraging smile. "Teamwork." Then he focused on the box.

Willie wet her lips, glanced at her time cuff. Eleven fifteen. She commenced to reading the combination—slowly, deliberately—whilst visions of her brother flashed through her mind. No one else said a word as Simon finagled each gold dial, although Willie's ears rang with the sounds of childhood bantering and laughter. Where Wesley was concerned, the bad times had outweighed the good, yet this moment only the good resonated. Rattled, she pushed Wesley from her mind, but her angst remained. She realized she'd been anticipating the sound of hostile footsteps . . . or an explosion.

Simon tweaked the last dial and tripped a switch.

A compression valve hissed and groaned.

Eli utilized a compact bolt cutter and the iron lock clanged and thudded to the ground.

Sweat trickled down Willie's back as they cautiously swung open the iron-grilled gate. No explosion. No footsteps. They shone their lights on a toddler-sized coffin.

"Seems small for an engine," Eli said.

"Remember," Gentry said, "I saw the plans that inspired this engine. Ain't size that matters. It's the inner workings."

"I'm dying to see it," Amelia said. "Imagine. An engine that enables people to soar through dimensions."

"We can gawk at it later," Willie said, anxious to meet with Strangelove and to vanquish the villain from their life. "Let's just get it out of here." She grabbed a handle just as everyone yelled, "Wait!"

Startled, she paused, but she'd already shifted the coffin and . . . "Oh, no." She heard a beep and then another. "What is it?" She looked around the vault, along with everyone else.

"It's a goddamned bomb," Phin said. "Here. Time detonator. What jolly good fun," he said with sarcasm. "Six minutes, fifty-five, nope, fifty-four seconds."

"Crikey," Amelia said, "we'll never make it out in time with the engine."

Simon dropped to his knees. "Eli, give me your tool belt. I've seen this sort of mechanism before."

"I can help," Phin said, stooping alongside him. "Wrangled some demolitions during the war."

"Ladies, run like hell," Simon said. "Gentry, Eli, grab the coffin. Get as far from us as possible. Just in case."

Sick to her stomach, Willie stared down at Simon. "I cannot leave you."

He cast her a confident, earnest look. "I cannot save us whilst you're here."

Amelia tugged at her brace. "Come on, Canary. My brother knows what he's doing."

Breaking free, Willie dropped next to Simon and framed the sides of his mud-streaked face. "I love you, Simon Darcy."

"And I you." Eyes dancing, he smacked a kiss to her mouth, then jerked his head. "Meet you topside, pet."

Heart battering her ribs, Willie flew out of the vault and down the corridor alongside her sister-in-law. Gentry and Eli were close on their heels, carrying the precious coffin between them. Amelia slipped in the muck of the sewage duct and Willie easily righted her with the aid of the Thera-Steam-Atic Brace. It would seem Simon's recent adjustments had afforded the brace an intensified means of strength. Willie's eyes burned as she thought about her husband's kindness, his genius, and she prayed to God his brilliant mind didn't fail him now.

"Haul butt, ladies," Gentry ordered from behind. Indeed, the cowboy and his crewmate fairly lifted Willie and Amelia off their feet as they whisked the coffin from the duct, up the moss-covered stairs, and through the rusted garden gate.

Lungs burning, Willie fell to her knees as the frigid fresh air chilled her sweat-soaked clothing. She checked her time cuff.

"What time is it?" Amelia asked, chest heaving from exertion and angst. "How long has it been?"

Willie sleeved tears from her eyes. "Almost six minutes."

"Crikey."

Gentry squeezed Willie's shoulder. "He'll prevail."

"How do you know?"

The man smiled down at her. "He's a Darcy."

As much as she wanted to trust in Gentry's confidence, Willie's world tilted as she braced for an explosion. She could not imagine her life without Simon. Envisioning his handsome face, she whispered a plea and prayed for a miracle. "I cannot change the world without you, my love. Come back."

"What time is it?" Amelia asked.

Willie could scarcely breathe, let alone move.

Gentry checked his pocket watch, as did Eli.

Amelia nabbed Willie's wrist, squinted at her time cuff, and squealed. "They're clear!" The young woman scrambled to the gate, yelled down.

Willie pushed to her feet, green with the collywobbles.

"They shouted back!" Amelia called over her shoulder. "Simon and Phin are on their way!"

Gentry flashed Willie a kind smile. "Never underestimate a Darcy." He winked, then looked to Eli. "Let's get this coffin to the dinghy before some copper spots us. We look like a pair of damned grave robbers. Come on, ladies!"

Willie palmed her forehead. Simon was alive. She thanked her lucky stars. She swore to tackle life along her husband's side. Freak and Vic, united forever and always. She glanced at her timepiece, then over her shoulder at Westminster Bridge. Would Wesley be alone? Would Strangelove be lurking? Or perhaps he'd hired a gunman. She remembered the first time they'd met, a murky memory of Strangelove and the whispered word: *assassin*.

Palming the bag slung over her shoulder, she verified the welfare of the memory disk.

One last obstacle. One more life to be saved. Then and only then could she embrace the future.

CHAPTER 36

Exiting the claustrophobic bowels of the catacomb and sewage tunnel, Simon had considered himself the luckiest bloody bastard on earth. This night alone he'd coldcocked the famous Sky Cowboy in defense of his sister's virtue, saved his wife from the clutches of a Mod's mind, located Briscoe's clockwork propulsion engine, and, along with Phin's help, disabled a ticking bomb. In addition to saving their lives, he'd ensured the well-being of a historical architectural treasure—Westminster Abbey.

In his somewhat dazed and euphoric state, it occurred that he'd spent the last few hours flirting with the kind of danger his brother, a secret agent for the Crown, no doubt faced every day. For once Simon's timing had been bang-on, and that constant nagging impulse to make his mark upon the world had been miraculously snuffed. In the instant he'd pushed through the garden gate, hugged his sister, then laid eyes upon his wife's beautiful tearstained face, Simon had imagined himself quite content spending the next few years engineering enhanced prosthetics and aiding Willie in the peaceful emancipation of Freaks.

He had not considered even an ounce more of excitement this night. So when Willie spewed an astounding tale of blackmail and deceit regarding a devious and powerful noble who went by the name Strangelove, Simon could not believe his ears.

"I never should have buckled under his threats," Willie said, her sole attention on Simon even though the others listened intently. "But given the circumstances at the time,

I could not afford involving the police. Please know I never truly intended to betray you. I *thought* I was protecting you as well as my family. I thought I could handle Strangelove, that I could somehow manipulate the situation. Then later, I worried if I told you, you'd be angry. That you'd never trust me again. That you'd . . ."

Her breath hitched and Simon pulled her into his arms. "You thought I'd leave you. Dammit, Willie." Simon dropped his forehead to hers, tucked her shaggy hair behind her ears, and willed his temper even. "Why tell me now?"

"Because I've changed. I don't want to go it alone. I don't want to endanger my brother's life, but I no longer want to surrender the ACC to Strangelove. What if he *can* access the data? What if he's a threat to the world? He swore once I complied he would leave me and mine alone. But I don't trust him." She placed her hand over Simon's heart. "I trust you."

Twisted up with emotion, Simon kissed Willie's forehead, then glanced over her shoulder at Clock Tower. "Less than thirty minutes to midnight. Not much time to devise a plan."

Phin crossed his arms and regarded the former air marshal with a cocky expression. "Tangling with all those Wild West outlaws, you've no doubt encountered hostage situations. Any bright ideas, cowboy?"

"I can think of one or two, Casanova." Gentry pulled a communication gadget from his pocket, and after seeing the one Strangelove had given to Willie, Simon decided he really needed to start shopping the black market.

"Tell them the weather could get rough," Willie said when she heard Gentry speaking with his chief navigator aboard the *Maverick*.

"Hold," Gentry said into the device, then turned his attention to Willie. "What do you mean?"

"Wesley's supernatural gift. He can manipulate the weather. He's been known to stir up violent storms when angered. If he's anxious because Strangelove threatened him . . ." Willie hugged herself against a blast of frigid wind. "Blizzards, whirlwinds, hailstorms."

"The Stormerator," Amelia said, wide-eyed.

"That'd be an all-fired coincidence," Eli said.

"What are you talking about?" Simon asked, pulling Willie close.

"Trouble in the form of a bastard sky pirate and his secret weapon," Gentry said. "Your brother a good sort, Amelia?"

She dipped her chin. "Not really."

"Think he'd use his gift for ill gain?"

"Unfortunately."

"Son of a bitch."

"But he's still my brother," she rushed on. "And he's still being threatened by Strangelove."

"Honey," Gentry said, tugging his brim low. "My gut says you've been hornswoggled. Eli, take the dinghy and hide the coffin in the *Maverick*'s cargo bay. Amelia, go with him and ready Peg." He spoke into the communicator. "Watch for a shark in a storm cloud, StarMan, and prepare to tussle."

Phin checked his personal arsenal and Amelia jammed her Remington Blaster against Simon's chest. "That derringer won't cut it with Dunkirk and his men, Simon. Listen to Tucker, and crikey, shoot to maim." She shocked Simon further by pulling Gentry down for a swift yet passionate kiss. "Hell of a honeymoon, Mr. Gentry. You owe me."

She raced off to join Eli, and Simon marveled at his little sister's transformation. She'd always been fearless, but smitten by a man? The equally besotted look on the former lawman's face went a long way to quell Simon's reservations regarding their whirlwind marriage. Although, good God, his own nuptials had been remarkably spontaneous.

He noted Willie's worried expression and strapped the blaster over his chest. Giving her hand a reassuring squeeze, he nailed Gentry with a look of fierce confidence and commitment. "I've studied the designs of Westminster Bridge as well as Clock Tower and all of Parliament and the Abbey. I know every crook and cranny."

"Then I'm in dire need of your intellect, Darcy." He looked to Phin. "Amelia says you're a crack aviator."

"Nice to know she thinks I excel at something."

"Catch up to her and tell her you need to borrow her pa's dig. With your military training I could use you in the air."

"Right, then." Phin dipped into his coat and handed Willie his cherished Knuckle Shocker Stun Gun. "For backup," he said. "I tweaked it a bit so it might actually pack the wallop Reggie intended."

Phin raced after Amelia, and Willie looked up at Simon, eyes bright. "Somehow it feels like your father is with us."

"He always was my greatest champion," Simon said, heart squeezing. He looked to Gentry, inspired and ready to kick arse. "So what's the plan?"

Bicycles were all the rage in London. Willie had pedaled more than a few, but none so furiously as the one "borrowed" from a passing citizen by Simon. Fortunately, Westminster Bridge was just down St. Margaret Street and to the east of Clock Tower. Unfortunately, an ominous fog was barreling toward her, obliterating the skyline and landscape, and obscuring even Willie's most excellent night vision.

She steered onto Bridge Street and at once was consumed in the dense, swirling mist. She knew the House of Commons and Clock Tower stood to her right, but she could not see either of the magnificent structures. Her mad dash became a perilous crawl as she strove not to veer into a random vehicle or a midnight-strolling pedestrian. Although, from the deafening quiet, Willie would swear she was alone in the world just now. She took comfort in knowing Simon and their band of musketeers were out there, somewhere, poised for a joint rescue and ambush.

Gentry had doled out direct instructions and Willie had thought his plan most sound, except they'd anticipated a violent storm of sorts, not this insidious, all-consuming pea soup. It occurred to Willie that even though she'd asked for help, she might be going it alone after all. How could anyone help her if they couldn't find her? The fog was not only blinding but disorienting.

A slight incline alerted Willie that she had reached Westminster Bridge. Her heart hammered against her chest as she now walked the bicycle whilst squinting through the supernatural veil in search of the glow from a streetlamp. Big Ben rang out, the first of twelve chimes, and never in her life had the Clockwork Canary been more aware of the time.

She saw it then, the hazy glow of three connected lamps atop the first pole. She quickened her stride, tempered her anxiety. This was her brother. Her blood. Even though they'd been at odds most of their life, surely he would not harm her. She'd hand over the memory disk as Gentry had instructed. Wesley would return to the *Flying Shark* and when he did, Gentry and crew would follow. The element of surprise was on their side and Gentry assured her and Simon that, in addition to reclaiming the Aquarian Cosmology Compendium, he would capture Strangelove. If the bastard was not on board, he would determine his true identity—information known to her brother as well as Captain Dunkirk—and hunt the man down. He strongly believed that the villain who'd masterminded the attempt to steal away Amelia's targeted invention was the same man who'd manipulated Willie in a bid to bamboozle Simon.

Spying the second streetlamp, Willie slowed, her bootheels sliding over the icy road, her mind replaying Gentry's instruction. *"Give Wesley the disk. He'll take it to Dunkirk. Lead us to Strangelove."*

Unless Wesley absconded with the disk himself.

She spotted her brother, leaning insolently against the lamppost, shrouded in a veil of fog and an arrogant manner. He looked much as he always had, dressed in ModVic attire, shocks of red hair stabbing out from underneath a purple fedora.

The last chime of twelve faded and Wesley's mouth quirked. "On time, as always." He held out his hand. "Fork over the goods, Sis, and I'll pass it on to Strangelove."

"The way you were supposed to pass my letter on to Simon?"

Wesley blinked.

Willie allowed the bicycle to tip over as she moved closer to her traitorous kin. "Why, Wesley? Twelve years ago, I entrusted you with an important letter, with my *heart*. You said you would take it to the rail station. You promised you would give it to Simon, but you didn't. *Why?*"

He stuffed his hands in his pockets, then shrugged. "I was saving you from your knobhead self. You're a Freak, Mina. You're meant for another Freak. Stick to your own kind and someday Freaks will rule this world."

"You're crackers!"

"I'm smart. Which is more than I can say for you. You could be capitalizing on your gift, yet you drudge away in a Vic's world, looking after the old man even though he barely provided for us."

"What are you talking about? We never wanted for anything."

"Didn't we? They doled out attention and affection with an eyedropper. They moved us all over hell's half acre and then some. Dad was obsessed with Mom. Mom was obsessed with protecting some twentieth-century icon. I knew it was volatile, maybe valuable, but I never guessed it was the compendium. Now give it to me and be on your way before my employer intercedes and takes a shine to you. He happens to like pretty young things."

Reminded of her present mission, Willie scrambled to focus. She envisioned her brother and the pirate escaping under this suffocating cloak of supernatural fog and taking the ACC and Strangelove with them. In order for Gentry's plan to succeed, he had to be able to see the *Flying Shark*. In order for her and Simon to move on, they had to put Strangelove behind them.

She needed to break the fog, and that meant breaking Wesley's concentration.

"Mom never told us what it was that she was protecting," she prodded. "How did you know it was from the twentieth century?"

"Because I followed her one day and overheard her talking to two other Peace Rebels. Because I cornered her later and told her we should sell whatever it was, make a fortune, and if she didn't, I would. I'd find a way."

"My God, Wesley! *You're* the traitor!"

"Matter of perception, although I guess that's how she saw it. Our tiff rattled her enough to consume her thoughts. She walked in front of that automocoach and my plan died with her. Those other two PRs disappeared with the stash, Dad went bonkers, and we were left high and dry. I tried tracking those Mods for over a year before giving up and making my fortune my own damned way."

Shocked and sickened, Willie squeezed back tears. "How can we possibly be related?"

"Something I asked myself the day you took on the mundane job of a pressman." Stone-faced, her brother pushed off the lamp pole. "Give me the bloody ACC."

"Go to hell."

He reached for her and she swung out with her injured right arm. The Thera-Steam-Atic Brace offered strength and her smack landed hard, knocking Wesley into the pedestrian wall.

Her brother roared and the fog diminished by half. Lightning cracked, illuminating the hazy night sky, and there it was, hovering over the Thames—the *Flying Shark*!

Willie heard the scraping of an iron grate and she knew it was Simon, beneath the bridge. She knew he'd heard enough and that he was coming to her rescue, only the fog started to thicken as Wesley shook off her blow. She dipped into her pocket, slipping her fingers through Reginald Darcy's invention just as Wesley charged. Her swift uppercut connected with his chin with a loud *ZAP!*

Hair smoking, he literally sailed through the air, plowing once again into the bridge's wall, only this time the force sent him toppling over.

Willie lunged, catching his arm before he plummeted into the dark, wintry river. *Deadweight*. The Knuckle Shocker had stunned the marbles out of her brother and if she lost her grip, her brother was fish bait. Thank God for her enhanced strength via Simon's brace.

"Let me help." Simon was there beside her, reaching down, grasping her brother's arm.

Willie heard horse hooves clopping against the pavement. She glanced over and saw the Sky Cowboy galloping toward them on a black steed. She could see him clearly. No fog!

She heard an explosion and looked up to see the *Flying Shark*'s zeppelin in flames and the *Maverick* flying out from behind Clock Tower, cannons blasting.

Her muscles screamed as she held tight to Wesley whilst Simon tried to haul him up.

Wesley stirred and suddenly he was pointing a gun at Willie with his free hand.

She was trying to save his wretched arse and he wanted to *kill* her?

He spared Simon a glance, then looked back on Willie. "You're a traitor to Freaks, Mina."

"You're a traitor to mankind," Simon said, swinging the Remington Blaster over the wall and taking aim. "Drop your peashooter into the drink, Wesley."

"I have a better idea, Darcy." He jerked out of Willie's grasp and plunged, gun and all, through the dark, through the air, into a watery grave.

Willie's heart jerked as she heard the splash. At once a raging whirlpool erupted, blasting them with icy water before fizzling into snowflakes. "Oh, God." Willie collapsed against Simon just as Gentry reined in.

"We good here?" the cowboy asked, flicking his gaze to the air skirmish.

"Willie's in my care, as is the compendium," Simon said. "You see to Strangelove."

"One way or another," he promised. "Don't worry about Amelia or the engine. Meet you back at the ranch, Darcys." He tugged at the brim of his Stetson, then kicked the horse into a dead run.

Willie turned just as feathered wings appeared and the horse and rider took flight.

Simon leaned forward, squinting into the dark. "Did I just see what I thought I saw?"

"Astonishing," Willie said, her night vision enabling her to watch as the Sky Cowboy navigated some sort of Pegasus into the ensuing sky battle.

"No wonder my sister's smitten with the man. He owns a flying horse. Blimey."

Emotions churning, Willie leaned into Simon. "I tried to save him. Wesley."

"Yes, you did. We both did. He made his choice, Willie. Not you."

"That's just it. He was too selfish to choose death." She glanced toward the Thames. "I'm not sure that he perished, Simon. I cannot explain, but I don't feel as though Wesley's gone."

"Just as I would know if Jules was no more. I understand." He held her close, kissed the top of her head. "If he comes back into our life, we'll tackle that obstacle together."

She looked up at him and forced a small, brave smile. "Everything will work out."

"Yes, it will." He brushed a kiss over her mouth and she felt her world settling into something good and right. "Ready to go home?" he asked.

"Not quite yet," she said, smiling into his eyes. "I have an adventure to pen and I haven't seen the end of the story yet."

Huddled together against the wintry mix, they gazed up into the dazzling night as the Sky Cowboy tussled midair with the Scottish Shark of the Skies.

"I do hope Phin doesn't steal all of Gentry's glory," Willie said as their friend roared by on some sort of kite flying contraption.

Simon winked down at her. "I hope he does."

EPILOGUE

ONE WEEK LATER . . .
MCSTEAM'S COFFEEHOUSE

"How did it go?"

"Surprisingly well."

"It could have gone better."

Simon squeezed his wife's hand, then held out her chair as she sat across a table from Phin. "Willie's disappointed because the queen refused to recognize our marriage."

Phin snuffed his cigar and regarded Willie with a furrowed brow. "You thought she'd overturn a long-standing law just for you."

"*No*, not just for me. For all Freaks."

"We live in a country where people are still frowned upon or penalized for marrying outside of their social class," Phin said. "The kind of change you're suggesting won't happen overnight."

"I realize that," Willie said. "I was just . . . *hoping*. Part and parcel of my new optimistic attitude."

Simon smiled whilst signaling the server for two more coffees. "At least she didn't ban you from the room."

"Aye," Willie said as she removed her derby and smoothed her hair. "Although Queen Victoria was wary of my race and the powers we possess, I confess she was most tolerant. And, in the end, somewhat reasonable, although I wish she were more so."

"I must say, I'm impressed that Gentry was able to arrange a private audience for you," Phin said. "Although it did take a bloody long week."

"Apparently the queen spent the last few days deliberating with an adviser," Simon said. "Given her views on time travel and the Peace Rebels in general, I'm grateful she didn't act in haste and order the artifacts destroyed."

"What did she decide?"

Simon waited until the server had placed two fresh cups and a small pot of aromatic coffee on the table before plunging into what he considered to be a fantastic tale. Never had he thought to meet Queen Victoria face-to-face, let alone receive a royal invitation to share his sketches and plans for Project Monorail. Indeed, his shock and elation were such he'd found it most difficult to fully concentrate on the legendary submissions. Thankfully, Willie, Amelia, and Gentry had been present, keeping the task at hand on track.

"Not so surprisingly," Simon said, "although the queen believed the engine and compendium to be worthy of submission for the Triple R Tourney, she did not deem a formal submission wise. Publicly declaring the PR's engine had not in fact been destroyed and that it was indeed the original engine used by Briscoe Darcy? Governments across the globe as well as assorted criminal kingpins would be vying to pinch the engine for God knows what use."

"So the queen and her adviser, the director of Her Majesty's Mechanics," Willie said, "decided that the best course was to lock away the clockwork propulsion engine in a secret vault, a royal vault. I cannot think of a better solution. It is safe. It is sound. And it is no longer my responsibility," she said. "I firmly believe my mother can now rest in peace, and that is a great comfort to me as well as to my father."

"What of the Aquarian Cosmology Compendium?" Phin asked.

"Curious, that," Simon said. "The director of HMM was not aware that the data of the ACC had been divided amongst three disks. Apparently the agency is in possession of one-third, compliments of guess who?"

"Thimblethumper?"

Willie nodded. "So now only one disk is at large and they believe that disk is in the possession of Professor Maximus Merriweather."

Phin drummed his fingers on the scarred table. "Did the director say? Is that what they sent Jules to procure?"

"The director and indeed the queen were loath to talk about Jules and his mission," Simon said. "Frustrating to say the least."

"The best news," Willie said after giving Simon's hand a supportive squeeze, "is that Queen Victoria was most pleased that Tucker and Amelia convinced Captain Dunkirk to hand over the antiquity he'd stolen from them. Leonardo da Vinci's ornithopter will be returned to the Italian government and that international incident will be put to rest."

"She was also pleased that Gentry apprehended one of Europe's most wanted sky pirates within a day of being commissioned to do so," Simon said.

"And," Willie said, her rainbow eyes sparkling with the sensation of it all, "she agreed to consider pardoning Captain Dunkirk of his past crimes *if* he apprehended and delivered Lord Bingham to the director of Her Majesty's Mechanics."

"Dunkirk only made that offer to keep himself out of the Tower," Phin said.

"Clearly," Simon said. "But Dunkirk's holding a colossal grudge against Bingham, and Gentry, who seems to hold some sort of professional regard for the pirate, thinks he'll make good on the promise."

"I'm still shocked knowing Strangelove and Bingham, a titled noble who actually owns land near Ashford and who had designs on marrying Amelia, are one and the same," Willie said. "I will not rest until I know the whole of his story."

"I'll not rest until he's crushed," Simon said.

"Speaking of Amelia," Phin said. "I thought they were going to join us."

"I daresay Tucker's not up to socializing," Willie said.

"He received news of his sister this morning. Unbeknownst to him Lily had been aboard the dirigible transporting Prime Minster Madstone across the Atlantic."

"The airship attacked by Freak Fighters?" Phin asked.

"The same," Simon said. "Without getting into the long of it, she was badly injured and Gentry's former ship's doctor was pulled into the scene."

"Doc Blue," Phin said. "The Freak who betrayed Gentry and his crew."

"The Freak who saved Gentry's sister, returning her sight and her will to live. The Freak who married her."

Phin blinked. "So now Gentry's wrestling with the knowledge that his little sister married a dubious sort?" He snorted. "You just made my day, Darcy."

"I have faith that it will all work out," Willie said.

Phin toasted her with his coffee. "Compliments of your newly adopted optimistic attitude."

Simon regarded his friend with intensified interest. "Willie has given her notice at the *Informer*. She'll be penning a memoir, a novel about the Darcys and our past and present adventures, whilst working diligently, peacefully," he said, squeezing her thigh as a private reminder, "to advance the emancipation of Freaks. A cause I support. Meanwhile I'll be pouring my energies in advanced prosthetics and perhaps Project Monorail." He raised a brow at Phin. "And you?"

The man leaned back and regarded Simon a moment before speaking, a quiet connection that knotted Simon's gut. "I'm leaving for Australia this afternoon," Phin said.

"Because we've lost touch with Jules?" Simon asked.

"Yes. And because Bella Caro's ship went down in Queensland. Her pilot was killed. She's missing."

"How awful," Willie said.

Simon frowned. "The director of the HMM said nothing of losing his Freak surgeon."

"Naturally," Phin said. "Bella's journey was unsanctioned." He rose, kissed the back of Willie's hand, then gripped Simon's shoulder. "I'll be in touch."

A moment later he was gone and Willie leaned into Simon. "I feel awful," she said.

Simon took a deep breath, searched his mind, his heart. He listened to his gut and heard nothing. "As it happens, I feel hopeful. I don't know what's going on with Jules, Willie. I don't know what he's up to. But knowing my brother, it's something great."

Willie smiled, then stole a brief kiss before looking out the window and across the bustling street. "I'm glad we decided to buy Thimblethumper's Shoppe of Curiosities. Wherever Ollie Rollins is, I'm sure he'd be most pleased to know my father agreed to step in as the proprietor. If anyone appreciates twentieth-century wonders and historical oddities, it is Michael Goodenough."

Simon wrapped his arm around his wife, marveling that he felt as though he'd made his mark upon the world simply by focusing on family. "I'm glad your father agreed to move back to Notting Hill. And I'm relieved the queen's gratitude extended to securing Ashford for my mother. We may not be legal, Willie, but we're blessed."

"Aye," she said, smiling and leaning into his kiss. "We are blessed."

Read on for a look at the first novel
in the Glorious Victorious Darcys series
by Beth Ciotta,

HER SKY COWBOY

Available in print and e-book from
Signet Eclipse

Prologue

GREAT BRITAIN, 1887
THIRTY-ONE YEARS AFTER THE INVASION OF THE TWENTIETH-
CENTURY PEACE REBELS

"Could you have been any more rude?"

And here I was congratulating myself for being so astonishingly polite. "Apologies, Mother." Repressing her frustration, Miss Amelia Darcy endured her mother's disapproving glare—she was well used to it—and moved to the rear of Loco-Bug, the family's one-of-a-kind steam-powered automocoach. Stoking the coal in the firebox, she simultaneously praised her papa's ingenuity and cursed the extraordinary and unreasonable price of gasoline.

Since the Peace War, only the very rich could afford petrol for everyday use. Others, like Papa, hoarded such fuel for special occasions or, in his case, special projects. She supposed she shouldn't complain about their fickle and sluggish mode of transportation. If her mother, who resisted anything relying on cogs, pipes, and belts, had her way, they'd be traveling by horse and buggy. The woman feared progress as though it were the plague. The only thing that vexed her more was her daughter's emancipated mind-set.

Whilst Amelia replenished the boiler's water supply, her mother stood by, tugging on her fur-lined gloves, tightening the sash of her ridiculously frilly bonnet, and arranging her thick traveling cloak to accommodate her portly frame. "I spent two months cultivating a relationship with the dowager Viscountess Bingham," she grumbled under her breath, "and you managed to ruin my matchmaking efforts in less than two hours."

"Proof of my restraint. Otherwise we would have earned the boot much sooner." Not that Lady Bingham had physically shown them the door, but she'd certainly expedited their exit.

Speaking of which, Amelia glanced over her shoulder and saw the dour-faced woman in all her straitlaced glory standing on the front steps of the magnificent country estate alongside her son—the Viscount Bingham. Decorum dictated that they oversee their guests' departure, no matter how tedious the process. Whereas Lady Bingham was no doubt scandalized by Amelia's determination to fire up and drive a horseless carriage like an unrefined commoner, she could feel Lord Bingham studying her every move. She knew he was fascinated by her passion for aviation and flair for mechanics and somewhat amused by her father's Frankenstein version of an automocoach. Influenced by sketches of Bollée's La Mancelle and a time-traveling Mod's psychedelic Beetle Bug, Papa's hybrid, built from available scraps, was a visual curiosity. However, to someone like Amelia, who had not experienced life before the invasion of the Peace Rebels, Loco-Bug just was.

What really irritated Amelia was Lord Bingham's keen fascination with her bountiful bosom. Even the modest and hideously constricting visiting gown she'd donned to appease her mother had not detracted from her bothersome "fine figure." Most women would have been flattered by his attention, she supposed, especially since Lord Bingham was a man of great wealth and influence. But he was also an arrogant and crafty sod, and it was for that reason that Amelia had striven to alienate Lady Bingham and her son with her fervent utopian ideals. Influenced by the cautionary tales of the Mods, she took her role in policing the fate of the world most seriously.

The steam engine finally puffed to life and Amelia burst

with joy. The sooner she distanced herself from Wickford Manor and the pompous Binghams, the better. She'd been duped into believing Lord Bingham was a fellow utopian, a New Worlder. After an hour in his company Amelia suspected he was, in fact, a Flatliner, someone who cared only for his future—and not the future of mankind.

Learning that he'd employed an entire staff of domestic automatons had singed Amelia's bustle. How insensitive to purchase robotic domestics at a set cost when so many living, breathing Vics were desperate for employment! It was just one of the things that had soured Amelia on the man her mother had envisioned as her husband. Not that Amelia had any intention of marrying. Ever. Why tie herself down when there was so much of the world to see? Why bend to a man's will and agenda when she possessed her own dreams and goals? As she lived and breathed, someday she would pilot her own airship and experience grand adventures! She imagined her exploits being reported alongside the colorful escapades of the Sky Cowboy, an American outlaw who flew the fastest airship in all of Europe. If only her mother would match her with that fearless aviator. Horrid husband material to be sure, but since she had no designs on being a wife—ever—she cared not about his notorious and scandalous reputation and only for his superior knowledge in aeronautical engineering.

Sighing, Amelia shoved aside that whimsical scenario and helped her mother up into the rear seat of the six-person cab. As the prim woman fussed and fidgeted, Amelia gathered her own bothersome skirts, compounded by the added layer of her leather duster, and climbed aboard the open-air driver's throne. She pulled on her leather gauntlets and tinted fur-rimmed goggles, then tugged her worn top hat, a gift from Papa, over her blond coiled braids. Unfashionable perhaps, but comfortable. Sensible as well—which was more than she could say for bustles and bonnets. Grasping the steering wheel, she rolled back her shoulders, feeling deliciously in control. Why anyone would prefer the role of passenger to pilot was beyond her imagination. Loco-

Bug vibrated and puffed, primed for action—same as Amelia. She would have smiled were she not conscious of Lady Bingham's scorn and her own mother's disappointment; were she not repelled by Lord Bingham's lecherous attention, damn his eyes. "Are you going to glare at me for the entire journey home, Mother?"

"Quite possibly."

At least she knew what to expect. Unlike with Lord Bingham. She'd expected—or, perhaps more accurately, hoped for—a tour of his collection of aerostats and aeronefs—flying machines of all manner, each a technological marvel—but she'd never gotten farther than the drawing room, and tea and watercress sandwiches. Her own fault, true. Still . . . *Blast*.

"You are a beautiful young woman, Amelia, in spite of your peculiar taste in fashion. Well educated. Charming, when you strive to be. Yet you are twenty summers old and without a husband."

Smiling now, Amelia breathed in the crisp winter air and engaged the clutch, setting them on a course for home. "Life is good."

"Why in heaven's name did you even agree to this meeting, only to sabotage it? You could have saved me the humiliation by simply refusing."

"If I had refused you would have pressured me until I relented," she said reasonably as they rolled through the ornate iron gates. "I know this, since you have tried to match me six—"

"Seven."

"—times before. This time I bypassed prolonged misery by giving in at the outset."

"I would have preferred an outright refusal. At least it would have saved me the embarrassment of being tossed from the grounds." Her mother sniffed, and Amelia knew without looking that she was using a dainty handkerchief to dab away tears. "Honestly!" she said, choking back a dramatic sob.

Since her back was to the woman, Amelia indulged in a

disrespectful eye roll. She'd never outwardly insult her mother, but blooming hell, it was difficult to hide her frustration. Anne Darcy possessed the extraordinary skill of crying at the drop of a hat. It was a weapon she used quite often against Amelia's father, Reginald Darcy, a baron by happenstance, an inventor by choice, and it drove Amelia to distraction, because her papa always relented. Always. Whatever Anne wanted, which was faithfully more than was reasonable, given the family's status and moderate wealth, her dear, sweet, brilliant, yet ofttimes scatterbrained husband strove to deliver.

Amelia, who could scarcely remember the last time she'd cried, rarely put stock in her mother's tears. This time, however, she acknowledged a morsel of guilt. True, she'd hoped to circumvent her mother's nagging by giving in and agreeing to at least meet with the viscount. But she'd also been driven by her desire to see and to perhaps climb aboard his magnificent zeppelin.

Oh, to pilot an airship of superior design, one that stayed afloat for longer than thirty minutes. Amelia had been obsessed with flying since she was a little girl. Thanks to her papa, who shared her obsession, she'd had the opportunity to sample the skies in his assorted flying machines. Unfortunately, like most of his inventions, his aerostats malfunctioned with extraordinary regularity, and her flights were thus often quite short.

"He was perfect for you, Amelia."

Meaning Lord Bingham. Although she wished her mother would dismiss the thought, she could not wholly disagree. His worldviews, or lack thereof, aside, she supposed he was perfect in that she could discuss aviation with him for aeons and he wouldn't grow bored. He could expose her to advanced technology and she would be mesmerized, but other than that, she saw no sense in the union. She did not love, nor was she even physically attracted to the man—in spite of his handsome features. Not to mention their extreme social and political differences. She didn't bother to explain those differences to her mother. She wouldn't understand. As an Old Worlder, Anne expected Amelia to conform to convention. She had no interest in technology or saving the future from chaos and destruction. She wanted everything to move forward with the natural march of time, the way things used to be, before the Peace Rebels.

As they chugged along, the vibrations from the engine invigorating Amelia's good senses, she cursed herself for giving in to her mother. For giving over to her curiosity regarding Lord Bingham's personal air fleet. Instead, she could've spent the morning assisting Papa, who, day by day, had become almost psychotic in his mission to fly to the moon. Although he'd promised not to tinker with *Apollo 02* (his second attempt at a futuristic rocket ship) until she returned, she didn't wholly trust his word or judgment of late.

"Can't you make this thing go any faster?" Anne asked, sounding suddenly anxious to return home.

"Regrettably, no," Amelia said as Loco-Bug's iron wheels rolled over the pitted, snow-dusted road. As with most of the shires, Kent had fallen upon hard times, and the much-traveled roads had fallen into ill repair. Not to mention that Loco-Bug was simply not made for great speed. "For what it's worth, the journey would have been half the duration if we had taken Bess." Her papa's one-of-a-kind kitecycle. Unfortunately, among other things, Anne Darcy was aerophobic.

"If people were meant to fly," she said with a sniff, "we'd have been born with wings."

If only, Amelia thought with a wistful sigh.

They fell into a sullen silence. Really, what was there to say? Old Worlder and New Worlder, fatalist and utopian, repressed and emancipated. They would never see eye to eye. For the next hour they rode in tense silence—Amelia contemplating her papa's moonship obsession whilst her mother no doubt plotted her next marriage match.

A short mile from their home, Loco-Bug stalled for the second time in thirty minutes.

Anne ridiculed her husband's automocoach as Amelia

hopped out to inspect the engine. Unlike her mother, she had faith in Papa's inventions. Sometimes it just took a lot of positive thinking and a bit of elbow grease. And in this case, a hair ornament. Pulling a decorative comb from her braided hair, Amelia probed and unclogged a valve. Though pleased when Loco-Bug coughed back to life, she glanced at the sky, thinking how much more enjoyable it would have been to soar the seamless air as opposed to driving along rutted roads.

A deafening boom blasted her eardrums, tripping her pulse and stealing her breath.

Pushing her goggles to her forehead, Amelia gaped at a large plume of smoke and fireworks marring the near horizon—a mushrooming cloud littered with fragments of brass, iron, and clockwork.

It came from Ashford. The Darcy estate.

Her mother gasped. "What in heaven's name?"

Apollo 02, Amelia thought, stifling a scream as she imagined Papa tinkering, then . . .

Please, God, no.

Refusing to think the worst, Amelia scrambled back into Loco-Bug, intending to push the machine to its limits. Upon reaching Ashford, she would find Papa singed and discombobulated but very much alive. She willed it with all her heart.

Amelia refitted her goggles, then engaged the clutch. "Hang on to your bonnet, Mama."

Also available

HER SKY COWBOY
The Glorious Victorious Darcys

by BETH CIOTTA

Amelia Darcy has no interest in marrying well. Her heart belongs to the sky and the dirigibles of brass and steel that swoop over Victorian England. But when her father, an eccentric inventor, dies, the Darcy siblings are left with scrap metal—and not a penny to their names. Their only hope to save the family name and fortune is to embark on a contest to discover an invention of historical importance in honor of Queen Victoria.

Armed with only her father's stories of a forgotten da Vinci workshop, a mechanically enhanced falcon, and an Italian cook, Amelia takes flight for Florence, Italy. But her quest is altered when her kitecycle crashes into the air ship of ex–Air Marshal—and scandalous dime novel hero—Tucker Gentry.

Challenged by political unrest, a devious sky pirate, and their own sizzling attraction, Amelia and Tuck are dragged into an international conspiracy that could change the course of history…again.

"Pure charm…you'll be hooked!"
—*New York Times* bestselling author Heather Graham

Available wherever books are sold or
at penguin.com

S0471

Also available

HIS BROKEN ANGEL

A Glorious Victorious Darcys Novella

AN EXCLUSIVE DOWNLOADABLE PENGUIN SPECIAL FROM SIGNET ECLIPSE

by BETH CIOTTA

Doc Blue has never had it easy. Born a Freak, the offspring of a Vic—a native Victorian—and a Mod—a time traveler from the future—he's lived on the fringes of society, hiding his true identity and preternatural healing abilities from even his closest friends. His brief support of the Freak rebellion has only left him with even more problems, losing him both his job and one of his greatest allies, the Sky Cowboy, Tucker Gentry. So when Tuck's kid sister, Lily, ends up blinded in an air skirmish on her way from America to England, Doc jumps at the opportunity to be the one to rescue her and use his powers to mend her wounds.

Curing Lily proves harder than anticipated, and Doc realizes that to restore her sight he will have to spill his biggest secret and embrace his true nature like never before. But, with Lily's help, Doc may be able to reach the full potential of his abilities, heal Lily's broken heart—and learn, finally, how to open his.

Available wherever e-books are sold or at penguin.com